SECOND CHANCES AT
CHERRY TREE COTTAGE

JO BARTLETT

Boldwood

First published in Great Britain in 2021 by Boldwood Books Ltd.

Copyright © Jo Bartlett, 2021

Cover Design by CC Book Design

Cover photography: Shutterstock

The moral right of Jo Bartlett to be identified as the author of this work has been asserted in accordance with the Copyright, Designs and Patents Act 1988.

Every effort has been made to obtain the necessary permissions with reference to copyright material, both illustrative and quoted. We apologise for any omissions in this respect and will be pleased to make the appropriate acknowledgements in any future edition.

A CIP catalogue record for this book is available from the British Library.

Paperback ISBN 978-1-80162-000-0

Large Print ISBN 978-1-80162-001-7

Hardback ISBN 978-1-80048-999-8

Ebook ISBN 978-1-80162-003-1

Kindle ISBN 978-1-80162-002-4

Audio CD ISBN 978-1-80048-994-3

MP3 CD ISBN 978-1-80048-995-0

Digital audio download ISBN 978-1-80048-997-4

Boldwood Books Ltd
23 Bowerdean Street
London SW6 3TN
www.boldwoodbooks.com

For the old school friends, who are still part of my life, and the school-run mums who made the experience much more bearable! You know who you are, but I'm going to name you anyway – Claire, Sarah Katy, Kate, Sheila, Ros, Vicki, Caroline S, Vanessa, Kerry, Nikki, Bev, Jennie, Toni, Michelle, Caroline D, Shelly and Angie xx

PROLOGUE

Opening the door of the fridge, I pulled out the carton of eggs. It was empty; I could tell before I even flipped it open. There were eight people already seated in the dining room, eagerly anticipating the full English breakfast we promised on our website, and we were out of eggs. Again.

'Luke, where did you put the eggs you said you'd get yesterday? Only it doesn't look like they're in the fridge.' I looked across at my husband, who was staring at his phone and barely seemed to register that I'd spoken to him. 'Luke, the eggs? Where are they?' My voice was rising and I didn't want another row. But if he'd forgotten to get the most basic of supplies again, I wasn't sure I was going to be able to stop myself.

'Oh Christ, I forgot. Sorry.' He finally looked up at me and gave the smallest of shrugs. If there'd been any eggs left in the carton, he'd have been wearing them by now.

'You forgot? Sometimes I wonder if you're doing this on purpose, sabotaging the business, so that—' I couldn't finish the sentence.

'So that what?'

'I don't know. I just can't believe you can forget stuff this important.'

'It's only some eggs; jeez Scarlett, you're so uptight. I've been under a lot of pressure.'

'And I haven't?' My voice was rising again, and Ava looked up from the colouring book that had been keeping her occupied. She was only three years old and she'd already got used to sitting in a corner, keeping quiet and colouring in, whilst her dad and I tried desperately to keep our bed and breakfast business afloat. At least, *one* of us was trying desperately.

'All right we both have.' Luke's tone softened as he walked over to me, putting his hands on my shoulders. 'I'll nip out now and get some. I'll be five minutes at most, just ply that lot with an extra round of tea and toast and they'll never even notice the delay.'

'What about Ava? I thought you were going to keep an eye on her whilst I did the cooking?'

'She's a good girl, aren't you, sweetheart?' Luke looked across at her, and Ava gave him a serious nod. 'Anyway, Maureen will be in soon, won't she? So it'll be all hands on deck and you can get on with the breakfasts in peace.'

'I suppose so. Just be as quick as you can, okay?' I turned towards him again and he planted a kiss on my lips, most of the anger and resentment I felt melting away the moment he did. Luke had always had that effect on me; trouble was, he knew it as well as I did.

'I'll be back before you know it. Scout's honour!' With that he was gone, slamming the kitchen door behind him, as I pulled out an uncut loaf from the bread bin and set about making another round of toast.

* * *

'Cooee!' Ten minutes later, just when I was on the edge of hyper-ventilating, the back door from the yard to the kitchen flew open. Maureen, who came in four mornings a week to help with the cleaning and room change-overs, gave me a cheerful wave. 'Sorry I'm a couple of minutes late, Scarlett, but that hubby of yours rang me and said you needed me to pick up some eggs on the way over. I was only a few doors down by that point, so I had to walk back to Boscawen's on the corner. Thankfully they still had some of the free-range eggs left from yesterday's delivery.'

'Thanks, Maureen.' I forced a smile. Where the hell was Luke?

'Are you okay, my love? You look a bit stressed.' Maureen's lilting accent was almost too much. I wanted to burst into tears and tell her I definitely wasn't okay, but I bit my lip instead.

'I'm fine, it's just that Luke said he was getting the eggs.' I forced another smile. 'Still, it doesn't matter. At least I've got them now; there are only so many rounds of toast I can give the guests before they start to get suspicious.'

'He said something had come up, but that he'd be back as soon as possible. You know Luke, there'll be something to explain it all when he gets back!' She smiled and I nodded my head. That was the thing with my husband, he always had a plausible explanation.

'I'll get on with the breakfasts then, Maureen, thanks. Could I be really cheeky and ask if you'd help Ava get ready for nursery? Luke was supposed to be doing it and then taking her in for ten o'clock, but it looks like I'll need to do that when I'm finished up here. I know it's not part of your job, but if you could just get her dressed and ready, I'll really owe you one.'

'It'll be my pleasure, my love. Me and Ava always have so much fun, don't we darling?'

'Yes, Nanny Maureen.' Ava took her hand and I felt another pang of guilt – that someone I paid a wage to for cleaning the B&B had become a stand-in grandmother for my daughter, when I barely got the chance to be a proper mother to her lately. Something was going to have to change, and I was determined to speak to Luke about it as soon as he got back. It had gone on for long enough.

* * *

It wasn't a surprise when Luke wasn't back in time to take Ava to nursery, but that didn't make it any less infuriating. I barely had time to stack the dishwasher after breakfast before heading out the door with Ava to go to the nursery three roads away. She was skipping along, singing a song about a frog on a log, all the way there. Poor little thing probably couldn't wait to get to nursery, where she'd get some one-to-one attention for a change.

'See you later, darling.' I knelt down to kiss her cheek, as one of the nursery assistants took her backpack and coat.

'Bye, Mummy.' She threw her little arms around my neck and I felt another pang. She never held how distracted I was against me, but somehow that just made the guilt worse.

'Have lots of fun with your friends today.'

'I will, Mummy. Are you picking me up, or is Daddy?' Suddenly her little face clouded over. Luke had missed more than one pick up slot, resulting in frantic calls from the nursery and a one pound fine for every minute we were late past their closing time. Worse than that was the look on Ava's face when I finally got there. She never said anything, but she didn't need to.

'I'll be here, darling, I promise.'

'Love you, Mummy!' With the smile firmly back on her face, and with one last wave, she disappeared into a group of other preschoolers. Worries she shouldn't have had, about whether her daddy would remember to pick her up from nursery or not, were forgotten for now.

Heading home towards the B&B, I thought about what I was going to say to Luke when he got back. It wouldn't be an easy conversation, but I needed to have it for Ava's sake. I wanted the B&B to work, but I wanted my marriage to work more. Most of all, I wanted Ava to have the childhood she deserved.

I stopped to pick up some more eggs from Boscawen's on the way, as I knew they had a delivery from one of the local farms at ten every morning. At least that was one less thing to worry about. Taking my mobile out of my pocket, I checked my messages. There was still no reply from Luke about where he was, or what time I could expect him home.

Then I saw him; he was getting into the passenger side of a bright red sports car with the sort of throaty exhaust that vibrated through your whole body when it drove past. Breaking into a run, I called out his name and waved my free hand in the air, clutching the carton of eggs in the other. He must have seen me. The front windscreen was facing in my direction, but the sun was shining on it, so I couldn't see who was driving.

I wanted to speak to my husband now, though, and I wasn't going to wait. Stepping out into the road, as the car pulled forward, seemed like the only option. Except it didn't work. The car revved hard and shot down the road, so close to me that I fell backwards, landing on the carton of eggs as I did.

'Oh God, are you okay?' A woman about my age, who'd been walking along the pavement opposite, dropped her shopping bags and rushed into the road to help me up.

'I'm not hurt, I've just broken my eggs.' It was then that I started to cry, as I looked back at the mess of broken shells and raw eggs running along the middle of the road in the direction of the B&B.

'Did you get the number plate?' The woman patted my back gently, as she led me out of the road and onto the safety of the pavement.

'No, it was all so quick.'

'Well, I'll keep an eye out for them, and note the plate down if I see them again. If you report it to the police, I can let them know.' She looked outraged on my behalf, but I just shook my head.

'It's okay, I'm okay. I don't want to make any fuss and there's nothing the police could do.'

'If you're sure. I suppose you're right, anyway. They were almost certainly tourists, driving like that around here.' She tutted. 'It's probably the last we'll see of them.'

I nodded, but I had no way of knowing at the time how right she was, and that it would turn out to be the last I saw of my husband for quite some time.

1

'I've made you a packed lunch.' Mum pushed the lunch box across the kitchen island. It had a picture of the boyband *Blue* on the front, the same one I'd had when I started secondary school. I suppose I should have been grateful that it wasn't the *Care Bears* one I'd taken as a six-year-old to Appleberry Primary School, where I was now about to start work. Although it wouldn't have surprised me if she'd kept that too.

'Thanks, Mum.' I opened it up; two scotch eggs, a tube of Petit Filous and an apple were wedged up against a carton of orange juice. It really was the nineties all over again. All I needed to complete it was a Cheese String.

'I don't want you getting into the habit of eating a school dinner every day, it's all too easy to pack on the pounds.' She swore by a low carb diet and even the scotch eggs were made with high fibre coconut flour. I was lucky I had an apple instead of a couple of chicken drumsticks; she'd offered me those for breakfast instead.

'Have you made a lunch for Ava?'

'No, I thought you should be the one to do that. What with it being her first day at school and everything.' Mum squeezed my hand and we exchanged a look. Just occasionally she knew when to step back.

'Thanks again, Mum. *For everything.*' I moved over to the fridge and grabbed what I needed to make Ava's lunch. Turning back to face the kitchen window, I could see Ava skipping around the garden with my Dad. It had been the right decision to come home – even if it had been my *only* choice at the time.

'Are you excited about starting your new job today?' Mum hovered behind me as I made Ava a sandwich. I was half expecting her to give me the usual speech about how all carbs were poison, so talking about my new job was a welcome surprise.

'I am, but you know what it's like. Starting something new is always a bit scary.'

'We've loved having you and Ava home, but I'm hoping today will help you kick start the next stage of your life. You don't want to end up like Auntie Leilah.'

'Mum, please.' She must have said that sentence at least three times a day, in the six months I'd been back in Appleberry. There should have been a plaque with it engraved on, under the ones that read *Home is Where the Heart is*, and *Family Comes First*, which hung on the kitchen wall under the shelf of cook books.

'Oh, I know, I know. I'm not supposed to mention you finding someone new, but it's been over a year, Scarlett. And that *man* isn't worth wasting another second on.'

'I'm not wasting anything on him, Mum. Ava and I are getting on with our lives, but if I end up like Auntie Leilah that's okay with me. She's happy, she does a job she loves and she's always out and about with friends. It sounds pretty good to me.'

'Yes, but then she goes home to her cottage and she's on her own, except when she's fostering one of those dogs. That was the reason she didn't come for Easter, do you know that?' She tutted, but I suspected Leilah's dog-sitting wasn't the only reason she'd avoided Easter at Mum and Dad's. A no-carb roast dinner was no one's idea of fun. 'And I'm convinced that's why she overeats too. Deep down she's lonely, however much she bangs on about not being the marrying sort, and I don't want you to end up like that.'

'Mum!' I couldn't even find the words to reply. I didn't have the headspace, and she'd never understand anyway. Aunt Leilah wanted different things to her, she always had. And so did I from now on. Relationships were overrated.

'All right, all right. I won't mention it again.' We both knew she was lying.

'I'll have to head off in a minute. Are you going to wish me luck?' Nerves fluttered in my stomach. And thinking about the scotch eggs again, as I picked up the lunches, a wave of nausea swept over me.

'I don't need to wish you luck, you'll do brilliantly. You've always been a success at everything you've done.'

'Not everything.' I squeezed my eyes shut. It was always going to be an emotional day, dropping my little girl off for her first day at school. But her dad should have been there to see it too, and I'd failed at that – I'd failed her.

'None of that was your fault.' Mum hugged me, and it was a bit like cuddling an ironing board. There wasn't an ounce of fat she'd allowed to make itself at home. But I was so grateful that she and Dad had always been there for me. I had to do the same for Ava now, and nothing was ever going to get in the way of that again.

It was a beautiful day. And for once I didn't mind that I'd had to sell the car, along with everything else that wasn't bolted down, before I'd moved home. The early autumn sun was warm on my back as we made the short walk up to Appleberry Primary. The school was on the side of a narrow country lane, opposite the sixteenth century church which clung to the hillside like a mountain goat. Dad said it had been built there so the worshippers would be closer to God, but it had always looked to me like it had been carved out of the hillside itself.

Beyond the village were miles of open farmland, hop gardens, some trendy new vineyards that had started to gain favour in this part of Kent – to make the most of the climate, and the hundreds of orchards which leant Appleberry its name. Rumour had it that Henry VIII himself had christened the county the Garden of England after tasting a bowl of the undeniably delicious local cherries. I'd always thought that when I grew up, I'd buy one of the cottages dotted around the village and have my own cherry and apple trees in the garden. But then I'd met Luke.

'Mummy, is it true that you have to keep your finger on your lips all day at school?' Ava looked up at me, jolting me back to the present, her blue eyes round with concern. The nerves were obviously starting to get to her too.

'Who told you that?'

'Archie.'

'Well, it's not true, darling.' Archie Green had been at nursery with Ava two villages away. There hadn't been a space for her at the nursery in Appleberry when we'd come home, and I'd been worried that it might make the transition to primary school more difficult. But I was glad she'd be getting away from Archie. He'd also told her that eating fruit could give you head lice, and that monsters waited behind your curtains at night, until your parents turned out the light, and then came out to scare you. 'Sometimes children who don't know how to listen are asked to put their fingers on their lips for a few minutes, to remind them not to talk whilst the teacher is talking.'

'I'm good at listening, aren't I, Mummy?'

'Yes, darling.' My eyes were burning again. She was such a good girl and, from the moment I'd set eyes on her, she'd always seemed perfect to me. If I lived to be a hundred and ten, I'd never understand how anyone could walk out of her life without a backward glance.

'I can't wait to play in the sandpit like before.' Ava was skipping again, the worries Archie had planted easily forgotten. She'd had a couple of taster sessions at the school in July, after I'd been offered the job as the Year 1 and 2 teacher. It was such a small school that only the reception year had a class of its own. The other three classes were made up of two year groups combined. It would give me some challenges as a teacher, but I was looking forward to getting back into the classroom on a permanent basis. I'd done a bit of supply work in the six months we'd been home, but this would give us both some stability.

'I'm sure you're going to love lots of things about school. I'll take you into your classroom, darling, but then I've got to go and see the children in my class, and their mums and da— their parents.' I stopped myself on the word *dads*. It was stupid. It was hardly as if I could protect her from every mention of the word for the rest of her life, or even the rest of the day. But I hated reminding her of what she didn't have.

'Okay, Mummy. I like being with Mr Ellis anyway, he's nice.' As we rounded the final bend in the road, the school came into view ahead of us, and there were other parents already waiting to drop off their children. The reception class had been asked to come in half an hour early to avoid overwhelming the children on their first day with the usual chaos of drop off. There was one dad, clutching the hand of a tearful looking little boy, with what I assumed was his mother on the other side. But the rest of the children were just with their mums, so I needn't have spent half the night before worrying that Ava would feel singled out. It was one of the downsides to a tiny village school with less than seventy kids, where at first glance everyone seemed to have a Range Rover and a traditional family set up. I could claim ownership of a fifteen-year-old mountain bike, languishing in Mum and Dad's shed, and a husband who'd apparently fallen off the face of the earth. I wasn't exactly flying under the radar, and experience had taught me most children just wanted to fit in.

'Good morning, Mr Ellis.' I smiled at Ava's teacher, who was also my new boss, as we went into his classroom. Appleberry had been federated with another small primary school in a neighbouring village a few years before, so the head teacher split her time between the two schools. Cameron Ellis was the assistant head of Appleberry and had day-to-day responsibility for the school as a result. He'd been on my interview panel and had observed me teaching the year 1 and 2 pupils, before they'd offered me the job.

'Good morning, Mrs West.'

I'd agonised over whether to start the new job using my maiden name. But that might have thrown up more questions for Ava, and I wanted us to have the same name. Maybe I was more like my mother than I wanted to admit.

Cameron bent down to draw level with Ava. 'I'm really pleased you'll be joining my class. Do you want to sit next to Daisy?'

Ava nodded and I planted a quick kiss on top of her head as she walked towards a table covered with paper and colouring pencils. I was determined not to cry.

'Are you okay?' Cameron touched my elbow and I swallowed hard, nodding my head.

'It's just a big day for both of us.'

'I think you're doing great. The children are usually fine, and we only ever get a few tears from them. But sometimes I actually have to ask the parents to leave because they're upsetting the kids!' Cameron laughed and I couldn't help smiling. He was right, all of this bothered me far more than Ava. 'Good luck with your first day, and you know where I am if you need me.'

'Thank you. And you'll let me know if there are any issues with Ava?'

'Of course.'

I crossed the corridor towards my classroom. It was an old building with heavy flagstones on the corridor floor, and the walls on either side were lined with the children's artwork and tiles decorated by Year 6 students moving on to secondary school.

My teaching assistant, Ruhan, was already in the classroom, and she smiled when she looked up and saw me. We'd been introduced after I was offered the job, and I'd discovered she'd been a TA at the school for over ten years. So at least I had someone to lean on until I found my feet again.

'Morning, are you excited about your first day?' Ruhan carried on setting out laminated labels with the children's names on as we spoke.

'Excited, terrified... nauseous!'

'It'll fly by and by the time you've been here for a week, you'll feel as if you've worked here forever.' Ruhan smiled again, and I set my bags down by the desk at the front of the classroom. It suddenly felt very real, but I'd always found the best way to deal with fear was to tackle things head on – at least until recently.

Within half an hour, we had the classroom set up how I wanted it, and we were talking through my lesson plans for the first day. There were a couple of children who Ruhan would support more closely. But with a total of twenty children in the class, including two new starters, I'd be monitoring her input over the first couple of weeks to see if we needed to make any adjustments. Ruhan had explained there were also some parents and grandparents who came in to do reading with the children, so I'd be assessing the children who would benefit from that the most. If the first thirty minutes were anything to go by, Ruhan was right – time really was going to fly.

'It's show time.' She grinned over her shoulder and unlocked the door at the far end of the classroom, which led out onto the playground. As soon as she pulled it back, a line of parents and their children started to file in. I could see Natasha Chisholm out of the corner of my eye, chatting to Ruhan, and another wave of nausea surged in my stomach. But I pushed it down, getting on with the business of speaking to the parents who hadn't just dropped their children and bolted.

'Scarlett! It's lovely to see you.' Natasha seized her chance the moment Henry Baxter's dad walked away after he'd filled me in on the triggers for his asthma. She threw her arms out and, for one horrible moment, I thought she was going to hug me. 'I couldn't believe it when I found out that you were going to be Ode's teacher! I was so sorry to hear about what happened between you and Luke, and I just wish James had been able to tell you something that might have helped. It must be just *tragic* for little Ava.'

'She's taken it all in her stride.' I forced such a tight smile onto my face that my lip felt like it might actually split. A few of the other parents were openly staring at us, and somehow, I resisted the urge to tell Natasha to mind her own bloody business. I should have known it was coming. She'd been at school with Luke, and had ended up marrying his best friend, James. They'd all been five years above me, so I hadn't really known any of them at the time. But James was the best man at our wedding and I'd got in contact with him the week after Luke walked out. Despite Natasha's see-through sympathy, I was sure they knew more than they were saying.

'Aww, I don't know how I'd cope if James left me. You and Ava are both being *so* brave.' And she was being *so* patronising.

Maybe I'd been wrong. Maybe coming back to Appleberry hadn't been such a great idea after all. There was a good chance the parents in my class would all know the intimate details of my personal life before afternoon pick-up. I might as well have got some flyers printed and put them in the kids' book bags.

'Is there anything you'd like me to know about Ode?' *Other than the fact that she's got a ridiculous name.* My internal monologue was working overtime, but I couldn't say any of the things to Natasha that I wanted to. Getting back at her wouldn't change the fact that Luke had left, and it might even lose me my job. He was the one I should be focusing all my anger on, anyway.

'According to Cam, she's an absolute dream to teach because she picks things up so quickly, and I'm sure you'll find the same.' Natasha smiled and I was silently praying she'd have a bit of lipstick on her teeth, but she was far too perfect for that. 'I suppose I should say *Mr Ellis* when the children are around, but when you're a lynchpin of the PTA you develop a much closer relationship with the staff.'

'Are you the chair then?' It was a perfect, if slightly pathetic, opportunity to get a tiny bit of revenge. I'd heard all about the power struggle in the PTA via one of Mum's friends, and how desperate Natasha apparently was to step into the role of chair.

'Just a matter of time.' Natasha tapped her nose. 'And I hope you'll be joining us. Cam – *Mr Ellis* comes to all the meetings.'

'And that's why the size of the PTA has more than doubled since he started. He's your classic tall, dark and handsome, and it's definitely worth volunteering to run the tombola for a chance to stare into those eyes!' A woman in what looked like a hand-knitted jumper, which stretched down to just above the top of her wellington boots, laughed loudly at her own joke, earning her a dismissive look from Natasha.

'The first meeting of this term is on Friday after school, so I'll look forward to catching up with you properly then?' Natasha raised an eyebrow and I found myself nodding, despite the fact there was almost nothing I wanted less than to give her another chance to tell the world what a total balls-up I'd made of holding on to my husband.

2

On the Thursday of my first week at school, Mum picked Ava up to take her to see the latest Disney movie, and I was using the opportunity to get some marking done in the quiet of an empty classroom. If I took it home, Dad would want to chat about my day, or invite me out to the garden to see if I thought his giant squash had got any bigger. He'd entered it into the church's annual Harvest Festival contest, and Mum frequently complained that he spent more time with it than her.

It wasn't that I didn't like spending time with Dad, or even pretending to be interested in weighing up the pros and cons of natural and synthetic fertilisers – all I knew for sure was which one smelt worse – but I was trying my best to keep my home and work life separate, to give Ava some quality time. And the chance to get some of my marking out of the way was too good an opportunity to miss.

'I'm not interrupting anything, am I?' Cameron knocked on the frame of the open classroom door, and I shook my head. I wasn't about to tell my new boss I was too busy to speak to him, even if I was.

'I was just doing some marking. Do you want to sit down?' I smiled and gestured to one of the kids' chairs. It was bright red, and about half the size of the one I was sitting on. But Cameron sat on one of the tables instead, and I grabbed my chance. 'How's Ava doing?'

'Really well. She's always trying to help the other kids out, and she seems to be interested in every topic we tackle. I could do with a whole classroom full of Avas.'

'That's good to hear.' My shoulders relaxed. It didn't matter what else Cameron wanted to talk about, as long as Ava was happy. 'So, did you want to speak to me about something in particular?'

'I was wondering if you'd be willing to do a joint performance with the reception class for Harvest Festival? If every class does their own thing, the service can end up being painfully long, and I mean *painfully*! It also means not every child gets a chance to have a speaking role if they want one.' He shook his head. 'You wouldn't believe the fall out that causes with some of the parents.'

'Oh, I would. I've already been asked by at least three of the mums whether their child is doing a reading at the service. I hadn't realised it was such a big deal.'

'It is to some of them, and it's actually caused some nasty arguments in the playground in the past. The parents are far worse than the kids. So I've decided to take the easy way out this year and give everyone the same opportunity.'

'Coward.' I laughed and instantly regretted it, hoping I hadn't misread Cameron's sense of humour and pushed it too far with a new boss I barely knew.

'You wouldn't say that if you'd ever been pinned into the corner of your classroom by Claire Winters, for not giving her son a big enough role in the nativity play. I actually thought it was going to get physical at one point.' It was his turn to laugh.

'I think it would be fun for the kids to do something together. I know Ava loves it when the older girls let her join in with them at playtime.' I wrinkled my nose. 'Sorry, I know we're supposed to be gender neutral and all that, but she just gravitates towards the girls. It probably means I'm a massive failure as a modern mother.'

'From what I've seen, you seem to be doing everything right.'

'Thanks.' I looked down at the colourful stick-man drawing in front of me, hoping Cameron was right. 'Have you got anything in mind for Harvest Festival, then?'

'I was hoping you might have a folder full of ideas you were just dying to share.'

'Sorry, no folder, but I was thinking of doing something to celebrate Harvest Festival around the world, like the Festival of Yams in some African countries, and Oktoberfest in Germany. We should be able to find enough places to give all the kids a couple of lines each. And if there are some who don't want to speak, they can hold up the pictures instead.'

'That sounds perfect, I knew I could rely on you.' Cameron smiled and I tried not to blush like a twelve-year-old.

'We could get really ambitious and make some of the fruit and veg out of papier-mâché. I think that would be right up Ruhan's street.'

'The kids would love that.' Cameron stood up. 'I'll email you, so we can set aside some time next week to plan it properly. You're doing a great job so far, by the way.'

'I knew I was on to a winner when I suggested papier-mâché yams!'

'There's a lot more to you than papier-mâché yams.' His words forced me to look down at the stick-man again. It was proving hard to take a compliment after so long without one. 'But the question is whether you're ready to pass the real initiation test and go to the PTA meeting tomorrow night?'

'I didn't think I had a choice, at least not the way Natasha

Chisholm explained it to me.' I shrugged, passing her off as just another pushy parent. There was no need for him to know we had a shared history of sorts. I wanted to keep my private life private, if Natasha would let me. I'd just have to keep my fingers crossed that opening her big mouth once would be enough.

'So you've had the royal command then?' Cameron laughed, Natasha's reputation doing all the work for me.

'It was something like that. But as a teacher *and* a parent, I really should join the PTA, shouldn't I?'

'Absolutely. And it will be nice to have another teacher there, to help me manage some of the parents' expectations.'

'I'll see you there then, if I don't catch up with you during the day tomorrow.' I didn't want to admit that a Friday night PTA meeting was the only thing in my diary for the whole weekend. It was probably time to make some new friends, and the PTA meeting was as good a place to start as any.

* * *

The meeting was being held upstairs in a private room at one of the two pubs in Appleberry. The Gamekeeper's Arms was an old-fashioned country pub, with low lighting, a wide selection of real ales, and ancient, dusty hop vines hanging from the beams in the main bar. Ruhan had told me the meetings were held there during the evening, so that some of the working mums could go, and to make it more of a social occasion. It made me feel slightly less of a loser to know I wasn't the only one whose social highlight was a PTA meeting.

Hesitating outside the door of the pub, it was like I was about to go on a blind date rather than meet up with other parents from the school. So it was a relief to see Ruhan already waiting when I finally pushed the door open.

'Let me get you a drink,' I offered, joining her at the bar.

'You don't need to do that, I'll get you one.' Her ready smile rarely left her face, even when the kids were doing their best to test her patience. I'd overheard her telling one of the children that her name meant kind-hearted in Hindi, and her parents had definitely made the right choice.

'No, it's the least I can do. I can't tell you how much help you've been this first week.'

'I've got to be honest, I was a bit apprehensive about working with a new teacher, after working with Lizzie for so many years. But it's been like a breath of fresh air, and Cam can't stop talking about you.' She dropped me a wink and I laughed. Despite my intentions, I'd found myself sharing the details of my marriage breakdown with Ruhan, but I didn't have much choice after Natasha had more or less announced it on our first day of working together. Ruhan was clearly cut from the same cloth as Mum, though, and she'd decided that the only single man who worked at the school would be the ideal match for me. Poor Cameron, he'd probably be as horrified as I was if he found out. But protesting too much just seemed to add fuel to the fire. The best thing to do was ignore comments you didn't like, that was what I always told the kids in my class.

'What can I get you, then?'

'Just a lime and soda, please,' Ruhan said, and I just hoped she wouldn't judge the vodka and tonic I'd ordered – I needed it if I was going to face Natasha again.

Drink in hand, I followed Ruhan across the bar and upstairs to the private function room. It was clad with dark wood panelling, and a mismatched selection of tables and chairs had already been organised into a U-shape.

'Evening, Ruhan.' A plump woman with unruly salt-and-pepper curls came over from behind the top row of tables and held out her hand to me. 'And you must be the new teacher I've heard such good things about. I'm Dolly Swan, chair of the PTA.' She had the hint of an Australian accent, and a relaxed demeanour that immediately put me at ease.

'Lovely to meet you. I'm Scarlett West, I teach Years 1 and 2, and I've got a daughter Ava, in reception.'

'Double bubble then!' Dolly had deep lines around her eyes, which made her look as if she spent most of her life laughing. 'I really miss having little ones in reception. My youngest, Billy, has just started Year 6, and I'm already dreading the day he leaves and I've got no excuse to attend the nativity play any more. I'm just hoping my eldest, who's twenty-six, won't wait too long before she makes me a grandma. I'd have had another one when Billy started in reception, if this old bugger of a body hadn't let me down.'

'You won't be saying that when you have to carry your bladder around in a Tesco's carrier bag because having so many kids has ruined your bits and pieces, like my poor old mum!' Molly Dawkins' mother said, as she came towards us. I recognised her from when she'd dropped Molly off in my class on the first day of term – she'd been the one wearing a hand-knitted jumper that reached down past her knees.

'So you're telling me your mum carries her bladder around in a carrier bag?' Dolly was still grinning, and this was already turning out to be a lot more fun than I'd thought.

'All right then, not exactly, but she had six kids and they had to prop it up in a hammock just so she didn't have to buy shares in Tena Lady. You should be grateful you stopped at five, one more and who knows!' She held out her hand to me. 'Kate Dawkins, my daughter Molly is in your class. And she told me last night that she prefers you to me.'

'Oh, dear. I'm sorry about that.' I didn't know what to say, but Kate just laughed.

'Don't be. It's a step up from her preferring the dog and the Dominos delivery driver, both of whom I've been compared to unfavourably in the last week. God help me when that girl turns thirteen.'

'If it's any consolation, she's an absolute pleasure to have in the class.'

'Well that's something. I don't need Natasha Chisholm and her gang to have any more ammunition. I'm already a shoo-in for the bad mum of the year award. I've tried teaching Molly and Barnaby that the *organic farmers' market* is code for McDonalds, but the little sods are always dropping me in it.'

'I don't know why you worry so much what they think.' Dolly looked up as she moved around the tables, putting a set of papers in front of each chair.

'That's easy for you to say, because you know you're nearly out of here. Nine more months and you're home free. I've got to have her looking down her nose at me for another five years. I can't wait until Molly is in Year 5, like Barnaby, and I can let her jump out of the car by the school gates and take herself into the playground. But even that's four years away.'

'She's not *that* bad when you get to know her.' Ruhan's tone was reasonable, but Kate was having none of it.

'She's not bad, she's worse.' Kate crossed her arms. 'I decided I didn't like her when I first saw her, and she's done nothing to change my mind since. Oh, but don't feel bad for her, the feeling is entirely mutual.'

'I went to school with her, but she was five years above me.' There was so much more I could have said, but there was no way I'd bad-mouth a parent in public.

'Ooh, I bet she hates that, you being five years younger than her. That's why she had to get that snide comment in about your ex-husband doing a runner.' Kate gave me a sympathetic look.

'Did she really say that?' Dolly's face dropped, but sympathy was the last thing I wanted.

'She blabbed about what a tragedy it was or something, but then I heard her filling her cronies in on the details out by the school gate.' Kate narrowed her eyes. 'See, I've always said she was bitchy.'

'So everyone knows what happened with Luke?' My voice sounded small, even to me. But I'd had enough of Luke making me feel small. If this was going to be out in the open it was going to be on my terms and with *all* the facts. Not just Natasha's version.

'They know he left you high and dry, but don't worry, no one else is gossiping about it, they're just sorry for you, that's all.' Kate cocked her head to one side. I'd been about to tell her that sympathy was my kryptonite, when Natasha Chisholm threw open the door of the function room. She was carrying a bottle of Prosecco in an ice bucket and three other women followed her in, all sitting together on one side of the arrangement of tables. They had expensive looking haircuts and had clearly mastered the art of contouring – which had left me looking like a road map of spaghetti junction the one and only time I'd tried it. The way they looked everyone else up and down made it hard not to take a leaf out of Kate's book and decide to dislike them on sight.

'Where's Cam?' Natasha directed the question at Dolly, as her friends giggled about something that was on one of their phones and casted glances at Kate. It was like going back to secondary school, and it seemed not much had changed if you didn't wear the right clothes or fit in with the in-crowd. I didn't want to think back to the times I'd done that to someone at school, but once or twice I'd been guilty of being as much of a cow as Natasha's friends were being right now. Except I'd been all of thirteen at the time.

'He said he might be a bit late; he had to go and fix a leak at his mum's place, but he'll be here as soon as he can.' Dolly took her seat in the centre of the table and Ruhan and I sat opposite the yummy mummies, while Kate sat next to Dolly. 'Katrina Polinski and Laura Brown have both sent their apologies along with Miss Wallace and Mrs Salter from Class 3 and 4, so it's only Cameron we're waiting for. Seeing as he's already said he'll be late, I think we should make a start.'

'So neither of the junior school teachers *or* Mrs Davy could be bothered to put in an appearance, then?' Natasha actually made a note in the jotter in front of her, and I couldn't help wondering if my name was already in there too.

'They've both got things going on at home which mean they can't be here tonight, and Mrs Davy is on a weekend training course in Milton Keynes, so she's travelling up there this evening.' Dolly's perfectly reasonable explanation did little to appease Natasha.

'Funny how she never misses a PTA meeting at Oaktree Forstal.'

Ruhan had already warned me about the tensions with the other school in the federation. A lot of the parents resented the fact that Nancy Davy seemed to spend more of her time at the bigger of the two primary schools she oversaw. My guess was it had more to do with the fact that Cameron was a really capable assistant head, rather than any favouritism, but clearly not everyone felt that way.

'Let's press on then, and you can raise any concerns you've got with Cameron, when he arrives. Let's leave that until the end of the agenda, though, so we don't get side-tracked by the same old discussions.' Dolly was a surprisingly authoritative chairperson, which made her more than capable of dealing with the women on Natasha's side of the table, despite their best efforts to take over. They'd apparently all been elected class reps at the end of the term before, so they had a big say in how any funds raised by the PTA ended up being spent.

Clare Winters was rep for reception, Danni Bennett for Years 3 and 4, and Tanya Slater for Years 5 and 6. Typical of my luck,

Natasha was class rep for Years 2 and 3, so I'd have to put any requests for PTA funds to her and, worse than that, we'd have to meet once a month. My instant reaction was to consider asking Janey Salter if I could swap with her and teach Years 5 and 6 for the rest of the school year, despite the neurosis of parents whose children were prepping for grammar school entrance tests. The prospect of meeting up with Natasha Chisholm on a regular basis was that bad.

'Agenda item three is the autumn fundraiser.' It was forty-five minutes into the meeting and, as Dolly started to outline the next item, Cameron finally arrived. Along with Ruhan, I'd been trying to contribute from the school's point of view, but I was relieved to see him. After only a week in the job, half the time I wasn't even 100 per cent sure if what I was saying was true.

'I'm really sorry. Things at Mum's were worse than I thought.' Cameron held up his hand in my direction and I couldn't help but wonder if I looked the way I felt – like a rabbit caught in the headlights.

'No problem. I hope everything's okay now?' Dolly turned to Cameron, who nodded. 'We were just about to start on the autumn fundraiser.'

'Great.' Cameron took a seat as he spoke. 'Well, I know from Mrs Davy that Oaktree Forstal are planning a copper snake in the playground.'

'And I heard they're planning to break the county record!'

I had no idea what they were talking about, but whatever it was had caused Natasha's voice to raise at least an octave.

'What's a copper snake?' Thankfully Kate looked as confused as me.

'Oh, you *must* remember, Kate!' Claire Winters, who was siting to the right of Natasha, gave her a withering look. 'We did one for the last autumn fundraiser, and we had the second spot in the county. It's where all the kids bring in as many copper coins as they can find, and we curl them round to look like a snake. Then we measure it to see how long it is. Trust the bloody Oaktree lot to want to go one better.'

'Does it matter, as long as we're both raising funds for the schools?' I might as well have admitted I deliberately ran over people's pets for kicks, given the expressions on the faces of the women sitting opposite me.

'Of course it matters. Just because Oaktree Forstal is a bit bigger than us, they think they're better too, and as for the chair of their PTA...' Natasha shook her head, her hair flicking from side to side so that Claire had to duck out of the way. This was more than just a bit of friendly competition, and I caught Cameron and Ruhan exchanging a look.

'Let's not get personal.' Dolly's tone was calm, but Natasha pursed her lips. 'Worrying about what they're doing isn't going to help us achieve our best, is it? I'd rather spend the time thrashing out our own ideas.'

'We could do "fill the bag" again; I've got loads of old clothes I could collect for it.' Kate's suggestion was met with more sniggers from Natasha's friends, but if it bothered her she didn't let it show.

'That's a great idea.' Dolly scribbled a note on the end of the agenda in front of her. 'But seeing as we had one just before the end of last term, it might be better to wait until nearer to Christmas when everyone is ready for another wardrobe clear out?'

'How about giving out tubes of Smarties again, and getting the kids to fill the empty tubes with silver coins to bring back in? Didn't we do quite well out of that last time?' Ruhan's hopeful expression didn't last.

'Been there and done that. And, anyway, not everyone wants their children to be loaded up with sugar and e-numbers.' Claire Winters was *really* starting to get on my nerves.

'Actually, there aren't any e-numbers in Smarties, we checked before we sent them out.' Even Dolly was starting to lose her cool. 'But we did have some complaints that we were contributing to childhood obesity.'

'Please tell me you're joking?' I'd been out of full-time teaching for almost five years, but surely things hadn't got this bad?

'You'd be amazed at the things we get complaints about, Scarlett.' Cameron raised his eyebrows and for the first time I noticed what an unusual colour his eyes were – grey with flecks of amber and, at that particular moment, more than a hint of amusement.

'How about an exhibition of the children's art? I did one at the last school I worked in and you raise money by charging an entry fee to the children's families, and for a programme with photographs of all the artwork in. You can also do prints for people to buy, or other things like calendars and tea towels.' I waited for the disparaging comments from the other side of the table, but Natasha and the others were actually nodding.

'Great idea. Ode is always drawing in her spare time.' Every time Natasha said her daughter's name, I had to suppress the urge to smile. Then I remembered the poor kid was stuck with that for life.

'Brilliant, so we've got our idea.' Dolly was smiling again. 'Is there anything in particular the money is being raised for this time?'

'Mrs Davy asked me to mention the possibility of buying some more picture books for the infants' school, with a focus on diversity of family type.' Cameron looked directly at Dolly as he spoke, but there were still mutterings from across the table.

'I'm not being funny,' Claire Winters said, and I doubted she was capable of being funny if she tried, 'but I think we already spend far too much on this sort of stuff. We funded the food from around the world day last term, and most of the children at Appleberry come from *normal* families anyway. So why can't we do something for all the kids?'

'And how exactly would you define *normal*, Claire?' Kate was visibly bristling, and I had a horrible feeling that at least part of her outrage was for my benefit.

'Oh, you know what I mean!' Claire threw up her arms. 'Stop being so bloody precious about it, just because you want to suck up to Scarlett. I'm sure she hasn't got a massive chip on her shoulder about being a single mum. It's not like she did it by choice.'

'That's enough!' Dolly actually slapped her paperwork on the table and looked pointedly at Claire. 'This is not about anyone's personal circumstances, it's for the benefit of *all* the children, to help make them accepting of everyone.'

'It's okay, Dolly. I think it's best if I get things out in the open, then people can find something else to talk about.' I cleared my throat, wondering if the words would actually come out. But honesty was supposed to be the best policy, and if it gave Natasha and her friends something to laugh about in the bar later, then at least some good had come of my crappy situation. 'Some of you know that I went to school in Appleberry myself and, even back then, I always wanted to be a teacher. I stayed on in Exeter after my degree, when I got my first teaching job down there, but I ended up meeting my husband when I came back here for the holidays one summer. Some of you knew Luke too – Natasha was even at our wedding – but we decided to move back to the West Country after we got married and open a bed and breakfast and run it together, so we could fit the hours around Ava and have time together as a family. But I'm sure you already know that Luke walked out at the end of the summer, last year and just never came back. I won't bore you with the details of how I ended up back here, but it hasn't been easy. I know most people at the school don't look like they've been through anything like that, but I'm sure there are children whose families have far more to contend with than we know about. So if buying a few books makes a difference to those children, then I'm all for it.' By the time I finished speaking, I was breathless and couldn't look at anyone. If I'd seen any hint of a smirk from across the other side of the table, I wouldn't have been responsible for my actions. But at least they knew everything now.

Nobody said anything for what felt like forever, until Dolly reached across Kate and put her hand over mine. 'Thank you, Scarlett. You didn't have to tell everyone that, but I think it goes to show how important these sorts of resources are for all the children. Regardless of what we think we know about them and their home lives.' Dolly moved the agenda on and everyone agreed to the purchase of the books. Even Claire Winters seemed to go quiet.

* * *

'Did I just make a complete idiot of myself?' I turned to the others, after the meeting had come to a close and Natasha and her friends had disappeared downstairs to the bar.

'Well I thought you were brilliant.' Kate clapped a hand on my shoulder. 'That Claire Winters could do with putting in her place more often.'

'I don't want to cause a rift in the PTA, though. It sounds as though there are enough issues with Oaktree Forstal.'

'That's all on Natasha. I don't know why she hates their PTA chair so much, but whatever it is, it's definitely personal.' Dolly shrugged 'But you did the right thing. There's nothing for them to speculate about now, they know it all.'

'Let's forget about them, they're probably downstairs now rating all of our outfits out of ten and I've almost certainly got minus points! Are we still doing supper club this month?' Kate dropped me a wink.

'I did tell you about supper club, Scarlett, didn't I? There's been so much going on since the start of term that I can't remember if I said it, or just thought about saying it.' Ruhan was packing up her bag, but she stopped to look up at me.

'I don't think so.'

'We meet on the third Saturday of every month, just me, Kate and Dolly, and we go to a restaurant. It's a way of making sure that we still get the occasional night out, without the kids in tow. We keep asking Cam, but for some reason he never seems keen to hang around with a bunch of women outside of work!' She laughed as Cameron shook his head. 'It no use, Cam, we've heard every excuse there is from you now, so we'll just have to work on Scarlett instead.'

'I'd love to.' They were the sort of women I could definitely imagine being friends with, and they knew my most embarrassing secret already.

'That's brilliant! We're definitely on then.' Ruhan grinned. 'So, go on then, Cam, what *is* your excuse going to be this month?'

'All right, you've worn me down, I'll give it a go this month, as long as you promise to steer clear of certain topics. And I don't just mean work.'

'Text me a list!' Ruhan laughed. 'Miracles never cease, I didn't think you'd ever cave in and join us.'

'I think I can guess why.' Kate muttered the words, and then dropped another perfect wink. My mother wasn't the only one with the subtlety of a brick, and with Ruhan that was three of them on my case. Sadly, they were all in for a big disappointment.

3

'What's wrong sweetheart?' It was a month before Ava's fifth birthday. But even working her way through the Smiths Toys' catalogue, circling everything she wanted to add to her wish list, wasn't cheering her up.

'Nothing, Mummy.' The wobble in her bottom lip said otherwise.

'Promise?'

'It's...' She shook her head again.

'You can tell me anything, darling. But I can't make things better unless you do.'

'It's just that Margo's mummy and daddy are taking her to the zoo, because it's her daddy's birthday and...'

'And that makes you feel sad about your daddy?' If a single look could break a heart, it was the expression on Ava's face when she nodded. I'd wrestled with how much to tell her about Luke's disappearance, but the one thing I was determined to do was make sure she never thought she was to blame for it. I'd panicked and told her he was ill, and that had somehow made him forget he had a family. It was the idea I'd clung to in the first few days, too. That maybe he'd had an accident and taken a knock to the head, and was in hospital somewhere not knowing that his wife and daughter were crying themselves to sleep at night.

But after I'd contacted the police and checked every hospital in the area, I'd discovered he'd drained the last of the savings account two weeks before he left, which meant I had to accept he'd been planning it for a while. So I clung on to the hope that he was ill in another way. He had to be. The Luke I'd fallen in love with would never just disappear – something had to have happened to change him. If it wasn't a mental breakdown of some sort, then that meant it had to be because of me. And I wasn't sure I could live with that, any more than I wanted Ava to.

'I just wish I had a daddy.'

'You have, darling, he just isn't well enough to see you right now.' I massaged my temples. Was it wrong to keep telling her that? It'd been more than a year and he'd made no attempt to get in touch. None of his friends or family would admit to knowing where he was, and I'd gone and opened my mouth at the PTA meeting and admitted he'd walked out on us. Now there was the chance that someone would tell one of their own kids, and it would get back to Ava that way. But in that moment I just wanted to put a smile on my little girl's face. 'How about we ask Nonna and Gramps if they'd like to come to the wild animal park with us, and we could go out for ice cream afterwards?'

'You're the best mummy ever!' Ava threw her arms around my neck and I pressed the side of my face against her head. I wasn't the best mum, I was just trying to get by, and hoping I wasn't messing up my beautiful little girl in the process.

* * *

A trip to the wild animal park had been the perfect thing to do as a short-term fix. Ava dashed between the enclosures – where the animals had open, safari-park-style habitats – leaving the rest of us trailing in her wake. The park had been set up as a conservation project, with breeding programmes for endangered species. And with all the baby animals around, it was Ava's idea of heaven. But whenever she slowed down, her hand would snake into her grand-father's. Thank God we had him.

There was a little café just after the Great Apes Nursery, and we were all ready for a break after keeping up with Ava's frantic pace. It was still warm enough to sit on the tables outside, opposite the big sandpit and play area.

'Tea for you, Scarlett?' Dad still insisted on paying for every-thing whenever we went out together, as if I was still a child too.

'Yes, please. Do you need a hand?'

'No, you stay here with your mother, I think she wants a word.' There were few sentences in the world more ominous than that.

'Don't look at me like that.' Mum squared her shoulders as Ava skipped along beside Dad into the café.

'Why do I get the feeling I know what you're going to say?'

'All right, you don't want me to keep nagging, but you've got to accept that Luke's never coming back.'

'I have accepted it.' I couldn't keep the sigh out of my voice, I knew exactly where this was going. 'And I'm not even sure I'd want him to come back now.'

'*Not sure*! Of course you don't want him back.' Mum ran a hand through her thick sandy hair, which Ava and I had both inherited – although Mum's colour was out of a bottle these days.

'He's still Ava's dad.'

'Not so you'd know it. What kind of dad does that? Your dad would have died rather than leave you behind like that.' Mum's voice was getting louder, and I didn't want to argue with her, because she was right. Only Ava wasn't as lucky as me, and I still thought having Luke was preferable to no dad at all.

'Why are we talking about him anyway?'

'Because until you accept that he's gone, *for good*, you won't realise I'm right about you putting yourself back out there.'

'Mum, not this again, please.'

'I'm not expecting you to find another husband or anything.'

'Well, that's good, because I'm still married and, until I find out where Luke is, I can't do anything about changing that. At least not for two years.'

'That gives you the next year to start dipping your toes back into the water then, doesn't it? And before you say you haven't got time for dating, I've downloaded an app. I've already written the profile, all I need to do now is take your picture.' She pointed her phone towards me. 'There you go. It's best if it's a natural shot anyway.'

'You are joking, aren't you?' This was a new level, even for Mum. 'If you think I'm signing up to Tinder just to make *you* feel better, then I'm afraid you're going to be very disappointed.'

'It's not Tinder, it's a dating app for professionals. And you won't even have to bother keeping up with it all, I'll just let you know if I think there's anyone worth replying to.' She turned the phone towards me, my mugshot from a few seconds before in the centre of a profile *written by my mum*. The word tragic might be overused, but not this time. The only consolation was that the photo made me look like I'd escaped from a secure unit, so the chances of anyone contacting me were negligible. If doing this would keep Mum off my back for a bit, then I was going to let her have her fun. I'd obviously failed to convince her that Ava was enough for me, but maybe a few weeks in the minefield of internet dating would do it for me.

* * *

'This has been my best day ever!' Ava was still clutching Dad's hand as we walked along the pavement to the ice cream parlour in Pudstable, the nearest town to Appleberry that had a decent range of shops and restaurants. Marisetti's ice cream parlour, which had been my favourite place as a child, was still there.

'I'm really glad you're having such a good time, Ava, but I think it was a good idea to leave Mr Stripes in the car, in case he got broken.' I couldn't help smiling at the thought of the porcelain tiger, which she'd insisted she preferred to any of the soft toys in the gift shop. She was a funny kid sometimes, but her little quirks made me love her even more. Mum was right; Luke was an idiot to miss out on all this.

'Look, it's Mr Ellis!' Ava was already tugging on Dad's arm by the time I realised she was right.

'Hold on, Sweetpea, you can't just run off.' Dad pulled her back towards him and Cameron waved as he spotted us.

'Hello, Ava.' I loved the way he always spoke to her first, and her face lit up as she looked at him. Exactly the way it had when she'd pointed to Mr Stripes on the shelf. 'Are you having a good day?'

'We've been to the zoo and Gramps came on the tyre swing with me.'

'Wow, that sounds brilliant. Where are you going now?'

'To get ice cream!' Ava was almost dancing on the spot. 'Do you want to come?'

'I'd love to, but I've got somewhere to be, unfortunately.' Cameron looked up at me, and my gaze slid down towards the carrier bag in his hand. There was the top of a bottle of wine sticking out of one side, and the end of a loaf of French bread visible on the other side. It looked like the basis of a cosy meal for two.

'Mr Ellis has probably got lots of marking to do, too. It's what all teachers have to do at the weekend.' I wasn't sure if I was trying to convince myself or Ava.

'Are you going to introduce us before Mr Ellis has to go, then? I've seen you briefly when I've picked Ava up, but we haven't met properly.' Mum was actually tugging on my sleeve, too, as she looked at him. She was worse than Ava.

I figured I might as well get it over with, since she wasn't going to take no for an answer. 'This is my mum, Christine Rush, and you've already met my dad, Steve, when he came in to school last week.'

'Cameron Ellis. Nice to meet you.' He held out his hand to shake Mum's, and I braced myself for the avalanche of questions that would come my way as soon as he headed off. 'Nice to see you again too, Mr Rush.'

'Steve, please.' Dad smiled. He might not be as blatant as Mum, but they exchanged a look. What was it with everyone assuming I needed pairing off? No one seemed to understand that I might actually want to go it alone.

'We won't hold you up any longer.' I placed my hand in the small of Mum's back in an attempt to get her moving again. But she was almost as firmly fixed to the spot as the lamppost to the right of where we were standing.

'You'll have to come to dinner one evening. We always enjoy meeting Scarlett's friends.' Heaven knows what my dating profile said, if she was this forward in person. My cheeks went hot at the thought.

'That would be great. I'm really sorry, but I've got to get off. Enjoy your ice cream.' Cameron held up his hand again, edging past us on the narrow pavement, and I made a mental note to text him later to apologise for Mum. I didn't want him thinking I'd put her up to it, but even contemplating how to word that text made me sweat.

'No problem, see you Monday.' He turned and nodded in response, as Mum finally followed Dad and Ava towards Marisetti's. The barrage of questions I'd expected when I caught her up were strangely absent. Maybe she'd picked up on the same thing I had; Cameron couldn't wait to get away. But why should it be any different for a man I worked with, when my husband had felt exactly the same?

* * *

Ava was out for the count by the time I'd got to the bottom of the second page in her bedtime story. Sneaking out of the room, I cursed under my breath as the mobile phone in my jeans' pocket pinged loudly with the arrival of a text. Ava didn't even stir, and I closed the door quietly behind me, waiting to check my phone until I was back downstairs.

✉ Sender not in contact list
Be careful what you wish for.

'Something wrong?' Mum came into the kitchen as I was reading the message, and I shook my head.

'No, I think it's just a text from a wrong number.'

'Well don't furrow your brow like that, it'll give you wrinkles. And that's the last thing someone in your position wants.'

I wasn't going to ask her what she meant, not least because I already knew, and I wasn't going to show her the message either, even if it did sound a bit odd. It probably was just a wrong number, or some weirdo texting random numbers and hoping for a *you've sent this to the wrong number* or a *who is this?* text, so they could reply and start a stalking campaign, or drain my bank account of its non-existent contents. Okay, so maybe I'd seen too many police dramas, but my mother had definitely watched too many rom coms, and she'd probably end up suggesting I texted back, just in case the message was from Mr Right. As far as I was concerned it was more likely to be from the Easter Bunny.

Deleting the text, I stuffed the phone back in my jeans' pocket, before she could grab it and start showing me some dating profiles I might be interested in. At that point, even starting a conversation with a potential stalker seemed preferable. But I had no idea how weird things were about to get.

4

By the end of September, the leaves on the trees we passed on our morning walk to school were starting to change to autumn shades, and my pockets were already filled with the shiny conkers that Ava collected like a magpie every time she spotted one.

After three attempts, I'd found a way to word the text to Cameron apologising for the inappropriateness of Mum's dinner invitation, that I hoped wouldn't make the situation more awkward. But he'd brushed it off, saying he'd love to do it some time. It was just that incurable British politeness, though. Everyone knew that *some time* really meant never, and that was fine by me. Having him come to dinner out of a misplaced desire to do the right thing, and sending Mum into a frenzy of false expectations, was something I was more than happy to avoid.

Ava was making friends, and she was always talking about Kate's little girl, Molly, and what they'd got up to at playtime each day, so it finally felt like we were settling in. My confidence in the job grew every day, and Ruhan was still proving to be indispensable. Almost a week had passed without Ava mentioning Luke, and there were some days when I barely thought about him either. I was sleeping better too, and so far Mum hadn't mentioned the dating app again – probably because my photo had put off anyone within a 100-mile radius.

There was a big notice outside the church advertising the Harvest Festival service, a reminder that the weeks were peeling past and it would be Christmas before we knew it. Ava had her birthday first, though, and the thought made my stomach turn over. It would be devastating if Luke let another milestone go past without getting in touch, but the prospect of seeing him again was almost as terrifying. I had no idea how I was supposed to feel. Never mind how I was supposed to react, if he did finally put in an appearance. Although God help him either way if my mother got to him first.

I could hear raised voices before I even got to the playground. And when I spotted Kate, standing on the edge of a group of other mums, including Natasha Chisholm and Claire Winters, she was waving her arms around like a one-woman-wind turbine.

'Have a good day, darling.' Bending down, I planted a kiss on Ava's forehead. 'Go into your classroom, I just need to talk to Molly's mum.'

'Bye Mummy, love you.' Ava rushed off towards one of her friends, before I could answer.

'You're being sodding ridiculous as usual!' Kate's voice was carrying across the playground, and a couple of the kids started giggling as they walked past. It might not be the worst word she could have used, but I was going to have to step in.

'Is everything okay?' I stood next to Kate, confident she'd realise I was her ally, whatever the argument was about. Even if I had to pull her up on her slightly colourful language.

'You're never going to believe what this lot are whinging about now!' Kate shot me a look. 'Or maybe you will. They've got form after all!'

'Oh well, you would say that. You two are thick as thieves and it's no wonder Molly's one of the favourites!' Claire Winters glared at me and the back of my neck prickled. As much as I didn't like her, I never let that interfere with how I treated the children. If anything, I was overly careful not to show favouritism – especially with Ava at the school.

'You're going to have to tell me what's going on.' I kept my voice level as I spotted Cameron crossing the playground towards us.

'You tell her, Nat, I can barely get the words out. I'm so angry.' Claire was actually doing a very good job of getting the words out, seeing as I'd heard her from right down the lane.

'We've just had enough of certain kids always getting the biggest parts in school events.' Natasha dropped her gaze, as if she realised how ridiculous she sounded once she'd said it out loud. 'Claire's son has got the highest reading age in the class, and he was in tears last night because you've got him playing a sheaf of wheat. Especially when there are other children, like Molly, who can't read as well, doing some of the narration.'

'Really?' I had to swallow hard not to laugh. Cameron had warned me, but I'd assumed he was exaggerating at least a bit. We'd worked really hard at planning Harvest Festival so that no one would feel left out, too. 'Jules seemed really happy about his part when I spoke to him yesterday. And he's got a solo verse in the harvest song, which is why he isn't doing so much reading.'

'He didn't mention the song, but...'

Kate cut Claire off, before she could finish. 'Probably because you didn't give him a chance; I bet it was you who made him cry with the way you reacted.' She crossed her arms in the way I'd quickly come to realise she did when she knew she was right.

'I think this has gone too far.' Cameron's tone was firm, and for a moment I thought he was going to ask us all to put a finger on our lips, until we could learn to stop talking over each other. 'As Mrs

West said, Jules has got a very good part in the show and we've made sure everyone has a speaking role, or a singing role, if they want one. I'm sorry if you feel he hasn't been treated fairly, but I can assure you there's absolutely no favouritism going on. And this really isn't an appropriate way to air your concerns, by confronting other parents. So perhaps you'd like to make an appointment to meet with myself and Mrs West to discuss this further?' At the PTA meeting everything had been on first name terms, but Cameron wasn't sounding nearly so friendly now.

'It's not so much of an issue now that I know about the solo.' Claire stuck her chin out and I waited for the apology. But if a tumbleweed had come rolling across the playground, it wouldn't have surprised me.

'Well, if that's it, I've got a class to get to and I'm sure Mr Ellis has too.' I turned to Cameron, who nodded in response. I couldn't tell from his expression whether he thought I'd handled things okay, but I wasn't sure what else I could have done.

Kate's arms were still firmly crossed, and I made a mental note to tell her how much Molly's reading was picking up. She was a bit behind most of her year group, but we'd extended the volunteer reading programme, which seemed to be making all the difference. All children progressed at such different rates, and Kate didn't strike me as one of the competitive mums. But having your child singled out as being behind the others, wasn't something anyone wanted to hear in the playground.

Just as I reached the door of the classroom, I felt a hand on my shoulder, and my spine stiffened in response. If Claire Winters had followed me in for round two, I wasn't sure I could keep my patience.

'I'm sorry about that, but I did try to tell you.' Cameron shook his head as I turned to face him. 'Although a row as loud as that is a new one, even for me.'

'I just hope they haven't fed those views down to the kids. I'll have to keep an eye on Jules and make sure he doesn't tease Molly about her reading when we practise.' I sighed, despite my best efforts to keep it in. 'Some people need more to worry about.'

'I sometimes wonder if people focus on the small stuff to distract from bigger problems.' Cameron put a hand on my arm again. 'But you handled it really well. And there was nothing Claire Winters could do in the end, but back down.'

'Thank you.' It was nice to have his support, but in a weird sort of way it made me miss Luke. There was no one I could go home to, any more, and ask for a hug, while I offloaded about Claire Winters and what a complete pain in the backside she was. Ava was always up for a cuddle, and I could moan to Mum and Dad about demanding parents, but it wasn't the same as sharing all of it with someone.

Luke hadn't been there when I'd really needed him, though – so it was just the idea of him I missed. I was determined not to read anything else into it.

* * *

'Could I have a quick word, please?' Natasha Chisholm strode across the playground back towards the classroom at pick-up time, as one of her friends took Ode in the opposite direction. '*In private?*'

'Don't mind me.' Ruhan looked in my direction. 'I need to go and speak to Dolly anyway, to let her know I'll be a bit late getting to her place. I'll see you there later then, Scarlett?'

'Absolutely.' At least I hoped so. It was reliant on me surviving the next five minutes. 'Please can you ask Dolly to hold on to Ava for me, whilst I have a word with Mrs Chisholm?'

'Of course.' Ruhan headed over to where Dolly was standing,

with a group of other mums, and I turned towards my classroom, Natasha following close behind.

'If it's about this morning, as Mr Ellis said, I think it would be better for you to make an appointment to see us both.' I was following his lead and keeping it formal, but Natasha was already shaking her head.

'It *is* about this morning, but I've already apologised to Cam.' Natasha made the exchange sound uncomfortably familiar. I didn't call him by the shortened version of his name, but perhaps she knew him a lot better than I did. The thought annoyed me far more than it should have.

'*You* apologised?' She'd definitely got under my skin, not least because she always looked so irritatingly perfect, but she wasn't the one who needed to say sorry.

'I know Claire can be blunt, but she's got some difficult things going on at the moment and that always seems to put her on the defensive.' Natasha ran a hand through her hair. 'She's been having some tests; it seems there's a good chance the BRCA gene might run in her family, which means she's potentially at increased risk of developing certain types of cancer. She's lost a couple of aunts and her grandmother to breast cancer already, and her older sister was recently diagnosed with ovarian cancer. She's just struggling with handling it, which is making her lash out.'

'That must be a real worry for her.'

'It's not just that, though, and I know you won't tell anyone this bit...' Natasha looked over her shoulder, as if double checking no one else would overhear. 'But Claire's not even that worried about her own results; her daughter Amber is twenty-one and just going into her last year at uni, and Claire's terrified she might have passed the gene on to her.'

'Claire's got a daughter at uni?' It was a good job Mum couldn't see me, because I was furrowing my brow pretty damn hard. 'She only looks mid-thirties at most.'

'She's thirty-six.' Natasha shrugged. 'Being a teenage mum threw all her plans into chaos, so Claire's parents more or less raised Amber as their own. Her parents live up in Yorkshire, which means most of Claire's friends around here don't even know about it. She'd kill me if she knew I'd told you, but I wanted you to understand that there are reasons why she acts the way she does. She had to make some tough choices to do what she felt was right by Amber, and she's probably over protective of Jules as a result, but I guess that's understandable. As you saw at the PTA meeting, she also gets on her high horse about what she thinks is pandering to people's *issues*. Because she's had to deal with her past and get on with things, she thinks other people should too. That's why she gets so defensive. Add to that the pressure of these genetic tests, and she's really struggling at the moment.'

'Poor Claire; I can't imagine what it's like to have something like that hanging over your child's health.' I had to sit down on the edge of my desk. It was obvious now she'd said it that Claire seemed to be permanently on edge. But what surprised me was Natasha wanting to protect her, even if that meant trusting me with a secret that could potentially put their friendship at risk.

'I know. I keep looking at Ode and wondering how I'd even sleep at night if we were going through something like that.' Natasha gave a half-smile. 'Seeing how you are with Ava, I knew you'd understand. And I thought it might help you a bit to realise the way Claire speaks to you sometimes is nothing personal.'

'Thank you.' I didn't know what else to say. Every time she mentioned Ava, the topic of Luke's disappearance seemed to hang over us like a bad smell I didn't want to mention. But Natasha clearly had no such qualms.

'We don't know where he is by the way – Luke, I mean. I'd tell you if we did. He rang James to ask if he could borrow some money when he first left, just after you contacted us to see if we'd heard anything. But he wouldn't tell James where he was. He still logs in to our Class of 2003 Facebook group every now and then, but no one seems to know for sure where he's staying. I even got James to ask around with some of the others, but if they know anything they're keeping it to themselves.'

'I knew he'd changed his number. I tried calling him every day for the first month.' I wanted to clamp my hand over my mouth. Why I was opening up to Natasha was beyond me. But she'd taken me so much by surprise, with her insight into Claire's behaviour, that I just didn't seem able to see her as the enemy any more. She and James were the closest link I had to Luke in Appleberry, too. 'At first he just didn't answer my calls, and then the number was disconnected. Even his parents said they hadn't heard from him, other than to let them know he was alive.'

'At least we know he's okay then. James didn't have the sort of money he wanted to borrow available just like that, and he's felt terrible ever since.'

'How much did he ask for?'

'Ten thousand pounds.'

'Oh God, I'm sorry.' What could he need that sort of money for, after he'd already drained our account? Given the circumstances, I couldn't bring myself to agree with Natasha that knowing he was alive was an entirely good thing. But why he needed so much money, raised a whole host of other questions. Maybe he had other debts I didn't know about – aside from those we'd racked up trying to get the business on its feet. That might explain things. Or maybe he'd got hooked on something. If he'd run away from a bunch of drug dealers threatening to smash his kneecaps, would that make what he did any more acceptable? Sometimes, in the months since he'd left, I'd found myself thinking that it would have been easier if he'd died. It was a horrible thing to think, but I couldn't help it. At least then we'd have closure. This was all such a mess and, by involving the Chisholms, he'd made sure I couldn't leave it behind me and make a fresh start.

'You've got nothing to apologise for.' Natasha smiled again, which almost made it worse. 'And I promise you'll be the first to know if we hear anything from Luke.'

'Thank you.' I was repeating myself, but what else could I say – that a big part of me hoped Luke never got in touch with any of us again? My life in Appleberry might not be perfect, but I was happier than I'd been in a long time and I didn't want anything to come along to change that. Not even if it was Ava's father.

* * *

Kate looked up from the table, where she was surrounded by off-cuts of material, and she'd somehow acquired a lump of bright yellow paint in her fringe. 'Whose idea was this again?'

'Dolly kindly offered to help with the costumes for Harvest Festival and, if you remember, you couldn't wait to volunteer!' I laughed as she pushed her fringe off her forehead, putting another streak of paint through it in the process.

'She's right, you did offer. No one had your arm up your back.' Dolly came into the kitchen, her mobile phone still in her hand.

'Please tell me, that once you finished with whoever it was that called, you ordered us a big juicy pizza, with extra cheese?' Kate held up the sheaf of wheat costume she'd made for Claire Winters' son, Jules. 'I don't know why, but this is really making me crave a big slice of four cheese pizza.'

'Maybe it's the shape? I just hope you've never eaten cheese quite that shade of yellow. You'd be radioactive by now, if you had.' Dolly put her phone on the counter and flicked on the kettle. 'I'll happily order us a takeaway in a minute, but I've got something to tell you first. About that phone call.'

'Oh, God, let me guess... It was Claire and Natasha again, to say Jules has got one less word in his solo than Molly.'

'Come on, Kate, we talked about this. Natasha was just supporting her friend, and there are reasons why Claire acts the way she does.' I bit my lip, still feeling guilty for the assumptions I'd made about them both. But Kate wasn't as easily convinced. Maybe it was because she only knew half the story, but I'd had to keep my promise to Natasha. I'd told the others about Claire's genetic tests and her sister's cancer diagnosis, which was more than enough to explain her irrational behaviour. There was no need for them to know about what Claire had been through as a teenager too. That was her story to share, not mine. I couldn't imagine what it like for her, waiting to hear if she'd passed on a faulty gene to her daughter, through absolutely no fault of her own. But looking across at Ava, on the walk over to Dolly's, the thought had made me shudder – like someone walking over my grave.

'All right, maybe I can forgive Claire for being a total pain in the arse, but what's Natasha's excuse for being so bloody competitive? Did you get that email she sent out about making sure we bring in at least ten items each for Harvest Festival? And how we've got to beat Oaktree Forstal at *all* costs.' Kate wrinkled her nose. 'Does she know not everyone earns a six-figure salary, or has a husband that does? Her obsession with beating Oaktree is bordering on the psychotic.'

'The email was a bit OTT, but I think she's just one of those people who has to be the best at everything they do.' I shrugged my shoulders, but Kate's arms were already folded across her chest.

'So what do you reckon? Poor little Nat wasn't given enough love as a child, or her husband used to date the chair of the Oaktree

Forstal PTA and she's never quite forgiven either of them?' Kate's
eyes lit up. 'Now there's some gossip I'd like to hear!'

'Well you'll have to leave your detective work for another day.
Clear a space and I'll tell you what the phone call was really about.'
Dolly came back to the table with the tray of drinks, and Kate
pushed the sheaf of wheat to one side.

'Is everything okay?' I was suddenly worried it might be bad
news, and Dolly's eyes had gone a bit glassy looking. Here we were,
banging on about Natasha and Claire being insensitive, and our
friend was waiting to tell us something important.

'I'm just a bit shell-shocked, I suppose. I didn't really think it
would happen.' Dolly took a sip of her drink, her knuckles turning
white from gripping the mug so tightly.

'I don't think I can take the suspense, if you're going to finish
your whole coffee off before you tell us, Doll.' Kate pushed her
drink away. 'Are you going to put us out of our misery, or do we have
to play twenty questions?'

'Sorry, I'm still trying to get my head around it, and wondering if
I've done the right thing. But that was my social worker.'

'Your *social worker*?' I had no idea what was going on, but Dolly
was the last person I'd have expected to have a social worker.

'We were approved for adoption a few months ago, but I didn't
want to tell anyone until we were matched with a child, just in case
it jinxed it.' I didn't know whether Dolly saw the expression that
crossed Kate's face, but surprise didn't come close. 'When I realised
there wouldn't be any more kids for me and Greg, I just felt like our
family wasn't complete. With only Billy and Maggie still at home,
now that Jodie and Tim are both at uni, and Sally has moved in
with her boyfriend, it just feels empty. I didn't think they'd want us
at our age, and then they said we could only have two children over
the age of six, because they're harder to place.'

'*Only* two?' Kate was still wearing her *are-you-out-of-your-mind* expression. She'd made it clear, more than once, that having two children was already pushing it for her.

'Well, that was the plan. But then we went to one of the adoption parties, where they introduce approved adopters to some of the harder to place children, and we fell in love with this group of siblings.'

'Do they really do that, parade kids around at a party, and see if anyone wants to take them home?' Kate's shocked expression had finally been replaced with a scowl, but I couldn't help agreeing with her. It sounded pretty awful for the kids, especially if no one picked them. Like a speed-dating disaster – where no one wants to meet up with you again – only with much higher stakes.

'It's not like that. They have games for the kids, and we all just join in and get to know each other more naturally. It's much better than just seeing things on paper, and it can work really well with the children who it's usually more difficult to find a family for.' Dolly smiled and Kate's scowl relaxed a bit. 'In all honesty, we'd never have looked at our four on paper. But when we met them, it just felt right.'

'There are *four* of them?' Kate's facial muscles were getting the workout of their lives.

'Yes, two boys and two girls, between the ages of one and six.' Dolly took an audible gulp. 'The social workers were desperate to try and keep them together, but nobody seemed to want to take on all four siblings.'

'There's a reason for that!' Kate wasn't holding back, but I didn't know what to say. Dolly was so relaxed and the children who were still at home obviously took after her, too. They were entertaining Ava and Molly in the playroom, along with Kate's son, Barnaby, who was twelve, whilst we got on with the Harvest Festival costumes. So the chances were they'd be more than willing to muck in and help when the other children arrived. But taking on four siblings was a huge commitment, and Dolly's husband, Greg, worked long hours. He was away a lot and I still hadn't met him, so most of it was going to fall to her. I was barely managing work and Ava, and I had Mum and Dad on hand whenever I needed them. Dolly deserved a medal. But for now she'd have to make do with my unswerving admiration.

'I didn't think they'd let us have all four, but we're the only adopters who've expressed an interest. The kids were even featured in a documentary on one of the satellite channels, but in the end it was a choice between us and splitting them up.' Dolly widened her eyes. 'And that was the call we've been waiting for; they've agreed to change our approval so we can take all four of them.'

'That's amazing.' I put my hand on Dolly's arm and she turned towards me again, blinking back tears. 'And you and Greg are even more amazing for doing it.'

'We're not amazing. We've got six bedrooms and three of them are empty almost all of the time. But more than that, I just felt like there was space in here.' Dolly put her hand over her heart and I wanted to throw my arms around her.

'You know what else this means, don't you?' I braced myself for whatever comment Kate was about to make. It could have been anything.

'What?'

'It means you won't have to resign from the PTA. I can't wait to see Natasha's face when she finds out; she's been waiting to be chair since the day her eldest started!'

'I think Dolly might be a bit busy.' I couldn't even imagine the impact of adopting four children. I probably wouldn't brush my hair for a year, never mind find time to chair the PTA.

'I'd like to keep doing it if I can, and Greg's going to cut down his hours at work, but we'll have to see.' Some of the colour had come back into Dolly's face. 'And the social worker said the docu-

wouldn't be with anyone from Appleberry. I didn't want to ruin the life I was making, if things went wrong, and I didn't want anyone else to let Ava down.

'Tough meeting?'

Cameron nodded. 'Oaktree Forstal have had their Ofsted notification, which means we'll almost certainly have ours next week.'

'Do they always go in tandem like that?'

'They always have done in the past.' Cameron drew level with me as he stepped into the hallway. 'You don't look too bothered; most teachers start hyperventilating at the mere mention of the O word.'

'I thought it might be something worse.'

'Worse than an inspection?'

'I thought they might have called a meeting to talk about ending my probation period. After the whole Claire Winters thing.'

'I think even she realised she was being out of order in the end.' Cameron caught my eye. 'And they'd have to get rid of me if they wanted to get rid of you. I knew at your interview that you'd be good, but you've made more progress with Class 2 in half a term than even I expected.'

'Thanks.' I really was going to have to learn how to take a compliment with more enthusiasm. 'You're not worried about the inspection, are you?'

'I think we're a great little school, and I can't see any reason why our good grading from last time would be reduced. But James Chisholm's made it clear he'll be disappointed if we aren't graded as outstanding this time.' Cameron shrugged. 'He didn't actually come out and say that heads would roll if not, but it was definitely implied.'

'Sounds like James and Natasha are quite the power couple.' Mrs Chisholm might have shown her softer side, but there was no doubt she'd back her husband all the way on this. Especially if Oaktree Forstal achieved an outstanding grade.

'They are. But do you know what? I think having you on board could make all the difference. If we get enough outstanding teaching grades, it could just about swing it.'

'No pressure then.'

'None at all.' He laughed as he followed me down the corridor to join the others, but I still wasn't worried. Whatever happened with Ofsted, I knew Cameron would support me. And I hadn't had a partnership like that – professionally, or personally – for a very long time.

* * *

Mum and Dad were already in bed by the time I got home, so I took the opportunity to catch up on a bit of trashy TV. For once, I didn't have to contend with Dad channel-surfing in the hope of finding something – *anything* – featuring Alan Titchmarsh, or Ava begging to watch *Frozen* for what felt like the millionth time.

I was curled up on the sofa, with a cup of tea and a packet of chocolate biscuits, when my phone pinged. I'd have bet every last biscuit the text was going to be from Kate, asking me what I really thought about Dolly adopting four children. But it wasn't.

✉ Sender not in contact list
Remember, every action has a consequence.

I shivered, my eyes darting towards the French windows, the darkness of the garden outside suddenly far more sinister than it had been only a moment before. Getting up, I pulled the curtains shut and looked at the text again. It wasn't really threatening, but for some reason it felt like it. I tried to remember if it looked like the same number as the text I'd deleted before. I was pretty sure the last three digits of both numbers had been 982, but I couldn't be certain. Either way, two weird messages were more than enough, so this time I blocked the number and deleted the message. If someone wanted to chat, then they were going to have to reveal themselves. And if it was Luke, he'd have to grow a spine and make contact like a normal person. Switching the phone off, I tried to get back into the reality TV show I'd been watching, but all I could think about was whether the messages really could be from my husband. And if they weren't, I just had to hope that blocking the number would be enough.

5

Mum and Dad's poodle-cross terrier, Jasper, stuck his head into a hole near the base of the tree in front of us. There was no way he was ever going to catch the rabbit that had shot down there, but no one could say he gave up easily.

'How are things at school?' Mum was marching on the spot as we waited for Jasper to stop yapping at the hole, in the misguided hope that it would encourage the rabbit to pop up and let him have his moment. There was only a week until the clocks went back, so there was just about time to squeeze in a walk after work.

'Busy. We've got the Harvest Festival show coming up, and the Ofsted inspectors will be in for the best part of next week too.'

'And what are you going to do this weekend? It won't do you any good sitting at home watching *Strictly* with Ava every Saturday night you know. One day, she'll be off, out on the town with her own friends, and you'll realise you forgot to have a life while you were young enough.'

'Can't you keep still for a minute?' The marching on the spot was relentless, but even a conversation about her daily step count was preferable to discussing my love life. Or, more accurately, the complete absence of it.

'I'm beating your father's count by five thousand steps now. It's a new personal best.'

'Great. Well you better hope Ava doesn't rope him into a Just Dance session on the Wii while we're out, then, or he could easily catch you up.' I could have sworn she doubled the pace of her marching at just the thought of it.

'There's a cookery class for singles at the community centre in Pudstable tomorrow night, hosted by the dating site from that app I downloaded. They're making a curry, apparently.'

'Good for them.' I whistled at Jasper; it was time to move on before Mum got really stuck into her favourite subject and I wanted the Friday night wind-down to start as soon as possible. When Mum had asked me to take Jasper out, I'd thought she meant on my own, and the idea of a bit of a walk to clear my head had been quite appealing. This definitely wasn't what I'd had in mind. At least if we were walking, she couldn't give me *that* look.

'The class could be good for you, too.'

'Mum, I can't have this conversation again. It's been so busy at school this week, I just want to relax this weekend and, anyway, I didn't sit home last Saturday night. If you remember, I had supper club with Dolly, Kate and Cam.' I'd found myself using the short-ened version of his name since the supper club, because everyone else seemed to do it, and he signed his emails off that way. It didn't signal anything more, but Mum picked up on it all the same.

'It's Cam now, is it? You don't want to hang around waiting for him to make his move, either. From what I heard, when I asked around, he's not the settling down type.'

I actually laughed; her persistence was breath-taking. 'Neither am I! Not again anyway.'

'I keep telling you, you don't have to find Mr Right, you just need a bit of practice getting back into the swing of things with *Mr Right Now*.'

'And what makes you think they'll be lining up waiting for me to arrive at this curry night? There'll probably be ten women to every man there.' If I could have guaranteed that was the case, I'd have happily gone along. At least if I showed willing, at an event where I had absolutely no chance of being asked out, it might get Mum off my back for a bit. I could have been blunt and told her to butt out of my life, or even shouted at her until she finally got the message, but deep down I knew she just wanted what she thought was best for me. The same as I did for Ava.

'They've got a limited number of spaces, and they only ever book in the same number of men and women, to maximise the chance of more matches.'

'And how do you know all this?' Jasper ran across the path in front of me, chasing another rabbit into a patch of brambles. I stopped to look at Mum, a horrible realisation dawning on me.

'Because I spoke to the woman organising it, when I booked you a place.' At least she had the decency to look at bit sheepish. 'Well strictly speaking, I spoke to the woman when I was pretending to be you.'

For a moment I was actually speechless, until Jasper emerged from the bushes and started to drag his bottom along the ground, desperately trying to dislodge the clump of thorns that were tangled up in the fur under his tail.

'Even the dog has more boundaries than you, Mum. I'd like to say I can't believe you did that, but sadly I can.'

'I'm only doing it for your benefit.' I knew I'd really got to her when she stopped marching on the spot.

'No, you're doing it because you're terrified that I'm going to end up on my own like Auntie Leilah, but I'd much rather be on my own than settle for just anyone.' I bent down and pulled the clump of thorns out of Jasper's fur and he was immediately on the hunt again. I envied the blind enthusiasm undented by his persistent failure. If only I could be more like Jasper, then Mum would be happy.

'I'm not asking you to settle for anyone, I just want you to have someone like I've got in your dad. And for Ava to have someone like him too.'

'She's already got Dad in her life.'

'You know what I mean.' She was right, I did know what she meant, and she knew exactly how to press my buttons, too. 'She deserves a father who adores her, even if it's not her biological father. I'm not saying you're going to meet him at this curry night, but he definitely won't drop into your lap whilst you're watching *Strictly*.'

'If I go to this curry night, do you promise not to book me into something without asking, ever again, and not to even mention dating this side of Christmas? Even if it doesn't work out?'

'I promise.' Mum pulled me into a hug and, despite my initial resistance, I eventually let my body relax. It was one night and at the very least I'd come home with a recipe for making a decent curry. It wouldn't be that bad – what was the worst that could happen?

* * *

'Did you know that turmeric plants were cultivated by the Harappan civilisation as early as 3000 years BC?' Lyle had introduced himself to me as soon as I'd walked through the door of the cookery class. He couldn't help the nasally twang in his voice, and I was determined not to hold it against him, but it would have been easier if he hadn't insisted on imparting not-so-fascinating facts about every ingredient we picked up. Especially as it sounded like he'd made a list from an internet search, just so he could share his new-found knowledge at the class. Not that there was anything wrong with trying to impress, but it would have done more for me if he'd actually asked me a question instead, or told me something about himself. He was nice looking, but we were only halfway through the class, and I was already wondering if I could excuse myself to go to the loo and never come back.

'Right, now you've got the chicken or vegetables for your curry marinating in the spices, we'll move on to preparing the accompaniments.' The class leader's tone demanded attention, which thankfully called a halt to Lyle's monologue on the health benefits of ginger. 'I think it would be a good idea for people to move around and work with someone else on the side dishes, so that you get the chance to meet as many people as possible.' I could happily have kissed the class leader, as Lyle moved to a different table and a new audience.

'You look like you've had enough already. Is it not turning out to be your thing?' I looked up at the man who'd spoken, and my shoulders sagged with relief. He had a rich, deep voice and a look of amusement that suggested he knew exactly *why* the curry class wasn't turning out to be my thing. He held out his hand. 'I'm Xander, by the way, pleased to meet you.'

'Not as pleased as I am to meet you.' For some reason I did a weird sort of bob when I shook his hand, like I was meeting the queen. 'I'm Scarlett.'

'So tell me, Scarlett, do you feel your life's complete now that you know garam masala contains cassia bark?'

'You could hear it too?'

'I think most of the room could hear him, but I couldn't stop looking at you.' Xander paused. 'And that wasn't completely down to how funny your attempts to look interested were.' Lyle was on the other side of the room, holding up a pot of cardamom pods. I couldn't hear him, but I'd have bet a month's wages he was telling his new cookery partner that they were one of the most expensive spices around.

'He's a very nice man, just not for me. But hopefully he'll have more luck with someone else.'

'I'm hoping you might have more luck with someone else, too, or at least lose that desperate-to-escape look you've been wearing for the last forty-five minutes.'

'It wasn't that bad.' Poor Lyle. I really hoped he hadn't been able to read my expression as easily as Xander obviously had, and it made me smile when Lyle's new cooking partner laughed at something he said. 'It looks like he's having more luck already.'

'That makes two of us then.'

* * *

There were three missed calls on my phone by the time I left the cookery class, and six text messages. All from Mum. She'd wanted to drop me off and pick me up from the class, which I'd flat out refused. So it was no surprise how impatient she was for a match report. I was just about to text her back, when the phone rang again.

'Why haven't you answered any of my calls?'

'I've just this minute come out of the class, Mum.'

'You could have texted me.'

'The cookery teacher asked us to put our phones away at the start and, in any case, it would have looked really rude if I'd broken off from a conversation with someone to text you back.'

'So there were people you wanted to have a conversation with then?' Mum instantly sounded much more upbeat.

'There was one.' I'd slid Xander's business card into the pocket of my jeans, and promised to give him a call about meeting up. It was more than I'd expected from the class, but I didn't want to say as much to Mum, or she'd be booking us in to have our banns read at the church opposite Appleberry School.

'And?' I obviously wasn't going to get away with not giving her any details at all.

'And... he's thirty-five, never been married or had any kids.'

'Sounds like a commitment-phobe to me. Same as Cameron – in their thirties and not a sniff of ever having had a serious relationship. It's a big red flag.'

'I thought we agreed I wasn't looking for commitment.'

'Hmm, so what about his family, do they live locally?'

'He's not got much of a family from what I can gather. His mum passed away a couple of years ago and he's not close to the rest of them.'

'You definitely want to avoid him then.' Mum tutted. 'It should have been a big warning that Luke wasn't going to be a family man, because of what your in-laws are like. You don't want to get involved with another man who's got a weird relationship with his family.'

'Luke's dad didn't go out to buy eggs and never come back.' I couldn't keep the emotion out of my voice. 'And just because someone isn't close to their parents or siblings, it doesn't mean they aren't capable of having good relationships. I spoke to Xander for all of about an hour and I certainly don't know him well enough to jump to the sort of conclusions you are.'

'I still think you should steer clear. Never trust someone who says they aren't close to their family.'

'There are lots of reasons people don't want to see their family.' I could think of a few myself at that point. 'But I suppose I was being naïve, thinking you'd be pleased that I wanted to go on a date with someone.'

'I'm just thinking of Ava.'

'Are you saying I'm not?' Suddenly an evening of listening to

Lyle, explaining a hundred things I'd always wanted to know about cumin seeds and been afraid to ask, seemed preferable to talking to Mum for a moment longer.

'Of course not.'

'Well, that's what it sounds like, and I never even wanted to go to this cookery class in the first place, if you remember? But now I've held up my end of the bargain and you promised not to mention anything about dating again.'

'At least not until you come around to my way of thinking.'

'Don't hold your breath.' I was definitely going to drive the long way home; I was in no hurry to get back and carry on this conversation. 'They're going to close the barrier to the car park in a minute, so I'll see you when I get home.'

'Okay darling and you know I've only got your best interests at heart, don't you?'

'Yes, Mum.' Deep down I did, but the constant interfering had also made me realise that it was time for me to move out. Otherwise one of us was going to say something we couldn't take back. Maybe Cam would let me pitch a tent in the playground – with the financial state Luke had left us in, it was about all I could stretch to.

Concentrating on negotiating the country lanes, in the dark, was quite a good way to clear my head. I had to work out a way to manage my relationship with Mum before it imploded altogether. Despite her frequently voiced good intentions, what she *thought* was best for me and Ava, wasn't the same thing as what *was* best for us. When Luke left, the bed and breakfast was just about starting to break even and, although we'd borrowed the maximum the bank would lend us, we'd kept some funds in reserve in case things went wrong. But when I'd checked our account after he disappeared, he'd withdrawn every penny. We had a huge mortgage to pay, as well as suppliers and some casual staff. He'd timed it impeccably, too, leaving just as the season was drawing to an end, and bookings over the winter were barely enough to keep us afloat. I didn't sleep for more than about an hour at a time in the first couple of weeks, but somehow, we made it through. I had to give the casual staff more hours, whilst I went back to supply teaching. I could earn more that way, and ensure I made the minimum payments on all the debts. But it wasn't sustainable, and I'd had to come to terms with giving up the business pretty quickly.

The only way we could avoid having the bed and breakfast repossessed, and risk losing everything, was to find a tenant who wanted to take it on as a going concern. I'd been close to giving up and just dropping the keys in to the bank, when one of the casual staff said he wanted to take it on with his brother on a two year lease. Even losing twenty pounds in weight, with the sheer stress of it all, didn't feel like a silver lining. It felt as if I'd been wrung through a mangle over and over again until there was nothing left of the old me. Coming home to Mum and Dad had been our only real option. I loved them, more than I could ever express, but it had been harder to go back to that parent and child relationship than I'd ever dreamt. Especially when Mum still didn't trust me to make my own decisions. Maybe that grated as much as it did because half of me thought she was right, after so much had gone wrong. But I didn't feel like a child any more, sometimes I felt a thousand years old.

Driving home from the cookery class, I started doing calculations in my head – October should see us in the clear, and by Christmas we'd have enough saved for a rental deposit. I'd asked around if anyone knew whether there were any houses coming up in the village; I couldn't wait for Ava and me to have the new beginning we really needed. I didn't want to think about what might happen if the tenants in Cornwall didn't want to renew their lease at the end of the two years, because that would completely derail my plans, but I was going to make an appointment to see a solicitor and talk through what my options were if I never found Luke. It was time to move on.

I was so lost in thought, I didn't see the pothole in the dark. But the car bounced in and out of it so hard, it jolted my neck. It was another downside to living in the countryside, the roads were last on the council's list for any repairs, and heavy frosts the winter before had resulted in more holes than a wheel of Swiss cheese.

Silently praying there wouldn't be any damage to Mum's car, I slowed down, but then I felt it. The distinctive drag of a flat tyre. I'm not ashamed to admit that more than a couple of swear words escaped from my lips, as I pulled into the next passing place and took out my mobile phone.

I was perfectly capable of changing a tyre, but doing it on a country lane in the pitch black held very little appeal. It was what roadside recovery had been invented for, anyway. I might not have a car of my own any more, thanks to Luke, but Mum and Dad's policy would cover me.

No service.

I should have guessed it would happen, before I even picked up my phone. There'd been several occasions since I'd got back to Appleberry, when I'd had to do an impromptu jig around my parents' house, until I found the sweet spot with my mobile, and could actually make a call or send a text. I'd cancelled the mobile data; yet another cost-cutting exercise I had to thank Luke for. So, without Wi-Fi to connect to, I was reliant on my mobile provider's signal. It was just my luck that the connection in Appleberry was the modern day equivalent of two polystyrene cups and a piece of string, but even worse in the woodland where I'd come to a stop. It was definitely turning into one of those nights.

I was still four miles away from the village and there was barely a house, never mind a phone box, between the passing place and home. Not that I would've had the guts to knock on someone's door to ask for help, anyway. The biggest crime the village had seen for years might have been the theft of a chicken coop from Appleberry Farm, but I wasn't going to take a chance. There was nothing for it, but to walk home in the dark. I was a grown up, though, and the sound of an owl hooting, and the screaming of a fox in the dense woodland was just part of country life. Wasn't it? There was nothing to be afraid of. I knew that logically, but with the curse of an overactive imagination every shadow looked like it might be harbouring an axe murderer. And the text messages I'd been receiving recently hadn't helped much either.

I'd only been walking for about five minutes when I heard a car. Stepping onto the verge, as far away from the road as I could get without falling into the dyke, I held my breath. *Please just let them drive by.*

The car whizzed past, and there was no way it could have seen me going that quickly, thank God. But, no sooner had I let out a breath than it stopped. And, worst still, it started to reverse back towards me. This was it, I was going to have my throat slit, and be found dead in a ditch on the side of the road by a passing tractor driver the next morning. And Ava wasn't going to have either of her parents.

I should probably have started to run, but my legs wouldn't move, and all the time my brain was working through every possible way I could be killed. It was ridiculous I know, but as the car drew level with me, I let out an ear-piercing scream. I wasn't going without a fight.

'Scarlett, what's wrong? It's only me.' I couldn't make out the man's face as he got out and came around to my side of the car, taking hold of both my arms. It took a few seconds for me to stop screaming, even when I realised it was Cam.

'I thought you were a...' I couldn't say it out loud now that I was staring into those hypnotic grey eyes of his. He'd think I'd lost the plot, and I was beginning to think he might be right.

'What are you doing walking out here at this time of night? Is that your car, in the passing place?'

'It's Mum's car, I hit a pothole and it's got a flat.' I was shivering, but I wasn't sure if it was down to the temperature or the fact that I'd succeeded in scaring myself half to death. I hadn't bothered to bring a coat out, but Cam took off his jacket and put it around my shoulders. 'And then I couldn't get a signal in the woods.'

'So it's not been the best of nights?'

'You could say that.'

'Come on, let's get you home, you can get the car sorted in the morning.' He opened the door and I slid into the passenger seat, my teeth still chattering. 'Are you okay, you look a bit freaked out?'

'I kept telling myself there was nothing to be scared of, but it wasn't working all that well and then when you stopped...'

'You're safe now.' Cam smiled, and I had to stop myself from telling him that he always made me feel safe. It would have given him the wrong idea, and I wasn't attracted to anyone in that way, not any more. He always seemed to be there, though, supporting me at school and now rescuing me when I needed it most.

'Have you at least been out somewhere that was worth all this trouble?' Even the tone of his voice was reassuring.

'I was at an Indian cooking class in Pudstable.'

'I love a good curry, although I'm better at dialling the takeaway than I am at trying to cook one.'

'Me too, but it was Mum's idea. It was actually a singles event, where you do an activity and get the chance to chat with other single people. I told her I wasn't interested, but she has a way of grinding me down. And, while I'm living with them, sometimes it's just easier to give in.'

'So did it live up to your expectations, this singles thing?' Cameron kept his eyes firmly on the road. 'Or more to the point, to your mum's?'

'Unfortunately, it lived up to what I was expecting. I chatted to a couple of nice people, but there was no one I desperately wanted to meet again. And that was before I got the flat tyre and the fright of my life!' I finally managed a smile.

'You wouldn't recommend it as a way to meet someone, then?'

'I exchanged numbers with one guy, but I'm perfectly happy being single. Even taking his number was more for Mum's benefit than mine.' I hesitated, wanting to ask Cam why he was interested. By all accounts, he didn't need any help getting a date.

'I suppose it'll take a while before you're ready to move on from your husband.'

'Uh-huh.' I wasn't sure if it was that any more. Sitting next to Cam, for just a moment I could imagine myself with someone else. Someone who made me feel safe, someone I could rely on. It might not sound romantic but, after Luke, I wanted someone I could trust with my bank account *and* my heart. Even more than that, I wanted someone I could trust with Ava's heart. That was far too much to risk, though. We were safer on our own.

'What about you, what have you been up to tonight?'

'I was just at Mum's. Patching up the damage the leak did now that it's been properly fixed.'

'You're very close, you and your mum, aren't you?' I might have taken Mum's theory about a man needing to be close to his family with a pinch of salt, but I liked that about Cam.

'We are. After Dad walked out when I was eight, I suppose I just became the man of the house, and I still feel the need to look out for her.'

'I'm sure she loves that.' As we got closer to the village, I changed the subject. It didn't seem right to ask him more about his father leaving, even though I was far more interested than I wanted to admit. So we talked about the inspection instead, but I couldn't help wondering if his dad's disappearance had made Cam reluctant to settle down. I'd obviously spent far too much time listening to Mum's insights from questionable internet sources, where she regularly quoted 'research' about family dynamics that supported her point of view. It was none of my business why Cam didn't have a partner. There were already a million things for me to worry about, so the space it was taking up in my head made no sense at all.

6

The playroom at Dolly's house could restock Hamleys toy store if the need arose. One wall was filled with a bank of books, and the opposite wall had a huge rack of shelves stacked with poster paints and boxes of glitter. Dad would have hated it. He had a thing about glitter and, much as he doted on Ava, it was the one thing he wouldn't let her have in the house. So I wasn't surprised when she dived on it, as soon as she spotted the jar on the shelf.

'Mummy, can I paint a fairy's house and put some glitter on top of the paint?'

'Oh I don't know, darling. It's not fair on Dolly to get all of that out, too. There are so many toys to play with, look at that lovely pirate ship for a start.' It was a huge wooden boat, with linen sails. The deck was lined with pirates, led by a girl with a shock of curly blonde hair escaping from her three-cornered hat, a very fierce expression on her face. Even as a grown woman, I could see the appeal of playing with it. Not Ava, though, she shook her head, and I recognised that single-mindedness.

'It's fine to get the paints and glitter out. You'll give Ava a hand, won't you, Maggie?' Dolly looked at her teenage daughter.

'Yes, and I can get the stickers out too, if Ava wants some?'

'It'll be good practice for her, seeing as she wants your job when she's older, Scarlett.'

'You want to teach in a primary school?' I was impressed as Maggie nodded. I'd had no idea what I wanted to do at that age. Maybe that was why I'd let Luke talk me into giving up my job to follow his dream so easily. Teaching was supposed to be a vocation, but I'd have done anything to make him happy back then. 'Well if you're really sure you don't mind supervising Ava, and your mum's sure she doesn't mind about the mess?'

'It's what playrooms are for! Come on, let's go and put the kettle on, while we wait for Kate and Ruhan, and you can tell me all about what happened at the cooking class.'

I'd just finished filling Dolly in on everything – even the part where I'd screamed like a banshee after Cam stopped his car – when the others turned up. By the time Kate had got her two settled in the playroom, Dolly was already pouring out more tea.

'If the kids weren't having a play date, I'd offer you all something stronger.'

'That's usually my idea, Dolly.' Kate laughed. 'But even I draw the line at starting before half past ten on a Saturday morning.'

'I know, but sometimes a cup of tea just doesn't seem enough.' Dolly had an unusually serious expression on her face, and I crossed my fingers under the table that they hadn't had bad news about the adoption. It would be disappointing for Dolly and Greg, but it would be a disaster for the kids who could have had a home with them, if they missed out on that.

'What's wrong, love? You look like you've seen next door's cat taking a dump in your garden.' Kate was up on her feet and had already slung a comforting arm around Dolly's shoulders. She wasn't slow in venturing an opinion, but she was just as quick to offer support.

'Mrs Davy rang me yesterday, apparently she's had some emails about me.' Dolly pulled a face.

'What sort of emails?' I couldn't imagine what Mrs Davy would have to complain about. Dolly only had Billy at the school and, if Ava turned out like him, I'd be patting myself on the back.

'Apparently someone's complained about the prospect of three new children joining the school at the same time, especially children who've been in care.' Dolly's eyes clouded and I wanted to cry for her, and those poor kids, who'd already been through more than enough.

'But they get priority admissions over everyone else. And so they should!' I was sure no one could prevent the kids getting into the school, but Dolly didn't deserve a moment's stress about it.

'They would get priority if there were any spaces up for grabs, but it's such a small school that adding three children will make it oversubscribed by almost 10 per cent, especially as it's already got a couple more than it should.' Appleberry was only supposed to have seventy pupils and there'd already been seventy-two when they'd squeezed Ava in, because Cam had known I wouldn't take the job if they couldn't.

'Somehow I doubt being oversubscribed was the real reason people complained.' Kate narrowed her eyes. 'And I bet I know who's behind this: the bloody Chisholms.' I hoped she was wrong. If Natasha could support Claire Winters in the way she had, surely she could see these kids needed someone on their side too? I was sure Cam would support Dolly, but this decision was going to be out of his hands.

'Mrs Davy wouldn't say who complained, but she did say there was more than one email.' Dolly sighed.

'And what did they suggest you do instead? Home school?' Kate's voice was tight. 'We should all bloody well take our kids out of Appleberry and home school them together. That would show them.'

'And they'd fill the places from the waiting list in five minutes.' Ruhan shook her head. 'Did Mrs Davy say what *she* thought?'

'She's going to talk to the local authority. There might be a possibility of getting two of the children into Oaktree Forstal and one into Appleberry, which would keep it within the allowed limits.'

'I'm so sorry you've got this added pressure, Dolly. I wish there was something we could do.' I couldn't bring myself to admit that using Ava's admission as a bargaining chip was probably part of the problem.

'I think we should go to the papers and expose the Chisholms, and the rest of that bunch of hypocrites, for what they are. They're the first to say they want to help the community by volunteering to head up the PTA and governors, but they drop all that do-gooding like a hot potato when it counts.' Kate was well and truly on her soapbox now.

'I don't think going to the papers would help, even if they were remotely interested in a story about a village school in the middle of nowhere. And we're not even sure it was the Chisholms.' Dolly took the words out of my mouth. 'I've just got to hope Mrs Davy can find a workable solution, and that the social workers don't pull the adoption as a result.'

'Can they do that?' I couldn't believe they would, but Dolly was obviously worried.

'I really hope not.' She forced a small smile. 'But can you see why I felt like a gin might help more than tea?'

'I think letting the tyres down on a certain someone's BMW would be even more satisfying.' Kate might have laughed, but I wasn't entirely convinced she was joking.

* * *

'How did the observation go?' Cam was waiting for me in the staff room, after the Ofsted inspector had spent the morning watching me teach.

'Okay, I think. She even smiled a couple of times, but she's meeting me to give me some feedback at the end of the day.' I took the cup of coffee he'd made and sank into one of the chairs that were squeezed into the tiny staff room, the springs determinedly pushing up through the worn seat. 'It's certainly not the worst observation I've had, anyway.'

'Funny, you didn't mention any terrible observations at your interview...' Cam grinned.

'I'm not sure if it was terrible, or just really boring. It was during my first ever inspection, and, when I looked up at the inspector about halfway through the lesson, he'd nodded off!'

'At least he found it relaxing.'

'My only consolation was that I was doing a lesson on story-telling. And he must have quite enjoyed it, because he graded the teaching as good.' I returned his smile. 'Have you had your feed-back now?'

'Yes, and so have Janey and Emily. We got two outstandings and a good between the three of us.' He didn't say he'd got an outstanding grade, but I knew he had. I'd seen him come alive when he was in front of the class and, unlike me, there was no doubting it was his vocation. I just had to hope I wasn't going to let the side down.

'That's brilliant. Do you know what the inspectors' plans are tomorrow?'

'They're going through all the parental and community feed-back.' Cam paused. 'And at least one of them is going to come in to watch Harvest Festival.'

'We'll just have to hope that Stanley doesn't announce he needs a *poo* in his loudest voice again, then, like he did in the middle of the dress rehearsal.'

'I'm more worried about the parents showing us up than the kids, after the latest.'

'What now?' I wouldn't have put it past Kate to follow through with her threat to start letting tyres down.

'The Dobsons are emigrating to Australia, which will free up two more places in the school. So we should be able to make a case to admit all three of the school age children Dolly is adopting. And the toddler will automatically get a place later on.'

'But that's great!' I leapt up to give him a celebratory hug, but then I remembered where we were, and the fact that it was Cam, and I dropped my arms to my side with an awkward jerking movement.

'I think so too.' Cam shook his head. 'But let's just say, not everyone thinks it's good news and I've got a feeling it could all kick off in the playground again. Especially if Kate Dawkins and Claire Winters aren't kept apart.'

7

I'd almost lunged at the Ofsted inspector, in the second misjudged hug of the day, when she'd said my teaching was being graded outstanding. I was so glad not to have let the others down. But, unlike Cam, I was willing to tell anyone who would listen – even the postman was in danger of getting a blow-by-blow account, when Ava and I set off for school the next morning.

In the run up to Harvest Festival, the church had a big hand-painted sign outside, advertising the service and asking for donations. Mum had taken up Natasha's challenge with relish and had gone through the cupboards clearing out anything she thought was too high in carbs. It looked like we'd all have to get used to spaghetti bolognese without the spaghetti. I tried to convince myself that courgette spirals were just like the real thing but, when Ava had wrinkled her nose, I'd struggled not to agree with her.

On the morning of Harvest Festival, there were plenty of parents heavily laden with donations, and a group of mums were standing by the church noticeboard as I walked past with Ava. Natasha Chisholm and Claire Winters were among them. It was obviously an animated discussion, and it didn't take a rocket scientist to work out what it was about, especially when they stopped abruptly once they'd spotted me.

'No donations, Scarlett?' I had to hand it to Natasha, the change of subject was seamless, and all eyes were instantly on me.

'Of course, just too much to carry. Mum's bringing it up in the car later.'

'Excellent, as long as you're being a team player. We've got to beat Oaktree Forstal.' Natasha's face relaxed into a smile. 'Although from what I hear, you really impressed Ofsted yesterday.'

'Thanks.' I didn't return her smile and, judging by the look on my daughter's face, I gripped Ava's hand a bit too tightly as we crossed the road. The inspection might have been the hot topic of conversation in the Chisholm household the night before, but I didn't want Natasha's approval. Especially if she was planning to make things difficult for Dolly.

* * *

The church was full to bursting, with parents and other family members who'd come to watch the service. The infant school was putting on the 'harvests around the world' show, and the juniors were singing harvest hymns, and telling the audience all about where their donations were going and why it was so important. I half hoped the inspectors might change their minds about coming to watch, so we could all be a bit more relaxed. But when I looked out from behind the curtains, which screened the nave off from the sanctuary, two of them were taking their seats in the front row, which had been reserved for their benefit. I wouldn't have been surprised if it was the head's idea to invite the inspectors along. Mrs Davy might keep a low profile, but she was nobody's fool.

By the time the juniors had finished their part of the service, the little ones were starting to get restless, and Ruhan had already done three toilet runs.

'Miss, something's poking me.' Jules Winters pulled at the sheaf of wheat costume he was wearing, just where it curved under the armpit. It was made of strips of cardboard, topped with cotton wool ears of wheat. But one of the cotton wool balls was missing, and the cardboard was poking into his skin. Ripping the top off the offending strip, I hoped it wouldn't unravel the whole costume. Making outfits to represent harvest items from around the world had seemed like a good idea at the time. But having a group of four-to six-year-olds, running around in them, and rolling about on the floor if they got half the chance, wasn't something we'd properly thought through.

'Is that better, Jules?'

'Yes thanks, Miss.' He gave me a gap-toothed grin, and he had the best manners of any kid in my class. Whatever I thought about his mum and her objections to Dolly's new family joining the school, she obviously couldn't be all bad.

'Do you ever get the feeling you should have stuck with tradition? There's a reason why the infant school kids usually perform first.' Cam walked up behind me and I turned around to face him. There was a big brown smudge on the front of his shirt, like a muddy football had hit him square in the chest.

'They're definitely struggling with waiting around. I'm just hoping the costumes are going to hold out for another half an hour.' I glanced at my watch. 'Do I even want to know what that stain is?'

'Daisy Hughes brought in some face paint to finish off her yam costume. But she decided to run at me full pelt to prove to Josh Summers, once and for all, that yams are stronger than potatoes.'

'Well, if it was an important scientific test, then you've got to live with the consequences!' It was one of the things I liked about Cam

– he never took himself too seriously, and was able to deal with whatever the kids threw at him. Even in the middle of an Ofsted inspection.

'It's our turn!' Ruhan took hold of one of the children's hands as she spoke, and led them through the curtains.

The first few children read or recited their pieces well, and Jules did a fantastic job of singing his solo verse, which was all about growing wheat. Ava's class came on next, and I could see my parents, in the second row; Dad was pointing his camera phone at the action, just as I'd instructed. I couldn't help feeling sad about Luke and all the things he was missing. But I had to shake it off – it was his choice after all.

The children were sitting on the sort of tiny chairs you only ever saw in an infant school and, when they were halfway through the song, Jack Day began to sob. Cam knelt down by his chair, whispering encouragement, but Jack just wailed all the louder, wrenching the woolly hat he was wearing off his head. It was covered in green tassels, which were supposed to be the crowning glory of his carrot costume. Squeezing between the chairs, Cam lifted Jack up and sat back down on the seat with the little boy on his lap. The wailing stopped as quickly as it had started. When Jack picked up the carrot topper and perched it on top of Cam's head, then laughed in that distinctive way four-year-olds do, Cam seemed to find it just as funny.

Luke had never been like that with Ava; he had never had the patience. I didn't want to compare Luke to Cam. I didn't want to think about Cam like *that* at all. I was just spending too much of my time either at work or thinking about it, that was all. Maybe it was time I rang Xander and arranged to go out for that drink.

* * *

By the end of the week, we'd had the verbal verdict on the inspection, which had been shared with the governors. We weren't allowed to tell anyone, but if the grin on my face didn't give away the fact we'd been awarded an outstanding, then I was a better actress than I thought. It felt so good to be part of something that was a success, after the struggles with the business in Cornwall. And I was starting to believe that teaching was what I'd been born to do, after all.

Ava woke up at seven on Saturday mornings, just as she did every day, but she was always happy to climb into bed with me at the weekend, so I could read one of her favourite books. We must have read *The Gruffalo* hundreds of times, and she knew it word for word, but we still had to do at least one read through every Saturday, and she'd tell me off for being inconsistent with the characters' voices. But it was our special time, and I usually managed to get downstairs to make us tea and toast, using Dad's secret stash of bread, as Mum wouldn't have it in the house any more.

'Are you excited about your birthday tomorrow?' I looked down at Ava munching on her toast. I was going to be finding crumbs in the bed until I changed the sheets, but it was a small sacrifice to make to have these moments with my daughter – moments I already knew I'd miss when she was a teenager, glued to her mobile phone. I had to grab them while I could.

'I can't wait! Is Mr Ellis still coming to the party?'

'I think so, darling.' I'd felt awkward asking Cam and had kept putting it off. But then Ava had taken the situation into her own hands and turned the painting of the fairy cottage she'd done at Dolly's house into an invitation just for him. When he'd told me what she'd said as she handed it over, I'd been lost for words. She'd said she wanted him to come because she'd have all her friends there, but I wouldn't have her daddy and she thought I was missing him. As Ava looked up at me again, it was as though she could read my mind.

'It's good that he's going to be there, if Daddy's not, isn't it?'

'Yes darling, but I've got lots of friends, plus Nonna and Gramps, so you don't need to worry about me missing Daddy.' I took a deep breath. 'Do *you* miss Daddy?'

'Sometimes.' Ava shrugged. 'But he's all wobbly in my brain if I try to think about him.'

'You know you can talk to me about it any time, don't you?'

'Uh-huh.' She picked up another piece of toast and the subject was closed; I just wished it was that easy for me. But the spate of recent calls to my mobile, which cut off as soon as I picked them up, was making me edgy. Getting the texts had been creepy enough, but the calls felt even more intrusive. If Luke ever wanted to come back into Ava's life, he needed to get a move on. As for coming back into mine, he'd left that too late already.

* * *

'Knock, knock, only me.' For some reason, Mum rapped her knuckles against the door even though she'd announced the knocking. 'There's been a delivery for you.'

'Me or Ava?'

'Not the little bookworm over there.' Ava was curled up on the window seat, lost in a new picture book, and she hadn't even looked up at the mention of a delivery. 'It's for you.'

'I don't think I'm waiting for anything else...' I'd ordered far too much for Ava's birthday, though, so there was a definite possibility I'd forgotten about some of it. Mum had told me I was overcompensating, but I wasn't going to admit it.

'It's not something *you've* ordered. Unless you're in the habit of buying flowers for yourself.' Mum went out into the corridor and came back in with a huge bouquet she could barely see over the top of. But I could still make out the hopeful expression on her face. 'Have you got an admirer you haven't told me about?'

'Not unless they're keeping it a secret from me, too.' I raised an eyebrow. 'Are you telling me you haven't read the card?'

'What do you take me for?' She couldn't quite look me in the eye, though. Picking up the card, I could see why she hadn't read it. It was in an envelope sealed with a flower sticker, so it would have been a dead giveaway if she'd ripped it open.

'They're from Natasha and James Chisholm, to congratulate me on being part of an outstanding team.' I didn't read Mum the last line about showing Oaktree Forstal who were best. Although I could almost hear Natasha saying it.

'That's nice, even if they aren't from someone special.' Mum looked like she wanted to say something else, but she shook it off. I'd already had to remind her three times about our agreement not to mention dating again, but it looked like she might finally be getting the message.

'Thanks, Mum. I'll put them in some water and then I've got to nip into Pudstable and get some more bits for Ava's party.' She'd invited her whole class, as there were only ten of them, and half of my class too. We'd hired the village hall, a bouncy castle and a children's entertainer, but there was still one big hurdle to get over. The morning's postal delivery. It was Luke's last chance to send his daughter a birthday card, and it might be his last chance altogether. I couldn't keep making excuses for him. If he'd left for good, then Ava deserved to know, so we could both move on. 'Are you and Dad okay to look after her?'

'Of course, darling. Take as long as you need, and I'll keep an eye out for any post.' Mum put an arm around me and squeezed. We were careful not to talk about it in front of Ava, but Mum understood, in the way only someone who loved Ava as much as I did, could. She might drive me mad sometimes, but I wouldn't have swapped her for the world, not even to give Ava her daddy back.

* * *

The noise in the village hall had reached a crescendo by the time the children's entertainer unfurled a giant parachute. With the kids kept busy, I took the chance to go through to the kitchen, and I was just uncovering the party platters when Cam walked in.

'Can I do anything to help?'

'You've already done loads.' I turned to smile at him. Kate and Dolly had both been planning to help out, but Kate had come down with a sickness bug, and Dolly had been asked to go a meeting with the foster carers who'd been looking after her new family. She'd apologised about a thousand times, but there was no way I was going to let her rearrange the meeting. I had Mum, Dad and Ruhan to help out, and Cam had been a star – organising games of musical statues and pass-the-parcel, when the entertainer had phoned to say she was running late.

'Can I at least make you a cup of coffee?' He was already over by the kettle. 'I've promised your mum one.'

'You promised, or she twisted your arm? She has ways of persuading people to do things they hadn't planned to do.'

'No arm twisting needed, I just wanted to make myself useful.'

'Mum is going to love you!' *Why the hell had I said that*? Turning back to the platter, I straightened the row of cupcakes that were already perfectly aligned.

'Ava seems to be enjoying herself.' Cam took a step towards me. 'Did her dad get in touch?'

'No.' Tears stung the backs of my eyes, and I swallowed hard, determined to get them under control.

'Then he's an idiot. I'm sorry if that's out of line, but I can't believe he doesn't want to be here for Ava.'

'Right now I couldn't agree with you more. It's difficult though. A big part of me never wants to see him again, but I don't want Ava to miss out either.' I turned back to look at him. 'I know thousands of people go through this, and a lot of them have it much worse. But it feels pretty crap, letting your child down.'

'You haven't, and Ava doesn't have to miss out on having a dad, although I'm sure she'd have a brilliant childhood if it stayed just the two of you. But when you find someone new, they'll love Ava just as much.'

'Do you really think so? I just can't imagine anyone growing to love Ava as much as I do. It was instant for me, but it won't be like that for someone who comes into her life now. I know it's wrong to say it, but it just feels like she'd be getting second best, because I messed up first time around.' Even saying it made my cheeks go hot; I was being more honest with Cam than I'd been with anyone. I knew amazing stories unfolded every day – stepparents who raised their families with as much love as any child could want, and adopters like Dolly and Greg. I wanted to believe that one day *we* could have that, too. But what if I made the wrong choice again and Ava had someone else walk out of her life? I'd rather be on my own forever than do that to her.

'I know they can. I've seen it so many times at work over the years, and then there's Mike. My stepdad.'

'I thought your mum was on her own?'

'She was, for a while, after my father left. But then Mike came along and I found it hard at first. I was a teenager, and I didn't want some bloke coming along and getting in the middle of our little family. I was vile for about two years, but he kept trying. He'd drive me to rugby training and stand there on the touch-line in the freezing cold, never taking the bait when I more or less threw my dirty kit at him after the end of each game.'

'Maybe I shouldn't wait until Ava's a stroppy teenager then!'

'If it's the right person, they'll work through it. Mike just kept showing he was there for me and Mum. He took me to visit all the universities I wanted to apply to, and he helped me get my first part-time job when I was still at school. Gradually I accepted how happy he made Mum too, and that he was going to be there for her when I went away to study. At first, I was just grudgingly grateful, but when he suffered a minor heart attack, in my first term at uni, I realised I loved him. I had a father out there somewhere, who hadn't bothered to stay in my life. But more importantly, I had a dad, who was slap bang in the centre of it, even if we didn't share the same genetic makeup. That's what's more important in the end, just look at what Dolly is doing.'

'You're right.' I really hoped the answer to my next question was going to be yes. 'And is Mike still around? I know you've been helping your mum out a lot lately...'

'Yes, thank goodness. He's had a few problems with his heart over the years, which is ironic because he's got the biggest heart of any man I've ever met. Even if that sounds cheesy as hell.' Cam gave a half-smile. 'But he's recovering from a triple heart bypass at the moment, so I've been going over to help out as much as I can, and cooking for them at the weekends to give Mum a break.'

'Oh, God, and here we are, dragging you to Ava's birthday party, which must just be like another day at work.'

'It's fine, honestly. There's nowhere else I'd rather be.' He put his arm around me, but only the way Dolly or Kate might have done if they'd been there, and I leant my head against his shoulder just for a second.

'I'm not interrupting anything am I?' Ruhan had a knowing look on her face as she walked into the kitchen. Thank goodness she didn't know Mum that well, or they'd have both ended up jumping to ridiculous conclusions.

'No, we were just talking about Ava's dad.' I pulled away from Cam, and the smile melted off Ruhan's face.

'I'm sorry, it must be pretty tricky on days like today. I was just coming to say there was an incident during one of the games, and Ava's got a bit of a graze on her knee. It's nothing really, but she's asking for her mum.'

'Oh bless her, I'll go and sort it out, if you two don't mind getting the rest of the platters ready?'

'No problem, only a mum will do at a time like this.' Cam smiled again, and I was tempted to say that someone like Mike could do just as good a job. He obviously had with Cam. But I still wasn't convinced I'd ever be able to introduce someone new into Ava's life, and risk her being hurt again. For now there was a grazed knee that needed my attention, so the rest would just have to wait. And, like Cam, there was nowhere else I'd rather be.

8

The parents' consultations for the end of the first term were being held in the church hall and it was absolutely freezing. The ancient heating system barely took the edge off, and I could see why Emily Wallace, who taught Class 3, had come in bundled up like Paddington Bear on the piste.

Wrapping my hands around yet another cup of tea, I scanned the list of parents to see who was next. Natasha and James Chisholm were already waiting across the hall, staring in my direction, like two birds of prey ready to pounce. I was running five minutes early and I briefly considered holding off until their allotted time. But there was every chance they'd have a lot to say. So starting ahead of schedule was probably my best chance of keeping the rest of the evening on track.

'Mr and Mrs Chisholm.' Getting to my feet, I called their names. James returned my smile, but Natasha's mouth was distinctly down-turned. 'Please, sit down. I'm running a bit early, so I thought we might as well make a start. Have you had a chance to look at Ode's books?'

'Yes, and I'm not happy.' Natasha's mouth dragged further down at the corners, backing up her words.

'Ode's doing really well. Hopefully you'll have seen that from her books? There are some very nice comments in there.' I racked my brains trying to remember if I'd written anything negative in their daughter's book. Even where a child was struggling, or not doing what was asked of them, I tried really hard to put a positive slant on my comments. But with a child like Ode that had never really been a challenge.

'It's that *What I Want to Do When I Grow Up* story. I'm not happy with what she's written.' Natasha scowled, and even James looked nonplussed. As far as I could remember, most of the kids had given the usual answers about wanting to be singers, racing car drivers or YouTubers. But I couldn't have recalled what Ode had written if my life depended on it.

'Sorry, let me just go and grab her book, so we all know exactly what we're talking about here.' Walking over to the table where the children's work books were laid out, I picked out Ode's and brought it back over to the consultation table. Natasha snatched it out of my hands and turned to the offending page before slapping it down in front of me.

'There! See, look what she's written.'

I scanned down the page. There were more pictures than words, and the labels under them were big and disjointed, as you'd expect of a six-year-old. But it was clear what she wanted to be: a mother.

'Look, I'm sorry. I'm really not sure what the problem is. And the whole point is that the children were asked to decide for themselves.'

'I don't want Ode growing up with those sorts of limitations. I bet none of the boys wrote being a father as the number one thing they wanted to grow up to be!' Natasha sat bolt upright in the chair, still as rigid as a telegraph pole, even when James put an arm around her shoulders.

'I don't think they did. But Ode certainly wasn't the only girl to mention motherhood.' I took a deep breath. 'I wouldn't read too much into it, though. I think it's a compliment to their mothers, that their daughters see being a mum as such an important job. She just wants to be like you.'

'But I run my own image consultancy. I'm not *just* a mum.' Natasha gave me a pointed look. 'If I was some sort of earth mother, like Dolly, I could understand it. But I want more for Ode than that.'

'Stop it, Nat. You're overreacting.' James took his arm off his wife's shoulders. 'You can't foist your ambitions on her, darling, she's just a kid. And I doubt many six-year-olds stick to the career choices they make at that age. God knows, I'm six times her age and I still don't know what I want to do some days!'

'James, that's not helping and it's not funny either.' Natasha turned her body away from her husband, and I felt sorry for them both. There must have been something in her that drove that furious ambition, an empty place she just couldn't fill. And it must have robbed them both of the freedom to choose what they *really* wanted, along the way. He'd definitely have to bury any ideas he might have for taking a less corporate path than the one he was chained to – like a secret desire to take up beekeeping, or set up his own micro-brewery – but it would be awful if Ode was robbed of her freedom to choose, too. It was hard to believe anyone grew up dreaming of becoming an image consultant. But poor Ode was probably going to end up spending her life trying to live up to her mother's expectations.

'Mr Chisholm is right.' I closed Ode's book. 'In my experience, children of Ode's age change their minds every day about what they want to grow up to be. But with a child as bright as your daughter is, there's nothing she couldn't grow up to achieve. If she *wants* to.'

'And what about her test results? Do they suggest she'll be in the top 10 per cent for the SATs in May?' Natasha didn't pause for breath and I looked down at the list of results. I might only have a fifteen-minute appointment with the Chisholms, but I already knew it was going to be the longest quarter of an hour of the night. If not my whole life.

* * *

There was a knot at the top of my spine I didn't think any amount of yoga could untie. Especially given that my attempts at downward dog, in the classes at the village hall, looked like someone had left the resuscitation dummy from the first aid classes behind to fend for itself. Thankfully I'd finished the last of my parent consultations and there had to be at least one chocolate digestive with my name on, left on the refreshment table. I should have known better. By the time I got there, all that was left were a couple of broken custard creams, and a chocolate chip cookie with what looked suspiciously like bite marks on one side.

'Ah, the glamourous life of the teacher.' Cam laughed as I gingerly picked up a custard cream, trying to decide whether or not I was desperate enough to eat it.

'I think we should have a secret stash of chocolate Hobnobs at least. After the grilling I've had about SATs preparation, and whether we've made any decisions yet for the casting of the nativity, I could use a bit of chocolate.'

'That's nothing.' Cam flicked the lever on the urn, pouring hot water on the teabags. 'I had one set of parents ask whether I'd thought about introducing end of term tests for the reception class with a league table shared amongst all the parents, so they could be clear about their child's position in the class.'

'Oh God, really?' Nothing much surprised me any more, but I

couldn't help sighing as he nodded. 'Still, at least for every parent like that, there's someone like Dolly, whose primary concern is her children's happiness. I'm so pleased we're going to be able to have all the children she's adopting in the school. It means she'll be one of my parents next term too.'

'But you'll lose the Chisholms at the end of the school year.' Cam grinned. It was win-win, but he didn't need to say it out loud.

'I suppose this is my opportunity to grill you over Ava's progress? I hope you're going to be able to reassure me that she is in at least the top third of your class.' I folded my arms and took a step backwards, but I couldn't keep a straight face.

'She is actually, she's a bright kid.' He paused. 'She must take after her mum.'

'It's certainly a better option than taking after her father.' I shouldn't have said it, but it still felt uncomfortable when Cam paid me a compliment. Looking back, things had slipped with Luke over a long period of time, but I'd been too busy with Ava and the business to notice. If I was really honest, my last memories of us being a family were blurred by arguments and constant subtle sniping. The signs that he was withdrawing from us had been pretty obvious, I just hadn't wanted to see them.

'I've heard we're going to be landed with all three of those bloody kids now.' A woman who I didn't recognise was standing at the other end of the refreshment table, her voice rising to a level I couldn't ignore, as she handed the man beside her a cup of tea. 'If I wanted Poppy and Lily mixing with those sorts, I'd have moved to an inner city. You'd think you'd be safe somewhere like this, wouldn't you? Mark my words, if the girls come home from school effing and jeffing as soon as they start, I'll take it to County Hall if I have to.'

'Don't get yourself all wound up about it again, Felicity. I thought you had a petition up to stop them coming here?' The man's cup rattled against the saucer as his hand shook.

'Fat lot of good that will do. Claire Winters took the petition to Mrs Davy, but she just said it was out of her hands.' Other people were starting to look over at the tea table. 'Bloody do-gooder, but it's not her children who'll be mixing with these kids, is it? She'd soon find a way to put a stop to it then, I bet.'

Cam stepped forward, and, even as I put a hand out to stop him, I could tell I was wasting my time.

'Mr and Mrs Douglas, isn't it?' He kept his voice steady, but his hands were clenched into fists by his sides. 'Aren't your girls both in Class 4?'

'That's right.' Mrs Douglas smiled – she obviously had no idea what was coming.

'I'm sure you want the best for them, don't you?'

'Of course; the twins mean everything to us.' Mrs Douglas smiled again. Her husband still wasn't saying anything and I had a feeling it might have been his default setting.

'And don't you think *every* child has the right to a good education and to go to the same school as their siblings, especially if that school happens to be in the village they live in?' Cam's voice had taken on an edge. 'Or is it okay for those places to be taken up by families who ferry their kids in from miles around, to take advantage of the better Ofsted rating Appleberry offers?'

'I'm not sure exactly what you're insinuating Mr Ellis, but we're certainly not the only parents who have concerns about *those* sorts of children coming into a school like this, in such large numbers. And the impact it might have on our children.'

'I would ask you what you mean by *those* sorts of children, but I don't think I want to know the answer.' Cam squared his shoulders. 'But you're entitled to your opinion and if you don't think Appleberry is the right place for your girls, there are plenty of people on the waiting list who do.'

'And if you take that attitude, you might soon find your school half-empty!' Mrs Douglas had drawn quite a crowd. 'Claire Winters had plenty of signatures on that petition. I bet the Chisholms signed it too. Didn't you?' She shouted across to Natasha and James, who'd been talking to some other parents since the end of our consultation. Natasha looked up and I braced myself for her response.

'Actually, no we didn't.' Natasha was speaking, but it was like watching a badly dubbed movie. Her lips were moving, but what I expected to hear wasn't coming out. 'I've had several heated discussions with Claire about it, but unfortunately I wasn't able to change her mind, any more than she was able to change mine. James and I both fully support Dolly's decision to adopt, and we're really glad that Appleberry is going to be able to accommodate the three children who are ready to start. In fact, it was James who petitioned the other governors about making an exception to the maximum roll numbers, before we found out the Dobsons were emigrating.'

James Chisholm nodded and walked towards Felicity Douglas. 'I can assure you, though, that the governors gave equal consideration to your petition to block the oversubscription. But I'm happy to say it was dismissed once the Dobsons' departure freed up two more spaces.' For a minute I thought James was going to stick out his tongue. 'And if it hadn't been, I was more than ready to resign as chair of governors.'

An uncomfortable silence briefly descended in the hall. I was gutted Dolly and Kate hadn't got to hear Natasha's speech – they were never going to believe it. I'm not sure I'd have believed it myself, if I hadn't been there.

'You haven't heard the last of this.' Mrs Douglas finally recovered her voice. Slamming her cup and saucer down on the refreshment table, she caught hold of her husband's arm, dragging him towards the door so quickly he had to give his cup to Louise Down-tree, the school secretary, as he passed her in the doorway.

'Do you want to go for a drink?' Cam turned towards me, as the buzz of conversation finally restarted around us. There were no prizes for guessing the main topic of conversation.

'I'd love a drink.' I could hardly wait for the chance to ask Cam if he'd had any idea the Chisholms felt like that. But if we'd gone outside and found a load of little green men waiting to beam us up to Mars instead, it would only have surprised me marginally more.

'So the two of you finally went out for a drink by yourselves, then? I'd given up hope of it ever happening. Even if everyone else can see you're perfect for each other.' Kate smirked at me as the waiter put a plate down in front of her. It was the second supper club I'd been to since starting at the school, but this time it was just me, Dolly and Kate. Ruhan had come down with a rotten cold and Cam had cried off too.

'It wasn't like that.' I shook my head as the waiter moved away. 'We were both so shocked about Natasha's outburst, we just needed a debrief.'

'But you do like him, don't you?' Kate topped up our glasses as she spoke and I shrugged.

'He's a nice guy, but I'm married.' I realised, as I said it, that I didn't really feel like I was any more. I just wanted Kate to stop going on about it. Even if I did admit I liked Cam, I'd stopped trusting my judgement a long time ago. And the excuse he'd made about not being able to make it to supper club hadn't helped.

'And when exactly was the last time you heard from your *husband*?' Kate wasn't going to let it go.

'For goodness' sake, let the poor girl eat her food in peace.' Dolly was always so reasonable, but for once her tone was sharp and I loved her for it.

'So what's the latest with the adoption?' I wasn't going to give Kate a chance to take control of the conversation again.

'It's all really good.' Dolly beamed, making her look ten years younger despite the dark circles under her eyes. 'We had another contact visit at the weekend, and it was the first one without their foster carers, or the social worker. It felt like we were a proper family and we went to the conservation park near Pudstable, but I'd almost forgotten what it felt like to try and keep an eye on so many children all at once. Maggie was like a second mother to them, though, bless her. And Greg was brilliant – although he did have to rub anti-inflammatory cream into his back after going on the rope swings! I think we've both got to accept we're not as young as we were first time around.'

'You're not having any second thoughts, though, are you?' Kate put down her fork.

'Not at all. We can't wait, but this weekend was a reminder that nothing worth doing is ever easy.' Dolly shot me a look and I had a feeling she wasn't just talking about the adoption.

'Do you know when they'll be moving in yet?' I couldn't even imagine how life-changing it was going to be for them all.

'We're hoping it'll be next Friday.' Dolly's voice caught. 'Sorry, I don't know why I get so emotional thinking about it.'

'I wouldn't expect anything less.' As I spoke, Dolly was still struggling to hold on to her emotions and she wasn't the only one. 'I feel a bit choked up myself. Those children are so lucky to be coming into a family like yours, and you'll be able to transform their lives.'

'We're the lucky ones.' Dolly smiled. 'And Cam has been great. He came with me to meet the teachers at their current school last week, and the children couldn't stop talking about it, and saying they can't wait to start at Mr Ellis's school!'

'I hope the twins won't be too disappointed they're going to be in my class.'

'Of course they won't, they'll love you just as much as Cam.' Dolly shook her head. 'I still can't get over Natasha and James Chisholm defending Mrs Davy's decision to let the kids join the school. I tried not to assume it was them blocking it, but deep down it's what I thought.'

'Me too.' I still felt guilty about it.

'Me three.' Kate pulled a face and I had to laugh – she was clearly a bit disappointed to be proven wrong.

'Everyone knew what you thought, Kate. You said so often enough!' Dolly was laughing too.

'True. Even the Chisholms probably knew. Maybe that's why they suddenly changed their tune, to make themselves look more caring... Or maybe they found out about the documentary and thought there was a chance they could end up in it!'

'I don't think it had anything to do with that.' I hadn't always thought the best of Natasha, but I couldn't let Kate continue to see the worst in her, not now. 'There were tears in her eyes when she'd finished putting Mrs Douglas in her place. And she ought to be auditioning for acting work, if she didn't genuinely mean what she said.'

'I get the feeling there's a lot below the surface with Natasha Chisholm and that she might actually be lacking in confidence, deep down.' Dolly laughed again. 'Although God knows why. If I had a figure like hers, I'd be far too confident for my own good!'

'You might be right.' I screwed up my face. 'Although did you see that email from her, suggesting a PTA spa day to celebrate the school's Ofsted results?

Kate almost choked on her dinner. 'Is that what that email was about? I've started deleting the ones from her without even reading them. I can't think of anything worse than letting stick insects like Natasha Chisholm and Claire Winters see me in a swimsuit. I probably weigh almost as much as the two of them put together.'

'You look lovely. Besides, who'd want to deny themselves all this fun, just to look like that?' Dolly twisted strands of creamy pasta onto her fork as she spoke. 'She even included Cam in that email. Can you imagine it, poor bloke, surrounded by us lot at a spa? He might never recover if he saw how many stretch marks having five children can give you!'

'Wow, I've just thought of something worse than letting Natasha and Claire see me in a swimsuit... letting Cam see me!' Kate cut into another slice of pizza all the same. 'But it's a shame you won't get a day at the spa with him, Scarlett.'

'I thought we were done with this subject?' I loved my new friends, I really did, and it was great to go out to dinner and not get lectured for ordering carbs. But it looked like I was going to have to spell things out to Kate. 'Even if I ignore the fact that I'm married, Cam isn't interested.'

'Well that's a load of crap. In fact, it's even harder to believe than Natasha Chisholm suddenly coming over all sweetness and light.' Kate blew out her cheeks.

'But it's just as true.' I clutched the stem of my glass. 'He said he couldn't come tonight. And when I asked him why, he couldn't even come up with an answer. He eventually mumbled something about needing to help his mum out, but I've spent long enough teaching to know when I'm being lied to.'

'Maybe he's doing something embarrassing he didn't want to tell you about.' Kate peeled some salami off her last slice of pizza. 'Like going to a tap dancing lesson, or having something lanced off his bum.'

'Trust you, Kate!' Dolly grinned.

'Google Dr Pimple Popper and you'll see what I mean. It's the best thing ever!' It was the most animated I'd seen Kate all evening, but I'd suddenly lost my appetite. I'd been so enthusiastic about getting together for supper club, and Cam had clearly felt bad about letting me down. *Poor dumped Scarlett.* I hated that label more than anything, but it could have been even worse. *Poor dumped Scarlett with a hopeless crush on Cam.* That was a label I definitely wasn't willing to wear.

'Anyway, if you must know, married or not, I've got a date tomorrow night.' I pushed my knife and fork together at the same time as Kate dropped hers. I hadn't actually set up the date yet. But, if it meant getting everyone off my back, I was more than willing to do it.

'Right, you're not leaving this table until you give me all the details.' Kate leant forward in her seat.

'His name's Xander and I met him at that speed-dating cookery lesson I told you about.'

'And? Have you got a picture?' Kate had already grabbed my phone.

'I've got him on Instagram. If you give me my phone back, I might even let you have a look. Just don't accidentally start liking all his photos. I don't want him thinking I'm stalking him.' I took the phone back from Kate and opened the app, clicking on Xander's profile. His Instagram feed made it look like he had the perfect life. Mine was a private account, that I only shared with friends, and it was filled with pictures of Ava.

Side by side, our profiles would suggest we had nothing in common. And I couldn't help wondering if Instagram knew more than I gave it credit for. Not that it mattered; whatever Mum's hopes, I wasn't going on the date thinking anything would come of it. I just wanted to convince everyone, Cam included, that I wasn't sitting around waiting for him to notice me.

'Very nice, look at those muscles!' Kate tapped on the picture to try and make it bigger. 'Oops, I've lit up the love heart by accident.'

'Click it again.' I shook my head, already beginning to regret even mentioning Xander, who was being pawed over like a stripper at a hen party. Even if it was only in the virtual sense.

'He's a fireman?' Dolly was looking at the phone over Kate's shoulder. 'Gorgeous and a hero too.'

'If you're a good girl, he might even let you see his hose!' Kate laughed so hard that someone on the table behind turned round and shot her a dirty look.

'He's just a nice guy and he wants to take me out. I wouldn't care if he was a fireman or a bin man.' I widened my eyes when Kate laughed again. 'It's true! If by some miracle this does go anywhere, I just want someone reliable, who Ava likes as much as I do.'

'You can't just settle for someone you *like*.' Dolly frowned. 'You deserve more than that. I don't know whether it's because he's away working a lot of the time, but I still get butterflies when I see Greg.'

'Pass me the bread basket.' Kate gestured to the wicker basket in front of Dolly.

'It's empty.'

'I know it is, but I need something to throw up in!' She mimed sticking a finger down her throat. 'Scarlett doesn't want all that hearts and flowers stuff. What she needs is a damn good shag. It must have been ages!'

'Kate!' Dolly sounded like she was telling one of her kids off.

'Oh come on, don't be such a prude. Everyone knows it's good for you. Why else do you think I have so many early nights with Alan? It's definitely not because he looks like Channing Tatum in Magic Mike. But if I close my eyes, and hum the music in my head, he can be for ten minutes.' She rolled her eyes. 'Well, all right, more like five.'

'Sex is pretty near the bottom of the list of things I miss about being in a relationship. So I'm afraid I won't have anything to report on Monday that's going to interest you, Kate.' I made a pattern in the leftover risotto with my fork, hoping she'd let it go now.

'What do you miss, sweetheart?' Dolly furrowed her brow as I looked up at her.

'Some of the things I miss are for Ava. When she asks why her daddy doesn't come and see her, or whether he'll make it for Christmas, it's almost unbearable. But there are things I miss for me too. When it was good with Luke, we'd sit up and talk late into the night, hatching plans for the future, or working through whatever was worrying us, together. I don't know when we stopped doing that, but it was probably not long after we moved to Cornwall if I'm honest. That's what I miss most – someone to talk to in the dead of night.'

'You can always call me. Alan's usually asleep five minutes after he unwittingly finishes pretending to be Channing Tatum!' Kate grinned and I knew she meant it. She might say the wrong thing half the time, but she'd definitely be there for me if I needed her.

'Me too. Well not the Channing Tatum bit, but the calling me in the middle of the night if you need me.' Dolly squeezed my hand. I was lucky to have made such good friends so quickly, after returning to Appleberry, especially with my friends from the old days all having moved away. But, with everything she had on her plate, I wouldn't dream of taking Dolly up on her offer. Or Kate come to that.

'I appreciate it. I don't know what I'd do without the two of you. But, honestly, I'm fine. I've got Mum and Dad if I do ever feel like waking someone up in the night just for a chat.' They didn't have to know that hell would freeze over before I confided my worries to Mum – it would just give her another excuse to start matchmaking. Ava and I were doing just fine, on our own, and it wouldn't be long before I'd have enough money put by to move out of my parents' place. Making a new start was all we needed to finally draw a line under Luke's disappearance.

'As long as you have a good time with Xander tomorrow night, that's all that matters.' Dolly passed my phone back to me and I ran my finger up the screen to close the app. I was glad Cam didn't seem to use social media – I wouldn't have been able to resist checking his updates. I might have found out why he'd really missed supper club then, too. And even though we'd only ever be friends, there were some things I was better off not knowing.

* * *

'What are you doing?' Coming into the kitchen, the smell of cooking hit me like a wave. It wasn't a weekend treat of bacon and eggs, though, but a huge pan full of chicken breasts sizzling on the hob, whilst my mum stood over them, jogging on the spot.

'Meal prepping and getting my steps in.' Mum pursed her lips. 'I know you think I'm over the top with all of this, but I'm doing it for your dad's benefit as well as mine. He likes my tight new bum even more than I do.'

'Oh God, Mum, please don't.' That was an image I really didn't want to have in my head.

'Don't be silly. If you stay flexible and lean, you can do things in your sixties you wouldn't have believed possible.'

'I wouldn't have believed this conversation was possible.' Thank goodness Ava was having a rare lie-in, I didn't want her scarred for life from overhearing a conversation about her grandparents' sex life. I reached into the back of the kitchen cupboard and took out one of the pods for the coffee machine. At least Mum hadn't banned coffee yet.

'You might not think it matters now, but when you've got a man again, you'll want to make sure that side of things stays good for as long as it can.' The sizzling in the pan was getting louder, but sadly not loud enough to drown her out.

'Don't start all that again, either. I keep telling you, all I need is Ava. I tried the dating app, and the events they ran, but only because *you* wanted me to.' I could have told her about my plans to go out for a drink with Xander, but I'd thought better of that too. Using him just to convince Cam I wasn't interested would have been wrong.

'Do you know what you said to me all the time when you were growing up?' Mum flipped the chicken breasts over and turned towards me.

'No, but I'm guessing you're going to tell me?' I waited, expecting to hear I'd been the sort of kid who spent every spare minute dressing as a bride and waiting for my Prince Charming to turn up. Unfortunately, he'd turned out to be Houdini instead.

'At least once a week you'd tell me you wished you weren't an only child.'

'I still wish I wasn't a lot of the time, but we both know things are more complicated than that.' I reached out and touched Mum's arm briefly. She hadn't told me, until after Ava was born, what a tough time she'd had giving birth to me. So tough it meant she'd never been able to carry another child.

'But the thing is, Scarlett, *you've* got a choice. If you find the right person.'

'If it happens it happens. If not, Ava will just have to be an only child like me, and I turned out okay in the end, didn't I?'

'Mostly.' Mum looked at me deadpan for a moment and then laughed. 'Of course you turned out okay, more than okay, but I also know you want another child. Don't let Luke take that from you, too, and don't hang around too long, that's all I'm saying. Look at Auntie Leilah, she'd have made a great mum, if she hadn't convinced herself she wasn't the marrying kind.'

'I got a text from her yesterday, actually. From New York.' I tilted my head to one side. Mum was always talking about *'poor Auntie Leilah'*, but if there were benefits to not having a family, Leilah was making the most of them.

'Deep down, I bet she'd give all of that up for a grandchild.'

'And you've already got one.' I took two cups out of the cupboard. 'Can't we just be thankful about that for now, and take what comes?'

'I just don't want you to give up on any more of your dreams because of what Luke did. I could happily punch him in the face as it is. If you can honestly turn around and tell me you've changed your mind about wanting more children, I'll stop going on about you meeting someone new.'

'Do you want a coffee?'

'I do, but I also want a straight answer.'

'In an ideal world, of course I'd like more children.' I concentrated on the coffee machine, so I wouldn't have to see the *'told you so'* look on her face.

'Unfortunately, my darling, an ideal world won't just turn up on your doorstep. But if you want something badly enough you can go out and get it. And I'm afraid I'm just going to keep on nagging you until you do.'   `

'I don't doubt it, Mum.' Maybe I should give Xander a call, after all. It would almost certainly lead to nothing, considering I'd barely thought about him much since the cookery class, but deep down I had to admit Mum was right. The lump in my throat wouldn't let me deny it. I had always dreamt of having a big family. It might not be my destiny to have more children – and whatever happened I'd be forever grateful that I had Ava – but I wanted to be able to look back and say that I had at least tried.

9

'I know why my class have got the next two half-terms at the forest school; it's a rite of passage for the new teacher, isn't it?' I zipped up my puffer jacket and turned to Ruhan, who was pulling a woolly hat over her thick black hair. I had thermal underwear on under my jeans and jumper. But the thought of heading out to the forest for the day, following a drastic drop in temperature overnight, wasn't all that appealing. It might only be November, but winter seemed to have arrived early, on a blanket of frost.

'I think you may be right. Let's face it, Janey and Emily had first choice of the forest school rota, and they were hardly going to pick this term, or the one after Christmas, were they?' Ruhan pulled her hat down again, but there was too much hair and not enough hat to keep it in place. 'I think Cam's a glutton for punishment though, going to every single forest school session.' She pulled a face.

'Maybe he's a frustrated boy scout? Although he doesn't look the type to sport a woggle and know all the words to "Do Your Ears Hang Low".'

'No he doesn't, but he could probably pull off the look and, believe me, not many men could.' Ruhan handed me the keys to the mini-bus. 'He's told me before that he does it because he wants to get to know every child individually, as assistant head. And he thinks the forest school sessions are the best way to do that.'

'That sounds like him.' It was typical of Cam to do something like that. His teaching assistant covered his class for lesson preparation time, which we all had for half a day a week. But Cam was using his half-day, and the additional half-day's cover he got as assistant head, to go to the forest school sessions. Which meant he was doing all of the prep in his own time.

'And I can't imagine Mrs Davy even owning a pair of wellies, can you?' Ruhan looked down at her own boots, which were covered in pictures of Minnie Mouse and matched her coat. No one could accuse her of not being in touch with her inner child; it was one of the reasons why the kids in my class loved her so much.

'I suppose as head teacher of both schools, she wouldn't have time to attend many forest school sessions. But I've never seen her wearing anything other than dangerously high heels.' She was always in fitted dress suits too, which would have made it impossible for her to bend down and talk to one of the kids out in the playground, or tend to a grazed knee, even if she'd wanted to.

'Well you know what Natasha Chisholm would say – she favours Oaktree Forstal and she doesn't even try to hide it.'

'It's lucky for us that she does, otherwise we wouldn't have Cam.' I glanced at the clock on the wall above the whiteboard. 'We'd better get outside and gather the kids together before they use up all their energy tearing around the playground.'

'We should be so lucky!' Ruhan laughed as we headed outside into the cold. The sky was blue, but there was a bite in the wind that the weak winter sun couldn't even begin to contend with.

'Do you want me to drive?' Cam turned to look at me, as I followed Ruhan across the playground.

'That would be great, if you're sure you don't mind?' I'd taken my mini-bus test somewhat reluctantly, as I'd known the school might need me to drive it sometimes. It wasn't so much the driving of the mini-bus I minded, it was the responsibility of having twelve very precious pieces of cargo on board that freaked me out. The rest of the class were being transported in cars, by volunteer parents who came to the forest school on a rota, and Ruhan, whose trusty Land Rover could get the rest of the cars out of trouble if the weather caught us by surprise. The forest school was in a ten-acre piece of woodland just outside Appleberry, and I knew from my class's first visit that the guy who ran it, Jamie, was an old friend of Cam's.

'I'd much rather drive than try to keep a fight from breaking out between Caitlin and Ellie about who is going to marry Justin Bieber.' Cam gestured across the playground to where the two girls from my class, who until recently had been the best of friends, were pulling faces at one another.

'Oh not that again.' I wasn't sure whether to laugh or cry. The argument had been going on ever since half-term, but I thought it had peaked the week before when Ruhan caught Caitlin trying to flush Ellie's packed lunch down the toilet. 'I keep telling them they can both do better!'

'You're not a fan of JB then?' Cam laughed as I shook my head.

'I'm a bit old for that, but the girls are *far* too young. I know I'm going to sound ancient now, but I'm sure that boys weren't even on my radar at that age. And if I did notice them, I thought they were revolting. They always seemed to be making farting noises or punching each other for reasons I could never quite work out.'

'Not much has changed, has it? Rory and Josh have been seeing who can make the most realistic fart noise with their armpits for the last ten minutes. It's something else I'm looking forward to you sorting out on the mini-bus.'

'Thanks! And you're right, not much has changed.'

'So you still think boys are revolting?'

'Not all of them.' It was on the tip of my tongue to tell him that I had a date with Xander, but it didn't seem the time.

'I'm very pleased to hear it.' If I hadn't known better, I would have sworn he was flirting with me. But a split second later he almost knocked me off my feet in a very different way, when he blew a whistle to get the kids' attention. 'Right, everyone line up and take a high vis vest out of the box Mrs Acharya is holding.'

Ruhan handed out the orange vests and the kids started to squabble about who was going on the mini-bus and who was going in the cars.

'My mummy is driving and I want two of my friends to come with me.' Caitlin looked pointedly at Ellie. 'Not her, because she smells of cat's wee wee.'

'Caitlin, that's not a very nice thing to say.' I moved towards the girls, aware that I'd be subjecting Caitlin's mum to a nightmare journey if I tried to force them to make up by putting them in a car together. 'I'd like to choose you to come on the bus with me, Ellie. Is there a special friend you want to bring with you?'

'No thank you, Mrs West.' Ellie wiped her eyes with the back of her hand and I wanted to give her a hug. I could still remember what it felt like to fall out with your best friend when you were only six. Sammi Alexander had been my best friend at primary school, but on the occasions when we'd fallen out, and she'd seemed like my worst enemy, it had felt like the end of the world. Now we were barely Facebook friends, who probably wouldn't notice for months if the other one disappeared from our virtual lives. That definitely wasn't something you could explain to a six-year-old.

'Right, well, Ellie was going to go in the car with Mrs Campbell, so if you swap with her, please, Chloe then everyone should know where they're supposed to be going and who they're supposed to be going with.'

It took about ten minutes to organise the class and get everyone loaded up into the cars and mini-bus, which was longer than it took to get to the patch of woodland where the forest school was located. On the days when the primary school weren't using the woodland, Jamie ran sessions for the village nursery school and other groups who could see the benefits of outside education. It never ceased to amaze me how children, especially those who usually looked as though they'd rather be anywhere else other than at school, could become so engaged in everything the forest school had to offer. Much as I moaned about getting the autumn and winter terms, deep down I loved it. Ava couldn't stop talking about it, when it had been her class's turn to go, and her latest plan was to be a teacher with her own forest school when she grew up.

'Miss, I don't feel well.' Ellie called out in a wobbly voice, just as we got to the lane that led up hill to the forest school. Turning to look at her, it was obvious she wasn't just trying to get attention. Her face had turned a Kermit the Frog shade of green.

'We're nearly there, sweetheart. Do you think you can make it?' She shook her head and dry-heaved. Experience had taught me that if one of the kids was sick, there'd be at least three more who'd follow suit. 'Can you stop the bus, please, Mr Ellis?'

'There's a spot just up ahead.' Cam pulled into a slightly wider part of the road and I leapt out of my seat and grabbed hold of Ellie, opening the door of the mini-bus.

'Take some deep breaths sweetheart and when you feel ready, we can walk up the rest of the lane to the forest.' I looked at Cam through the open door. 'Is that all right with you Mr Ellis?'

'Of course; we'll wait for you up by the Blessing Tree.' Cam tilted his head. 'If you're sure you're okay with it?'

'Ellie and I will be fine, won't we?' The little girl nodded and I turned back to Cam again. 'Although I can't help thinking you knew what you were doing when you offered to drive.'

'You've discovered my secret.' Cam grinned as I slid the door shut and I took hold of Ellie's hand.

'How are you feeling now, sweetheart?' Her face wasn't quite so green, but she still looked as if she might burst into tears at any moment.

'My belly feels a bit wobbly, but it's not as bad as it was on the bus.'

'Do you get sick when you go in the car?' I was already thinking about the return journey and the best way of making sure Ellie got back to school without an incident.

'Not unless I watch my iPad. I'm not allowed to do that in the car any more, 'cos Daddy shouted at Mummy when I was sick on the way to holiday.'

'Oh dear, that doesn't sound good.' I couldn't help smiling. I'd seen Ellie's dad wiping non-existent smudges off the bodywork of his Lexus when he'd picked her up from school. 'We'll see if we can swap things around so that you can go back in one of the cars this afternoon, if you like?'

'Caitlin won't let me go in her car; she said I'm not her friend any more.' A tear slid down Ellie's cheek.

'You've got lots of other friends in the class, though. Don't worry too much about what Caitlin says, I'm sure you'll be friends again soon.'

Ellie shook her head. 'She said I'll never ever be her friend again.'

'And all of this is over Justin Bieber?' I had to press my lips together, hardly able to believe I was having this conversation with a six-year-old.

'She's just mean all the time. My mummy said she's probably sad because her mummy doesn't live with her any more, but she's only mean to me.'

'Your mummy could be right, Ellie.' I kept hold of her hand as we walked the last hundred metres or so to the forest school. Not sure what else to say, I couldn't help wondering if Ava ever lashed out because of what was going on at home. She was such an angel most of the time, and the tantrums I'd waited for had never come.

'How are you doing?' Cam walked down to meet us and Ellie looked up at him.

'My tummy's stopped wobbling. I think you were making the bus go too wiggly.'

'Well I'll do my best not to do that again.' Cam laughed. 'But are you okay apart from that?'

'I don't want to go up there.' Ellie pointed up towards the Blessing Tree where the rest of the group were gathered. 'No one likes me.'

'Of course they do.' Even as I tried to reassure her, she was shaking her head, the tears welling up again.

'Mrs West is right and we'll have lots of fun today. Aren't you looking forward to seeing how the worms are getting on?' Cam kept his tone light and Ellie eventually nodded her head. My class had started up a wormery during the first forest school session and had come up with a list of names for the worms, even though there was no way of telling which was which.

'At least they're nice to me.' Ellie frowned, determined not to be cheered up, but she didn't know that Cam had another trick up his sleeve.

'Do you want to know a poem about a worm?'

'Okay.' Ellie gave him a serious look and furrowed her brow in readiness.

'It goes something like this,' Cam pretended to clear his throat, 'I wish I were a glow worm, their day is never rotten. 'Cos how can you be grumpy, when the sun shines out your bottom?'

For a moment Ellie just stared at him and then she started to giggle. And once she'd started, she couldn't seem to stop. As we walked up towards the Blessing Tree, she ran towards the other children and, within seconds, she was recounting the rhyme to them, still giggling at the end of every line.

'You'll get emails about that, you know.' I smiled at Cam and he shrugged his shoulders. No wonder Ava loved being in his class. He just had a way of interacting with the kids on their level. And he'd managed the seemingly impossible task of cheering Ellie up, and restoring her confidence to approach the other children, all in one go.

'I've got plenty more where that came from!'

'It's just what Ellie needed, and she seems to have forgotten feeling so poorly on the way over, not to mention the fall out with Caitlin. I'm glad you're here today.'

'And now for the tree hugging.' Cam winked and I pressed my lips together again, knowing I wouldn't be able to look at him during the tree blessing that started off every forest school session. It was something Janey, the Class 4 teacher, had introduced. Having just taken on the role as reader at Appleberry church, she was keen to bring an element of praise to the forest school sessions. Cam had agreed, as long as it didn't exclude anyone, so Ruhan had been asked to work with Janey to come up with a non-denominational poem for the children to say. Everyone had to rest a hand against the big tree at the top of the woodland. But the first time I'd done it, I'd accidently caught Cam's eye, both of us struggling to take it as seriously as we should have been.

'Are you ready, children?' Ruhan was already standing by the tree, with the parent volunteers and the children in a circle around her. 'We all need to find a place to rest our hands, then we say the blessing together.' She waited while the children got themselves into position, and there was a bit of pushing and shoving until they were all happy with where they were. 'Right, now you remember what we're going to say, don't you?'

'Thank you for all the blessings on me and thank you for this beautiful tree. Thank you for all the oxygen it makes and for the unwanted CO_2 that it takes. Bless me please and bless this tree, and bless our friends and family.'

It was *the unwanted CO_2* bit that got me. I had to hand it to Ruhan – not only had she got a message of gratitude in there, she'd also ticked the environmental box. But there was just something so amusing about the way the kids said it, and the look on Cam's face, that made me want to laugh.

'Right, who's ready for some adventure?' Jamie, the forest school leader, called out to the children when the blessing was over, and was met with a chorus of excited responses. 'We're going to build some dens today and make a fire. If we've got time, we might even start building an extension to the wormery.'

'Mr Ellis told me a poem about a worm's bottom.' Ellie skipped alongside Jamie, as the rest of us followed them down the track, deeper into the woodland behind the farmhouse where Jamie lived.

'Did he now?' Jamie glanced over his shoulder at Cam and grinned.

'Guilty as charged.' Cam held up his hands as Ellie began to recount the poem again. I had a feeling that she'd never forget the poem he'd told her, and I couldn't help thinking about Ava and her dad again. Was there anything she'd remember about him, if he never came back?

* * *

'I was beginning to think you might never be free for a date.' Xander brought two plates over to the table and set one down in front of me.

'Sorry, it's just been busy at work and then Ava was poorly.' They weren't the only reasons I'd delayed arranging a date after the cookery class, but I'd probably been too quick to decide there just wasn't a connection. At least not the sort that would make me want another relationship. Unsurprisingly, it was Mum who'd convinced me I should give him another chance with her talk of having more children.

'So, was it the promise of trying out my curry that finally persuaded you to come over?' He smiled and lifted his glass. 'I knew that Indian cookery class would pay off in the end.'

'It certainly looks like it.' The food did look delicious and I tried not to feel irritated that he hadn't even asked how Ava was feeling now. It would have been the first thing Cam said, but that wasn't fair on Xander either. He wasn't a parent, and he didn't work with children, I couldn't expect him to prioritise them in the same way that Cam and I did.

'This is my chicken korma and I think it might be the best thing I've made so far. More wine?'

'I'd better not.' I put a hand over my glass. 'I've got to be up early tomorrow. Ava's got a rehearsal for a dance recital in the morning and even if she didn't, she's at the age where she doesn't really do lie-ins. It makes hangovers ten times harder to get over than they used to be.'

'Maybe next time you can stop over here and get your parents to sort all that out?'

'How's work?' If he could brush over Ava, I could avoid acknowledging his suggestion.

'It's been madly busy this past week and we were called out to a really nasty crash on Wednesday.' Xander topped up his own glass. 'We ended up having to cut three young lads out of their car, when one of them did his best to wrap it around a tree.'

'That must have been awful. Were the boys okay?'

'The lad driving was able to get up and walk away, but the other two were in a pretty bad way and they're both still in intensive care.'

Xander shrugged. 'Car versus a big oak tree is rarely a good outcome for the car.'

'Is it hard not to take that sort of thing home?' I skewered a piece of chicken with my fork. 'I think I'd be up all night worrying about what had happened to them.'

'It was tough when I first started, but it gets easier the longer I do the job. Put it this way, I wouldn't swap it for a class of screaming six-year-olds.'

'I think we're both in the right jobs then.' I didn't add that it was just as obvious we were both on the wrong date, but we were. I wasn't sure if Xander even liked children. But the way he spoke about them, we definitely weren't on the same page. Much as I fought Mum every step of the way about dating again, the main reason I'd let her grind me down and convince me to give it a go, was because we both knew I wanted more children. Having Ava was the best thing that ever happened to me and I'd never regret being with Luke because of her. But I was just wasting Xander's time. And mine.

'Do you think you'll stay in Appleberry or have you got ambitions to do other stuff? I've been looking at the possibility of applying to be a firefighter out in New York.'

'Wow, that sounds amazing.' We were a million miles apart already, and it didn't matter if he was down the road from Appleberry or in NYC. I'd been told by a colleague about a cottage that was about to become available and having walked by to take a look at it, moving in there with Ava was now my number one ambition. It was surrounded by the cherry trees that had given the cottage its name and I could already picture how the garden would look in every season of the year. I knew there'd be stunning cherry blossoms in the spring, in glorious shades of pink, the plumpest, dark red fruit in the summer, and even in the winter the empty branches of the cherry trees would make the perfect framework to hang outside Christmas lights from. I'd climbed cherry trees more times than I could remember as a kid too, sitting in a low bough with a book and eating some of the fruit straight from the source, before the birds got to it. That was the life I wanted for my daughter. NYC might be amazing, but it definitely wasn't for me. 'I'm really happy at the school at the moment and I certainly don't want to move away until Ava is ready to go on to secondary school. She's had enough upheaval in her life and, fingers crossed, we'll be moving into our own little cottage soon.'

'Just don't get tied into too long a contract. Things can change and you might find you're ready to move on from Appleberry sooner than you think.' Xander was already topping his glass up again. 'The world extends a long way from the edge of the village.'

'I know.' It was exactly what Luke had said to me when he'd persuaded me to move to Cornwall, and look how that had turned out. But I'd been in love with Luke, and I wasn't even convinced I liked Xander. Toying with my food and working out how quickly I could leave, without being rude, should have been a dead giveaway though. 'You're right about this curry, it's great.'

'You should see my red velvet pancakes – it'll be the best breakfast you've ever tasted.'

'I'm more used to making soft boiled eggs and soldiers. It's Ava's favourite.' I was hoping if I kept mentioning my little girl, he might get the picture that this wasn't going anywhere – least of all through to breakfast – without me having to spell it out.

'Have you ever been on a jet ski? I bought one last month and I thought we could get together and take it to the beach for the day?' Xander put his hand over mine and I pulled it away. I was going to have to be brutal after all.

'My husband got himself one of those when we were down in Cornwall. I'm sure they're great fun, but I always thought the sound of them buzzing like a giant angry wasp was too big a price to pay, especially for everyone else using the beach. I like to be able to hear the waves lapping on the shore, or the sound of Ava laughing as she digs in the sand.' I sighed. I'd never been good at saying no, or giving people the bald truth if I thought it might hurt them. And it was one of the things I hated about myself. I needed to draw on the half of the genes my mother had given me. She'd say anything to anyone if she thought she was right, no matter how uncomfortable it might make them feel, because she'd convince herself it was for the best in the long run. 'It's been nice to see you again and this is a lovely meal, but I just don't think we've got anything in common.'

'Of course we have. It's just because I mentioned the jet ski and it's reminded you of your husband, but not all of us are like him, you know.' Xander probably was a nice guy, deep down, but the touch of his hand on mine had made me shudder, rather than shiver. It might have been the same whoever I'd been with, even if they'd seemed the sort of person who could accept me and Ava as a whole package. I just wasn't ready; I might never be. And if that meant my biological clock tick-tocked all the way down to zero, then that was just the way it was going to have to be. All I wanted was to make the most of being Ava's mum, and I wasn't going to waste another minute on Xander, or any of Mum's other well-intentioned dating advice.

'It's not about Luke...' My mobile phone started to ring and I gave Xander an apologetic shrug. I didn't care if it was someone wanting to talk to me about PPI, or trying to sell me a pre-paid funeral plan, I was going to use it to my advantage.

'Sorry, I'm going to have to get this. Hello?' There was a long silence, just like with the calls that had been coming through since the texts had started. At first they'd been weeks apart, but I'd already had two in the last week. If it was Luke, he was doing me a favour for once, and getting me out of this dinner date. So I carried on my one-sided conversation for Xander's benefit.

'Oh no, really? What projectile vomiting *and* diarrhoea?' I shook my head at Xander, who'd put down his knife and fork with a clatter. 'Ten of them, already? Of course, no, you're right. Hopefully that will stop it spreading. Thanks for letting me know and I hope you feel better soon, bye.' I paused again, to make it look like the phantom caller was saying goodbye, and for a second I thought I heard someone say my name. Whoever it was, they'd have to wait for another opportunity to finally speak up. I was going home to Ava.

'I'm so sorry, Xander, but that was Ruhan, my teaching assistant.' I was already pushing my chair back from the table. 'It seems half my class has gone down with a horrible winter bug that affects *both ends*.'

'Oh God.' He pulled a face. 'This is why I don't want kids, they're like germ bombs.'

'Umm and the trouble is, I've obviously been exposed to it all. Ruhan's already suffering, so I'm guessing it's only a matter of time for me.' I stood up and clutched my stomach. 'I don't feel quite right as it is, and the last thing I want to do is to pass it on to you.'

'You'd better get yourself off home.' Xander stood up too, but instead of coming towards me, he turned back to the kitchen.

'Yes, of course. I just need to know where you put my coat?'

'It's hanging on the end of the banister at the bottom of the stairs.' Xander emerged from the kitchen with a bottle of Dettol anti-bacterial spray. Following me out into the hallway, as I picked up my coat, he started spraying the surfaces. 'I'll have to get everything you've touched. I can't get sick; I've got a bit of a phobia about vomiting.'

'I'm sorry Xander, I wouldn't have come round if I'd known.' I couldn't help feeling guilty. The poor man was in a panic now that he was about to develop symptoms of a horrible bug that didn't even exist. But it wasn't all lies. I wouldn't have come over if I'd known how the evening would end up. None of it was his fault; it was down to me for not following my gut. It was the last time, though. 'I'm sure you'll be okay.'

'I hope so.' I think he would have pushed me out of the front door if it hadn't meant touching me. It was a good job he didn't have a broom handy, or he'd probably have prodded me with it, like a farmer moving reluctant livestock. Although I was just as keen to get out as he was for me to leave.

'Take care, Xander.'

'You too.' He didn't mention another date, and I bet he looked as relieved as I felt when he pushed the door shut behind me.

Just as I got inside the car, my phone started to ring again. I hadn't had a chance to block the number and, emboldened by my success at shaking Xander off, I decided it was time to get tough with the mystery caller too.

'Hello?' There was no response. 'Look, whoever you are, and I think I know who it is, these phone calls are completely pointless. You don't say anything and I just block you. Either say something or sod off. You must have better things to do than this.'

'Scarlett, I know where you are.' Suddenly the sound of silence was infinitely more appealing than the robotic sounding voice at the other end of the line. If it was Luke disguising his voice, then he was doing a very good job.

'Who is this?'

'I'm coming to see you Scarlett. You and Ava.' The mention of my daughter's name made me shiver. I was certain she'd be safe with Mum and Dad, but I had to get home.

'Whoever this is, don't call me again.' Pressing the button to end the call, I activated the auto-lock for the car doors and started the engine, grinding the gears and over-revving it as I pulled away. Ignoring the mobile on the passenger seat beside me, which was already ringing again, I tried to steady my breathing. I didn't want to stop and block the number; it would have to wait until I got home. But by the time I pulled up at Mum and Dad's and picked up the phone again, there were twelve missed calls. Whoever it was knew my name, and much more worrying than that, they knew Ava's too. I was going to have to put a stop to it, even if that meant tracking Luke down myself – whatever that took.

10

Three hours of scrolling through Facebook and I was still no closer to tracking down my estranged husband than I had been at the start. I started with the Class of 2003 from Castonbury High, the nearest secondary school to Appleberry, where Luke had studied alongside Natasha and her husband. The Chisholms were both members of the alumni Facebook group, but Luke wasn't in there any more from what I could see. Although I wasn't about to send the administrator of the group a request to join and risk giving Luke the heads-up that I was looking for him again. I'd tried it all before, when he'd first disappeared, so I needed to find another way this time.

Looking up the names of his parents, I scrolled through a few matching profiles, but none of them turned out to be right. Most of his friends had private accounts and, even though one or two of them had more public posts and friends' lists, I still couldn't find any mention of Luke. After that I tried every other form of social media I could think of, as well as Googling his name and following up a load of red herrings. It was as if Luke had disappeared off the face of the virtual world, too, when he'd walked out on us.

Going through the profiles of the Class of 2003 group, I saw a photo of Jonathan Grant. According to his profile, we had a mutual friend – Phoebe Spencer. She'd been my best friend since secondary school and, although life had taken us in very different directions, we had the sort of friendship we could pick up as if we'd never been apart. If she was still in touch with Jonathan, who I knew for a fact had been on Luke's stag do, then she might be able to help me track him down and find out if he was making the calls to my mobile. It had to be worth a try.

'Scarlett, I was just thinking about you.' Phoebe answered her phone on the second ring. 'I was going to give you a call to see how things are going down there in the back of beyond.'

'Don't try and pretend you wouldn't give up your flat, on the doorstep of everything London has to offer, given half the chance.' I laughed; she'd told me often enough that they'd have to drag her back to the village kicking and screaming.

'It's not so much Appleberry, but some of the people who live there.' There was an edge to her voice and I knew exactly who she was talking about. It was selfish, but I didn't want to get into that until I'd had a chance to speak to her about Jonathan.

'You still keep in touch with some of the old crowd though, don't you? Have you heard much from Jonathan lately?'

'Jonathan Grant? We're friends on Facebook and I've got him on Instagram if I remember rightly, but I don't think I've even got it set up to see his posts. There were too many about kayaking and mountain biking, and it was starting to put me off unhealthy eating. What made you ask about him? Is this about Luke?'

'Kind of.' I took a deep breath. I hadn't wanted to worry Mum by telling her about the phone calls. But I needed to speak to someone, and it might as well be Phoebe.

'What do you mean "kind of"? Please tell me you aren't thinking about taking him back. You should tell him to drop dead, as painfully as possible.'

'Chance would be a fine thing. I've got no idea where he is and I haven't heard from him since he left, at least I'm pretty certain I haven't.'

'Have you been drinking, or is life back in Appleberry affecting your brain? You're talking in riddles.'

'Sorry, I just can't get my head around the fact that it might be Luke.' I paused for a second. 'I've been getting weird texts since I started at the school, and then phone calls. At first they were silent, but recently there's been someone on the line, making what sounds like veiled threats and mentioning me and Ava by name.'

'Does it *sound* like Luke? Or does it sound like some saddo sitting at home in his underpants, eating cold baked beans out of a tin, and getting his kicks from freaking you out? Although I'm not sure how you'd tell the difference.'

'It sounds a bit like Stephen Hawking... but seeing as he's dead, I think I can cross him off the list of suspects!' I felt a bit better already. Phoebe had always been able to make me laugh, and it all felt a bit less sinister now I'd told her. Except it hadn't felt that way when the voice mentioned Ava.

'It'll be one of those voice changer things like kids have. Are you sure it isn't just one of the children from your class messing about?'

'The kids in my class are only five or six!'

'It could be Luke; I wouldn't put it past him.' Even though I couldn't see Phoebe, I could picture the look on her face. She always wrinkled her nose when she mentioned Luke's name.

'You never liked him, did you?'

'In the beginning I thought he was okay, but then...' She hesitated for a few seconds longer than was comfortable. 'But then he did what he did and I went right off him.'

'You'd decided you didn't like him long before he walked out, though, didn't you?'

'What does your mum think about the calls?' Her attempt to sidestep the question wasn't exactly subtle. She hadn't liked Luke since more or less the time we got married. And seeing as she'd been proven right, there was really no point raking over it again. He'd turned out to be worthless as a husband and, even worse, as a father. Phoebe had just realised it a long time before I had.

'I haven't told Mum.'

'Why not?'

'You know what she's like. She already thinks I should have found someone else and moved on. If she hears about the phone calls, she'll double up her efforts to fix me up. Like I need a knight on a white charger to come and rescue me or something.' I sighed. 'I wouldn't mind, but she doesn't *need* Dad, she's the one who makes all the decisions and he just goes along with it. So the fact she thinks I need someone to look after me, is quite insulting.'

'I'd swap your mum for mine in a heartbeat.'

'I know and I'm sorry.' The first time I'd met Phoebe's mum she'd terrified me, and I'd had no idea why she spoke to her daughter the way she did. It was a long time before I discovered she had some serious psychiatric issues and it explained a lot about why Phoebe was the way she was, the barriers she put up to protect herself. 'Have you spoken to her lately?'

'No and it's why I haven't been down to see you either. If my mother got wind of the fact I was in Appleberry and hadn't visited her, all hell would break loose. But you know you're always welcome to stay up here, if you want a break from that place for the weekend or whatever.'

'Does Adam know you're making that offer?' Phoebe had lived with Adam for about three years, and I was never really sure whether they were flatmates, partners or somewhere in between.

The lines had been blurred somewhere over the three years, and Phoebe was insistent she didn't want a full-time relationship with anyone. I was pretty sure that decision led back to her mum, too.

'He'll be cool with it.'

'How are things between you two?'

'Fine. But if you mean, are we *together*? Then sometimes we are and sometimes we're not.' Phoebe laughed. 'I know you can't get your head around it, but it's just another version of what you're saying. I don't need a man, but from time to time I want one. I couldn't bear that sort of commitment anyway.'

'Do you think that makes us messed up?'

'Everyone's messed up, one way or another.'

'Maybe Luke left because deep down he knew I didn't need him in the way some men want to be needed.'

'That's bullshit and, if he did, then you're even luckier to be rid of him than I thought.' Phoebe's tone was sharp. 'But my mum definitely messed me up and she'd still keep doing it if I let her.'

'What if I do the same to Ava?'

'Now you're really talking crap. You love Ava, and everything you do is because of her. You shouldn't even mention yourself in the same breath as my mother.'

'But Lucy's doing okay with Darcy, isn't she?' Phoebe's sister still lived in Appleberry and I felt another twist in my stomach, at the fact I hadn't been to see her since I'd got home. Her daughter, Darcy was two years younger than Ava, and she'd be due to start school the September after next.

'Mostly, but I think she has some of the same worries as you. And, with our mother as a role model, she has far more to be concerned about.' There was a catch in Phoebe's voice. 'That's why I'm never having kids. But you'll be fine, you're great and so is Ava. Like I said, you're both better off without that arsehole. You should go and see Lucy, though.'

'I know and I will. I've just been so wrapped up in getting a rental place sorted and getting to grips with teaching again. But that's no excuse.'

'And when are you coming up here? Maybe you can bring Lucy up too, with the kids. We could go ice skating at the Natural History Museum or something, if you can get up before Christmas? I might not be mother material, but I can work on being a fun auntie.'

'That would be great.'

'You should report the calls, too. Just in case.' Phoebe suddenly sounded serious.

'I will. Do you think I'm doing the right thing, trying to find Luke in the meantime?'

'I'll speak to Jonathan, but why don't you just go and see his mum and dad again?'

'I'm not sure I can bear to speak to them after the last time. They cut all ties with me and Ava when he disappeared. And they were hardly attentive grandparents even before that.' My stomach churned again. Luke's parents had been cold to me from the start, as if they thought I wasn't good enough for their only son. But their ability to just walk out of Ava's life, too, had floored me. Maybe that was where he got it from – it was another reminder of the influence we had on our children's lives and yet another reason to make sure I didn't let Ava down.

'What's the worst that can happen? Just do it, and prove to your mum and yourself that you don't need anyone to fight your battles.'

'I will.' My heart was starting to race, despite the bravado.

'Give Ava a hug from me and tell her Auntie Phoebe will take her to Hamleys when you come and visit.'

'We'll do it soon, I promise, and I'll give Lucy a call.' I knew I was wasting my breath saying what I said next, but I did it anyway. 'And don't work too hard, okay?'

'It's what keeps me going. I'll give you a ring next week and I want to hear that you've reported those phone calls.'

'Okay.' I ended the call without actually making her a promise. If I reported the calls, they might stop, and I wanted to find Luke before they did. I might not need him, but Ava needed a relationship with her dad, or at least the closure of knowing he was gone for good. I just wanted the best for Ava and that meant tracking down her dad, however hard he tried to hide.

The outside of their four-bedroomed detached house, on an estate in a town about ten miles from Appleberry was non-descript, aside from the boxwood hedge, which had been trimmed to look as though it had a row of bowling balls balancing on the top. They still had the same red Nissan Micra parked in the driveway that they renewed every three years. I'd parked Mum's car around the corner, so they didn't know they had a visitor before I was ready for them to.

There was no getting out of it now, though. If the car was in the driveway, then the likelihood was that they were home too. I must have walked up and down the pavement outside their house ten times, trying to psyche myself up to knock on the door, and earning a suspicious look from the man next door, who was raking up leaves in his front garden. If I didn't knock on their door soon, I'd be targeted by the Neighbourhood Watch.

Blowing out my cheeks with a long breath, I took a step down the path towards the house. It was stupid, but for the first time the realisation hit that Luke could actually be in there too. When I'd last seen them, just after he first disappeared, they'd claimed they had no idea where he was, but that he'd called them to say he was safe and not to worry. It was a damn sight more than he'd done for me. After that, their responses on the phone had become more and more monosyllabic, until they'd stopped taking my calls altogether and blocked my number. So I wasn't exactly expecting an effusive greeting when I turned up on their doorstep. It must have been what Jehovah's Witnesses felt like when they saw a Give Blood sticker prominently displayed on someone's porch window. And I was just as likely to get the door slammed in my face.

'Janice, how are you?' My mother-in-law was staring at me open-mouthed, as I spoke. I suppose I should have been thankful she hadn't shut the door straight away.

'What do you want, Scarlett? We've told you before, we don't see anything of Luke, and it just makes things worse you turning up here and phoning all the time. It's why I had to stop taking your calls.'

'Can I come in?' I fought to keep my voice steady. She had some neck implying that I'd bombarded them with calls and visits. I'd been to the house once, and called every couple of weeks to see if there was any news of my missing husband. Ava's missing father.

'I don't think that's a good idea.' Janice turned and called down the corridor. 'Colin! Colin!'

'Is Luke in there?'

'Of course he isn't. I've told you, all we get is the odd phone call and even we're not sure where he's living at the moment.'

'So you do have some idea then?' I paused as my father-in-law stepped heavily along the laminate flooring towards his wife, until he was standing by her side, physically blocking my entrance to the house, as if I might try and make a run for it and rugby tackle Janice out of the way.

'Scarlett, this is no good. If Luke wants to see you, he will. Just go please, or we'll have to call someone.' Colin at least had the grace to look down at the floor as he spoke. I wondered if he was proud of a son who could act the way Luke had.

'And what about Ava? If you've got an address for him, even if you're not sure that it's his latest, you owe her that, surely?'

'It's not our decision to make.' Janice folded her arms, and despite my mother's ill-informed well-intentions, I suddenly had a whole new appreciation for her. If things had been the other way around, and I'd run off and left Luke and Ava without a backward glance, she'd have done everything she could to make sure they were okay. And she'd have fought tooth and nail to ensure she still got to see Ava as much as possible.

'Can you at least pass this letter on to him, then?' I pulled the envelope out of my coat pocket and held it out towards them. For a few seconds, it looked like they were going to refuse to even take it, but Colin finally pulled it out of my hand and gave the smallest nod of his head.

'Thank you *so much*.' I layered the sarcasm onto the last two words as heavily as I could and turned back down the path, forcing myself not to break into a run. All I could do was hope they'd leave the decision about reading the letter to Luke. But even if they did, there was still no guarantee he'd get in touch.

11

The rehearsals for the nativity play seemed to eat up half the school day in the run up to end of term. Between that, getting the children to make gifts and cards for their parents, and trying to do some present buying of my own, preparations for Christmas seemed to have swallowed December whole. We'd cancelled supper club because everyone was so busy, especially Dolly who was trying to prepare for Christmas in a household that had more or less doubled in size overnight.

I was attempting to get ahead of myself by wrapping some Christmas presents on the night before the nativity, when Ava was safely tucked up in bed. I'd already decided to make a donation to a charity, rather than sending out cards. I told myself it was altruistic, but in all honesty I just couldn't find the right thing to say. I could hardly send one of those round robin letters out, filled with news – even if I didn't think they were completely naff. Not without spelling out in size 12 Times New Roman, to everyone who might be wondering, that I still had no idea where Luke was.

There'd been no reply to my letter, which hadn't really surprised me. I just wished I was sure whether Luke had actually seen it, or if Janice had stuck it in the recycling before I'd even got back to the car. Ava had barely mentioned her dad lately, not even to ask if he'd be coming 'home' for Christmas. Things had moved on since her birthday, and he was slipping further out of her thoughts on a daily basis. It was no less than he deserved.

'What are you doing, Mummy?' Ava's voice had the sleepy quality that only those aged five and under could really pull off, without sounding whiney. Whipping a piece of Christmas paper over the Play Mobil campervan I'd been halfway through wrapping, I held out my arms.

'I was just helping Dolly out and wrapping up some presents for Davey and Kylie.' They were the youngest of the Swans adopted children, so Ava could easily believe her gifts were meant for them. I knew, from talking to the kids at school, that every household handled Christmas differently. But in our house, Santa Claus brought the stocking gifts and one big present from under the tree. The rest were labelled up by whoever had bought them, so at least I didn't have to grab a pair of elf ears and pretend I was helping out the big man.

'Do you think they've written Santa Claus a Christmas list?'

'I'm sure they have, darling.' I pulled her onto my lap and she snuggled into me, her little arms snaking around my waist. Her hair smelt of the apple shampoo I'd washed it in before she'd gone to bed. I could never give up moments like this. Luke had no idea how much he'd lost.

'Do you think it's too late for me to change my letter?' Ava lifted her head slightly and looked up at me. 'Chloe said she doesn't do hers until the day before Christmas and they burn it on a fire at her nanny's house. So Santa should still be able to get me what I want if I change it.'

'Well, I'm sure he can... Probably.' I braced myself for what was coming – a puppy or a pony. She seemed to love both in equal measures, and I'd breathed a sigh of relief when neither had made it into her original letter. 'What is it you want to change, darling?'

'I'd like a sister. I don't care if I don't get anything else, I just want that.'

'Not a brother, then?' I don't know why I said it. I was in no position to give her either, and right then I'd have happily taken the pony option.

'Chloe's got a brother and she says he's really naughty. He put crayon on her dolly's face.' Ava knitted her eyebrows together and I suppressed a smile.

'If you had a little sister, she might do things you think are naughty too. She'd probably borrow all your things without asking as well.'

'If I had a little sister, I'd definitely share.'

'Well maybe one day, but babies take a lot longer than two weeks to arrive.' I put my hand under her chin, gently tilting her little face up towards mine. 'I don't think even Santa could pull that off.'

'Do you promise I'll have a sister *one day*?'

'I'll do my best, darling.' I stroked her hair, racking my brain for a distraction technique that might actually work, anything to get us off this subject. 'Are you nervous about tomorrow?'

'I'm just the donkey, silly.' She grinned, the dimple on the right hand side of her face the mirror image of mine. 'Donkeys don't speak, so it's not scary.'

'I'm sure you'll be the best donkey ever.' Her costume was hanging on the back of the door. I'd ordered it online, having neither the time nor the ability to make one from scratch. Natasha Chisholm had handmade all the angel costumes and had seemed almost disappointed when I'd told her the donkey costume was already in hand.

'What do you want for Christmas, Mummy?'

'Just to spend it with you.' I pulled her towards me. It was true, nothing else really mattered to me. But I couldn't shake the nagging feeling that Ava needed more. My conversation with Phoebe had reassured me for a little while, but at the back of my mind there was still that feeling of dread; the fear I'd emotionally suffocate Ava one day, by making her my everything. Holding her close, I shook the feeling off again. She was only five, after all. So how much harm could it do for now?

* * *

'Is there any reason why Jules Winters has got his hat pulled down over his eyes? I must have told him to push it back about twenty-five times,' Ruhan said, turning towards me as the parents began to file in to the church hall.

'He said he couldn't go on stage if he could see the audience, because his belly was doing somersaults, as he put it!' Jules was one of the three kings, and he was waiting at the other side of the stage for the big moment he didn't even want. It was strange when he'd been so calm about singing the solo at Harvest Festival, but kids were often unpredictable. 'I just hope he doesn't trip going up the steps... It was a choice of letting him wear the hat like that or finding a stand-in king at the last moment. Deep down I don't think he really wants to pull out, and his mother was waiting outside half an hour before the doors opened, to make sure she got a front row seat. So I can only imagine her reaction if he didn't have his promised part.' I definitely wasn't up for a confrontation with Claire Winters, I could barely keep my eyes open. There'd been another phone call at 2 a.m., but my mystery caller had gone back to saying nothing. Unfortunately, I hadn't been able to manage the same.

'If that's you, Luke, just bloody well say something!' When there was no response, I'd thrown the phone across the room and it had hit the wall, sending it crashing down onto the floor. Then I'd buried my face in the pillow, desperately fighting the urge to scream.

'What on earth's going on?' Mum had come hurtling into the room in about twenty seconds flat, as if she'd been stalking the corridor outside waiting to pounce, the moment she heard a bump in the night. Her hair was wrapped in what looked like a turban made from cling film and she had a sleep mask hanging lose around her neck.

'What have you got on your head?'

'Never mind that, what's the shouting and banging about? Are you getting into a state about Luke again?' It had become her go-to question when I showed the slightest sign of stress. So I wasn't surprised it was the first thing she'd thought of, especially as the mobile phone was still face down in the middle of the floor.

'No.' It was partly true. I had no way of knowing whether the mystery calls were from him or not, although I wouldn't have bet against it. 'I was having a bad dream that's all, and I must have knocked my book off the nightstand, and my mobile phone with it.'

'I know you've been trying to contact him again.' Mum sat down on the edge of my bed and started to stroke my hair, just like I did with Ava.

'What do you mean, you know?'

'Colin rang me and asked me to tell you not to go round there again, apparently it's too upsetting for Janice.' She rolled her eyes. 'And I told him to piss off.'

'Mum!'

'Well, what else was I supposed to say? How dare they put any blame on you? And how dare that bloody woman put her feelings first, when there's a child involved in all of this? It's no wonder Luke's turned out like he has with a mother like that.'

'I left a letter for him, but I don't even know if he'll ever get it.'

I leant into Mum, wanting to be a child again and for her to sort out this whole sorry mess for me. Sadly, it wasn't that easy any more.

'I know about the letter, too. And Colin promised they'd passed it on, before I told him where to go.' Mum sighed. 'Although I don't know that I'd trust anything they say. Why didn't you tell me you were going round there? I would have come with you and given them a piece of my mind, face to face.'

'That's exactly why I didn't tell you. I wanted to give them the chance to show they'd changed and to build bridges with Ava if they wanted to.' My eyes stung. I'd never understand them cutting Ava off, not in a million years.

'It's their loss, darling, and our gain.' Mum stroked my hair again and, for a few moments, I let the tears fall silently into the fabric of her silky pyjamas. If she felt them, she didn't say so. Eventually I pulled away.

'Is Ava going to be okay, do you think? It's my fault for picking someone like Luke, and now she's got to grow up and deal with his rejection. I've seen what that can do to people.'

'But she wouldn't be Ava if he wasn't her dad, and it's the one good thing the useless sod has done.' Mum took my face in her hands. 'But whatever happens she'll do brilliantly, you'll make sure of that.'

'Thanks, Mum.' For a moment I came really close to telling her about the mystery calls and texts, but after her response to Colin ringing, there was every chance she'd make things worse. Mum dropped her hands and fiddled with the cling film on her head. It might ruin the poignant moment we'd just shared, but I had to ask. 'Why *have* you got that on your head?'

'It's to stop my hair drying out. I soak it in olive oil once a week and leave it overnight, and your dad says I smell like a sun-dried tomato if I don't wrap it up this tight.' She tilted her head to one side. 'You should give it a go. I could feel how dry your hair's getting, when I was stroking it.'

'Don't ever change will you, Mum?' I laughed, despite the insult. Even if she did sometimes say things without thinking, I knew she loved me and Ava unconditionally. My daughter might have an absent father, and one set of grandparents who didn't seem to care about her at all. But all the time she had Mum and Dad she'd have as much love as she could handle from the three of us. And somehow, we'd make that enough.

Ruhan's voice jolted me back to the present. 'What happened to your phone?'

'I dropped it last night.' It had survived being hurled against the wall, but the screen was cracked like a bullseye to a car windscreen. At least it still worked, though. And I had it at the ready to record Ava, as she led Mary and Joseph down the aisle between the audience members' chairs and up onto the stage. Dad had dug out his old video camera, and he'd be filming it too, but I'd do it as a backup. Unlike Luke, I didn't want to miss a second.

'You've got to love Cam, haven't you?' Ruhan laughed as Cam started to marshal his class, including Ava, into position. Only the reception class and my class took part in the main nativity play, the rest of the school acted as the choir, who stood at the back of the stage behind the performers. 'He's really entering into the spirit of things, isn't he?' Cam was wearing one of the angels' halos, which he'd told us he might have to. In the name of gender equality, it had been decided that half the angels would be girls and the other half boys. Except some of the boys didn't seem to be quite so 'on message' and were refusing to wear the theatre-standard halos that Natasha Chisholm had fashioned out of brass wire. There was no tinsel taped to a reformed metal coat hanger for her. It was only when Cam had told his reluctant Angel Gabriel, and the rest of the boys, he'd wear one too, that the deadlock was broken.

'He looks great,' I whispered back, as Mrs Davy took her position at the front of the hall to welcome all the parents. It was show time again.

* * *

'You did a brilliant job, darling.' I gave Ava a hug, as the children came out to meet their parents after the nativity play was over.

'Did you see me pick up baby Jesus?' Ava grinned, and I couldn't help laughing in response.

'I did sweetheart. Isn't it a good job Mary had a donkey there when she dropped the baby, or who knows what might have happened?' I turned slightly and caught Cam's eye as he walked towards us.

'It's not a *real* baby, Mummy.'

'But if it had been, it would have been a good job you were there,' Cam said, when he came and stood beside us. Mum and Dad were queueing for coffee and cake from the refreshment table, and there was a buzz of conversation in the room, the children clearly excited that Christmas was officially just around the corner.

'Do you want a baby? My mummy does.' Ava looked straight at Cam and heat hit me square in the face, like stepping off a plane on a tropical island somewhere. At that point, even the ground opening up and swallowing me would have been a welcome holiday.

'Ava!'

'But you do, I heard you telling Nonna. And you told me you need a lady and a man to make a baby.' She looked at Cam again. 'Even Santa Claus can't do it on his own.'

'Ava, stop it. It's rude to ask people questions like that.' My tone was much sharper than usual, and a tightness settled in my chest as

Ava's face fell. If it had been anyone else, I'd have laughed it off, but I was taking my embarrassment out on her.

'It's fine.' Cam looked amused. 'I do want a baby. One day. But I'd need to find a mummy for the baby first and I'm not having much luck on that front.'

'Mummy hasn't got a daddy for her babies any more.'

'Right, darling. I think it's time I took you over to Nonna and Gramps to see if you can find a cake you'd like.' Taking hold of her hand, I glanced over my shoulder and mouthed the word 'Sorry' to Cam, determined not to overthink what he'd said.

* * *

Mum and Dad took Ava home and I headed back across the road to the school, to do a few bits of marking that had to be finished by the end of term. I was just writing a comment in the last child's book, when I looked up to see Cam standing in the doorway.

'Are you nearly done?'

'This is the last one. What happened to your halo?'

'I decided it didn't go with my shirt.' Running a hand through his just slightly messy hair, he walked towards me.

'I'm sorry about what Ava said earlier. We were having a chat about her Christmas list the other day and she asked me if she could have a baby sister, so I had to explain that it doesn't quite work like that.' I shook my head. 'But if I'd had any idea she was going to come out with that sort of thing, I'd have kept my big mouth shut.'

'There's no need to apologise. Ava always manages to brighten my day and she did it again today.'

'She is a happy little soul.' I swallowed hard, determined not to give Luke's absence one iota of space in my head.

'She's got a way of getting the truth out of people, too. Someone tipped a bottle of blue poster paint all over the dollhouse yesterday and everyone was denying it, but she got to the bottom of it in the end.'

'She's funny like that. I keep thinking she'll make a great teacher one day.'

'It's in the genes.'

'Thanks...' There was so much I wanted to say, but Ava had already embarrassed me enough for one day, I wasn't about to layer it on further by telling him I'd suddenly realised how great he was, too, but not just as a teacher. And it had taken seeing him in a halo to do it.

'She made me confess today too – to myself as much as anything.' Cam pulled out a chair and sat down close enough for me to have reached out and touched him if I'd wanted to. I clamped my hands by my sides.

'What was that?'

'How much I like you. I meant what I said about not being able to find the right person, but just lately I've been wondering if there's a chance it could be you.'

'Me?' I wasn't expecting that. 'I thought you were dating some-one, when you cancelled supper club last time?'

'I was trying to protect myself. And you.' Cam shook his head. 'I've been wanting to take you out right from when you started at the school, but it's complicated with things the way are.'

'Because of Ava?'

'No! Ava's a bonus. It's because of us working together. If you did agree to go out with me, and then you realised I'm not what you want, it could be really awkward.'

'I could say the same for you. But we'll never know unless we try, will we?' It was bravado I'd had no idea I possessed. But when I looked at him, I had to take the chance. 'And if we make a pact to go back to being friends, if nothing else comes from it, I think we're both grown up enough to stick to it. Don't you?'

'I'm sure we are. Although summoning up the courage to come in here and lay my cards on the table has made me feel like a thirteen-year-old boy again, asking for a dance at the school disco.'

'I'm glad you did.'

'Me too.' Cam finally took my hand, setting off a reaction in my body which seemed to have no concept of taking things slowly. 'I've had a few thoughts about what we could do on our first date, on the slim chance you'd agree.'

'Okay.' After the experience with Xander, I wasn't holding out much hope.

'I thought we could take Ava up to Winter Wonderland, if you're up for it?'

'She'd love that and so would I.'

'That's good, because I took another chance and booked an ice-skating session and tickets to see Cinderella.'

'I don't think you could have chosen anything better.' I'd have kissed him there and then, but I had no idea who else was still in school. And if we had any chance of keeping this low key, then we were going to have to be careful.

'So it's a date then?'

'Definitely.' Ava was going to be so excited, but probably only half as excited as Mum when she found out. Persuading the pair of them to see this as just a slow step up from friendship was going to be tricky, especially as I wasn't even sure how I was going to manage that myself.

12

Ava placed the plate of carrots on the table in Mum and Dad's hall-way, next to the mince pies and a bottle of beer.

'Are you sure that's enough?' I tried not to laugh as she rearranged the carrots on the heavily-laden tray.

'How many reindeer are there again, Mummy?'

'Eight, or nine if you count Rudolph.' We'd already read *The Night Before Christmas* together and she wanted to make sure that everything was ready for Santa's visit before she went to bed.

'Nonna said there were eighteen carrots. Is that enough?'

'That's two carrots for each reindeer, and don't forget they'll be stopping at an awful lot of houses tonight, so I think that's probably more than enough.'

'I think we should take the lid off Santa's beer, in case he's in a hurry.'

'What if he wants to take it home and drink it later?' Reliving the magic of Christmas with Ava was even better than I'd hoped it would be. 'How about if I leave the bottle opener right next to it, so Santa can decide for himself.'

'Okay, Mummy.' Ava yawned and I scooped her into my arms.

'Wow, you're getting big.' The days of being able to carry her up to bed were numbered. 'You need to get tucked up in your room, sweetheart, because Santa can't come until you've gone to sleep.'

'I'm too excited.' Even as she said it, Ava was yawning again. I'd give her ten minutes at the most before she dropped off to sleep, and I didn't think I'd be far behind her.

'Can Gramps tell me another story?'

'I'm sure he will, darling.' Carrying her through to the kitchen, I found Mum and Dad debating the merits of double-wrapping the turkey in bacon.

'It'll dry out if you don't.' Dad turned to me and winked. 'We don't want a repeat of last year, the turkey was like a camel driver's flip flop.'

'And you'll be having a Pot Noodle for Christmas lunch at this rate, you cheeky so and so.' Mum flicked him with the end of the oven gloves.

'Ava thinks she might be too excited to get to sleep, so she wants one of Gramps' special stories.' I walked towards Dad and he lifted Ava out of my arms.

'Get him to tell you what he thinks of the England rugby squad this year, Ava, it's enough to send anyone to sleep. And he can go on about it all night long if needs be.' Mum laughed at her own joke and I shook my head. They were sparring partners, but the affection was still obvious.

'How about a *Hettie the Hedgehog* story?' Dad had been telling those stories for as long as I could remember, and I'd loved them just as much as Ava when I'd been her age.

'Yay!' Ava's face lit up. 'Night night, Mummy, night night, Nonna.'

By the time Dad and Ava disappeared upstairs, Mum was already following his advice, despite her protests, and wrapping the turkey in another layer of bacon.

'Do you need any help?'

'No, thank you, darling. I'm probably better off left on my own, it's been bad enough having two cooks in the kitchen with your father interfering, without adding a third one into the mix.' She stopped what she was doing. 'Why don't you go out and meet Cam for a couple of hours?'

'I saw him earlier, and he's at his mum and stepdad's place anyway.'

'Yes, but when you saw him earlier, you had Ava there. You always seem to have Ava there.'

'One of the things I like best about Cam is that he always thinks about Ava.'

'It's one of the things I like best about him too, especially as I believed all that rubbish from the village grapevine about him not being the settling down type. But you need some time on your own.'

'We've had a few evenings to ourselves and, anyway, we've agreed to take things slowly.'

'Just don't take it so slowly that you get stuck in the friend zone.'

'The friend zone? Have you been reading dating advice for teenagers?' I gave her waist a quick squeeze, picturing how my in-laws were probably preparing for Christmas, and remembering how lucky I was. 'Have you heard from Auntie Leilah?'

'She's ringing later, don't forget they're a few hours behind over there.'

'It'll be weird having Christmas without her, won't it?' I took a bottle of beer out of the fridge, as Mum nodded. 'Do you want one of these?'

'Better not, if I start now we might really end up with Pot Noodles for Christmas lunch and you know how I feel about carbs. I still can't believe Leilah isn't coming home, but I suppose I can't blame her for wanting to spend Christmas in New York.'

'I just hope she's not spending it on her own in some soulless hotel.'

'She's spending it with Nicky's family, apparently. I suppose that's what swung it, making a good friend out there and having the chance to experience a real American Christmas. As long as she doesn't make a habit of it. This is the first Christmas in over sixty years – my whole life, in fact – that we haven't spent together.'

'She'll be back in the New Year, Mum.' Leilah had her own jewellery design business, so she had the ability to work from almost anywhere. Ever since my grandparents had passed away, she'd had the freedom to travel, too, and she certainly seemed to be making the most of it. 'If you're sure you don't need me, I think I'll go and wrap the last of Ava's presents.'

'You've bought more?'

'Only one or two.' Mum knew as well as I did that I'd gone over the top, but despite the promises I'd made myself, I still hadn't quite cracked the over-compensating thing. I'd get there, though, and it was definitely getting better. Speaking to my horrible in-laws had actually helped me move on, despite their unwillingness to share any information about Luke. It had made me realise we weren't missing out by not having them in our lives. And the same could probably be said for him. 'Give me a shout if you need me.'

I was just folding the end of the last piece of wrapping paper into a triangular shape to seal the parcel up, when my mobile rang. It was an unknown number and I very nearly rejected the call. But curiosity got the better of me.

'Hello?'

'Happy Christmas, Lettie.' This time there was no disguising the voice, and only one person had ever called me Lettie.

'Luke.' I'd run through what I was going to say if I finally got the chance to speak to him again a million times. But when it came to it, I could just about get his name out.

'I know you probably just want to cut me off, but I'm hoping, as it's Christmas, you might find it in your heart to let me say what I should have said months ago. I'm sorry for leaving the way I did and one day I hope I get the chance to explain it to you, but I understand if you don't want to talk to me.'

'I don't, but it's not about me. If it was, the call would already be over.' Hearing his voice didn't seem real, but no amount of apologising would ever be enough. I was shaking, but determined not to let him know how much he was getting to me. 'How could you just leave Ava?'

'I don't want to try and explain it over the phone, but I want to see her so badly. I want to see you both, if you can face it.'

'And you just expect me to agree to that? When you haven't even got the balls to tell me why you left? I honestly feel like I don't even know who you are any more, so why would I trust you with my daughter?' I wanted to scream at him, but I couldn't risk waking Ava, or having Mum hurtle down the corridor to check on me again. This was hard enough as it was.

'*Our* daughter, you mean. Look, I know I fucked up, Lettie, but I never stopped loving you. I just don't want to get into it now and have you slam the phone down on me. I hate myself for leaving and I don't expect you to feel any differently. But I want the chance to explain what happened face to face and I promise to answer any questions you've got. Surely the eight years we were together is worth that? Please?'

My head was spinning and it had nothing to do with the bottle of beer I'd drunk whilst I was wrapping the last of my daughter's gifts. She'd been *my* daughter alone for well over a year, and now Luke just wanted to walk back into our lives on the strength of a phone call. But isn't that what I'd wanted? Wasn't that why I'd left the letter in the first place? Now it came to it, I didn't know what I wanted any more, except to end the call as quickly as I could. 'I need time to think about what's best for her.'

'Seeing her daddy *is* what's best for her.' Some of the softness had left Luke's voice. 'I get it, though. You've got my number now and you can give me a call when you're ready.'

'Okay.' It was such a bald little word and it was far from okay – I felt physically sick just thinking about it – but okay would have to do for now.

'Just don't leave it too long.' I couldn't tell if it was a plea or a threat, but I wasn't going to let him control me any more. He'd done that when we were together, and in lots of ways he'd even managed it when we'd been apart. Enough was enough.

'Goodbye, Luke.' Without giving him a chance to answer, I ended the call, my hands still shaking. I was almost certain of the right thing to do, but it had been such a shock to get the call, I wasn't sure I could trust my judgement any more. Especially when it came to Luke. I needed to run it by someone who could give it to me straight. And with Kate away visiting family in the Midlands, that only left one person. I just hoped Phoebe wasn't out at some sparkly party, celebrating a childless and carefree Christmas Eve. I needed my oldest friend more than ever and I just had to stop shaking for long enough to make the call.

* * *

'Are you at home?' I sounded as if I'd run up a hill, rather than up the stairs to my bedroom to make the call to Phoebe. I couldn't risk Mum overhearing it, and finding out that Luke had got back in touch, before I'd decided what to do.

'Yes, boringly enough. Adam and I decided we couldn't be bothered to go out tonight, so we're waiting for a takeaway curry to arrive. But we are at least drinking champagne.'

'Put your drink down. I need a straight answer to a straight question, and I want you to have a clear head for it.'

'What's up?' I could picture her cradling her mobile phone under her chin, and putting her glass down on the coffee table in the immaculate flat she called home.

'Luke just called me.'

'Are you sure it was him this time?'

'It was definitely him. He told me he was sorry and that he wanted to see Ava. And me.'

'Oh my God, what did you say?'

'Hardly anything, I was as close to being speechless as I've ever been in my life. I didn't even manage to find out where he's been all this time, I was just so shocked.'

'What does he expect, for you to invite him round for Christmas dinner? Arsehole.'

'It's what I've been wanting all this time, though. For him to want to see Ava.' I pulled my legs up towards my chest, wishing I could curl up into a ball and sleep. Maybe then I'd know for sure what to do in the morning.

'Don't rush into it. You don't owe him anything after what he's done, least of all a quick decision. You've got to do what's right for you and Ava. Get through Christmas first, and New Year if you want to, and then give him an answer.' Phoebe made it sound more like an order than a suggestion. 'He's kept you two hanging on for over a year without even a word.'

'You're right. I need to make sure whatever I do is for Ava. Thank you.'

'No thanks necessary. You know I'm always here if you need me, just like you've been for me so many times.'

'Thanks again for everything Phebes, and have a good Christmas, won't you?'

Ending the call, I put the wreckage of my phone into the

bedside drawer, switching it to silent. I'd got into the habit of doing that in the months since the texts and calls had started, but I wouldn't have to do it any more. At least that's what I'd thought.

* * *

The church hall looked like something you'd see on Pinterest, and it was almost unrecognisable from the place where we normally held school assemblies. There were fairy lights everywhere and little glass jars dotted around holding tea lights. Potted trees were positioned in groups in each corner of the hall, providing yet more hanging places for the lights. Somehow a forest wonderland had been created inside the hall, and there were more glass jars lining each side of the pathway, enticing guests in. At least I hoped they would, since they were my one contribution to the New Year's Eve forest school's fundraiser. As always, the powerhouse driving it was Dolly. How she'd managed to do so much whilst her new family were still settling into the household was beyond me. The evening was being arranged in two parts – the first celebration of New Year was going to be at 8 p.m., for the families with young children who wanted to head off early, and everyone else could stay on until the second celebration at midnight itself. Ava definitely wouldn't make it past the first celebration, much as she might want to.

'Do I look like a princess, Mummy?' She did a twirl in her party dress, when we'd finished setting up for the party. I'd got to the church hall early to help set up for the evening, with Jamie, who ran the forest school, Kate, Dolly, Cam, and Natasha. Ava had insisted on coming with me, so she'd been dressed and ready for the party since about 2 p.m.

'You look beautiful, darling.'

'I love my dress.' She did another twirl in the outfit Cam had bought her for Christmas. It was just like Cinderella's dress from the final scenes of the show he'd taken us to see. He'd also bought her ice skates and some lessons to go with them. So much thought had gone into it and, without a shadow of a doubt, they'd been her favourite gifts. A card had arrived from Luke the day after Boxing Day, with a crumpled twenty-pound note in it. It was a stark contrast that had nothing to do with the amount of money spent.

'It's an amazing dress.' I looked over towards Cam, who was talking to Dolly's husband, Greg, and laughing at something he'd said. We'd been taking things slow, but any doubts I'd had about him taking me and Ava as a package had been blown out of the water. It helped that she'd already loved him as her teacher, but now he was so much more than that. I'd worried she might not be able to separate the Cam she knew outside school, from the teacher who had to treat her exactly the same as everyone else. But, just like she had so many times before, Ava had amazed me with her maturity, and it had also allayed my fears that she'd be able to cope with being in my class the following year.

Cam and I had told her we were good friends, but we were careful not to do anything that would make Ava think we were more than that, when she was around. We didn't even hold hands. There weren't many men who'd be that patient, but he'd never once made an issue of it.

'He's looking very handsome your other half, tonight, isn't he?' Kate sidled up to me with a silly grin on her face and I shook my head. She could do with a few lessons from Ava on how to behave.

'He's not my other half.'

'Ooh, okay, your *boyfriend* then.' She sounded even more like her inner thirteen-year-old, which was never that far from the surface.

'He's not that either, he's just a friend.' I shot her a look, inclining my head towards Ava and hoping she might actually get the message for once. Kate and Dolly knew we were dating, but we were keeping as low a profile as possible.

'Is this woman bothering you?' Dolly came over to join us, as Ava skipped off to play, and she grinned at the affronted look on Kate's face.

'Of course I'm not bothering her. We were just talking about the delicious Cam.'

'*You* were, you mean.' I was just staring at him, which was probably worse.

'How's it going?' Dolly's question was one I could cope with. It didn't label us, along with the pressure that added. I didn't know how I'd describe my relationship with Cam, if I had to, but I knew what I thought about it.

'It's great. We love spending time together and he understands Ava is the biggest part of my life. He also knows he's got to take it slow with her and, as far as she's concerned, we're just good friends. I don't want her getting too attached to him, in case things don't work out. He's been brilliant about that too.' I couldn't help smiling and it was hard to play it down when my face was such a big blabbermouth.

'Every time I look at him, he seems to be staring in your direction.' Dolly squeezed my shoulder. 'You've got a good one there.'

'So have you.' I looked over to where Greg and Cam were carrying the disabled ramp towards the doors of the church hall, making sure everyone could get access. 'You both seem to be coping with the adoption really well.'

'I can't say there haven't been some teething troubles. Thank God for under eye concealer, or I'd have to pretend tonight was fancy dress and that I'd come as a zombie.' Dolly smiled and looked across at Greg again. 'But it's worth every moment. Davey told me he wanted to stay with us forever last night. The older two are a bit more suspicious, but I can understand that. They've been moved from their home, to foster care and then on to us. I think they'll need to keep testing us for a while, before they trust we're in it for the long haul.'

'You're amazing, do you know that?' Kate took the words right out of my mouth.

'I can't get over the fact you've organised this fundraiser for the forest school with all you've got going on.' I shook my head again, it really was staggering. If it had been a fancy dress party, Dolly could have come as Wonder Woman.

'She can't afford to let Natasha think she's slipping, or she'll have the PTA chair role wrestled out from underneath her before you can say tea-light.' Kate had that familiar look on her face again, as if she'd trodden in something she couldn't scrape off her shoe.

'Actually, Nat's been great.' Dolly shrugged. 'I'm sorry to disappoint you, Kate, but I'm not going to lie.'

'Yeah, but there'll be some motive behind it.' Kate was like a one-woman conspiracy theorist when it came to Natasha Chisholm.

'I think you'd like her if you really got to know her.' Dolly might as well have talked to the wall. 'Anyway, it's five to six now, and people are going to start arriving any minute, so I reckon we should grab one of the cupcakes Natasha made before they all go.'

'Go on then.' Kate wrinkled her nose. 'As long as you know it's for re-fuelling purposes only, and not because they look and taste like something Mary bloody Berry would knock up.'

* * *

'Ava's doing her absolute best to pretend she isn't tired.' I turned to Cam with an apologetic smile. 'But it's the yawning that gives it away, I suppose I'd better take her home.'

'Do you want me to give you a hand? I could give her a piggy-back if you don't think she'll be able to walk all the way back?' He was already putting down his hard-earned drink. He'd hardly stopped all night, but he was more than willing to end his night now, just to help me out and make sure Ava got home okay. And it was really hard not to fall a little bit in love with him every time he did something like that.

'I believe it's a grandfather's prerogative to carry his grand-daughter home to bed on New Year's Eve. And no one does a fire-man's lift like me, do they Scarlett?' Dad seemed to have appeared from nowhere, with Mum right behind him. Probably propelled by her hand in the small of his back.

'They don't, Dad, and I can still remember you carrying me up to bed like that, when I'd dropped off downstairs. Although I'm not so sure you could manage it now!'

'Oh God, don't challenge your father like that!' Mum shook her head. 'Last week some young lad down at the rugby club bet your dad a tenner he could beat him in an arm wrestle. It got very ugly.'

'What? I won the tenner, didn't I?'

'Yes, and took all the skin off your elbow and put that poor lad in a sling!' Mum pursed her lips. 'But even if you do try and pretend you're still twenty sometimes, I think you're more than capable of carrying Ava home if she's too tired to walk.'

'Don't you want to stay on until midnight?' They shook their heads in unison, with overly enthusiastic grins on their faces – like a couple of well-practiced synchronised swimmers.

'No, we want to catch the fireworks display on the BBC at midnight, don't we Steve?' Mum nudged Dad, who nodded again.

'Yes, and your mum has promised me I can open a packet of French Fancies as a New Year treat.' This time Dad's smile was defi-nitely genuine. 'You two can stay on here and see midnight in properly.'

'Are you sure you don't mind?'

'Of course we don't.' Mum gave me a pointed look. 'We've seen in thirty-five New Year's Eves together, but you two hardly get any time alone.'

'Thanks, and I'll make sure Scarlett gets home safely. Happy New Year.' Cam kissed Mum on the cheek and shook Dad's hand.

'I know you will, son. Happy New Year to you too.' Dad nodded and turned to envelop me in his arms. It was somewhere I'd always felt safe and I wanted that for Ava too. Whether Luke was up to it remained to be seen, but, as Dad pulled away, I knew I had to at least give him the chance. 'I'll go and get Ava and bring her over to say goodnight.'

'Happy New Year you two, make sure you have a good night.' Mum raised her eyebrows and I was just grateful she didn't give a pantomime-style wink.

'Thanks, Mum, and thanks for everything this past year.' I pulled her into a hug and caught a waft of the Chanel No. 5 perfume she'd worn for as long as I could remember.

'Here she is.' Dad walked back with Ava, just as I let Mum go. 'Come and give Mummy a kiss and say Happy New Year.'

'Happy new 'ear, Mummy.' Ava's words were slurred with tiredness and she rested her little head on my shoulder briefly, as Dad lifted her up to kiss me goodbye.

'Happy New Year, my darling. I love you.'

'Love you too.' She lifted her head, her eyelids drooping as she did. 'Love Cam too.'

'Happy New Year, princess.' Cam ruffled her hair and I watched his face. Was this all too much for him, too soon? We'd promised to take things slowly, and I'd wanted that as much as him. Trouble was, Ava and I were both struggling to keep to the plan.

* * *

The sky was a perfect inky backdrop for the blanket of stars that were doing their best to steal the show. They might well have managed it, too, if the Chisholms hadn't paid a small fortune for a fireworks' display to light up the sky at midnight. Sparkles of frost crunched under foot as the remaining party-goers moved a safe distance back from where the display was about to start. I shivered and Cam pulled me closer towards him.

'Do you want my coat?'

'I'm fine, but thanks anyway. Were you Mr Darcy in a past life or something?'

'Are you taking the mickey?' Cam laughed. 'I was just brought up that way, I guess. It's all down to my stepdad, it's the way he is too.'

'I've got to meet this man; he should be giving lessons.'

'I'm glad you want to meet him; they've both been nagging me non-stop about it.'

'I didn't know if you were ready for all that meet-the-parents stuff?'

'I am, if you are?' Cam studied my face. 'But I've had the advantage of knowing your parents for almost as long as I've known you.'

'Are you sure that's an *advantage*? Especially with my Mum!' I tried to read his expression.

'They're great and they love you and Ava more than anything.'

'They're pretty keen on you too. Although you could probably tell, by the way Mum engineered things tonight so we could spend the evening together.'

'That's another thing in her favour as far as I'm concerned.'

'About what Ava said earlier...' I couldn't finish the sentence because I had no idea how it had made him feel. Love was such a big word and I was terrified, partly that it would freak him out, but more that I might be setting Ava up for another fall. The one thing I'd wanted to avoid was someone else she loved walking out of her life one day. But it turned out I had even less control over her feelings than my own.

'It was the best start to seeing in the New Year I've ever had.' Cam pulled me into him again, as the first of the fireworks lit up the sky. 'And it's getting even better. Happy New Year, Scarlett.'

'Happy New Year.' I stood on tip-toes, kissing him on the mouth and trying not to think about how many people had seen us. I was never going to be famous, but being a teacher in a small village school, and dating the assistant head, gave me some idea what it was like for your every move to be watched. I didn't want the whole world to know about us just yet and, glancing around, it seemed most people were more interested in the fireworks, thank God.

'Can we get a photo, so I can text Mum and Mike Happy New Year, and put them out of their misery now that you've agreed to meet them?' Cam took his mobile phone out of his pocket.

'As long as you tell them my selfie face isn't really what I look like?' Somehow, I'd never quite got to grips with the perfect pout that everyone else was so good at. I usually ended up looking like I was recovering from a serious neurological episode, or at best like I was badly constipated. Neither one was a good look.

'That'll do it.' Cameron snapped a blissfully speedy selfie and, as he sent the message, I took the opportunity to text Phoebe and wish her a Happy New Year, too, before I headed over to do the same with Kate and Dolly. I was about to shove the phone back into my pocket, when a notification appeared on the screen – it was a new message.

✉ Sender not in contact list
Make good decisions in the New Year or you and Ava might regret it.

I didn't recognise the number and it definitely wasn't the one Luke had used to call me the week before, because I'd stored that in my phone. I wanted to believe it was just a badly worded wish for a safe New Year, but no one could get it that wrong and I still had no idea who was behind it. I shivered again, wishing that Cam's offer of a coat could make me feel better, but some things weren't that easily fixed.

13

I'd been staring at the phone for about half an hour. Several times my fingers had hovered over the contact list, but I couldn't do it. Once I called Luke, he'd be expecting a decision. But I needed to ask him, first, about the message that had made me lie awake worrying several times since New Year's Eve. Ava and I were moving into our new home, a little cottage less than half a mile from the school, in a matter of hours. Finding Cherry Tree Cottage had felt like the most amazing piece of luck; it was the perfect place for the two of us to have our fresh start and it was more idyllic than anything I thought I'd ever be able to provide for her, after what Luke had put us through. I just wanted everything sorted before then, to give us all the clean slate we needed. As it was, the thought of leaving my childhood bedroom was suddenly almost as daunting as it had been when I'd first left for university. And I'd only had myself to think about back then.

'Right, come on, you can do this.' Speaking out loud to the empty room, I scrolled through the list of contacts again, until I found where I'd saved the number Luke had used on Christmas Eve. Mum and Dad knew now that he'd phoned, and that he'd sent

Ava twenty pounds, because they had a right to know what was going on. Mum had done that pursing her lips thing, which was always a tell-tale sign she was annoyed, and she'd been adamant I should only arrange contact if Luke made a legal approach. Dad was a bit more even-handed, suggesting that giving him a second chance would be good for all of us. If the worst happened and he let Ava down again, I'd know for certain I'd done the right thing in stopping contact. But if it worked out, then Ava would have her dad back. None of us were any the wiser about why Luke had left in the first place. But since no excuse would be good enough, I couldn't factor that in to the decision.

Cam had said more or less the same as Dad, when I'd confided in him too. But I hadn't told any of them about the latest threatening text message, not even Phoebe. I wanted to believe it was a one-off and pretending it hadn't even happened seemed the best way.

'Hello, Lettie, I was beginning to think you might never call me back.' The familiarity of his voice wasn't quite the shock it had been on Christmas Eve, but I could still barely manage a squeak in response. 'Lettie, are you there?'

'Sorry, I've got a bit of a sore throat.' There was no way I was giving him the satisfaction of knowing how much I was struggling.

'Me too, I've had flu since Boxing Day, it really knocked me off my feet this year. I think it might be the stress I've been under, waiting for you to get back to me.' I'd forgotten about Luke's yearly assertion that he'd come down with the flu. I'd only had it twice in my life and I'd genuinely felt like I was dying. Luke's version of flu involved a lot of lying around feeling sorry for himself, but he'd still managed to watch TV and eat as normal – as long as I'd carried the food up to him on a tray. He'd taken to his bed a week after Ava was born, for the best part of a fortnight. And it had felt like I was nursing two babies, until I got an infection myself and the health visitor had shouted at Luke for letting me work myself into that state. She'd taken me to one side later and said that some men struggled to adjust to not being the centre of attention any more. It looked like she'd been spot on with him.

'I don't think you can get stress-related flu.' He hadn't even asked about Ava, and he was already blaming me for his illness. It was doing very little to convince me he'd changed.

'I'm not saying it *caused* the flu, just made it worse.'

'Are you staying with your parents?' Somehow, I doubted his mother would be waiting on him the way I had, and it was why I'd made so many excuses for him over the years. He hadn't had the nurturing I'd had with my parents, and I'd filled that void for him when we first got together.

'Yes, I've been with them since Christmas, but I miss you.'

'And Ava?'

'Of course.' He hesitated for a moment. 'Did she like the money I sent her for Christmas?'

'I haven't told her about it yet.' It was something I'd struggled with. If I'd told Ava about the money from her father, she might ask about seeing him and I hadn't been ready at that point to set it up. Especially as she still thought he hadn't contacted us because he was ill and couldn't remember who we were. It had been a stupid lie to tell, in a moment of desperation, and it was hard to take back. But after the text on New Year's Eve, I wasn't even sure I wanted to.

'Why haven't you told her?' Luke's tone was hard.

'Because you disappeared out of her life – our lives – overnight, and you can't just send twenty pounds in a Christmas card and think you can pick up where you left off. It's more complicated than that when a little girl's feelings are at stake.'

'I'm not going to make the same mistake twice.'

'So it was a *mistake*?' I'd made a lot of mistakes in my life, but none that involved me disappearing without a trace.

'Of course it was.' Luke's voice softened. 'You know I don't want to get into this over the phone, but I had a reason for going. I left to protect you and Ava.'

'In what way could walking out on us, without any contact, possibly have been about protecting us?'

'If you insist on hearing it like this, instead of face to face, I had debts – big ones. And not just the money we'd borrowed for the B&B, but other debts you didn't know about. And the people I'd borrowed money from, weren't the sort who just sit around patiently waiting to be paid.'

'Debts for what?'

'Gambling.' He paused and I was speechless for the second time in a matter of moments. 'It all started one night when I couldn't sleep, worrying about how much longer it was taking to get the B&B off the ground than I'd expected, and I found a poker site online. I won a thousand pounds that first night, and I got it into my head I could gamble my way out of our financial problems. Except it turned out to be beginner's luck but, even when I started losing, I couldn't stop. I was desperate to win back the money I'd lost and then it spiralled out of control. I ended up borrowing off a money lender and his methods of collection were less than conventional, put it that way. I had no choice but to disappear, and letting you and Ava know where I was, would just have put you at risk. I wanted everything to be back square before I got in touch again. I got a job back in IT consulting, because it was the only way I could think of to make enough money quickly. But I didn't want to come back until I could be the husband you deserved again, and I was sure there wouldn't be any repercussions from the money lender. That's why I just disappeared and it's why I wouldn't let Mum, Dad, or anyone else tell you where I was.'

'Why didn't you just tell me when you first lost the money?' I didn't know what to believe, much less how to feel. It might just be a plausible lie, but Luke had a history of being impulsive and self-sabotaging just when things were going well – it was why we'd given up well paid jobs to start the B&B. I also knew for a fact he'd sat up late at night on his computer in the months before he'd left. He'd told me at the time he was working hard to market the B&B, and after he'd left I'd wondered if he'd been having an affair. But there'd have been no reason for him to go to the extremes he had. Plenty of people walked out on marriages for that reason, but they didn't completely disappear. If he'd got us into even more debt, I could almost comprehend why he'd wanted to run away. And it might even explain the threatening phone calls.

'I couldn't bring myself to admit what a bloody idiot I'd been. You were working all hours to make the B&B a success and I'd dragged you into that. I didn't want to drag you into another mess I'd made.'

'We were married, you should have been able to tell me anything.'

'*Were* married. I was under the impression we still are?'

'Technically, yes, but whatever happens between you and Ava, we can't go back to that.'

'Not even now you know why I went?'

'You couldn't trust me with your biggest secret, and it turned out I couldn't trust you with my heart. You might be able to justify what you did to yourself, but if you'd really loved me, you wouldn't have been able to walk out like you did.' I was making the right choice, but that didn't stop the lump that was forming in my throat feeling as though it might burst through the skin at any moment. 'I want you to have a second chance to be the dad Ava deserves, but I'm telling you now there won't be a third chance.'

'I wouldn't expect one. I'm not going to mess up again, I can't lose you both.'

'You're going to need to prove that. But there's something else I need to know first, and I want the truth.'

'Okay, but I've already told you the worst and I've got no secrets from you any more.'

'Have you been calling me and not saying anything? Or sending texts from multiple phone numbers?'

'Of course not!' Luke's reaction was instant. 'Why the hell do you think I'd do something like that? I've been wanting to talk to you every day since I left and now you know why I couldn't contact you. Hearing your voice and not being able to speak to you would have been the worst kind of torture.'

'I was sure it was you. The messages mentioned Ava and they were weird.'

'What did they say?'

'They were warning us to be careful. I don't know, they just felt threatening.' I didn't want to say too much, hoping that if I just gave him the bare bones, he might say something to give himself away. The idea they might not be from him was infinitely worse.

'I know your opinion of me has sunk as low as it possibly could and I can't blame you for that, but you don't really think I'd ever want to hurt you or Ava, do you?' He didn't sound angry any more, just sad, and I felt a familiar prickle at the back of my eyes. How had we come to this? Two people who'd promised to be together forever and now I'd convinced myself that he was more or less a stalker.

'I just can't imagine who else it could be. Unless it's the debt collector, trying to get to you through us?'

'The debts are paid off and there's no way it could be him anyway. I went to the extremes I did to make sure he didn't even know you and Ava existed. But, what about this Cameron guy you're seeing? How much do you really know about him?'

'How do you know about Cam?'

'It doesn't matter *how* I know, and I can hardly blame you the way things were.' The sharp tone of Luke's voice contradicted his words. 'But what if it *is* him? Trying to make you think it's me, to push the two of you closer together.'

'He'd never do something like that.' This was all too much to take in. Luke's gambling confession had been huge, but he knew about Cam, too, and I wanted to know how. Not that many people knew how close we'd got... Had someone I trusted told Luke? Maybe Phoebe had let it slip when she'd contacted Jonathan from the Class of 2003 Facebook group. Or maybe one of Luke's old friends who still lived in Appleberry had seen us on New Year's Eve and put two and two together. The Chisholms would have been Kate's number one suspects. Whoever had told Luke, it was none of his business, and I wasn't going to let him make me doubt my new relationship. Cam had proven over and over again that I could trust him, and he couldn't have been more different from Luke. Thank God.

'How long have you known him, six months? You can't be sure you can really trust him so soon.'

'I knew you for over eight years and that didn't exactly work out well, did it?

'I just think you should be careful, Lettie, you don't want to rush into anything you might regret.' Luke's words made me shiver, the parallels with the text surely more than coincidence.

'I don't need your advice. And who I see, or don't see, is none of your business any more. If you want to see Ava, then I'm willing to let you have some contact. But it's got to be on my terms, and we'll have to take it slowly, until I'm sure I can trust you not to hurt her again.'

'I keep telling you, I'd never touch a hair on her head. Or yours!'

'I'm not talking about physically. You just don't get it, do you?

You've broken her little heart once, and I swear to God I won't be held responsible for my actions if you do it again.'

'Fair enough.' The fight had left Luke's voice, and some of the tension left my body with it. It was always easier to run than face up to the consequences of your actions, and, whatever his excuses, walking out had been cowardly. The messages and silent calls still felt threatening, but Luke couldn't hurt me any more than he already had. I meant what I said, though. If he hurt Ava again, I could be capable of almost anything.

'I don't know what I'd have done without you here to help me.' I passed Cam a cup of tea and rested mine on the top of an unopened box. I'd hired a van to collect the stuff that had been in storage since we moved in with Mum and Dad. There'd only been a limited amount of room at Mum and Dad's place, and I'd wanted to take all of Ava's toys, so there were lots of things in storage I'd almost forgotten about. Some of it was Luke's, and I planned to unpack it all gradually and give him back his stuff when he saw Ava. In the meantime, Cam had helped me stack it all in the dining room of the cottage, which I eventually wanted to turn into a play room for Ava. I didn't want the cottage to look like a slimmed down version of our old home with Luke, so I'd had new beds delivered, and new sofas for our cosy front room. We might still be surrounded by unopened boxes, but thanks to Cam, we'd made a lot of progress.

I'd made a decision about the phone calls and text messages, too. Now that I was as certain as I could be that they weren't from Luke, I'd decided to report them. The police were sympathetic, but I could tell it was low down on their list of priorities, because of the relative infrequency of the calls and the fact the messages didn't suggest serious threat to life and limb, as the young PC had put it. I was given a reference number and told to keep a record of any more calls and texts, and to contact them again if they became more serious. Now Luke was back in touch, I'd decided the best thing to do was just to change my number and hope that it stopped the calls for good. If they carried on after I did that, it meant it had to be someone I'd given my new number to and I was sure that wasn't going to happen. For now, though, I just wanted to get settled into the cottage and put all the worries of the last year and a half behind me.

'I'm really glad you let me help. I had a horrible feeling you'd want to do all of this alone.' Cam opened the door of the woodburner and put a log on the fire he'd lit whilst I was making the tea.

'Part of me thought I should.' I shrugged. It was easy to be honest with him. 'Moving into this place is about me standing on my own two feet again, and not relying on Mum and Dad. So asking for help seems a bit of a cop out.'

'Asking for help isn't a sign of weakness.' Cam studied my face. 'You should be proud of everything you've achieved, after you were left to sort out the B&B. Your mum and dad have said as much. Sometimes I wonder if you choose not to hear the good stuff that's said to you.'

'Stop trying to psychoanalyse me!' Cam was studying for a postgraduate diploma in child psychology and sometimes his knack of uncovering the truth and laying things bare was uncomfortable in such a new relationship. 'I heard what Mum and Dad said.'

Dad had been fixing Ava into her booster seat before they took her out for the day so Cam and I could get on with the move, when Mum had turned to me and said how proud they were of the way I'd held it all together when Luke left. And how I always did the best for Ava. I hoped they were right, but I still hadn't told them about Luke and Ava's first contact, which I'd set up for Wednesday after school. The only other people who knew were Cam and Phoebe. I wanted to be able to see how it went, first, and there was every chance it might be a one-off. There were already too many people who could be hurt if it went wrong, and I didn't want to add Mum and Dad to that number.

'Okay, I promise not to psychoanalyse you any more.' Cam gave me a rueful grin and I realised there was one thing I did want to lay bare.

'What time have we got to get to the church hall by?' Putting down my tea, I stood up and crossed to where he was sitting. There was going to be a first screening of the documentary about Dolly's adoption, in the church hall, with donations to raise funds for Adoption UK. I'd decided not to let Ava watch it until after I'd seen it at the screening, in case there were parts I needed to explain to help her understand what had happened to her new school friends, as well as what she'd been through with Luke. I hadn't told her about meeting up with him yet either, and I wasn't going to until the day came. It seemed less risky that way.

'The church hall will open at seven and the screening's at half past.' Cam turned towards me, and I ran a hand through my hair.

'So we've got time then?'

'Time for what?'

'Time to make sure we've put the new bed in my room together properly.'

'You want me to go and test the bolts again?' Cam raised an eyebrow and my stomach flipped over. He knew exactly what I meant, but I suddenly wondered if he might not want it as much as I did.

'I'm asking you to come and test the bed. *With me.*'

'Are you sure you're ready?' Cam took hold of my hands. If he didn't move upstairs soon, it might be the new sofa we were testing. It had been well over a year and a half since I'd had sex with anyone, and over ten years since I'd had sex with anyone but Luke. There'd only been one other person before him, the boyfriend I'd had when I'd left for university. I just hoped I remembered what to do. Phoebe had laughed when I'd confessed my concerns a couple of days beforehand, promising me that it was like riding a bike and that you never forgot. Trouble was, last time I'd ridden a bike, I'd managed to fall into a blackberry bush, swerving to miss a rabbit that had shot out from underneath it.

'I'm definitely ready. If you are?'

'This sounds like a really bad chat up line, but I've been ready since the moment I saw you.' Cam was stroking the back of my hand with his thumb. 'But I haven't been through any of the issues you have.'

'None of that matters any more. This house is a new start and so are you.' Moving my hand, I caught hold of Cam's wrist, pulling him to his feet.

'You're really sure?' Cam put his arms around me and I nodded.

'I promise I won't regret it in the morning, or should that be this afternoon? I'm not used to any of this, it's been so long...' Nerves were getting the better of me and I couldn't seem to stop talking. But when Cam kissed me, I forgot everything else. We'd had very good reasons for taking it slow, but standing in front of me was an even better reason for breaking my own rule. And once I did, there'd be no going back.

* * *

'You two looked very cosy all the way through that screening; I saw you holding hands! You won't do a very good job of keeping it under wraps at this rate.' Kate nudged me, as Cam went to get some drinks from the refreshment stall that Ruhan and some of the other PTA members were running. I'd bought a box of cupcakes from the bakers in Pudstable and, even if I hadn't been in the middle of moving house, cake making wasn't one of my strong points.

'We're getting along well and he's brilliant with Ava.'

'He's also got a bum you could bounce a ball off.' Kate looked towards where he was standing and did a squeezing motion with her hands.

'Does your husband know you fantasise about other men's bums?'

'If he hadn't installed a radiator in the garage just to keep his car warm, I might be more tempted to find out if I still like what's under his overalls. Lately, not even pretending he's Channing Tatum is cutting it for either of us.' Kate shook her head. Her husband, Alan, had started renovating an old MG sports car and, from what she'd said, it had pushed her way down his list of priorities.

'It could be worse, he could be down the pub chatting up the barmaid, or down at the bookies blowing your next mortgage payment on the 3.45 at Kempton Park.'

'At least then he might be interesting. If I have to look at one more fabric sample to see if I think it's the right thing to cover the car seats with, I think I might scream.' Kate nudged me again. 'You don't know how lucky you are, having a bit of excitement in your life.'

'I'm in no position to give anyone marriage guidance, but have you told Alan how you feel? I know only too well that you can be in a relationship with someone and have no idea what's going on in their head.'

'Or I could just go out and get horribly drunk and find my own excitement.' Kate laughed. 'The look on your face, Scarlett! Of course I won't, really. But pretending there's a possibility keeps me going whilst Alan is out there sanding down the rust spots on Stella.'

'Stella?'

'It's what he calls the car.' She rolled her eyes. 'Oh God, look, the Chisholms are going up to the front. We're in for another one of their speeches by the look of it. This is supposed to be Dolly's night.'

'I thought you were going to try and give Natasha the benefit of the doubt?'

'Yeah well, I'm full of good intentions.' Kate crossed her arms over her chest like she always did at the mere mention of Natasha's name.

'Thank you all for coming tonight.' James Chisholm spoke into the mic. 'I think everyone here will want to join us in wishing Dolly, Greg and their family every bit of happiness following the adoption of Kylie, Davey, Chantelle and Matty. To mark the occasion, myself and my wife Natasha thought champagne would be a fitting way to toast the Swan family. So we've got some bottles cooling in the hall kitchen, or grape juice for those of you who'd prefer that, and we'll be coming around with glasses in a few moments.'

'See, I told you. Making it all about them.' Kate didn't bother whispering and a few people nearby turned to look. 'Just a way to show off how much money they've got again and offer a round champagne like it's lemonade.'

'Kate, don't—'

James cut off my response. 'And now Natasha would like to say a few words.'

'I'm sure some of you are wondering why I'm standing up here.' I might have imagined it, but I could have sworn Natasha looked straight at Kate. 'As James has already said, we're here to celebrate the fantastic commitment Greg and Dolly have made to their new family, which we've seen for ourselves, not only through the documentary but at school. I know from personal experience what a difference having fantastic adopters like Greg and Dolly can make.'

'Who does she think she is?' At least Kate muttered the words under her breath this time.

'I was adopted at three years old by my wonderful parents, Brenda and Joe, and I know all four of Dolly and Greg's adoptive children will be just as grateful as I am that they've had the chance of a new family.' Natasha's voice wobbled and, for a second, she almost lost her composure. 'I also know that sometimes children who don't understand adoption can make fun of others. I remember only too well being told by another girl at school that I was only adopted because my real family didn't want me. And I'm sure I don't need to tell you just how much that hurt. I'd hate for Dolly and Greg's family to go through that. So, as well as champagne, we've bought some books on adoption and fostering. We really hope you'll all take one from the boxes in the kitchen and share the stories with your children over the coming weeks. Thank you all so much for coming and congratulations again to the Swans.'

'Did you know she was adopted?' Kate's eyes were like saucers as she turned to look at me.

'No, but I've got a feeling Dolly might have known, and I think those books are a great idea.'

'Dolly's heading this way, I'm going to ask her.'

'Natasha and James are about to bring the champagne around for the toast. Can't you wait until later?'

'You should know me better than that by now!' Kate looked over her shoulder at me. 'Anyway, it's the perfect opportunity whilst the Chisholms are otherwise occupied.'

'Thanks for coming guys.' Dolly hugged us both in turn, but Kate was already cross-examining her.

'Did you know Natasha Chisholm was adopted?'

'I only found out last week. She told me when she asked if it was okay for her to buy the books.' Dolly smiled. 'Of course, I was delighted, and I asked Natasha if she'd mind saying something tonight, too. Although I had no idea about the champagne!'

'Typical flash gesture from them.' Kate still wasn't giving an inch. 'For all we know, she could be making the whole thing up.'

'It's definitely true, and she told me all about the bullying too.' Dolly furrowed her brow. 'The person who gave her the hardest time when she was at school was Belinda Fincham.'

'The chair of the PTA at Oaktree Forstal?' I'd barely got the question out before Dolly nodded in response. Some of Natasha's more bizarre behaviour suddenly made sense. It explained why she was so competitive with the other PTA – she still had something to prove.

'Yes and I'm sure Belinda's changed a lot since then, but it's obviously affected Natasha for her whole life. So she wants to do what she can to avoid that happening here.'

'I still don't buy all this charitable stuff. You mark my words, Dolly, she'll be making a play for your position as chair as soon as you let your guard down.' Kate wagged her finger.

'And she'd be welcome to it, I've got everything I need now.' Dolly smiled. 'You really should try harder to give Natasha a chance, Kate.'

'I've got to say I agree with Dolly.' I gave Kate an apologetic shrug and glanced over to where Cam was helping the Chisholms hand out champagne.

'Oh, you're just seeing everything through a lovesick haze at the moment!' Kate turned to Dolly. 'Have you seen her? She can hardly take her eyes off Cameron.'

'I have, and it's great.' Dolly squeezed my hand. 'Question is, what can we do for you, Kate, to stop you feeling so jaded about everything?'

'If you were my real friends, you'd help me bury Alan and his bloody MG underneath the patio.'

'I was thinking more along the lines of setting some dates for supper club this year?' Dolly laughed at the expression on Kate's face.

'I suppose it's better than nothing. Just about.'

'I'll get on to it. There is one thing I forgot to mention though.' Dolly knitted her fingers together. 'I've invited Natasha to join supper club this year.'

Thankfully the sound of a champagne cork popping masked Kate's response, but I could have guaranteed it was X-rated. The next supper club meeting was going to be an interesting one, I just hoped Kate's pride didn't get in the way of her coming along. If her marriage really was in trouble she'd need her friends to lean on. She'd helped me get through and, even when she was being snappy and difficult, it was something I'd never forget.

* * *

By the second week of living on our own, Ava and I had fallen into a sort of rhythm. That didn't mean there weren't still days when we found ourselves rushing out of the house. And even, one day, after a power cut, when my alarm had failed to go off, that she'd had to eat breakfast on the walk to school. If Ava had her way, she'd be quite happy to have a chocolate brioche and a carton of fresh orange juice on the move every morning.

She'd had two meet-ups with Luke. I'd gone along for the first session, as she'd been quite shy about seeing him, but she was still doing far better than me. I hadn't even been able to keep my breakfast down on the morning of that first meeting and my whole body had ached from trying to stop myself shaking when I saw him again. I didn't look at him properly either, keeping my focus on Ava, desperate not to let him see he could still make me cry, and terrified of how I might react if I really looked at him.

One thing we had managed to agree between us, was to keep to the story that he hadn't been well enough to see anyone. Luke was only too willing to go along with it, because it let him off the hook, and I felt Ava was too young to understand the truth, in a way that didn't end up hurting her. The first meeting had gone well, and they'd had two hours on their own the second time. I'd had to tell Mum and Dad about the contact starting up before Ava did, and they'd done their best to hide what they were thinking when she talked about him. But they were never going to be his greatest fans.

On the Saturday after Ava's second meeting with her dad, I'd gone into school to help out at an open morning. We had two open sessions during the year, where members of the community were invited to come in and see what went on at the school, to encourage them to support our activities, and where parents of prospective pupils could get a sense of whether it was for them. One of the open days was on a weekday, but the other one was held on a Saturday, so that those with full-time jobs didn't miss out. Some of the children had been asked to come in on the Saturday morning to give the school a realistic feel, and there'd been a surprising number of names put forward. But Cam had organised games and craft activities for the children to do, so it was probably a chance for parents to get other things done without having to worry about entertaining their kids. Ava hadn't taken much persuading to volunteer, which was just as well seeing as she didn't have much choice.

The children in my class were making Egyptian sarcophaguses out of papier-mâché, and Claire Winters' son, Jules, had taken it a step further and was attempting a whole pyramid. The poor kid had probably been put up to it by his mum, but whatever the reason, I was still tearing up extra strips of newspaper when Cam came around towards the end of the morning to let me know that the last of the visitors would be coming through my class in the next ten minutes, and I could pack up after that.

'How's it gone this morning?' He looked around. There was plenty of evidence that things had got messy with the wallpaper paste at one point, when some of the kids had decided that flicking it would be a lot more fun than using it to make papier-mâché.

'Apart from a minor riot midway through, it's been great. And at least five of the parents said this will be their first choice when they have to pick a school in November.'

'That's great. I just hope there's enough space for everyone that wants it, we've already got quite a few siblings coming in next year. All the visitors have been through my class now, so Mrs Davy has taken the kids outside to run off some steam in the playground.' He moved closer and picked up the newspaper, helping me tear off more strips.

'It's good she's here and doing her bit; I still get the sense that some parents think she puts us after Oaktree Forstal.' I kept my voice low, conscious that little ears were extraordinarily good at picking up on the things you didn't want them to, and passing that information back to parents. Bad-mouthing the head teacher was a definite no-no.

'She got here ten minutes ago and she still had her golfing glove on when she arrived, so she was either hot off the tee, or she's doing a very half-hearted tribute to Michael Jackson.'

'Eurgh, golf!' It had been another excuse Luke had made for disappearing at some of our busiest times at the B&B. Apparently eighteen holes with the local head of tourism was work too, if it helped put the business on the map.

'Are you still up for coming over to my parents' place for lunch today? You look all in.'

'Of course, but you're going to have to get used to this.' I circled my face with my hand. 'It's what a working single mum looks like, at least this one does. Shadows under the eyes are all the rage this season.'

'You can carry it off.' Cam had a way of making me believe I could, even if Mum had dropped off some under eye concealer the last time she'd popped round. It wasn't just combining work with motherhood that had me looking like this – I'd had another phone call, the last time Ava had been with Luke. I'd cross-examined the poor kid when I'd picked her up, asking if Daddy had spoken to anyone on the phone. She'd been insistent that he'd only got his phone out to take pictures of them together, and I'd ended up making her cry by asking her over and over again if she was sure.

'Maybe you should warn your Mum and Dad that I look like an extra from *The Walking Dead*.'

'They'll love you.' He hesitated for a moment. 'Everyone does.'

Not everyone. There was someone out there who hated me enough to put the frighteners on me and now I was almost certain it wasn't Luke, but I still had absolutely no idea who it was.

'I'll meet you in the playground as soon as the last of the parents has come through and we can scoop Ava up on the way.'

'I suppose we'd better stay for Mrs Davy's closing speech.' Cam's face revealed how little he was looking forward to the prospect.

'You should be doing her job, but I can't see her ever wanting to leave, can you?'

'No, sadly I think I'll have to move on if I want to get a headship.'

'Is that something you're thinking of?' The thought made my stomach feel like I'd swallowed the bucket of papier-mâché.

'Not at the moment. There's far too much to keep me in Appleberry.' He touched my arm briefly, as the children carried on with their craft projects, heads down.

'That's good to know.' We hadn't talked about the long-term, but I'd be lying if I said I hadn't thought about it. We'd been in agreement about taking things slowly at the outset, but that hadn't gone entirely to plan. The future was every bit as unpredictable, which made it even scarier than the mystery phone calls.

* * *

'That lunch was delicious, Heather. Are you sure I can't give you a hand with the dishes?' I stood in Cam's mum's kitchen, opposite the big picture window that looked out onto the back garden. Heather was really easy to talk to.

'You're a guest, hen, and I wouldn't dream of asking you to help. Anyway, Mike and I are a well-practised team at loading the dishwasher. And you like it just so, don't you darling?'

'Yes, it's one of my worst habits apparently!' Mike grinned and I couldn't help smiling back. He was even nicer in person than I'd expected him to be.

'I can't imagine you've got a lot of bad habits.'

'Apparently putting the wrappers back into a tin of sweets is potentially grounds for divorce.'

'Don't forget about putting empty packets back into the fridge!' Heather waved a serving spoon in his direction. 'But you're not so bad overall.'

'Praise indeed!' They reminded me of Mum and Dad in a way, and I'd caught Mike watching Heather several times over lunch, with the same sort of affection my parents shared. 'Look at Cam out there, I can't tell who's having more fun, our boy or little Ava.'

It was one of those mild winter days, when you could believe that spring might really be just around the corner.

'He's great with kids, isn't he?' I was watching Cam and Ava continue to race around the garden, playing a game of tag that had been accompanied by lots of excited squeals from Ava, regardless of whether she was being chased or doing the chasing.

'He's always been like that. He spent half his childhood begging me for a younger brother or sister, but life just didn't work out like that.' Heather sighed.

'I'm an only child too, but that wasn't my parents' choice either.'

'And what about you, hen?' Heather looked away from the garden, fixing her gaze on me instead. 'Do *you* want more children?'

'I'd love to, if I get the chance. A lot of only children love it that way and want the same for their own families.' I shook my head. 'But it's not what I want for Ava, or for me. I just want to get it right next time, and not put another child through the sort of family break-up she's had to deal with.'

'She looks the picture of happiness to me.' Mike squeezed my shoulder. It was the best thing he could have said.

'From what Cam's said you've done a brilliant job in a difficult situation.' Heather's tone was gentle. 'I know what it's like, I've been there, and Mike is living proof that better things can come your way.' She reached out to her husband. 'And in a funny way I'm glad Cam's dad put us through what he did, or we wouldn't appreciate what we have now, as much as we do.'

'I hope I can find that for Ava.'

'My guess is that you already have, hen.' Heather shot me a look. 'Now, why don't you go out there and join in their game, while Mike lectures me again about all the mistakes I'm making loading up the dishwasher!'

'Thank you. And thanks again for lunch.' I leant down to give Heather a hug and I tried not to imagine what it might be like to have lovely in-laws like them, next time around. But it was easier said than done.

* * *

I looked down at the text again, as Cam drove us back towards Appleberry. Mum sometimes had the tendency to be over-dramatic, but I didn't want to take the chance and now she wasn't answering her phone.

✉ Mum

I've had a call from Auntie Leilah and you'll never believe what's happened. Please come and see me as soon as you can xx

'Are you sure you don't mind calling in to Mum and Dad's before you drop us home?'

Cam turned his head briefly to glance in my direction. 'Of course not, if you don't think they'll mind me being there?'

'I doubt very much it's as important as Mum's made it sound.' I tapped my fingers on the dashboard in front of me, hoping I was right. 'She's probably just up in arms about Auntie Leilah's next trip away. I think she'd be happier if my aunt stuck to Saga holidays, instead of deciding, like she did last year, to spend two weeks sea-kayaking in Croatia with a bunch of twenty-somethings.'

'She probably just wants to protect her sister.'

'She's always worrying that I'm going to turn out like her.' I laughed. 'I'm far too knackered to go sea-kayaking, let alone with twenty-year-olds. But Mum seems to think that Auntie Leilah never getting married is the worst thing in the world. It was partly why she nagged me into speed-dating when I first came home.'

'Sounds like your aunt's pretty happy living the life she's got.'

'She is and she's great fun. I've never really understood why mum's so fixated on the fact that Leilah's single. And I sometimes wonder if she's the one who's jealous of Leilah's life.' It was a hard thing to say out loud, but I couldn't help thinking Mum might have more regrets than she'd admit to. Maybe that's why she got so obsessed with things – at the moment it was nutrition and fitness, but over the years there'd been a whole host of charity fundraisers and courses in everything from grief counselling to dress-making.

'I don't think so, you can see how much she adores you and Ava, and your dad.'

'Well, we'll see what the big news about Leilah is this time.' I'd texted Mum again to let her know we were only five minutes away. And when Cam pulled up outside the house, she was already waiting on the doorstep.

'Ava shall we go out to Nonna and Gramps' back garden and see if I can beat you at tag again?' Cam winked at her as we got out of the car, and she put her hands on her hips.

'I beat *you* at tag!'

'I know, sweetheart.' Cam took hold of her hand. 'But how about giving me another chance?'

'Okay, but you're not going to win!'

'I thought it might be best to leave you to it.' He looked over his shoulder, Ava already pulling him in the direction of the back garden.

'Thanks, Cam.' I walked towards Mum as they disappeared around the back of the house. 'Your text scared the life out of me, especially when you didn't answer your phone. Is Auntie Leilah okay?'

'That depends on how you define okay. Your father thinks it's great news, but I think she's completely lost her marbles.' Mum pulled open the front door and I followed her inside. There was an empty bottle of red wine on the coffee table and a glass with a lipstick stain in Mum's distinctive shade of rose pink.

'Where's Dad? Have you drunk all of that by yourself?'

'Not *all* of it. He's taking Jasper for a walk – he said my panicking was driving him mad.'

'You're going to have to tell me what's so bad.'

'Auntie Leilah's getting married.' Mum sat down in her favourite armchair with a thud.

'That's great!' I sat down on the sofa opposite her. 'But now I really don't understand what the problem is, I thought that's what you always wanted for her?'

'Yes, but she's always said she wasn't cut out for marriage and it wasn't something she'd do, with *anyone*.' Mum picked up her glass. 'Right from when we were young and... and your dad and I got together and decided to get married, she said it wasn't for her. But now she's met someone – who she's only known since just before Christmas – and she wants to come home and get married, in Appleberry in the spring. It's so out of the blue and so ridiculously quick.'

'I know it's quick, but sometimes these things work out better than they do for people who've been together years before they get married. Leilah's in her sixties, so if she doesn't know her own mind now, she never will.' My words seemed to be falling on deaf ears, as Mum took another slug of her wine. 'Who is her fiancé anyway?' I steeled myself, wondering if my uncle-to-be was some twenty-five-year-old cocktail waiter from a Manhattan bar.

'He's a retired curator from the art museum and they met in the New York library apparently. His name's Nicky, well Nicholas really. All the time she was talking about this Nicky and about spending Christmas with Nicky's family, I thought she'd made a nice female friend out there. But now Leilah's saying it was love at first sight and it just hit her like that. Bam!' Mum banged her wine glass down on the table to emphasise the point.

'If he's retired, he must be about her age? They sound like they'd have a lot in common too.' I softened my tone. 'I'm sorry, Mum, but I really can't see what the problem is.'

'You're just like your bloody father! But at least you've got an excuse, you weren't there when...'

'When what?'

'It doesn't matter, but your father should understand why I'm so worried about it. It's just easier for him to bury his head in the sand; he's always been better at that than me.'

'Why can't you just tell me what happened before, that's making you worry so much now?'

'Some things are better left in the past, that's one thing your bloody father is right about.' Mum shook her head. 'I just don't want Leilah to do anything she might regret.'

'You can't make everyone's lives right for them, Mum. Sometimes you've got to let people make their own mistakes, but let's meet this man before we decide if that's what Leilah might be doing. Do you know his second name?'

'Mulholland.' Mum pursed her lips. 'I've Googled him and it seems he's at least telling the truth about what he used to do, if he actually is Nicholas Mulholland of course. I've asked Leilah to send me a photo of him, so I can compare it to the ones I've found online. But she said she's bringing him over in a couple of weeks to meet us all, so I don't need a picture.'

'That's good news then.' I stood up and put an arm around Mum's shoulder, thinking about what Cam had said to me on the way over. 'I know you're only looking out for Leilah, but let's try not to worry about things before they happen, okay?'

'That's easier said than done.' Mum put a hand over mine, though. 'At least you having Cam gives me one less thing to worry about. What with Luke being back on the scene, there are hundreds of other things to keep me awake at night.'

'I'm fine and Ava is too, so you don't need to worry about either of us.' I definitely wasn't going to confide in Mum about the late night calls and messages now. Whatever it was she wasn't telling me about Leilah's past, my aunt's news was more than enough for her to deal with for now. I just hoped the calls and messages would stop as quickly as they'd started. But as Cam's mum had so rightly said, life didn't always turn out how you planned.

14

Luke was waiting in the small car park at the end of the high street in Appleberry. I'd decided from the outset that I didn't want him picking Ava up from Cherry Tree Cottage. It was all part of the fresh start I'd been so determined to create for us and having him there would have felt like blurring the lines with our old life. As an IT consultant, he'd told me he worked mostly from home, which I'd guessed was currently his parents' place, but I didn't ask. The less we spoke about them the better. His job meant he could be flexible about when he saw Ava, but this was the first full day they'd be having together. The Wednesday evening sessions had been going okay, so I had no reason not to keep my promise to gradually increase the amount of contact they had. Especially now I was convinced he wasn't behind the anonymous calls and texts, which were still coming through at least once a week.

Ava seemed to be enjoying seeing her dad, too, although she mentioned him far less between their meet-ups than I'd expected her to. I was finding it a bit easier every time, as well. Maybe because when I'd finally plucked up the courage to look at him full in the face, for the first time since he'd come back, I'd realised he didn't have power over me any more. I no longer cared that he'd left me either; how he treated Ava was all that mattered. As long as he did right by her, and didn't expect anything other than a civil exchange from me, we'd get along just fine.

'So what are you two going to be getting up to today?' I handed Ava's bag to Luke, after he'd strapped her into the back seat.

'We're going to London for the day. I wanted to take her up to see the changing of the guard at Buckingham Palace, and then we'll go on to Madame Tussauds.'

'I wondered why you wanted to leave so early.' I dug my nails into the palm of my hand to stop myself from telling him to make sure he was careful.

'It was one of the things my nan used to do with me when I went up to visit her.' Luke looked a bit misty-eyed. He'd loved his nan, but she'd died not long after our wedding, and we'd named Ava after her. She'd probably been the person he'd been closest to growing up and I knew she'd offered a balance to the hands-off approach his parents had taken to raising him. After she died was probably when Luke started to change into someone who could walk away from everything, but neither of us had realised it.

'I'm sure Ava will love it, it's the sort of thing memories are made of.' It was hard trying to be the bigger person all the time, and to remember that Ava's happiness was the most important thing, when I was the one who wanted to make all her childhood memories. I hadn't gone into motherhood thinking about sharing her, but it was just another one of those adjustments that had to be made.

'Why don't you come with us?' Luke held up his hands. 'It's all right, I'm not going to leap on you the moment you get in the car.'

'I just think it will send out the wrong signals.'

'To me or Ava?'

'Both of you.'

'I'm not going to give up on us, you know?' Luke tried to stroke my hair and I stepped back.

'It's never going to happen, Luke, but I'd like us to be able to be friends one day.'

'I managed to conquer the gambling problem, and I've got faith that I can make you change your mind too.' Luke gave me a lingering look and I wrapped my arms around my body, as if reinforcing my words.

'I'm glad you've sorted your problems out, but you've got to move on with the rest of your life.' I'd been putting off what I said next, but the message needed hammering home. 'You'll be hearing from my solicitor about selling the B&B and getting the financial agreement sorted for the divorce.'

'You don't really want to break Ava's family up, do you Lettie?'

'You did that a long time ago.' Turning away from him before I said something I couldn't take back, which would ruin any chance we had of eventually being friends, I opened the car door and bent down to kiss Ava goodbye. 'Have a good day darling, I'll see you this afternoon.'

'I'll call you when we're about twenty minutes away.' Luke closed the door again. 'Shall I drop her straight to your place?'

'No, I'll meet you back here. Be careful with her, Luke, won't you?' I couldn't stop myself saying it in the end. I was letting a man I didn't really trust any more take my daughter out for over eight hours and it was hard. 'She's the most precious thing in the world to me.'

'I know, she's the second most precious thing in the world to me too.' Luke walked around to the driver's side of the car. 'And whatever you think, Lettie, you're the first and I won't give up on us for as long as I have breath in my body.'

'Don't...' I wasn't sure if he even heard as he shut the door hard behind him. I knew he didn't mean what he said – something, or someone, would eventually come along to distract him from his mission of reuniting our little family – but I couldn't help wishing it would happen sooner rather than later.

* * *

Narrowing my eyes, I studied my reflection in the mirror again. 'Are you sure I look okay?'

Cam looked me up and down slowly. 'Okay doesn't really cover it. You look fantastic, but I've told you that already.'

'I know, sorry. I'm not usually one of those people, but I feel really nervous.' It was a slight understatement given the swarm of butterflies doing dive rolls in my stomach.

'It's not a job interview, you're meeting your auntie's fiancé.' Cam moved behind me and put his arms around my waist. 'I'm the one who should be nervous about getting your aunt's approval.'

'That's a given, but Leilah's never brought anyone home before.' Mum's reaction was what was really bothering me, though. I'd woken up in the night worrying that she might have another melt-down about the surprise engagement, in front of Nicky and Leilah. And I still couldn't get the truth about why she was so worried. Something significant had happened to convince Mum that Leilah would be single forever, and if she ever did get married it would be for the wrong reasons. But she didn't want to tell me what it was. All that time when she'd been banging on about what a shame it was that Leilah was on her own, just didn't make sense any more.

Every possible scenario had run through my mind. And, put it down to too many episodes of *EastEnders*, but I'd even got it into my head that Leilah might be my biological mother. When I'd asked Mum if that was the problem, she'd almost choked on her drink, and tea had actually come out of her nose. It was ten minutes before she recovered and dug out some photos of her in a bikini with a very prominent baby bump. So unless they'd gone to an awful lot of trouble to cover their tracks, I could at least rule that out.

'It'll be fine. You've spoken to your aunt anyway, haven't you?'

'Yes and she said Nicky's dying to meet us. She sounded so happy and excited, I just don't want Mum to put a dampener on it.'

'I'm sure she'll be okay when she sees how happy Leilah is.'

I leant back against Cam, wanting to believe it was that simple, but he didn't know Mum anywhere near as well as I did.

* * *

Leilah was outside when we arrived at my parents' place, filling up a log basket from the store at the side of the house.

'Ah, Red!' She dropped the log she was holding and threw her arms around me. She'd always called me Red, since I was a kid, not because I'd been blessed with anything as interesting as ginger hair, but because of my name. I'd been Scarlett, the little red hen, when I was tiny, and over the years it had just morphed into Red and stuck that way. It got on Mum's nerves, which I think was part of the reason Leilah did it, and it gave her another excuse to tell Mum to chill out. She might as well have given the advice to a doorknob for all the notice Mum took – she just wasn't the chilling out kind.

'Auntie Leilah, you look great!'

'I look like a beetroot, I'm boiling.' She yanked off the woolly hat she was wearing to emphasise the point. 'It's absolutely baking here compared to Manhattan, and I've brought all the wrong clothes.'

'Hark at you, talking like a native New Yorker.' I stepped back. 'This is Cameron.'

'Your mum was right about one thing, he's gorgeous.' Leilah

grinned, looking much younger than her sixty-four years. 'Pleased to meet you Cameron.'

'And you.' Cam held out his hand, but she was having none of it, instead pulling him into a hug he had no chance of resisting.

'Right, come on then, we'd better get in and rescue Nicky before your mum has him booking the next available flight back to JFK.'

'How has she been so far?'

'As you might expect.' Leilah laughed. 'She was giving us the third degree about why we'd got engaged so quickly before we'd even taken our coats off.'

'I'll take the logs in.' Cam had already picked up the basket. 'It'll give me something to do if things get awkward.'

'You might have to move every single log in that store if you want to avoid awkward moments for the rest of the day.' Leilah winked at him. 'My little sister seems to think she's my mother half the time, and the way she's been carrying on, anyone would think I was sixteen, not sixty-four.'

'Maybe I shouldn't have dragged you into all this.' I turned to Cam, as we reached the back door. I was just glad Ava was out with Luke.

'I wanted to come.' It was true and he seemed more than happy to get involved with my slightly dysfunctional family, as well as dealing with the reappearance of my ex. Maybe he was after some drama, having come from such a nice, straight-forward family. One thing I could guarantee about a family get-together with my mother hosting, was that it would never be boring.

* * *

'You don't think it's too young for me?' Leilah held up the picture of the dress on her phone again.

'I think you should wear whatever you want.' I looked more closely at the dress, it was boho-style with full-length lace sleeves, and the girl in the picture had a simple crown of flowers on her head.

'At least the sleeves will cover your bingo wings.' Mum leant over my shoulder to look at the dress.

'Mum!'

'Ha, she's right, Red. I missed the boat on being able to wear a strapless ball gown.' Leilah laughed. 'But some things are worth waiting for and I'm glad I waited for Nicky.'

'He's great.' I ignored the grunt from Mum. I couldn't see how she could possibly dislike him, he was charming, funny and a big cuddly bear of a man who clearly worshipped the ground Leilah walked on.

'He is, isn't he?' Leilah was ignoring the negativity too, as she'd somehow managed to do all afternoon, despite Mum being as forthright as I knew she would be. She had an opinion on everything, from the date of the wedding, to Leilah and Nicky's decision to have a tower of Krispy Kreme donuts, instead of a traditional fruit cake. 'It might have taken me over half my lifetime to find Nicky, but I can tell you've found a good guy in Cameron.'

Dad had announced after lunch that he was taking Jasper out for a walk, and Nicky and Cam had both jumped at the chance to go with him. It was no surprise, given that Mum was radiating tension and even her hair seemed to have taken on a static frizz as a result. Although that could have been down to the polyester yoga pants and matching vest she'd decided to keep on all afternoon, for reasons known only to her. Maybe it was to emphasise, as she'd already pointed out to Leilah, that she'd managed to keep her bingo wings at bay.

'It's early days for me and Cam.' I smiled at my aunt, knowing she'd understand what that meant and that I didn't want to say too much in front of Mum.

'You don't want to hang around. You won't do better than Cam, Scarlett.' Mum tapped me on the shoulder to make sure she'd got my attention and, unfortunately, I was nowhere near as good as Leilah at ignoring the things I didn't want to hear.

'So it's too soon for Auntie Leilah to be getting married, but I'm taking too long?'

'It's different.' Mum shrugged. 'And Leilah knows why.'

I looked at my aunt, trying to read the expression on her face, and waited for her to say something. But if I'd hoped she'd shed some light onto Mum's rambling, I was in for a disappointment.

'What do you think about this for your bridesmaid dress, Red? I thought it looked perfect for a spring wedding.' Leilah scrolled down to another picture on her phone and the split second opportunity I'd had was gone.

'It's great, if you're sure you want a soon-to-be-divorcee like me as your bridesmaid.' I shot Mum a look. 'After all, according to Mum, I might be a bad omen.'

'Bullshit!' Leilah scrolled down to a third photo. 'And what about this one for Ava, if you think she'll want to be a flower girl?'

'*Want* to? She'll be thrilled!'

'I'm glad you two are focussing on all the really important things, like the dresses you're going to wear, rather than the next twenty or so years Leilah and Nicky could face together.'

'You make it sound like a prison sentence, Chrissy.' Leilah sighed. 'I can't wait. And even if the worst does happen, we'll survive. After all, Red survived being married to that idiot, and what he did to her. And she's come out the other side.'

'And she was just like you, she wouldn't listen to the warnings. She still doesn't. She's got to start making good decisions.' Mum's lips disappeared into a thin line.

I didn't hear Leilah's response because Mum's last line was ringing in my ears. *Make good decisions*, that's what the text had said on New Year's Eve. As far as Mum was concerned, giving Luke a second chance with Ava wasn't a good decision. But surely she couldn't be behind the messages, could she?

15

Every time a car slowed down to negotiate the bend in the road, just before our cottage, Ava would go up on her tip-toes to peer out of the window.

'How late is Daddy now?'

'An hour and twenty minutes, darling.' Cursing him under my breath, I tried his number again. It went straight voicemail, like it had on the previous two attempts.

'Isn't he coming?'

'I don't think so, sweetheart.' I could almost hear my own mother's voice as I pulled Ava into my arms and sat down on the armchair with her, like I had done when she was a baby. *He'll let that child down again, you mark my words.* I'd so wanted her to be wrong, even though a big part of me had been worried she was right. Why couldn't he just ring? Even if it was to make an excuse that both of us knew was a lie, at least then I'd have something to tell Ava when she asked me the question I'd been dreading.

'Doesn't he want to see me?'

'I'm sure it's not that, darling. There's probably been an emergency or something.'

'Not a crash?' Ava's eyes widened with panic. A car had crashed on the bend in our road the week before, and it had still been embedded in the half-demolished wall when we'd walked by on the way to school. Ava had been full of concern about what had happened to the driver, and the elderly couple whose wall it was, and had kept asking questions about it for days afterwards.

'No nothing like that, but he might have broken down like Gramps did when he put the wrong sort of fuel in his car.'

'Is that when Nonna called him a silly old man?' Ava grinned at the memory, knowing she wasn't supposed to repeat what she'd heard, but just this once I was glad of the distraction.

'That's right and Gramps went for a very long walk with Jasper until she'd calmed down.' Poor Dad, he'd been on the receiving end of so many tellings-off from Mum over the years, but that one had stuck in all our memories. Not least because she'd reminded him that the car took diesel and not petrol every single time he'd so much as picked up his car keys since. 'Is there anything you'd like to do, if Daddy doesn't manage to get here to pick you up soon?'

'Can we go for ice cream?'

'It's trying to snow outside.' I caught the downturn of her mouth. The same expression she had every time she'd realised a passing car wasn't Luke's. 'But if that's what you want, sweetheart, then of course we can get ice cream.'

'You're the best mummy ever.' Ava snuggled into me, and I glanced at my phone on the arm of the chair. Still no message from Luke. It was my fault she was being disappointed by her father all over again, and I didn't deserve her praise. I felt like the worst mother possible.

* * *

Working in such a small school, the teachers at Appleberry were expected to take on extra-curricular activities. Ruhan and I had decided to volunteer to run the school magazine. So, on Tuesday afternoons, straight after school, we ran the media club. It was open to all year groups, except the reception pupils, so Mum always picked Ava up from school and took her to her dance class in Pudstable.

'Miss, I can't get the picture to line up with the text.' We were ten minutes into the club and one of the Year 6 students, Samira, who was working on an article for the magazine, called me over for help with the computer.

'You just need to click and hold the mouse button...' The squeal of brakes, followed by an almost animal-like wail cut me off midway through the explanation.

'What on earth was that?' Ruhan moved towards the windows, but the fence around the school was too high for us to see anything. There was more shouting and I felt a weird prickling sensation at the back of my head. A sense of dread I just couldn't explain.

'Shall I go and take a look?' Turning towards Ruhan, I tried to keep my voice level. It sounded like something serious had happened outside the school, but I couldn't make out the voices distinctly enough to be sure.

'Scarlett!' Kate burst into the classroom, before Ruhan even had the chance to answer me, her face drained of all colour and her eyes darting between me and the window. 'It's Ava, there's been an accident.'

'No!' I shook my head so hard it hurt. It couldn't be Ava. Mum would already be halfway to the dance class with her, in the safety of her people carrier, belted in and surrounded by air bags. Even if their car had been pranged, it wouldn't have sustained much damage. Not outside the school with its speed restrictions and the traffic humps that book-ended the site.

'She's been knocked down.' Kate's arm was around my shoulders, pulling me towards the door and I was vaguely aware of a classroom full of little faces turning to look at me.

'But she's with Mum.'

'She ran off and, before your mum could catch hold of her again, she'd shot into the road.'

'Is she...' I couldn't say the words and I wanted to run, but it felt as if I were wearing gravity boots, almost as if my feet wouldn't make contact with the ground.

'Your mum and Cam are with her. She's crying and asking for you, so that's a good sign.'

I finally managed to move my feet and I started to run, straight out of the front door of the school and along the inside of the small wall that separated the pavement from the road. Ava had begged to walk along the top of the wall, holding my hand, countless times. And I'd always said no, because it was far too dangerous... but I hadn't been there when it *really* mattered. Cars were at a stand-still and there was a group of people in the road up ahead. Some of the children were sobbing and, as I drew level with where my baby was lying in the road, I caught sight of the faces of other parents looking in my direction – pity, and relief that they were safely holding the hands of their own children, written on their faces. As wrong as it was, I'd have done anything to swap places with them at that moment, to be holding Ava's hand and praying hard that someone else's child would pull through. If that made me a terrible person, I couldn't help it. She was my world, and seeing her pale and almost motionless, her cries drowned out by my mother's hysterical sobs, was my worst nightmare.

'Scarlett, I'm sorry, I'm so sorry!' Mum could barely get the words out, but I didn't have time to comfort her. I needed to touch my child, to feel the warmth of her skin so I could convince myself it would be all right.

'Mummy.' Ava tried to move when I knelt on the tarmac beside her.

'Stay still darling, I'm here now.' I stroked her hair, watching her chest rise and fall.

'She just ran out in front of me.' I didn't recognise the man whose deep voice cracked on the words. 'There was no way of stopping in time.'

'It wasn't your fault.' It was Cam who reassured him. I couldn't let myself think about whose fault it was, because deep down I knew it was mine. I was Ava's mum, it was my job to protect her. But I couldn't absolve him of blame either, not while Ava was lying on the ground and I had no way of knowing if our lives would ever be the same again.

'Why wasn't anyone holding her hand?' The driver sounded desperate, and Mum's sobs increased in volume.

'I was just talking to Cam...' She took a shuddering breath. 'Ava said she could see her dad, he's got the same car as yours and she just wrenched free, I...' Mum was crying so hard it was impossible to make out what she said next, and Kate was trying to comfort her. I couldn't reach out, not even to my own mother. It was like I was watching the world from above and Ava was the only thing I could really see. Everyone else was blurring around the edges.

'Oh thank God, it's here.' I don't know who said it, but the wail of the ambulance siren was growing all-too-slowly closer. I couldn't let Ava go as I whispered to her, telling her how much I loved her. But I wanted someone else to take over, someone who could promise me it was all going to be okay and that it was just bruising, or at most a broken bone. Something Ava could get over, that would gradually fade to nothing more than a painful memory. I wasn't a regular church-goer, and I wasn't even sure I believed, but there was a prayer running through my head, a promise that I'd do anything if God saved my baby. I didn't care if it was the paramedics clad in dark green, who were running towards us, or some higher power – as long as someone gave me Ava back.

'What happened?' Someone answered the male paramedic and there was a flurry of activity as they started doing checks and asking more questions. I seemed to have lost the power of speech, so Mum had to answer when the female paramedic asked me if there was anything Ava was allergic to. Someone mentioned shock, and I didn't realise they were talking about me at first, or that I was shivering so much my teeth were chattering. It wasn't until Kate draped a picnic blanket over my shoulders and put her arm around me, that I realised how violently I was shuddering. But I still couldn't bring myself to speak.

The paramedics worked fast, strapping Ava onto a spinal board – I'd seen enough medical documentaries to know that meant she might have a spinal cord injury. My face was wet with tears, but if I spoke I'd have to ask whether she could be paralysed. My five-year-old little girl, who loved nothing better than dancing and climbing the apple tree in Mum and Dad's back garden.

'Who's coming with us in the ambulance?'

Kate turned to face me, shaking my shoulders. 'Scarlett, you need to go with Ava.'

'M-m-me,' I stuttered a response, meeting Kate's eyes, and I could tell she'd been crying too. Kate, who was always so matter-of-fact, had big fat tears rolling silently down her cheeks.

'I'll drive your mum to the hospital.' Cam's voice was steady and I nodded, not even looking in his direction as I was helped into the ambulance.

The female paramedic kept speaking to me, and telling me what she was doing, as her colleague slammed the door of the ambulance shut behind us. A strange sense of calm descended, when we finally left the crowd outside the ambulance behind –

until I looked across at Ava, lying on a stretcher bed, the spinal board she was strapped to keeping her still.

'Keep talking to Ava, Mum.' The paramedic put her hand on my shoulder, as the siren burst into life. 'She needs to know you're here.'

'It's okay, baby, we'll be at the hospital soon, and the doctors will make you feel better.' All I could hope was that I wasn't lying, as the paramedic flicked a switch that made the lighting inside the ambulance turn blue.

'This sometimes helps with the kids, it's a bit more restful.'

'Thank you.' It was going to take more than a blue light to stop my heart hammering so hard inside my chest that my ribs were in danger of cracking. I needed to hear the words 'she's going to be okay' and I was terrified they might never come.

* * *

'We'll know more when we get the results of the scan. There are consultants from several departments looking at them now and I'll come back to see you and explain it all, as soon as they've finished.' The doctor looked down at her notes, before I had the chance to respond. She was probably sick to death of the questions I'd been asking since the moment I'd met her. When they'd whisked Ava off, seconds after I followed the paramedics into Accident and Emergency, I'd finally found my voice.

Cam had arrived with Mum, and Dad, who they'd picked up on the way, whilst Ava was in the scanner. He'd also offered to go back to the house and pick up some of the things Ava might need, so it was just the three of us standing around Ava's bed, as she was hooked up to machines that bleeped and pulsed in ways I wished I understood. I didn't know if they sounded the way they should, or whether the things they did were just another reason to panic.

'But she's going to live, doctor?' Mum whispered the question and I barely resisted the urge to fly at her. I couldn't even contemplate the possibility of losing Ava altogether, the implications of any injuries she might have sustained already too much to bear.

'Mum, for God's sake!' Ava's eyes shot open as I shouted. She'd been given some mild sedation to help her cope with being scanned, and to stop her wanting to move so much whilst she was still strapped down. They couldn't remove the restraints until they were sure she didn't have a spinal injury, in case it made it worse. I moved closer and stroked her hand. 'It's okay, angel, shh, go back to sleep.'

'She's stable.' The doctor seemed completely unfazed by the way I'd snapped at Mum; she must have seen it all before. 'As I said, we can be much clearer about everything else once the consultants have reviewed the scan. I'll be back as soon as I have news.' Even the way she pulled back the curtain, as she left the cubicle, sounded efficient.

'Could anyone use a drink?' I turned to look at Dad as he spoke.

'How about a Valium cocktail? I don't think coffee's going to cut it, do you?'

'They said you were in shock, you could probably ask the doctor for something if you need it. But I don't know about Valium, darling...' Dear, sweet Dad just wanted to make things right for me, like I did for Ava. But popping a pill wasn't going to cut it either. I needed answers. 'I thought your mother might need something to calm her nerves, too. When they picked me up, she was crying so hard, but Cam managed to calm her down a bit.'

'I'll take a coffee, Steve.' I stared across at Mum, as if she were speaking a foreign language. Could she really be bothered about getting a drink at a time like this?

'I'll be right back. Are you sure I can't get you something, Scarlett?' I shook my head and Dad opened the curtain of the cubicle again, leaving me and Mum on opposite sides of Ava's bed. And what felt like opposite sides of the universe.

'I'm so sorry, darling.' She was already crying again. 'I shouldn't have stopped to talk to Cam, I just wanted to ask how he thought Ava was getting on.'

'Mum, don't.' I didn't want to talk about what could have been done differently. I'd already heard the story several times when we were waiting for the scan. The car that had hit Ava was the same model and colour as Luke's. She'd said she could see her dad just before she shot out in front of it. Mum might be blaming herself, but if I hadn't let Luke see Ava again, she'd never have done that.

'But it was *my* fault.' Mum didn't seem able to stop, but I didn't look up at her. I just didn't have the energy to make things right for her, not yet. 'I told your father this would happen. I knew I was going to have to pay for what I'd done one day, but I never expected this.'

'What are you talking about?' She wasn't making any sense and she didn't have the chance to explain, as the cubicle curtain swished open again.

'We've got some news for you. This is Doctor Daniels, one of the consultants who's been looking at Ava's scan.' The A&E doctor came back into the cubicle with another woman, who was wearing an expensive looking trouser-suit. She looked like she should be bidding for shares on the stock exchange.

'We've got the results of the scans now and the good news is that we can remove the board, as there are no injuries to the spine.'

'Thank God for that.' Mum's hand flew to her mouth, but as I turned back towards the consultant, the smile died on my lips. There was something else, something serious. I could see it in her eyes.

'What is it?'

'Shall we step outside a moment, whilst the nurses remove the board?' She looked towards where Ava was lying and then back at me. I knew what it meant: she didn't want to tell me what she had to say in front of Ava.

My heart was hammering even harder than it had been before, as we followed the doctors to a small room and the door closed behind us.

'I think it's best if Doctor Daniels continues to explain.' The A&E doctor gave me a sympathetic look. 'She's one of the urology consultants and I think it's important that you hear it from an expert.'

'What is it?' I repeated the question, not caring who the hell told me. I just needed to know.

'As I said, there's lot of good news. Amazingly there are no broken bones, and no damage to the spine or the brain.' The A&E doctor turned to her colleague. 'But Doctor Daniels spotted something else on the scan.'

'It appears that when the car hit Ava, the impact caused some blunt force trauma and what looks like a fairly serious tear to her right kidney.'

'So she's got internal bleeding?' It was scary, but it could have been worse. At least Ava had two kidneys. If it had been her brain or her heart, I'd have been much more terrified.

'She has had some internal bleeding, but it appears to have stopped now. Although we won't know the extent of the damage until we open her up to see if it can be repaired. The worst case scenario is that we'll have to remove her right kidney.' Doctor Daniels adjusted her glasses. 'Normally that wouldn't be too problematic, as it's perfectly possible to live a normal life with one kidney, but because Ava has kidney dysplasia...'

'Kidney what?' I didn't understand the terminology, but from the way the doctors were looking at me there was clearly more bad news to come.

'Ah, we assumed you'd already be aware. It's usually picked up on pre-natal scans, although obviously not always.' Doctor Daniels shook her head. 'It means that one of Ava's kidneys didn't form properly and, over time, because of the cysts caused as a result, it's stopped functioning altogether. As Ava had a fully functioning kidney on her right-hand side, she wouldn't have had any symptoms to alert you to the condition. Unfortunately, it's her healthy kidney that has sustained all the injuries.'

'What happens if you can't repair the healthy kidney?' I already knew the answer, but I was praying I was wrong.

'If we have to remove her right kidney, then Ava will have to go on dialysis and then onto the transplant list.'

'She can have one of mine!' Mum was up on her feet, and if she could have pulled a kidney out of her body, there'd have been a real danger of her handing it straight to Doctor Daniels.

'We can look into all the options when we know for sure what we're up against.' Doctor Daniels nodded slowly. 'We're just waiting for a theatre to become available and then we're going to take Ava straight in. They're preparing her for surgery now, but you can come up and kiss her goodbye before she goes down.'

I tried not to think about what the word *goodbye* might mean. I was putting my whole world in Doctor Daniels' hands, but it was the only option I had.

* * *

The words were starting to blur on the screen. I'd scanned what felt like hundreds of pages of information on my phone, between answering text messages from Kate, Dolly and Phoebe. As much as part of me wanted to murder Luke, I was also desperate to get hold of him. I wasn't sure he had the right, any more, to know that his daughter was in hospital. But if Ava needed a kidney, there was a chance he could be the best match. And he owed her that. Phoebe was doing her damnedest to track him down, by speaking to everyone she could get hold of from the Class of 2003 Facebook group. They might have protected him first time around, when it was just his angry estranged wife trying to get hold of him, but if they did the same when Ava was lying on the operating table, then they deserved to burn in hell. If I knew Phoebe, she was telling them as much too. Dolly and Kate were offering emotional support, but I didn't want anyone else at the hospital for now.

Dad had arrived back with the coffees and panicked when he'd found the cubicle empty. Once he'd tracked us down, he'd taken Mum home in a taxi, despite her all too vocal protests – recognising that I needed a break from her. Cam had come back and offered to stay, and I'd realised that I wanted him there, more than anyone else. He wasn't making it about him, or the fact that he'd been talking to Mum when she'd let go of Ava's hand. Instead, he was coming up with ways we might track Luke down. It was what I needed at that moment, someone who was putting Ava's needs before their own and taking action to make things right.

'It says here that dysplasia might have been caused by some-thing I did when I was pregnant with Ava.' My stomach turned over at the thought, and I handed my phone to Cam.

'Don't Scarlett.' Cam swiped the page so that it disappeared. 'I've been reading about it too and there are lots of possible causes, but it isn't your fault.'

'What if it is? What if it was that glass of champagne I had at my second cousin's wedding?'

'It wasn't. It's just one of those things that happens sometimes, and look how well Ava has been. You'd never have known about the dysplasia if it weren't for the accident. You've raised a happy and healthy child who's a joy to be around. I've seen the kids of parents who don't put them first and that isn't her.'

'I just wish the operation wasn't taking so long I need to know.' I laid my head on Cam's shoulder, overwhelmed with exhaustion. It felt like I'd lived a whole lifetime since half past seven that morning, when I'd been plaiting Ava's hair. It was like Groundhog Day – every morning I had to almost pin Ava down to brush her hair and wrestle her fairy wings off, which she always wanted to dance around the garden in, just as we were supposed to be leaving. She'd complain about sitting still, and the brush pulling at the tangles in her hair, and then we'd end up rushing to leave. Now I'd do anything to be plaiting her hair or watching her spin circles in the garden, pretending she could fly.

'I'm sure it won't be long now.' Cam stroked my hair and I listened to the steady rhythm of his heart. Somehow, leaning against the solidity of his chest, I could let myself believe everything would be okay – that Doctor Daniels would appear and tell us the operation had been a complete success, and we could take Ava home in the morning. I must have fallen asleep for a few moments because I was woken by Doctor Daniels coming into the relatives' room.

'Is she okay?' I was up on my feet in an instant, but Doctor Daniels gestured for me to sit down again, as she took the seat opposite.

'She's in recovery and she's stable again.' She gave me a brief smile. 'We've attempted a repair to the kidney and we're monitoring her closely. I think we're going to have to put her on dialysis, at least temporarily, whilst we wait to see if the kidney can recover enough function.'

'And if it doesn't?'

'We'll have to continue dialysis until a suitable donor is found.'

'I read something earlier about live donations from family members having the highest rate of success.' If we were going to have to face the worst case scenario, I wanted to be ready for it. 'Can I be tested now, to check if I'm a match?'

'I think it's a bit early for that.' Doctor Daniels smiled again, but it was okay for her to sit back and wait. It wasn't her baby we were talking about, and she didn't know our story – how hard it might be to track Luke down. But I was way past being embarrassed.

'Please! Her father's disappeared – it's the second time he's done it and I have no idea where he is. If I'm not a match, and with my parents the age they are, I need to go all out to find him. So I'd rather know as soon as possible.' If I sounded desperate it was because I was, and something in Doctor Daniels' face changed.

'We can organise an initial scan and kidney function test. I guess it can't do any harm to be prepared. But I'm still hoping we'll have the best outcome, and that Ava's own kidney will start working properly again.'

'Thank you.' I reached across the space between us. 'For everything.'

'It was a team effort.' Doctor Daniels stood up. 'One of the nurses will come and get you as soon as Ava's ready to come up from recovery, but she's quite heavily sedated. Unfortunately, we don't have any facilities for parents to stay overnight. So, after you've seen her, the best thing you can do is go home and get some rest and come back tomorrow when she'll be more herself. We'll give her the first session of dialysis overnight and hopefully she'll be able to sleep through that, too. I'll ask one of the nurses to book you in for a scan and blood test tomorrow as well.'

'Thank you, again.' Doctor Daniels nodded in response, and we were left alone in the silence of the room. Reaching out, Cam pulled me towards him and for the first time I really let myself cry. There'd been silent tears when I was kneeling next to Ava in the road, but I hadn't really been able to cry properly, not in the way Mum and Dad had. And even Kate. Now, in Cam's arms and more certain than I'd been for hours that Ava was safe, I finally let go. He didn't say anything to try and make me stop, he just held me and let me cry. And whatever happened in the future I'd always be glad it was Cam who was with me that night.

'Is that your phone?' I picked up the low buzz of Cam's mobile, which must have been on vibrate, when the tears finally started to dry up.

'It's fine, I don't need to answer it.'

'No it's okay, you should get it.' I peeled myself off him. His jumper was soaked through where I'd rested my head, and my supposedly waterproof mascara had streaked the fabric – it had probably never been tested to quite that extent.

'Hello?' He turned his body slightly away and I pulled my own phone out of my pocket, starting a text to update everyone on news of Ava's operation. 'Thanks for calling me back. Yes, that would be great. Do you want to speak to her?' Cam turned back to me. 'It's Natasha Chisholm.' He held out the phone.

'I don't...' I wanted to say that I didn't really want to speak to anyone, least of all someone I wasn't close to, who was probably only ringing so she could be in-the-know at the school gates in the morning. It was the sort of thing Kate might have said, but luckily Cam cut me off before I got there.

'It's important. She says she can find Luke.' I took the phone from him.

'Hello, Natasha?'

'Oh Scarlett, we are so sorry to hear about what's happened to Ava, we've been beside ourselves.'

'She's doing better than she was, but there's a chance she might need a kidney transplant.' I came straight out with it, I needed to find Luke and there was no point in sugar coating it.

'Cam told me. He thought I might know where Luke was, because of us going to school together.' Natasha took an audible breath. 'The truth is, Luke gave James his new number when he asked to borrow the money. We could have tried to get hold of him the first time he disappeared, but he asked us not to tell you.'

'I don't care about what happened before, this is about Ava.'

'I know, but I argued with James the first time around, because I really wanted to give you his number. This time I don't give a fuck what Luke wants.' I'd never heard Natasha swear before, and it sounded weird, like hearing your nan do it. 'I've told James to go and get Luke and get his arse down to the hospital; they should be there in the next hour.'

'Thank you.' I'd said the words so many times since Ava's accident, but it was all I could say. The Class of 2003 might have covered up for Luke in the past, but Natasha was a mum too and she'd come through when it really mattered.

'If you need anything else – *anything* – just let me know.'

'I will.' I handed the phone back to Cam and he ended the call. 'It's you I should be thanking, for contacting Natasha in the first place.'

'It was the least I could do.'

'Luke's going to be here in an hour.'

'Good.' Cam looked as exhausted as I felt. 'Do you want me to leave you to it, when he gets here?'

'You could probably do with getting home, anyway, couldn't you? Especially as you're going to have to arrange cover for me tomorrow on top of everything else.'

'Don't worry about any of that.' Cam took hold of my hand, and I wanted to ask him to stay – to arrange cover for us both, so he could be at the hospital with me and Ava. But that wasn't fair on him, and I wasn't sure how Luke would take it either. As much as I wanted Cam, I had to keep Luke on side until we knew if she needed a transplant, for Ava's sake.

'Do you want to go now?'

'I'll wait until the nurse comes to say you can go and see Ava, or until Luke arrives. Whatever happens first.'

I nodded, wanting to say so much, but it wasn't the time or the place. Once Ava was well, we could pick up where we'd left off. But things were never quite that easy.

16

'Did you stay here all night?' I nudged Luke's shoulder and he looked up at me, his eyes still heavy with sleep, looking so much like Ava had, when she'd been desperately trying to stay awake on New Year's Eve. When he'd arrived at the hospital, part of me had wanted to pummel my fists against his chest and scream in his face that all of this was his fault. If Ava hadn't run out after that car, she wouldn't be lying in a hospital bed. But I just didn't have the strength to row with him, not whilst every cell in my body was focussed on Ava making a recovery, and not when I was the one who'd allowed it all to happen by letting him back into our lives in the first place.

'I couldn't leave, not until I knew for sure that Ava was okay.' He put his head in his hands. 'This has made me realise just how much I've risked.'

'I told you last night I didn't want to talk about all of that, not now. We can't afford to start something that's going to end up in an argument.' I kept an empty seat between us, as I sat down on the line of brown plastic chairs. My class would be settling down in their chairs, waiting for the start of the school day. Cam had texted to ask how Ava was, and to say they'd arranged a supply teacher who could cover the next two weeks at least. It was one less thing to worry about. When Luke had turned up at the hospital the night before, Cam had already gone home. I was sitting with Ava in intensive care, but they'd said she could move down to the high dependency unit after her first session of dialysis. Doctor Daniels had stayed around too, until we could both be sure that Ava was definitely going to make it. That had meant a lot.

'I know you don't want to talk about it, Scarlett, but I just can't believe what an idiot I was.' Luke had been full of excuses from the moment he'd turned up, but I'd heard them all when he'd promised not to let Ava down again, and we both knew how that had gone. All that mattered was getting Ava better and there was a chance she might need him for that, more than she needed me. If he tried to justify his disappearance second time around, I wasn't sure I could hold my temper. And with his form, that could send him heading straight to the car park and out of our lives for the third time in eighteen months.

'Luke, just don't, okay?' If he wanted me to say it was all right, then he was out of luck. He deserved to feel bad for the way he'd treated Ava and, if it was genuine guilt, he'd have to learn to live with it. 'Has anyone told you what time we can go in this morning? They said last night that we might have to wait until after ten this morning, so they could get her moved down to HDU.'

'Yeah, the sister said the same to me, when the nurses had their shift change over this morning. She told me to wait in the relatives' room, but I didn't want to miss you when you came in.'

'I've got to go for a scan at nine thirty and then up to phlebotomy to have my blood taken.'

'Do you think I should push for a scan too, so we know which of us is going to be the best match?' Luke stretched as he spoke, his leg pushing out far enough to touch mine, and I suddenly remembered the way he used to lie in bed when he slept, with one leg draped across me – a memory from another life that I could hardly believe had ever been mine.

'Let's see how this morning goes.' I stood up, annoyed with myself for the petty thoughts running through my head. I wanted to be the one to give Ava the kidney, not Luke. We'd been a team since he'd walked out, and the thought of him coming in now and saving the day was driving me crazy. It was stupid, if Ava needed a kidney, it wouldn't matter where it came from. 'I might as well head up, just in case they can squeeze me in a bit early, then I can get back for when we're allowed in to see Ava.'

'I'll come with you. And then, if you aren't done by ten, I can come back down here and let Ava know you're on the way.'

'You don't need to.'

'I know, but I want to.' Luke was already on his feet. 'Sitting here, waiting for the clock hands to move around to ten is like some form of torture.'

* * *

There were three other women waiting in the ultrasound department when I got there. Two of them were obviously pregnant, but the other lady looked like she was in her eighties. If she was in there for an ante-natal check-up, she'd be booking her place in the *Guinness World Records* too.

'You don't have to wait with me.' I leant across Luke to pick up a magazine from the small collection on the table at the side of him. He still wore the same aftershave and a memory jolted my senses – the way Ava had always smelt of her daddy's aftershave when she was a baby, because she'd been snuggled in his arms at some point during the day. We'd been happy once, I'd almost forgotten that.

'I want to stay. Being here reminds me of when we went for that scan, when you were expecting Ava, and you squeezed my hand so tight I just knew what I was in for during labour.' Luke laughed.

'They make you drink so much water, and you've got a baby jumping up and down on your bladder. Then when they run late, which they always seem to, it's almost too much to bear.' I smiled at the memory too. 'It was either squeeze your hand or leave a big puddle in the waiting room.'

'Do you need to squeeze my hand now?' Luke looked at me. Ava was one of those children who was an instantly recognisable combination of her parents. She'd inherited my olive skin tone and slightly upturned nose, with the same full lips, but her eyes were all Luke's, blue with long thick lashes and even her brow line was unmistakably inherited from him. Looking into his eyes was like looking into hers and for a second my fingers twitched almost automatically, but I couldn't let him hold my hand. Those days were gone.

'I'm fine, thanks. Anyway, I told the receptionist about getting back for Ava and she said if the nine fifteen appointment doesn't turn up, I should be able to go straight in.' I lowered my voice, not wanting to drop the receptionist in it, with the other waiting patients.

'Shall I come in with you?'

'I think that's a step too far, don't you?' I didn't wait for him to answer. 'Why don't you read this while you're waiting?' Handing the magazine to Luke, I stared at the door, praying that whoever had the nine fifteen appointment didn't walk through it.

'Mrs West? We can see you now. Room two please.' The receptionist had obviously decided the nine fifteen had had their chance.

'You're still using your married name then?' Luke smiled and I shrugged in response.

'It's Ava's name. That's why.' Standing up, I walked to the other end of the waiting room and knocked on the door of room two.

'Come in.' It was dark inside and there were two members of staff, one already sitting by the scanner and the other seated at a computer. 'Pop your things on the chair, please, Mrs West, hop up onto the bed and we'll get started.'

'Thank you.' Lying down on the bed, I pulled up my top and undid my jeans, rolling my pants down as low as they could go without revealing anything the radiologist didn't need to see.

'So I understand we're doing an initial check of your kidneys to see if you might be suitable as a live donor for your daughter?' She had a reassuring smile, and I wondered how often she had to give bad news. There was a small tattoo of a heart just poking out from under her watch strap with a date printed underneath it. Everyone had a story to tell, and this was going to be part of mine. I just didn't know how big a part yet.

'Yes, that's right. We're still hoping she won't need it, but I'd rather make sure I can, so we're ready to go if we need to.'

'I'm just going to put a bit of gel on your tummy.' She tucked some blue paper towel into my knickers and squirted the gel onto my stomach. 'I'm sorry if it's cold.'

'It's fine.' My breath caught all the same, and I tried to keep still as she instructed me to move first onto one side and then onto the other. She seemed to spend a lot of time on my left side and I screwed my eyes shut, fighting the growing sensation of tightness in my bladder. Maybe I should have brought Luke in after all; squeezing his hand could have given me a tiny bit of revenge. When I opened my eyes, the radiologist's colleague was standing beside her.

'Have you ever had a kidney scan before?' The older woman looked at me and I shook my head, trying to read the expressions on their faces. 'I'm sorry but it looks like you've got kidney dysplasia, your left kidney doesn't seem to be functioning at all.'

'But I can't have.' I sat bolt upright, not caring when the end of the ultrasound scanner slipped off the bed and banged against the metal frame. 'I'm thirty, I'd know by now, surely?'

'Not necessarily, if your other kidney is functioning okay and you've never had to have a scan for anything related, you could easily live with the condition and not know. And you can live a perfectly normal life with one kidney.'

'But what about Ava? She's got dysplasia too and her good kidney's been damaged.'

'I'm so sorry, but this obviously means you're not going to be able to be her donor.' The younger woman's tone was gentle. 'The condition does sometimes have genetic links and it looks like that's what's happened.'

'I've let her down again, passing that on to her, on top of everything else.' I wanted to put my fist through the scanner, but I clenched them by my sides instead.

'No, you haven't.' The younger woman wiped the gel off my stomach and helped me pull my top down, which forced me to unclench my hands. 'And I'm sure there are other family members who can get tested as a match, aren't there?'

I thought about Luke sitting out in the waiting room and I nodded slowly. Saving Ava could be down to him now. 'Her dad wants to be tested.'

'If you speak to your daughter's urologist, I'm sure they'll set that up.' The older woman looked up from the computer, where she was no doubt recording the fact that I was useless as a donor.

Standing up, I fastened my jeans, scooping up the stuff that I'd left on the chair moments earlier. 'Thank you.' I mumbled the words and opened the door, the brightness of the waiting room making me blink.

'Do you need to go to the loo before you go and get your blood taken?' Luke walked towards me and I shook my head. 'What's the matter, Lettie? You look terrible.'

'I *am* terrible. I can't do it, Luke.' I was crying now, and I didn't care that everyone in the waiting room was staring in my direction.

'I know it's a scary prospect, but of course you can do it. Ava needs you.'

'Exactly! And I can't help because I've only got one working kidney, too, and it's my fault she didn't have a spare one when she needed it.'

'Lettie, don't, please. It'll be okay, I can do it.' Luke pulled me into his arms and I let him, leaning against the body that suddenly seemed to fit so well with mine, as though we'd never been apart. The achingly familiar aftershave still made it feel as if Ava were sandwiched between us, as she had been so many times when she'd woken in the night as a toddler, and wanted to sleep in our bed. 'It'll be okay, I won't let either of you down this time.'

'Promise?' The words were muffled against his chest.

'I promise.' He leant back, turning so that his arm was around my shoulder, and guided me towards the waiting room door. 'Show's over people, you can go back to your *Woman's Weeklies*.'

I let him protect me from the stares, and from the hollow feeling that had settled inside me, somewhere near my useless kidney. Luke was going to make sure Ava was okay and I was going to trust him to keep his promise – whatever that took.

17

Ava dropped the colouring book onto her bed with the sort of dramatic sigh that only a five-year-old could muster.

'Mummy, I'm *so* bored. When can I go back to school?'

'Soon, darling, you're doing really well.' I didn't miss the way she wrinkled her nose. *Soon* wasn't a good enough answer for her, but she was making amazing progress, and Doctor Daniels seemed to think her kidney had a more than 50 per cent chance of repairing itself. In the meantime, she was still having dialysis, which she hated even more than missing out on school.

'I miss Cam and my friends.' The constant grumbling was a clear sign she was getting better, though.

'We have to be careful that you don't get an infection, so it's probably best if we wait until you get home before your friends come round. That's why only me, Daddy, Nonna and Gramps can come and see you. But look at all the lovely cards your friends have made.' There were get well messages all around Ava's hospital room: drawings, paintings, and even some covered in dried pasta and cotton wool ball clouds. Cam had come over to the cottage the night before and dropped them off. Luke had asked if he could stay at my place, but I'd managed to persuade him it wasn't a good idea. So he was staying with the Chisholms. I was confused about how I felt, and my bond with Luke, through Ava, was stronger than I'd ever realised. But I missed Cam as much as she did.

Typically, Cam hadn't pushed me by asking where he stood. When he'd dropped off the cards from Ava's classmates, all he'd wanted to know was how she was, if I was coping and whether he could help in any way. I'd used the excuse of being exhausted not to spend too much time with him, but when I'd kissed him goodbye, it had felt as though I was cheating. I just wasn't sure who I was cheating on.

'Is Daddy coming up to see me later? He promised he'd play Snap.' Ava was getting fidgety, and every time Luke was late, I couldn't help wondering if this would be the time he'd let us down again.

'I'm sure he'll be here soon.' I glanced at my watch, whipping around as the door to Ava's room swung open.

'Sorry, we just need to take you down for a scan, sweetheart. To see how that kidney of yours is doing.' Sam was one of Ava's favourite nurses and he could do all sorts of accents; today he sounded like a cowboy from a western movie and Ava was already giggling. It made the constant tests, which more often than not involved a needle, a lot more bearable for both of us.

'Can I have some ice cream when I get back?' Ava was sharp as a tack, and she'd soon picked up on the fact she could ask for pretty much anything either side of one of the tests or treatments.

'I'm sure we can sort that out.'

'Come on then, princess, let's take you down there.' Sam helped her into a wheelchair and winked at me. 'I'll have her back in about half an hour. You'll have just about enough time to get that ice cream sorted.'

'See you later, Mummy.' Ava blew me a kiss. 'Can I have strawberry, please?'

'I'll see what I can do, darling. Be good.'

* * *

I'd taken to bringing a cool bag and freezer block into the hospital, since nine times out of ten Ava would ask for ice cream. The doctors were restricting her fluid intake, and there was also a list of foods she could only have in small amounts, including dairy products. But the supermarket around the corner from the hospital stocked a dairy-free variety, which had been a godsend. It was good to get out of the stifling environment of the hospital, too. My skin was tight and dry from hours spent in an airless room under strip-lighting, so the biting February wind was a welcome change.

I pulled my phone out of my bag, to check whether Luke had texted to say why he was running late. I was really trying to give him the benefit of the doubt, and let him prove he'd changed, but the trust wasn't there yet. The wind was whipping my hair across my face, but it wasn't lifting the fog in my brain. I couldn't seem to think straight any more. Luke being back in our lives, at a time when Ava needed him so much, had shifted our relationship. But I still wasn't sure what we were, or what I wanted us to be. And then there was Cam.

There were six messages on my phone, but none were from Luke.

✉ Kate

Hope Ava is still doing great. I've got her some sticker books as I know you said she's bored stiff. Best keep a low profile as Natasha is sending out orders about the summer fair already!!! Doesn't she know it's still bloody freezing!

✉ Dolly

We've been thinking of you and beautiful Ava and we loved the picture of her looking so much better. Davey can't wait to visit and he chose a paint-your-own-unicorn craft set for her too. Give Ava a big kiss from us and look after yourself as well. Let me know if you need anything xx

✉ Phoebe

U both okay?

✉ Mum

Can you ring me and let me know when we can come and see Ava again. Need to talk to you about the trip with Auntie Leilah too. Mum xxxx

✉ Cam

So glad Ava is doing so well. Mum made her a cake in the shape of an ice skate, not sure if she's allowed to eat it? But I didn't want to break that to Mum, I think she's been watching too many old episodes of Bake Off! The kids in your class have made you some cards too. Let me know when you want me to drop them off. Miss you both x

✉ Natasha Chisholm

Luke told us the good news about Ava's progress. Can't imagine how scary that was. We'd like you to use the villa for a family holiday when Ava's well enough. Will you make it to the first meeting about the summer fair? We've got to raise more than Oaktree Forstal this year. It's on!

It was funny how even such short messages could reveal so much about their senders, like the fact Phoebe struggled to show affection, and Mum still hadn't realised she didn't have to sign off her texts with her name. Kate clearly hadn't got over her issues with

Natasha, who was still fixated on outdoing the PTA at Oaktree Forstal. And Cam? He was still being about as perfect as it was possible to be, which just made things more confusing.

I texted quick responses to everyone except Phoebe and Cam. I'd call him later, but I needed to talk through my confusion about Luke with someone before I did. Going over and over it in my head was getting me nowhere. Kate would be too biased in favour of Cam, and Dolly had enough on her plate, but I needed to decide whether giving Luke another chance – not just with Ava, but as a family – was as bad an idea as I thought it might be.

'What's wrong?' Phoebe might not find it easy to show her emotions, but the concern in her voice was obvious.

'Nothing. I just needed to talk to you; I thought I'd have to leave a voicemail.'

'I'm working from home today.'

'In your PJs with *The Chase* on in the background?' I laughed, waiting for her to bite back. She had the opportunity, as a data analytics expert (whatever that was), to work from home a lot. And I'd tease her about it, but she always gave as good as she got.

'It's got to be at least a few days until your next half-term, hasn't it? Aww, poor over-worked teachers, it must be so hard.'

'You wouldn't last a week!'

'I wouldn't last ten minutes. Fond as I am of my niece and Ava, I couldn't be doing with all that snot and kids constantly whinging.'

'That's the easy bit, it's the pushy parents that make it hard work.' I thought about Claire Winters briefly and the fact she'd sent me a big bouquet of flowers after Ava's accident. It had been a real surprise, but Natasha was probably right about why Claire behaved the way she often did. If I could give someone like her the benefit of the doubt, then didn't I owe the same to the father of my child?

'I bet you'd give anything for Ava to be back to normal and for you to be back at work, though?'

'Yes, but she's making really good progress, so hopefully it won't be long.'

'You sound tired.' There it was again, the tell-tale concern in Phoebe's voice. 'You haven't been getting those phone calls again, have you?'

'Not since before the accident, no. I'm just, I don't know... I suppose confused is the best word for it.' I stopped behind a glass bus shelter, halfway between the hospital and the supermarket, to shield myself from the worst of the wind. There was an elderly couple sitting on the bench, who were doing their best to pretend they weren't listening, but the surreptitious glances in my direction every few seconds gave them away.

'Is this about Luke?'

'Don't say it like that. I need an objective opinion and you were right when you told me to think things over at Christmas, before I let him see Ava again. I know he's never been your favourite person, and in the end I can make the decision on my own, but you're the only one I can really talk to about it.'

'Okay. I can't promise to be neutral, but I'll do my best. Spit it out then.'

'It's just been so weird, since Ava's accident and spending so much time with Luke, I've started to remember what I saw in him. When I realised I couldn't give Ava the kidney, he was there for me, promising to make everything okay and I found myself believing him.' I cleared my throat, bracing myself for what was coming next. 'I found myself picturing us as a family again, too.'

'And how's he doing with living up to that promise to make things right? Any better than he did the first time around? Or the second?'

'He's not gambling any more; when he walked out on us he was in a bad place.'

'And what about the second time around, what brilliant excuse did he come up with for that?' There was a note of impatience in her voice and I could imagine what it looked like from the outside – gullible Scarlett falling for a line, yet again.

'I haven't asked him yet. When he first turned up at the hospital, I didn't want to row with him and make things any worse than they already were for Ava.'

'Well ask him now then. See what he's got to say about why he just stopped seeing Ava, and left her so confused she ran out into the road after a car that looked like his.'

'You sound like Mum.' I wouldn't have put it past them to have talked about it behind my back, but then almost everyone was blaming Luke. Except me, and maybe Luke himself.

'Just promise me you'll ask him before you do anything stupid and throw away everything you've built for yourself and Ava since he left.'

'Are you sure Mum isn't working you with a hand up your back?'

'No, but I know how worried she is, and she thinks you and Cam are made for each other. But I'm not even talking about you making a choice between him and Luke. You've seemed so much happier since you started at the school, and you and Ava have both made friends, not to mention getting settled in a place of your own. Don't let Luke ruin that.'

'He's Ava's dad.' I couldn't bring myself to admit it to Phoebe, but there was still a part of me that wanted the family I'd always pictured. A mum, a dad, and a couple of kids, fitting neatly together like something out of a breakfast cereal ad. I didn't want to be part of a mosaic, or a part-time mum – sharing Ava with Luke, and no doubt in time, his second family. It was ridiculous, there were millions of families like that, who wouldn't swap their mosaic for anything, but being with Luke again I couldn't let go of a tiny shred of hope that we could put our family back together. But then I thought about Cam and losing him was something I didn't even want to imagine. I'd always thought people on TV shows, who swore blind they were in love with more than one person, were either selfish or lying. Only now I wasn't so sure.

'Just because Luke was up for the bit of jiggy jiggy that resulted in Ava, it doesn't mean he's the best person to raise her.' Thank God the old couple, who'd given up any pretence of not listening, weren't able to hear Phoebe's side of the conversation.

'I know, I just...'

'You just want everything to be perfect, but you can't make Luke into something he's not. And I know better than anyone that being a good parent has nothing to do with biology.'

I leant against the back of the bus shelter, the old couple still staring at me through the glass.

'Thank you for being honest. You're right, too. I need to find out why Luke went AWOL again, before I can even think about what's best for us all. Whether we raise Ava together or apart, I've got to be sure he's going to give her the commitment she deserves.'

'That's the first sensible thing you've said.' Phoebe laughed.

'I'm going to speak to him next time we're together, and Ava's otherwise occupied. I'll text you later and let you know how it went, but I'm going to have to go now. I want to be there when Ava gets back from the scan.'

'Tell her I'll take her to the Greedy Goat for the best ice cream in London when you come up.'

Ending the call, just as my elderly audience got on the bus they'd been waiting for, I was already running through what I wanted to say to Luke. The conversation I might need to have with Cam afterwards was a lot harder to contemplate.

* * *

'At last! I was beginning to wonder if you'd taken Ava home without telling me.' Luke was sitting in the chair closest to the window by the time I got back to Ava's hospital room.

'They've taken her down for a scan and I went to get her some ice cream. You said you were going to be here this morning.' My tone was razor-sharp, but I'd been psyching myself up to challenge him about letting Ava down over contact and I couldn't hide the way I was feeling any more.

'Take it easy, I'm here aren't I?' He stood up and took the cool bag from me, putting it on top of the locker by Ava's bed, and resting his hands on my shoulders. 'Something came up with a client that I needed to sort out.'

'Something always comes up though, Luke, doesn't it?'

'What do you mean?' He took a step back, dropping his hands to his side.

'I mean you've let Ava down before.'

'I hardly think being a couple of hours late because I had to work is *letting her down.*'

'She wanted to play Snap with you.' Tears stung my eyes. It sounded ridiculous, but I didn't care. I had to get it all out. 'And walking out on her, then missing contact after you finally got back in touch, definitely warrants letting her down.'

'You know about the gambling. I was just protecting both of you when I left.' He had the same expression Ava always wore when she'd protest her innocence about a chocolate bar wrapper that had mysteriously turned up in her room, or how the toys littered all over the landing had got there.

'And the second time?' I watched his face, wanting to see if there was anything there I could believe.

'I couldn't handle it. Seeing you and Ava, but not having *all* of you. Knowing that there was some other man you were spending your time with, who you wanted to be with more than me.' Luke stepped towards me again. 'It was selfish and stupid, but I thought you'd be better off if I just left you to get on with it, to keep building the new life you'd started for yourselves without me to mess it up.'

'You must have realised that would hurt her? Especially going again without even saying why?'

'I wasn't thinking straight. But when I heard about the accident, I knew I had to be with her and that I wanted to be with you. I knew I'd made a massive mistake leaving the first time, but I didn't realise just how big until all of this. I love you both so much and I'd do anything to put it right, so we can be a family again. I know you've felt it too, Lettie – we're the only people in the world who know what it's like to see our baby lying in that bed, it's not something anyone else can really understand.'

'I know.' We were so close we were almost touching, and I could smell his aftershave again. I tilted my face up to look at him, a thousand memories of our life together bubbling dangerously close to the surface. I needed to know for sure.

'Right, here we go Ava.' Sam pushed her wheelchair into the room. 'She's been an absolute star, as always, so I hope you've got that ice cream at the ready?'

'Of course!' I turned away from Luke, the spell broken but my mind still whirring at what I'd been about to do. Moving over to the side of the bed, I caught sight of one of the cards Ava's friends had drawn. It had a group of stick people on the front, which was supposed to be Ava's class, and the biggest stick man was obviously Cam.

He was such a good man and the connection between us had developed pretty quickly over the limited amount of time we'd spent together. Whatever I decided, it wasn't fair to keep him in the dark about how conflicted I felt, but I didn't want to hurt him. I didn't want to lose him either, but if I chose Luke that was the price I'd be paying. I just had to make sure it was worth it.

'Did you get any results from the scan?' I shot Luke a look as he asked the question, hoping it would relay the message screaming in my head. *Not in front of Ava.*

'Not yet.' Sam smiled, at least he understood. 'But we'll have a chat later if there's anything new to report.' He ruffled Ava's hair. 'Enjoy your ice cream, sweetie.'

'I'm starving, Mummy.' Ava settled back against her pillows as I plumped them up.

'I've got your ice cream over there. Luke, can you get it, please?'

'Anything for my girls.' He passed Ava the ice cream, which was shaped like a foot.

'Thank you, Daddy.' She barely paused for breath, she was eating so fast, and I couldn't take my eyes off her. She looked so much better, and I hadn't realised how rigidly I'd been holding my body – and for so long – until my shoulders finally relaxed a bit. Luke was scrolling through his phone, occasionally stopping to show her a picture of a goat dressed in a onesie, or some other silly video he'd found online.

It was about an hour later when Sam stuck his head around the door of the room again.

'Everything okay in here? Did you save me any of that ice cream, Ava-quaver?'

'Sorry, Sam-bam.' She giggled. The way the nurses had been with her had made such a difference to all of us.

'I didn't think so, I'll just have to buy myself a big tub on the way home.' Sam winked. 'Can I borrow your mummy and daddy for a minute, I need them to show me where they get that fabulous ice cream from.'

'Okay, but Daddy's still got to play Snap.'

'We won't be long, I promise.' Sam looked towards me and inclined his head, indicating that I should follow him out of the door. My stomach seemed to lurch up towards my chest and back down again. It couldn't be bad news, could it? Not when she was looking so well.

'Let's go down to the relatives' room.' Sam glanced at me again as we followed him down the corridor. 'You don't have to look like that. It's good news.'

'Oh, thank God.' I wanted to reach out and lean a hand against the wall to steady myself, but Luke's hand had already closed around mine. He was right, we *were* the only people who could really understand what it felt like to hear those words.

'Do you want to sit down?' Sam gestured towards one of the small sofas in the relatives' room, as he closed the door behind us.

'I just want to know.' Luke squeezed my hand as I spoke, neither of us moving to sit down.

'Well the scan showed the kidney function has improved significantly, and whilst we can't be 100 per cent confident yet that Ava won't need a transplant, Doctor Daniels' team are delighted with the progress she's making.'

'That's amazing, thank you so much.' I pulled my hand free of Luke's for a moment and hugged Sam hard. When I pulled away, there were two bright spots of red on his cheeks.

'I'm just the bearer of good news, that's all.'

'You're so much more than that.' I couldn't stop myself from hugging him again. I would have kissed every single member of the team involved in getting Ava better, if they'd been there, but poor Sam had to take it all. And I barely even registered Luke putting a hand on my shoulder.

'Give the man some air, Lettie, he's just doing his job. He doesn't need you leaping all over him.'

'I'm sorry, Sam, I'm just so happy and so grateful. To all of you.'

'Hey, I'm not complaining.' Sam grinned, regaining his usual confident charm. 'It's not every day I get a hug from the nicest mum in the children's ward.'

'Much as I hate to break up this mutual appreciation society, it would be helpful to know what might be next.' Luke's tone was tight and, when he caught hold of my hand again, his grasp was tight too. 'Do you know when we might be able to take Ava home?'

Home. There was a loaded word. It conjured up an image of the three of us living together under one roof, and it was all moving so fast. It wasn't that I didn't want Ava to be released from hospital. I just wasn't ready for any of the decisions that would come with that. But then I didn't know if I ever would be. Not if it meant choosing between us being the family I'd always wanted, and losing Cam.

'Like I said, we can't be sure of that yet, but everything is moving in the right direction.' Sam smiled at Luke, who didn't return the courtesy. 'But you can probably start making plans, so everything is ready if things carry on the way they are, and she can come off dialysis.'

'Thank you again, Sam.' The words were inadequate, but I was going to keep on saying them. He and the rest of Doctor Daniels' team had given me my baby back.

'No worries. Right, I'll leave you to it, but I'll be at the nursing station if there's anything else you think of that you want to ask.' Sam closed the door of the relatives' room behind him.

'He's an arrogant prick, isn't he? I don't know who some of these people think they are, they can never give a straight answer to a straight question in this place. I just want to know when we can take our daughter home and start getting everything back on track.' There was a muscle going in Luke's cheek – otherwise I'd have been sure he was joking.

'Sam's great, in fact, everyone here has been amazing. Are you seriously telling me you can't see that? They just can't give us an answer yet, not until they're sure Ava is really okay.'

'Yeah, I can see you love him.' The tension radiating from Luke was tangible. It was like he'd had an entirely different conversation with Sam than the one I'd had. We should have been leaping around the room, whooping and high-fiving each other.

'I'm just grateful to him that's all. When Ava first came in, I kept thinking if she died that I would too. What else would I have to live for without her?' I didn't want to cry, but hot tears were already streaming down my cheeks at the memory; the possibility I'd be leaving the hospital without her. A childless mother. The very definition of an empty shell of all that I'd been. I was Ava's mum – nothing else I was, or did, mattered a millionth as much.

'I know and I'm sorry that I wasn't here for you both and sorry for what I just said. It's just the stress of all this, making me say stuff I don't mean.' Luke pulled me towards him, resting his head against the top of mine and murmuring into my hair. 'I wish we hadn't waited after Ava to have more children.'

'Me too.' I didn't ask him why, and I didn't tell him my reasons either. They weren't logical. If Ava had died, I'd have been just as bereft if I'd had other children, but at least they would have given me a reason for going on. And they'd have had the same genes as Ava, maybe that same upturned nose, or the way she rolled her eyes when things weren't going her way.

'It isn't too late.' He pulled away slightly, cupping a hand under my chin – those blue eyes I'd fallen for, before I'd noticed anything else about him, fixed on my face. 'I love you, Lettie.'

'I...' His mouth closed over mine before I'd had the chance to answer, before I'd even been sure what I was going to say. The kiss, when it finally happened, was urgent. His hands were in my hair and our bodies were pressed together as they had been a thousand or more times before. I waited for the thunderbolt of recognition from my body, that this was my other half finding the way back to me. But all I could think of, was what I was going to say when he finally stopped probing the inside of my mouth with his tongue, whilst I stood rigid, praying that no one would open the relatives' room door and catch us in what suddenly felt like an awkward teenage fumble. I wanted to rewind the clock and tell him that part of me would always love him for giving me Ava, but that we couldn't ever have what we'd had again. There was no *we*, except that *we* were Ava's parents. Despite the confusion that sharing the fear of losing her had raked up, I knew that now for sure.

'Oh God, I've been wanting to do that since the second I saw you again. His breath was hot on my neck and I was fighting the urge to bat him away like a fly that just wouldn't quit. I had to get this right, to find a way of letting him down so he could still be there for Ava and be the dad she deserved to have. If I came out with it and told him everything I wanted to say, he'd just disappear again, and I didn't want that. At least not for Ava.

'I think we should be getting back to her.'

'I know, I know, but I could stay here forever. I was beginning to think this might never happen again.' He was pressing himself into me, his obvious excitement making the hairs on the back of my neck stand up for all the wrong reasons.

'I need to be with Ava.'

'I know you do, when she gets home. But if they won't let her out for a while, maybe we could use this time to reconnect?' He actually jiggled his eyebrows and part of me wanted to laugh. The other part wanted to grab the bin from the corner of the room and throw up. It was like someone had taken the blindfold off and made me see everything that was wrong with our relationship, in one huge hit. 'The Chisholms have said we can use their villa whenever we want, so maybe we can have a few days over there before Ava gets out.'

'You can't seriously think I'd leave her?' I pulled away from him, unable to bear the touch of his skin against mine. I thought the kiss would be a catalyst. But, even if there had been thunderbolts, rather than toe-curling awkwardness, what he'd just suggested would have told me everything I needed to know.

'No, well, I suppose not. It was just a thought.'

'Let's just forget it and get back to Ava.' I opened the door of the relatives' room and strode off down the corridor in front of him. He could forget about the kiss, and more importantly about us ever being a family of three again. That was a conversation for another day, though – when the doctors were sure Ava's life didn't depend on him being in it. If he decided to bolt after that, it was his loss. But until she was off dialysis, I had to play it safe.

* * *

I pulled up outside the cottage, just as Cam was dragging my wheelie bin out to the pavement. I think it was the moment I realised that I loved him. Hardly the stuff of romantic movies or love songs, but it was when I knew for sure that he'd do anything for me and Ava, without even having to be asked.

'Are you nicking my bin?' I called out to him as I got out of the car, and he smiled.

'It's tempting, I think you can get fifty quid for them on eBay.' He laughed. 'I just didn't want it to sit there filled with rubbish for another two weeks.'

'You're so thoughtful.'

'It's hardly a big gesture!' His words mirrored what I'd been thinking. But I'd never be able to explain how much it meant, without telling him how confused I'd been. And now there was no need.

'Sometimes it's the little things that really count.'

'You know I'm happy to help any time. The truth is, I was hoping to catch you, that's why I came over so late. I've got some more bits for Ava, but I can just grab them from the car if you're tired?'

'No, I'd like you to come in if you've got time?' It was already nine o'clock. I'd waited until Ava had fallen asleep before leaving the hospital. Luke had wanted to come back to the cottage, but I'd told him I was going to see Mum and Dad, because the last thing I wanted was to be on my own with him. I wouldn't have put it past him to follow me, so I'd popped into my parents' place. Mum was still overwhelmed with guilt about Ava's accident and nothing I said seemed to make any difference. She'd been determined to cancel a trip they'd planned to meet up with Leilah and Nicky in Reykjavik, which was apparently the closest thing to a half-way point between the UK and New York. Auntie Leilah had rung to see how Ava was, and had told me she'd planned the trip so that Mum and Dad could get to know Nicky better before the wedding, and hopefully allay their fears. Mum's excuse was that they didn't want to go because they were so worried about Ava, but there was definitely more to it...

I hadn't had the chance to talk to her about the conversation we'd been having, when the A&E doctor had interrupted to tell us about Ava's kidney dysplasia. Things had been so hectic since then, and I didn't really want to ask what she'd meant about being punished, at least not in front of anyone else. All of that would just have to wait. I'd insisted they keep the holiday booking, though, even as Mum was shaking her head. Dad had always wanted to go to Iceland, and Ava was on the mend. Whatever the problem she had with Auntie Leilah getting married was, they needed to sort it out.

Cam's voice brought me back to the present. 'If you're sure you want me to come in? Of course I've got time.'

'I'm totally sure.' The central heating timer had come on a

couple of hours earlier, so the cottage was warm when he followed me inside. 'Do you want some tea? Or something to eat?'

'I'm good, unless you're hungry? Have you had time to get something to eat at the hospital? I could cook you something.'

'It's okay, Mum force fed me an omelette when I went to their place to let them know how Ava's doing.'

'I made Ruhan smash a mug when I got your message. I was so relieved, I leapt out of my seat in the staff room and it scared her so much she jumped backwards and knocked her mug off the side. Apparently I owe her a replacement, although we both agreed it was a small price to pay.' He grinned and handed me an envelope. 'And in the meantime, I got Ava these, so she's got something to look forward to.'

I slipped the contents of the envelope out and looked up at him. 'Disneyland Paris tickets? Thank you so much! But you can't give her those, they're far too expensive.' I didn't even want to think about how much they cost.

'Yes I can, and you can get the Eurostar straight to the gate. I got three tickets, in case you wanted to take your mum or...'

'Or you could come?'

'No pressure, but I know Ava loves Cinderella, and they do a princess parade at the end of the day.' He looked a bit sheepish. 'Not that I've spent hours researching Disney princesses or anything!'

Dropping the tickets onto the kitchen counter, I walked towards him. 'Can you stay?'

'What, tonight? You don't have to ask me, I know you must be exhausted.' I put my finger on his lips, acting with far more confidence than I felt.

'I want you to stay.'

'Then how can I say no?'

I took his hand, stopping at the bottom of the narrow staircase that led up to the bedrooms. 'Go up. I'll be two minutes; I just want to check there's nothing from the hospital. I'm sorry, I know that's a massive mood killer.'

'There's no rush. I'm not going anywhere.' He turned and kissed me, just a gentle brush of the lips that my body instantly reacted to.

I almost ran back to where I'd left my phone in my bag by the front door. There was nothing from the hospital and I ignored the texts from Luke and Mum. But there was one from an unknown number and, just in case it was from one of the nurses, I clicked on it.

✉ Sender not in contact list
You're making a mistake, but it's not too late to change your mind.

I shivered, despite the warmth of the room, but I wasn't going to let whoever was sending these messages win. Dropping my phone into my bag, I headed up the stairs to where Cam was waiting. With all the drama of Ava's accident, I hadn't got around to changing my number and I still had no idea who was sending the messages, but whoever it was, they were wrong. Being with Cam wasn't a mistake, I'd never been more certain of anything.

18

Cam was making a cup of tea when I came down the stairs and checked my phone again. There was still nothing from the hospital and I let out a breath. I had a landline by the bed, so they'd have been able to get hold of me if anything had happened, but I'd still woken up with a sensation of dread that I couldn't shake. I just had a horrible feeling the universe was going to make me pay for spending the night with Cam, whilst my little girl was still in the hospital. But I couldn't bring myself to regret it.

It was a bit weird having a man in the house again; I figured I could get used to it, though. Especially when that man looked like Cam and seemed to anticipate the right thing to do before I even opened my mouth. I was with Luke for the best part of eight years and I could probably count on one hand the amount of times he'd made me a drink in the morning without me asking. It was just another little thing, but they kept adding up.

'Thanks, I need to get off to the hospital in a bit.' I took the cup from Cam. It was the start of the February half-term holiday, so he wasn't under the usual deadline to get to work. I wanted to get in to see Ava as soon as the hospital would let me, and the days of the week had lost all meaning within the confines of its walls anyway.

'Is there anything I can do to help you out?'

'There is one thing, but it's a bit of a big ask.' Before Ava's accident, I'd promised to have Jasper, Mum and Dad's dog, whilst they were on holiday. And now Mum was using it as another excuse to cancel the trip. She'd sent me another couple of texts – on top of the one I'd ignored the night before – all saying they couldn't possibly go away now that there was no one to look after Jasper.

'If I can do it, I will.' Cam turned me around to face him.

,   'I promised to have Mum and Dad's dog, Jasper, whilst they're in Iceland, but obviously now it's a bit tricky because I'm at the hospital all day. If I bring him back here before I go, do you think you could pop in and check on him at some point during the day, and let him out to go to the loo?'

'I can do better than that. If it's okay with you, I can pick him up from your mum and dad's place and take him back to mine, then drop him here later. I don't mind having him for the whole week, if it's easier. I haven't got any big plans for half-term.'

'Are you sure?' I threw my arms around his neck as he nodded, and planted a quick kiss on his lips. He really was too good to be true. 'That would be brilliant. If you go and collect him, Mum won't want to turn down your offer. But If I go, she'll keep making excuses about why she can't possibly leave. I don't know what's going on with her and Auntie Leilah, but with everything that's happened with Ava, life's too short not to sort it out.'

'It's no problem and it gives me another excuse to come over and see you tonight.'

'You don't need an excuse.' I should have told him about Luke then, and explained why I was playing along with the prospect of us getting back together until I was sure Ava was okay, but it didn't feel like the right time. If I'd known what was about to happen, if

I'd have thought that the lingering kiss we'd shared would be our last, I'd have blurted everything out, and told him I'd never had the connection I felt with him with anyone else. It wasn't Cam who was too good to be true – having him in my life was.

* * *

'Oh, thank God! I've been trying to get hold of you for half an hour.' Sam, the lovely nurse who always seemed to brighten up the ward somehow, was looking serious for once, as we met in the corridor outside Ava's room.

'I was driving over and I must have had my Bluetooth switched off. Is everything okay?' Even as I asked, it was obvious from Sam's face that it wasn't.

'Ava was doing well overnight and first thing this morning, but in the last half an hour or so she suddenly started going rapidly downhill, and Doctor Daniels thinks she's contracted an infection that's threatening to shut her organs down. Her heart seems to be the main issue at the moment, and it's progressing so quickly, we're not sure...' Sam couldn't finish the sentence, but he didn't need to. I was already pushing past him into Ava's room. The bed was empty and my legs went out from under me. Sam caught me half a second before I hit the floor.

'Where is she?' It was more of a wail than a question and my legs still couldn't hold me up.

'We've moved her up to ITU, but Doctor Daniels wants her transferred to the Royal Brompton cardiac centre as soon as possible.'

'But she was fine, she was making so much progress getting her kidney working properly again, and there was nothing wrong with her heart. Are you sure it isn't a mistake?'

Sam sat me down on the edge of the bed, where I'd kissed my

daughter goodnight only hours before. How could so much have changed, so quickly?

'The infection could have started during dialysis, but Doctor Daniels will explain more to you. Ava's dad is up in ITU with her, and Doctor Daniels said she'd speak to you both as soon as you arrived.'

'Luke's with Ava?' I tried to stand up, but I was still wobbly. I was glad she had her dad, but I should have been there. Not in bed with Cam. I knew it wasn't logical to think like that – I'd have got to hospital even later if he hadn't stayed over and offered to pick up Jasper. But it just felt like the hammer I'd been waiting to fall had hit the ground with enough force to be picked up on the Richter scale.

'He's been there since they moved her up about ten minutes ago. I'll go up with you, just in case. You've gone a really funny colour.'

'It's my fault.' Sam took my arm as we went out into the corridor.

'Of course it's not your fault. It just happens sometimes, with dialysis, and it wasn't obvious because of everything Ava has been through. There wasn't anything anyone – least of all you – could have done to prevent it.'

'But I wasn't even here when they took her up. She must have been so scared.'

'Her dad was, but only because he happened to be here before we normally allow parents in for visiting. You got here as soon as you thought you'd be allowed in; you couldn't possibly have known things would be different today. Ava probably doesn't even realise you aren't there, anyway. She's had a lot of medication, but she'll need you on the other side. The last thing you should do is beat yourself up about not being here for the last thirty minutes, you've got to stay strong.'

'On the other side? She'll definitely get better then?' I turned to Sam as the lift doors opened.

'The Royal Brompton is the best place for her, if it turns out she needs surgery on her heart.'

'And she'll be okay, even if she does need surgery?'

'She'll be in the best possible hands.' Sam's smile was fixed, but he wasn't making any promises, and it took everything I had not to beg for an answer as the lift doors shut behind us. I needed a rock solid guarantee that Ava would eventually be coming home – I couldn't even contemplate another outcome.

* * *

Doctor Daniels asked to meet us in her office. The relatives' room in ITU was already in use by the family of a young man whose life was hanging by a thread, after a motorbike accident. His mother's strangled sobs echoing down the corridor as we passed, and his father ranting about how he'd told him to '*ditch the fucking motorbike for a car*', filled in enough of the gaps for us to know what had happened. They wanted to turn back time, to change things so that their son wouldn't be lying in a bed, covered in tubes and almost unrecognisable even to the people who'd held him in their arms the moment he'd drawn his first breath. I didn't have to meet them to know they wanted to turn back the clock, because I did too. If I hadn't volunteered to run an after school club, I'd have been the one to pick Ava up from school that night, and I wouldn't have let go of her hand. Mum was riddled with guilt about dropping her hand, even for a moment, but I didn't blame her. I blamed myself, and now Ava was hanging between life and death too, her miraculous recovery from the accident right back to square one, or maybe even worse. We'd know for sure when Doctor Daniels gave us her assessment, but my legs were still struggling to cooperate as we made our way down the corridor to her office.

We didn't speak to each other as Luke knocked on the door – trying to breath was hard enough. I wanted to be back by Ava's bedside, watching the machines that were keeping her alive doing what they were supposed to do. The comforting silence of the heart monitor, indicating that everything was stable, was my new favourite sound.

'Come in.' Doctor Daniels' voice was reassuringly authoritative, and we did as we were told. 'Please, sit down.'

I sat next to Luke and he took hold of my hand. I hadn't realised it was shaking until then. He was taking all of this much better than me, telling me, from the moment I got to him and Ava in ITU, that it was going to be okay. I was glad one of us was certain of that, but I needed to hear it from Doctor Daniels before I could even start to believe it.

'I'm sure all of this has been a horrible shock to you. Ava was progressing so well and we were really pleased with the recovery of her kidney.' Doctor Daniels looked directly at me. 'But unfortunately, it seems as if she's picked up an infection called endocarditis, possibly because of the dialysis. It's very rare, especially in children, but Ava's just been really unlucky.'

'And that's affected her heart?' Luke spoke first and squeezed my hand. Despite everything we'd been through, I was glad he was there.

'Yes, the bacteria enters the blood stream and travels to the heart, causing an infection to the lining.' Doctor Daniels' voice was even, as if she were talking about what she'd seen on TV the night before. Inside my head I was screaming, but I still couldn't seem to get the words out.

'But she can recover from it?' It was going to be down to Luke to ask the questions we both wanted answered.

'We've started the process straight away by administering intravenous antibiotics. If it's left untreated it can cause heart failure or a stroke. Our hope is that the antibiotics will resolve the infection, but it's quite common for patients to need surgery, unfortunately. If Ava does end up requiring that, then the Royal Brompton will be the best place for her and, either way, they've got far more expertise in this area than we have as a general hospital.'

'So if the antibiotics don't work, surgery will definitely resolve things?' Luke leant forward slightly in his seat, pushing for a definitive answer.

'The odds are good, about 80 per cent of people survive endocarditis. Ava is young, and kids are remarkably resilient in the main, so I'm very hopeful. But what we can't be sure of, is the effect it might have on Ava's recovery from the original damage to her kidney, so there's still a chance we might need to address that with more dialysis or even a transplant. If that's the case, then it's Luke who will probably make the best match, and the Brompton might even want to offer some initial tests. I know Ava's grandparents offered to be donors when she first went on dialysis, but at her age, the best chance of a good outcome is with a live donor under a certain age. I wish I could give you cast-iron guarantees, but we just can't be sure how this will impact Ava yet.'

'But she's just a little girl.' I finally managed to speak, tears spilling onto my cheeks at the unfairness of it. 'I wish it was me lying in that bed, going through all of this.'

'I know.' Doctor Daniels, who was normally stoic to the point of seeming almost emotionless, reached out and squeezed my arm, her eyes clouding too. 'But we're doing all we can and, like I said, she'll be in the hands of experts at the Royal Brompton, so the best thing we can do is to transfer her as soon as possible.'

'Today?' I searched her face as I spoke.

'We want to arrange it for as soon as we're sure she's stable enough, and we're really hoping that will be today.' Doctor Daniels looked from me to Luke. 'If there's anything you need to get sorted before you go up there, then I suggest you do it now, so we're ready to go as soon as we can. If you're both planning to go up, that is?'

'I'm definitely going.' I turned to Luke as I spoke, and he nodded.

'Me too, but you should go up in the ambulance with Ava, and I'll follow on by car.'

'I'm not sure what the accommodation situation is for parents. But, unlike here, hopefully there'll be a room available so you can stay on site. I'll ask my secretary to call ahead for you.' Doctor Daniels smiled for the first time. 'I know it's impossible but try not to worry too much. She's having the right treatment and she's a little fighter. Having her mum and dad there with her will really help too.'

'We're a team and we'll get through this together.' Luke squeezed my hand again and I nodded. If it took a united front to get Ava through this, then we both owed her that. I could do it and, even if it cost me everything else, it would be worth it.

* * *

My head dropped, jolting me awake, and for a second or two I didn't know where I was. It was a blissful interlude that passed in the blink of an eye, before I realised it wasn't all some horrible dream. I was sitting at my daughter's bedside, in a specialist London hospital, waiting and watching for a sign that the antibiotics were doing their job, and that she was going to turn the corner for a second time. How had I managed to fall asleep on a job as important as that? I looked over at Luke, to see if he'd succumbed to the same exhaustion that had overwhelmed my body, but the light from his mobile phone was illuminating his face. He hadn't fallen asleep, and he'd been there before me when Ava was taken ill for the second time. He might have let her down in the past, but he was making up for it now.

'Are you okay?' My voice croaked and my neck and shoulders were stiff with tension, and lack of movement, from sitting on a rock hard plastic chair at the side of Ava's bed ever since she'd been admitted. Luke was sitting in a bigger, cushioned chair, farther away, which was meant for the patients once they were able to sit upright and get out of bed. Seeing Ava sitting in that chair was all I wanted. It would mean we were on the road to getting her home again, which seemed a million miles away. But Doctor Daniels had said Ava was resilient, and there was every chance she'd bounce back from the heart infection. We could deal with the kidney issues then, if we needed to, and I was almost certain Luke wouldn't let her down on that front either, now. He hadn't left our sides since he'd followed the ambulance up to the hospital and I didn't want him to.

Phoebe only lived a short tube ride away from Chelsea, so she'd offered to let us stay there because there were no rooms immediately available in the relatives' accommodation. Sadly, Ava was far from being the only sick child they were taking care of. For once we had a bit of luck on our side, and Phoebe's flat mate – and on/off partner – Adam, was away at a conference in Rome. So there was a spare room and a sofa bed at our disposal, and there wouldn't be the same pressure for Luke and me to share, as there would have been in the relatives' accommodation. I was planning to tell him how things had moved on with Cam eventually, but that was the last thing I wanted to get into – even before he looked up from the phone.

'I *was* okay.' Luke's tone was bitter and he narrowed his eyes as he raised his head to look at me. It might have been tiredness, but it was clear from the rigid set of his jaw that it was more than that.

'Has someone been in about Ava?' I couldn't believe I'd have slept through that, but the fact I'd shut my eyes and stopped watching my daughter's every breath was unbelievable, too.

'No, but *you've* had plenty of messages come through.' He held up the phone and it took me a moment to register that it was mine, the cover on the back created from a picture of Ava dressed as a fairy, taken the Christmas before.

'Why have you got my phone?' I stood up and leant across Ava's bed, reaching out for him to give it to me, but he snatched it back towards him.

'I was going to play a game, but the battery on my phone's dead. I knew your passcode would still be Ava's birthday.'

'So how did you go from playing a game to reading my messages?' It was such an invasion of privacy. Especially from someone like Luke, who'd guarded his own phone like it was more precious than the Crown Jewels. The times he'd turned away from me, so I couldn't see over his shoulder, were probably when he'd been playing online poker. Was that what he'd wanted my phone for? Recovering alcoholics could easily fall off the wagon with the sort of pressure Ava's illness had put us under. Maybe it was the same with gambling.

'A message popped up when I was playing. It was from Cameron.' Luke shook his head, the pitch of his voice rising. 'Why didn't you tell me how far things had gone between you two?'

Curling my hand into a ball, and taking a handful of Ava's bedsheets with it, was the only way I could stop myself from saying what I really wanted to – that it was none of Luke's business any more. But he'd made it clear he wanted us to try again, and I'd let him believe that might be a possibility, to guarantee he'd stick around. Deep down, I had to admit I probably did owe him an explanation.

'We've been taking things slowly, but I really like him.'

'It sounds like more than that to me.' Luke spat the words out and heat flushed my face. I had no idea what the message said, but he seemed to have a far clearer picture of how far things had gone with Cam than I wanted him to.

'You shouldn't have read the message.'

'But I did. And that's how I have to find out that some other man is planning to take my wife and daughter off to Disney, like you're *his* family.' Luke slammed his fist, still curled tightly around my phone, against the arm of his chair. 'You and Ava belong to me.'

'We don't *belong* to anyone, Luke.' I was fighting to keep my voice under control. The last thing I wanted was for him to start shouting, and for Ava to wake up and see us like this. As angry as I was at him – and his breath-taking assumption that we could just take up where we'd left off – she was still my top priority.

'I can't hang around and see another man take over my life and my family, pushing me out like a cuckoo in the nest.' He stood up and moved towards the window. 'So you've got two choices. You can either watch me walk out of here, go down there to the car park, and drive out of your lives for good. Or you can tell Cam it's over and block his number from your phone. I can't share you, or Ava. It's either him or me.'

'You're not serious?' Even as I said it, it was obvious he was.

'Oh, I'm deadly serious. I've even typed the message for you. I was going to send it myself, but I need to see you do it. I need to be sure you mean it and you're not going to contact him behind my back.' Luke turned back towards me, and finally held out the phone. 'Do you really want Ava to wake up and find out I've gone?'

It wouldn't be the first time. The words I wanted to say were like bullets waiting to be fired, but it was different this time. If the virus that had affected Ava's heart had done more damage to her kidney, too, she was definitely going to need Luke far more than she needed me – for the first time in her life. He knew as well as I did that he was holding all the cards.

'What do want from me, Luke? You walk out on us and just expect things to go back to how they were?' I was shaking with suppressed anger, as I reached out and took the phone.

'I just want you to give us a chance, that's all. We owe that to Ava and ourselves. I know I've made mistakes and it's pretty obvious from Cameron's messages that you've made mistakes too, but I still think we can put that right.' Luke sighed. 'I've got to believe that, if I'm going to stick around. Just give me one more chance and, if that doesn't work out, we can both move on.'

'One chance. That's it. If you mess up again, we're done.' I was lying through my teeth. I wouldn't stay with Luke if he was the last person on earth. Even if I hadn't realised the strength of my feelings for Cam, after the stunt he'd just pulled I could barely even look at my husband. But he might be the only person who could give me back my daughter and for that, I'd do anything. Even play at happy families until I was sure she didn't need him to survive.

'I've saved the message in your drafts. All you've got to do is press send, block his number and delete the contact from your phone.'

'That's all?' I almost wanted to laugh, it was such a ridiculous thing to demand. Had I ever really known this man? The controlling, gambling addict, standing in front of me, was someone I couldn't even recognise.

'That, and I want to link your phone to mine, so I can see every message you send. And if I find out you've got another phone, I'll be heading up the motorway and out of your lives before you can even come up with an excuse.'

'If that's what it takes.' My hands were shaking even more, as I scrolled down to the draft messages. I wanted to throw the phone at the wall and tell Luke just how much I hated him. That I'd never hated anyone more in my life. But I opened up the message instead.

✉ Draft message

Seeing U was a mistake. We R over. Don't call or text. It is not 2 L8 to make a go of things with Luke + Ava. We R a family + we R sticking 2gether

It took me a couple of reads to work out what the message even meant. I never used text speak like that. Phoebe always laughed at me, and said I was the only person she knew who'd ever put a semi-colon in a text. When Cam read it, maybe he'd realise it wasn't really from me and text me back. Only his number would be blocked, and if I tried to get it back from Kate or Dolly, and texted Cam, Luke would see that message too. I doubted Cam would understand why I was letting Luke force me to do this either, it was totally spineless. And deceiving Luke so I could use him as a walking organ donor probably made me as bad as him. My finger hovered over the send button and my eyes slid towards Ava, her chest rising and falling in a reassuring rhythm, as vital to my survival as my own heartbeat.

'I'm sending it now.' I pressed the button, waiting until a message popped up to show that the text had been successfully sent.

'Give it back to me and I'll block his number and delete it.' Luke grabbed the phone before I even had a chance to answer. 'And I want you to resign from the school, as well. I'm earning good money now that the debts have been cleared and we can sort out selling the B&B as soon as possible too.'

'But I love my job.' Tears blurred my vision, but I wasn't just crying for the job that had given me back my self-esteem, along with a sense of belonging in Appleberry.

'I don't want you working there, with *him*, okay? Unless you want me to hit the road?' Luke smiled, looking suddenly like The Joker from *Batman*, sinister and smug all at the same time. He could blackmail me and I'd do whatever he said if it meant saving Ava's life. I shuddered. The thought of him touching me made bile rise in the back of my throat. With his track record, there was always a chance he'd let us down anyway. But at least if I ended things with Cam, there was a *chance* Luke would do right by Ava. What choice did I have?

'I'll email the head to resign on Monday, after the half-term holiday is over.' I didn't look at him, keeping my eyes on my daughter and willing her to open hers and look back at me. She was the only thing that mattered and when everyone else found out I'd agreed to try again with Luke, she might be all I had left.

19

'So you're really going to try and make a go of things with Luke?' Phoebe wrinkled her nose as she handed me a cup of coffee. It was six o'clock in the morning and Luke had already left for an early meeting in the Midlands, with one of his clients, so he could meet me back at the hospital later. Phoebe was up early every morning to get ready for work, so we were taking the chance to grab a quick catch-up before she headed off.

'It seems like the best thing for Ava.' I was desperate to tell Phoebe the real reason, but I couldn't risk her confronting Luke. And the chances were she would. As it was, the look in her eyes told me she thought I was out of my mind. She didn't need to say it out loud, but that didn't stop her.

'Really? Luke's hardly been dad of the year up until now, has he? And as for how he's treated you...'

'Since Ava's been ill, it's made me realise how much we need him.' I stared down at my coffee, so she couldn't read the expression on my face as easily as I could read hers.

'And how did Cam take it?'

'I don't know, I haven't heard anything from him.' For all I knew he might have sent me twenty texts and tried to call, but I was none the wiser about how he'd taken it.

'That's really weird! And he didn't say anything to your friend when she went to pick Jasper up?' Phoebe wasn't that easy to fool, and I suddenly felt overwhelmed with exhaustion again. Lying rigid, as Luke pressed himself up against me in the night, had meant I'd barely slept. I hadn't been able to think up a good enough excuse for me to take the sofa bed, whilst he was in the spare room, but at least I'd managed to keep his advances at bay for now. Ava was still making slow progress in the right direction and even he seemed to understand that not knowing for sure how things would turn out was enough for me to cope with for now, but I knew I couldn't hold him off forever. Not without telling him the truth.

'I asked Dolly to pick up the dog in the end; she's more discreet than Kate, and she wouldn't push Cam into talking unless he wanted to.' I shrugged. Dolly had told me when she'd called that Cam seemed okay and, as selfish as that was, it had hurt to hear. Just because I was cut up about finishing with him, I'd assumed he would be too. Maybe I'd read far more into where our relationship was at than he had. He was a nice guy and all the things I'd thought he was doing because of how he felt about me and Ava, might just have been an extension of that. My text clearly hadn't been earth-shattering, as far as he was concerned. He was *okay*. I just wished I could say the same.

'Perhaps he's just waiting until Ava's better.' Phoebe's eyes lit up suddenly. 'Ooh maybe he'll challenge Luke to a duel like something out of *Poldark*...'

'You've got to stop watching the DVD of that series. It's making your imagination run wild.' It was nice to laugh, and think about something other than Ava's progress, and the situation with Luke and Cam.

'But he's just so... shirtless!' Phoebe grinned again.

'I'll give you that, but real life isn't like that sadly.' I'd fantasised about pulling a gun out on Luke myself in the early hours of the morning, when he'd pressed his erection into my back for the fourth time.

'I know, but a girl can dream, can't she?' Phoebe leant against the kitchen counter. 'Can I get anything for Ava before I come in and see her after work?'

'Thanks, but I don't think so. Is it still okay to take your car and pick up some more of her stuff later, though? Luke said he'd stay with her at the hospital until I get back.' We'd left for London in such a hurry that there hadn't been time to get any more of Ava's things to bring up with us. Now that she was starting to show some signs of fighting off the infection, she'd asked for a few of her toys. It was a relief and I was hoping, by the time Mum and Dad got back from Iceland on Sunday, that the news would all be positive. I'd decided not to tell them about Ava being moved to London, or the problems with her heart. There was nothing they could do anyway, so there was no point upsetting them before they got home, or adding to the guilt Mum already felt.

'Of course you can. I hardly use the bloody thing anyway, living up here. The run out will probably do it good.' Phoebe took the keys off a hook in the kitchen. 'So will you be back at the hospital by the time I get there?'

'Yes, I'm just going to wait there until Luke arrives, then shoot straight down to Appleberry and back again, as soon as I've grabbed Ava's stuff and some more clothes for me, so I don't have to keep borrowing yours.' I forced a smile. It wasn't like I had a reason to stop in Appleberry to see anyone, and the last thing I wanted was to bump into Cam. Maybe I should ask Phoebe if she had a balaclava she could lend me.

* * *

Luke was almost an hour later getting back from his breakfast meeting than he said he'd be, but I could hardly blame him when there'd been an accident on the M40 and he'd not only got stuck in it, but also seen some of the aftermath. It sounded like another family would be sitting by a hospital bed praying, if it wasn't worse than that. I was so desperate to hear some good news. It just seemed to be one thing after the other lately and Luke was still pushing me to send the email to resign from school. I was holding out for Monday, and, in truth, I was holding out for something else: the hope that Luke might stop acting like a control freak and change his mind.

When he'd finally got to the hospital, I'd had to leave almost straight away to stand any chance of getting to Appleberry and back before rush hour kicked in. Not that driving in London was ever that easy, but I wanted to spend some time with Ava in the evening before she fell asleep. She seemed to drift in and out of sleep all day long as it was, but there was a small window between about 6 p.m. and 8 p.m., when she seemed more alert, more like the vibrant little girl I'd assumed she'd always be.

I was still fobbing Mum and Dad off with texts saying that Ava was making progress. It wasn't a lie. The doctors were pleased with how she'd been doing since she'd started the intravenous antibiotics. But my parents still had no idea about the virus itself, and I wanted it to stay that way. Kate and Dolly were texting all the time too, but neither of them had mentioned Cam again. It wasn't like Kate not to question my decision to end things with him, she was very similar to Phoebe in some ways and she normally had an opinion about everything. I think Ava being so poorly had just realigned everyone's priorities. Most of all, mine.

Auntie Leilah had texted some photos from Iceland and told me she'd ordered the bridesmaids' dresses she wanted me and Ava to wear. It was something to focus on, the belief that Ava would be twirling around in a dress covered in tiny rosebuds, like the princess she longed to be. It was the bright spot I needed as I headed back to Appleberry and I selected the feel-good playlist I'd set up on my phone when Luke had first disappeared. It had got me through some dark days back then, too.

I hadn't told anyone I was coming back to Kent. It was easier that way. If I saw Kate in person, she might not be able to help giving me the third degree about finishing things with Cam. And if I saw Dolly, I might well burst into tears and tell her everything. But I couldn't afford for anyone to know what I'd done – when I'd all but sold my soul to my estranged husband.

For once, things went to plan. The cottage might look like it had been ransacked by a burglar on speed, but I was in and out within twenty minutes, and back on the road to London. I forgot to re-start the playlist on my phone, so the Bluetooth selected random tracks and, three songs in, Ava's favourite song from the Cinderella movie came on: 'A Dream is a Wish Your Heart Makes'. It was what I'd sung to her, really badly, when she couldn't sleep, in the weeks and months after Luke had first left, and we must have watched the movie close to a hundred times over the years. Now there were other memories tied up with the song too. Cam hoisting her up at the Cinderella on Ice show so she wouldn't miss anything, and our plans to take her to Disneyland.

I was glad when the song stopped and Stormzy's 'Shut Up' came on instead. The Apple music app had taken the definition of 'random play' to the max and it made me smile – another brief spot of brightness. But it didn't last, and two minutes later the music stopped altogether. I didn't want to pull over to sort it out, I just wanted to get back to the hospital. So I listened to the radio instead, with some DJ wittering on about the phone-in competition his station was running to win Taylor Swift tickets, and then talking about his plans for the weekend, and asking listeners to text or call in and share theirs. I could never understand why people bothered to do that. I wondered how the DJ would react if I called in to say my plans involved sitting by my daughter's hospital bed in the day, and avoiding my husband's attempts to reignite the physical side of our relationship at night. Would Stevie, the DJ who sounded all of about nineteen, have any advice?

It was just as I decided to risk taking my eyes off the road for a split second, to switch radio stations, that it happened. When I looked up, the cars up ahead were slowing for an upcoming exit and I put my foot on the brake. As I went to change down a gear, I realised the clutch had gone completely floppy, and the car was revving like it had no power at all. Coasting towards the slip road, I prayed I could at least roll out of the way of the heaviest traffic. Just before the slip road, there was an exit with a big warning sign making it clear that it was for emergency vehicles only. But if this wasn't an emergency, with an HGV lorry getting ever closer in the rear-view mirror, I didn't know what was. Turning the steering wheel I rolled to a stop at the bottom of the slope, just far enough off the road to be out of harm's way.

'Shit.' My heart was racing as I unpeeled my fingers from the steering wheel to pull up the handbrake. I'd never broken down on my own before. The night I'd hit the pothole, Cam had driven by and rescued me almost straight away. And, other than that, the worst I'd ever had was a flat tyre on the outskirts of Appleberry, when I'd been about twenty, and I'd just walked home and gone back with my dad later, where he'd proceeded to teach me how to change a tyre. I didn't like to tell him that I'd been planning to call the AA, especially as he was of the generation who weren't afraid to kneel down on the hard shoulder of the M25 to change a tyre, never mind in the quiet lanes around Appleberry. I'd have to call Phoebe and see if her roadside rescue would cover me whilst I was driving her car. If not, at least she could call a recovery truck for me.

Picking up my phone, it was painfully obvious why my music had stopped playing. The battery was flat, and the lead I'd thought was plugged in to the charging socket was hanging loose. All that feel-good music might have lifted my spirits temporarily, but it had well and truly landed me in it. I was in a layby, thirty miles from Appleberry, and at least as far from London. There were only three numbers I could remember off the top of my head – presuming I could even find a phone box to call them from. Unfortunately, one of those numbers was for my parents' house, which left just two numbers to try, and I'd have to be truly desperate to take the second option.

Locking up the car, just in case a joy rider with the ability to fix a busted clutch decided to check out the emergency-vehicle exit, I headed up the slope away from the main road. There was a sign for a rugby club about a hundred yards up ahead and a narrow ledge of grass between the road and a drainage ditch. I had no idea if there'd be anyone at the club on a Friday afternoon, or if they'd let me use the phone if there was, but I was desperate. And if it took tears for them to take pity on me, I didn't think I'd struggle much to summon them up.

'Can you help me?' I pushed open the doors to the clubhouse and a young girl looked up at me from behind the bar.

'Yes, what can I get you?' She smiled, already moving towards the row of optics behind her.

'Sorry, no, I don't want a drink. My car's broken down, just off the main road on the emergency exit and the battery's died on my phone and I...' My voice had gone like Mickey Mouse on helium.

'Don't worry, you can use the phone here.' She looked over her shoulder, as if expecting to see someone watching her every move. 'My boss isn't in for half an hour and the lads from the first fifteen team don't finish practice for ten minutes, so no one will be any the wiser. Not that the lads would care, but my boss is a bit of an arse, so he'd probably want you to pay.'

'I can pay, it's not a problem.' I would happily have given her a twenty-pound note for one phone call at that point.

'Don't be daft.' She grinned again.

'Thanks so much. I wasn't sure if I'd have to walk for miles to try and find a phone box.'

'Do people even use those any more?' She gave me a funny look. 'I'm Chloe by the way. There's a phone here behind the bar. You can use that.'

'Perfect, thanks Chloe. I'm Scarlett and I'm forever in your debt!'

She laughed as she handed me the phone and I tapped out the first number. I'd called it so many times in the past week to check on Ava's progress late in the evenings, when I was at Phoebe's flat, it had stuck in my head. All the other numbers I called on a regular basis, were programmed into my phone, but the hospital number was engraved in my mind already.

'Can you put me through to the children's ward please?' I glanced at Chloe as I spoke, her eyebrows shooting up. I guess it must have seemed odd, a woman turning up to say her car had broken down, and then calling a children's ward. It was a long story and I'm sure she wouldn't want to hear it. 'Oh, hi, this is Ava West's mum, I just wanted to see if I could speak to my husband, Luke, please? I'm sorry to go through you but I need to speak to him urgently and my phone has died.'

'I'm sorry, but your husband left about an hour ago. He said he'd been called out urgently for work.' The intonation of the nurse's voice made it sound like a question, as if she didn't believe him any more than I did.

'Did he say when he might be back?'

'No, sorry, but the doctors were hoping to speak to at least one of you.'

'Is Ava okay?' I went cold and I could sense Chloe watching me.

'She's fine. In fact, she's better than that. She really seems to have turned a corner today, it looks like the antibiotics have done their job and she's definitely not going to need any surgery on her heart.'

I clutched the edge of the bar with my free hand. 'That's brilliant, and what about her kidney, is she out of the woods with that yet?'

'You'll need to speak to the doctors to get the whole picture, but Ava is asking for you. So it would be great if you could get in by the time they do their rounds this afternoon?'

'My car's broken down, but I'll make sure I'm there, somehow.' In that moment, I felt as if I could run all the way there without stopping, if it came to it.

'Oh no, what a nightmare. I hope you can sort something out, but maybe your husband will get back here first anyway?'

'Maybe.' I sighed, but shook it off. Luke might be as flaky as a Gregg's sausage roll, but I'd just been given the best possible news, and I didn't even care where he was. 'Thank you, so much.'

'No problem. We'll see you later.'

'Everything okay?' Chloe stopped polishing the pint glass she was holding and raised a questioning eyebrow, as I put down the phone.

'I was trying to phone my husband. Our daughter's in hospital and I thought he'd be there, but he's had to go out urgently for work.' My voice was flat, the words sounding as unconvincing as they felt.

'Oh God, is your daughter okay?'

'The nurse said she's doing a lot better today.' I smiled. 'Look, I'm really sorry, I couldn't make one more call, could I? I need to get a recovery truck out here to pick me up, so I can get to the hospital.'

'Of course you can. Do you know the number?'

'No, I'm sorry to ask, but I wondered if you might be able to look it up?'

'I would, but my data is all used up for this month already and, my boss won't give me the passcode to the Wi-Fi or unlock the office when he's not here.' She shrugged apologetically. 'But if you can wait until the lads come in from training, I'm sure one of them can look it up on their phone for you.'

'There's a number I can try first if that's okay?' I didn't want to get Chloe into trouble by using one of the premium directory enquiry services, that might show up on the bar phone bill. And I didn't want to wait for the team to finish their rugby training, either. So I'd have to phone the only other number I could remember. Hopefully, the school secretary would be in the office, as she often was in the half-term holidays. Louise would definitely look up the number for me, and probably even call the recovery truck out. Then I'd just have to sit tight until they arrived. I dialled the school's number, which I'd got to know by giving it out to parents more times than I could count, crossing my fingers that Louise would be there.

'Good afternoon, Appleberry Church of England Primary School.' I'd recognised the voice by the time he got to the second word, and I almost dropped the handset.

'Cam, it's Scarlett.'

'Scarlett.' He repeated my name as if it was a word he couldn't quite get to grips with.

'Yes, look, I'm sorry to ask, but is there any way you could ring a recovery service and get them to come out to me? I've broken down in Phoebe's car, my phone's dead and Luke's gone AWOL again. I've got to get to the hospital so the doctors can give me an update on Ava, and I'm borrowing the phone at a rugby club in a place called Kingsbarr.'

'Is Ava okay?' It was the same question I'd asked the nurse and there was the same urgency in his voice. This wasn't a polite enquiry. He really cared.

'Much better, I think. But I won't know everything until I can get to the hospital.'

'I'll take you. I know where the club in Kingsbarr is, we used to play rugby against them when I was a teenager. I can get the recovery service to pick up the car afterwards, but you need to get to the hospital.'

'Are you sure?' I had to ask, even though I was just as desperate to accept his offer as I had been to find a working phone. I wouldn't have had the bare-faced cheek to ask him, not after everything that had happened. But typically, he was putting Ava first.

'Of course. I'll be there as soon as I can. Are you okay to wait at the clubhouse, if I head straight off?'

'Yes, I can wait here.' I paused for a second. 'And, Cam?'

'Yes?'

'Thank you.' The words didn't even come close to what I really wanted to say, but they were all I had.

'I'll see you in about forty-five minutes, just sit tight, okay?'

'Did you manage to sort things out?' Chloe took the phone as I passed it back to her side of the bar.

'Yes, thank you. My friend's coming to get me.'

'Your *friend*?' Chloe gave me a half-smile. 'I know it's none of my business, but you just got this look on your face when you were talking to him.'

'Not much gets past you, does it?'

'You'd be surprised how much I see working behind this bar.' Chloe grinned again. 'I'm also a very good listener.'

I opened my mouth, realising I really did want to tell someone the secret I'd been hugging to myself since ending things with Cam. And who better than a stranger behind the bar of a rugby club that I would never visit again? But then the doors behind me were suddenly flung open and a cloud of testosterone seemed to fill the air.

'My nan could tackle with more impact than you did today!'

'Yeah and you run like Graham Norton!' The rugby club's first fifteen had clearly finished their training and were winding each other up, doing almost as much pushing and shoving as they did on the pitch, as they headed into the bar.

'Right you lot, before you start on the beers, I've got a job for you.' Chloe held up her hand, stopping them dead in their tracks, with all the efficiency of the opposition's burliest tighthead prop. 'Scarlett here had her car break down on the emergency exit, so we need to move it up to the club and out of the way. I'm guessing you boys can handle that? There's a free pint in it for whoever helps get it shifted.'

'I think we can, don't you, lads?' One of the men turned to the others and then laughed. 'Maybe not you though Tommo, you couldn't push a door shut the way you've been playing.'

'Yeah, all right Dean, you take the easy job and steer the car like you pretty boy wingers always do, and those of us with the muscle will push.'

'Just get it done boys and the beers will be waiting.' Chloe held out her hand. 'Pass us the keys then Scarlett and we'll get it sorted.'

'Thank you all so much.' I handed over the keys and watched as the whole team disappeared back out of the clubhouse. 'Did they all need to go?'

'No, of course not. But everything's a competition with that lot. Even how far they can pee! I knew the offer of a free beer was one way of getting them all to go, too.'

'Let me pay for the beers.'

'Don't be silly. Some of them drink so much when they get started, they'll have no idea how many beers they've had. I'll just sneak the "free" beers onto the tab.'

'You really don't miss a trick, do you?' Anyone who underestimated Chloe or made assumptions about the pretty blonde barmaid working at the rugby club, would do so at their peril.

'Nope and now you can tell me all about this friend of yours before the boys get back.' She opened one of the drinks' fridges behind her and took out a bottle of wine, pouring out two glasses. 'And I promise I won't judge.'

I took a deep breath and started to speak.

* * *

'Do you want me to wait here?' Cam turned to me as we pulled into a space in the hospital car park.

'You don't have to hang around. I can get a tube back to Phoebe's place from here.' I kept my gaze fixed on his left shoulder. I'd been avoiding looking him in the face since he'd turned up at the rugby club and seen me sitting at the bar, chatting to Dean, the captain of the first fifteen, who seemed determined to get my number for some unfathomable reason. I couldn't bring myself to admit to him that I didn't even know what it was. On the drive up to the hospital, Cam didn't mention the text Luke had made me send, and neither did I. If it really hadn't bothered him, then what was the point in raking over something that was obviously far more painful for me?

'I'd like to stay and hear how Ava is, if that's okay?'

'Why don't you come up with me, then?' I finally looked at him, just in time to see his eyebrow shoot up.

'What about Luke?'

'He won't be there.' Suddenly I knew it with absolute clarity – just as I knew that wherever he was, he definitely wasn't at a work emergency. He didn't have that sort of job.

'I don't know, what if he turns up? I don't want to get in the way of things. Again.'

'I'd like you to come, and Ava will be really happy to see you.' I watched his face and it was almost as if I could see him weighing everything up, but he nodded finally.

'Okay, but if Luke's there, I'll leave you two to it. *Like you wanted.*' There was a sting in the tail. Even Cam wasn't perfect, and in a weird sort of way I was glad. There was a big part of me that had started to wonder if he might actually be relieved I'd called things off. But it had obviously affected him, just maybe not as much as it had affected me.

* * *

'Mummy!' Ava held up her arms as I walked into her room. The colour was back in her cheeks and I didn't need the doctors to tell me she was getting better, I could see it for myself.

'I've brought Pinkie in to see you.' I pulled her into my arms, sandwiching the soft unicorn toy I'd been holding between us. 'He was missing you.'

'I missed him too, and all my toys. But I missed you most, Mummy – where did you go?' Ava stuck out her bottom lip.

'I had to go back and get some of your things, but especially Pinkie, because he needed one of your special cuddles.' I didn't want to tell her about the car breaking down, or my stupid phone battery going flat. It had been a bit of a nightmare, but it meant I had something far more exciting to tell her. 'I've brought someone else to see you, too.'

'Who?' Ava started scanning the room and I just hoped my instincts were right. I'd already put Cam through enough, so if Ava's reaction to seeing him fell flat, that would just pile on the guilt. I needn't have worried, though.

'Hello sweetheart.' Cam, who had been waiting outside the door

– partly to make it more of a surprise for Ava, and partly to make sure Luke hadn't come back – walked into the room.

'Cam!' Ava tried to get out of bed and I had to hold on to her. 'I've missed you loads and loads and loads!'

'Everyone at school has been missing you, too.' Cam wiped his eyes and I could have burst into tears for what I'd thrown away. Seeing the two of them together again, I couldn't pretend that what Cam and I had started to build was just a fledgling relationship, something that could be easily replaced down the line. He was perfect for Ava, and he was perfect for me.

'Can I go back to school soon, Mummy?' Ava widened her eyes and I nodded.

'I hope so, darling. I really hope we both can.'

'Sorry to interrupt.' Ava's consultant knocked on the open door to her room. 'I just wanted to catch up with you for an update?'

'Shall I come out to you?' I looked towards Cam, as the doctor nodded. 'Are you okay to keep Ava entertained while I have a quick chat with the doctor?'

'Of course.' He smiled and Ava did too. I could have left them together for a lifetime if I had to, and I knew she'd be okay. More than okay.

'Are you happy to chat out here?' The doctor was smiling too and I nodded. I'd already been told it was good news, I just wanted to know how good. 'We've been really pleased with the progress Ava has made over the last twenty-four hours and I think we can be completely confident now that the antibiotics have cleared the infection up, and her heart should make a recovery to full function without any surgical intervention in a matter of days.'

'Thank God.' It was greedy to ask for more, but so much hung on my next question. 'And what about the kidney?'

'We've got to run a few more tests, but it doesn't look like the infection caused any further damage. So if she continues to recover from the accident in the way she has been, her kidney should eventually recover to full function too. In the meantime, it's certainly functioning well enough for her not to have to return to dialysis, which means she should be able to transfer back to your local hospital over the weekend. And, if things keep going the way they are, she should be able to go home fairly soon.'

'Do your patients' parents often hug you?' I thought briefly about Sam, the nurse at our local hospital, who'd I'd hugged half to death when Ava first started to make a recovery, before the virus. Consultants weren't always as approachable as nurses, though, and I didn't want to embarrass him.

'Sometimes.' The doctor held out his arms. 'But sometimes I hug them. Especially when we have news as good as this.'

'Thank you so much.' I seemed to have said those words a million times since Ava's accident. But for the first time in my life I really understood what gratitude meant, and I'd never stop being thankful for the second chance I'd been given to be Ava's mum.

* * *

'I can't believe Cam's gone out to pick up a takeaway.' Phoebe pulled a face. 'I told him one of the joys of living in London is that you can have almost anything delivered within twenty minutes.'

'I think he wanted to give us a bit of time to chat by ourselves.' I curled my legs underneath me on the sofa. Cam had brought me back to Phoebe's place, once Ava had started to drift off for the night. By the time I'd filled her in on everything that had happened, and Cam had said he'd sorted out a recovery truck to take her car to the garage to be fixed, and that it would be dropped back some time the following week, they'd been chatting like old friends. We'd been so excited about the news from the consultant, it was all Cam and I had spoken about on the way back to the flat. So the text still hung between us, like a hornet's nest neither of us seemed ready to poke. When Phoebe had invited Cam to crash on the sofa if he wanted to – conveniently forgetting that she'd already promised a room to Luke for the night – I'd expected him to say no, or at least mention the prospect of Luke turning up, but he hadn't. Not that there'd been any sign of my husband. I'd charged my phone as soon as I got back to the flat and texted to tell him the good news about Ava, but there'd been no reply.

'I don't think you gave Cam full credit when you described him.' Phoebe topped up both our glasses with the hastily purchased bottle of champagne I'd picked up to celebrate the news about Ava. 'He's gorgeous.'

'I know, and Ava loves him too.'

'You *love* him?' Phoebe slammed her glass down on the table, champagne spilling over the sides.

'I, er...' The alcohol hitting my system only half-explained the heat rising up my neck. 'Okay, I'm pretty sure I do.'

'So why on earth did you ditch him for Luke?'

'It's a long story.' I thought back to my conversation with Chloe at the rugby club, and her promise not to judge me. I'd wondered if she would, though, when she found out I was only using my husband as a living organ donor, and lying to everyone else I cared about to pull off the deception. But she was true to her word, she hadn't judged me, and she'd even said she would have done the same thing. So if I could trust a virtual stranger with the truth, surely I could trust my oldest friend?

'I never wanted to get back with Luke, but when I found out about the kidney dysplasia and the hospital told me he was the best chance of being a perfect match with Ava, I couldn't afford for him to disappear again. So when he said I had to commit to making a go of things or he wouldn't hang around, I didn't feel like I had a choice.'

'What an arsehole!'

'What, me?'

'No, you silly cow, Luke! You just did what you had to for Ava, but for him to blackmail you like that... I'd like to say it's out of character, but—' She suddenly stopped, and shook her head.

'But what?

'Oh God. I've been thinking about telling you this ever since Luke did a bunk, but I just thought it would pile the hurt on. Especially when I should probably have told you years ago.' Phoebe picked up her glass and took another swig of champagne.

'Told me what?'

'Just before your wedding, Luke made a pass at me.' Phoebe visibly shuddered. 'I should have told you then, and I could have saved you all this shit with him, but I knew how much you loved him, and when I told him where to get off, he apologised and said it was down to the drink. But, the thing is, I didn't really believe him, not even then. I didn't want to risk losing you, but I should have put you first.'

'But then I wouldn't have had Ava.' I waited for the sick feeling to hit me in the stomach, but finding out that my husband had made a pass at my best friend didn't seem to be having any effect.

'I still should have told you.'

'I wouldn't swap having Ava for anything. I'm glad you didn't tell me then, but I am glad you've told me now.'

'Can you forgive me?' Phoebe held out her hand and I took it.

'There's nothing to forgive.' I squeezed her hand and then let it go, picking up my phone from the table in front of us. 'In fact, maybe I should order a second bottle of champagne, there must be someone who can deliver that? Oh, speak of the devil, there's a text from Luke.'

'What does it say?'

I handed the phone to Phoebe, so she could read it for herself.

✉ Luke

Great news about Ava, babe. Got 2 go away on a top-secret job 4 a wk. But I will text or call u back when I can xx

'I thought he did something to do with IT systems? Unless it's for MI5, I can't see what's so secret?' Phoebe was pulling that face again, the same one she almost always did when she spoke about Luke. Now I knew why.

'Because it's bollocks, just like almost everything he's ever said to me. But do you know what? I really don't care. The longer he's away, the better.'

'You just need to sort things out properly with Cam now.' Phoebe pushed my glass towards me, as if sensing I might need some Dutch courage. 'Just tell him what you told me.'

'What if he hates me for it?'

'Am I going to have to keep calling you a silly cow tonight?' Phoebe nudged me, spilling a bit more of her champagne. 'Of course he isn't going to hate you. He loves you too, it's bloody obvious.'

'I'll do it later; I just need to pick my moment.' I took a sip of my drink. This was going to take more than Dutch courage.

* * *

'Is that you, Scarlett?' Cam whispered as I tip-toed past the couch where he was lying, to get to the kitchen.

'Yes, sorry, did I wake you?' It was dark, but I could make out his outline, as he shifted into a sitting position.

'No, I can't get to sleep.'

'Neither can I, so I was going to get a drink. Do you want one?'

'I'd rather have a chat.' Cam's voice was barely a whisper, but I shivered. He was right, we needed to have the conversation I'd avoided all night, telling myself it was too difficult to explain what had really gone down with Luke whilst Phoebe was around. But if I was in Cam's position, I was pretty sure I wouldn't even be in the flat. I'd probably have left him stranded on the side of the road.

'Shall I put the light on?'

'No, in case it wakes Phoebe up.' Cam patted the end of the couch nearest to me. 'Just come and sit down.'

'What do you want to talk about?' Sitting down, I turned towards him in the dark, already knowing exactly what he was going to say.

'What's going on, Scarlett? With you and Luke?'

'He made me send the text.' I sounded about twelve years old, but I didn't care. I was going to have to tell him the *whole* truth, but at least I could start out by making him dislike Luke as much as I did.

'I guessed it wasn't really you by the wording, but then I called and my number was rejected, so I didn't know what to think. With Ava being so poorly, I just had to sit it out and wait, you had enough to worry about without me turning up and demanding an explanation. But what I don't understand is why you went along with it?' Cam's voice was steady, but I wished I could see his face.

'Luke threatened to disappear again if I didn't give us another chance.' I wasn't explaining myself properly, but it was hard.

'And would that bother you? Enough for us to finish?' Cam sighed. 'I know it's complicated with him being Ava's dad, but I wanted to work through all of that. Together.'

'Me too.' I was close enough to reach out, but I knotted my hands together. 'Ava needed Luke around and I couldn't risk him disappearing until I was sure she was okay. Oh God, this is going to make you think really badly of me, but when I found out there was a good chance she might need a kidney, and the doctors said he'd probably be the best match...'

'So it was his kidney you wanted? Nothing else?'

'It makes me sound so mercenary, doesn't it? But I'm not going to lie. I'd do anything to make sure Ava is okay, and it's not like Luke's been straight with me either.'

'It doesn't make you sound mercenary, I know you'd do anything for Ava. I just wish you'd been upfront with me.'

'I should have told you straight away, when it was just Ava's kidney we were worried about, before she picked up the infection. But I thought I might never have to tell you that I'd let him think there was a chance for our marriage.' I curled my hands into an even tighter ball. 'Then when they transferred her up here, Luke got hold of my phone and read some of our messages. That's when he said that if I didn't finish things with you, he'd have to leave. Ava was more poorly than ever at that point, so I just couldn't risk it. But I never wanted to lose you.'

'I would have understood.'

'And now?' I held my breath, waiting for Cam to answer.

'It depends on what you want. I wanted to drive to the hospital when I got your text, and tell Luke that he'd had his chance and blown it. Twice. But he's Ava's father and she's got to come first. The last thing I wanted to do was turn up in her hospital room and cause a scene, so like I said, I just bottled it up and waited. But even Louise in the school office picked up on it. Apparently, I've been a miserable sod this last week and I was trying to bury myself in work, by spending the half-term holiday at school. If you'd just told me, it would have been so much easier. I didn't know what was going on when I got the message, but I was sure you couldn't really mean it – not if you felt even half as much for me as I did for you. But I'm too old to play games, Scarlett.'

'So am I, and you're right, Ava does have to come first. You know I didn't want to start a relationship without being as sure as I could that it was right for her.' I finally reached out and caught hold of his hand. 'You've done nothing but prove that I made the right decision to let you into our lives, and I really want to pick up where we left off. But after everything I've put you through, that decision has got to be down to you.' It could all still be too little, too late.

'What if he disappears again because of us?' Cam didn't pull his hand away, which was something.

'If he can't put Ava first after nearly losing her, then I think she's better off without him.'

'He can't really mean what he says about leaving, surely?'

'I wouldn't put it past him, but it doesn't matter.' I held something back: the confession that deep down I wanted Luke to disappear. This had been about Ava from the start, though, so I pushed the thought away. Just because it would have been easier for me, that didn't make it right. 'I've really missed you.'

'I've missed you, too, and it's driven me crazy not knowing for sure what was going on with Ava. I know I'm not her dad, but...'

'You don't have to say it. Words are easy and even Luke can talk the talk, but it's the little things, like just being there, that really make the difference in the end.'

'And there's nothing else you want to tell me, about what happened, or how you're feeling now? If there's anything else, I'd rather we just got it out in the open, so we can start afresh.'

'Nothing at all.' There *was* something else I was keeping from him. But he didn't need to know about the turmoil I'd felt when Ava was first ill, when I'd been sure only Luke really understood what it was like to watch our daughter lying in that bed. He didn't need to know about the kiss, either. Both of those things had been nothing more than half-remembered memories in the heat of the moment, and a reminder that the past was so often better left where it was.

'So, do you want to make it official?'

'What do you mean?' My stomach flipped over. He couldn't mean what it sounded like. There was no doubting now that I was in love with Cam. But I definitely wasn't ready for *that*. For a start, I was still married to Luke. Although not for much longer if I had my way.

'I wanted to organise a party for Ava, when she gets home, and all the kids in my class have been coming up with ideas. It would mean a lot of the parents from school would be there too, and I'd like to throw the party as more than just your colleague. But it would put *us* out there, with everyone. Not just the select few who knew before, or those who thought they did. There's no way that won't get back to Luke at some point.'

'I haven't got any secrets I need to keep any more, least of all about us.' I leant into his chest as he pulled me towards him. 'It sounds perfect to me.'

'Just promise you'll tell me first if anything changes, next time?' Cam kissed the top of my head.

'I promise. From now on things are only going to change for the better, though, with everything out in the open.' Lying in the dark in Cam's arms, I was certain of it – but I never had been that good at predicting the future.

20

Once Ava started to get better her recovery amazed us all. The nurses explained that it was often like that with children, they were more resilient and able to bounce back far quicker than adults who'd been through the same thing.

Ava's kidney function continued to improve after she was transferred back to our local hospital, and it was obvious she was better when she started to complain about how boring it was and to kick up a bit of a fuss when it came time for the latest round of blood tests. So we were both relieved when Doctor Daniels told us she could go home. She'd need regular check-ups to monitor her kidney function until they were sure she was fully recovered, and she had to take it a little bit easy at first, but going home was a huge step in the right direction.

Luke had texted a few times and, despite how angry I was with him for disappearing again, I'd replied to let him know about Ava's progress. He'd said he'd be back by the weekend and asked if I'd handed my notice in yet. My texts couldn't have been any blunter, but he still seemed to be under the illusion that we were going to make things work. My responses got starker as the week went on, but despite the fact he'd emotionally blackmailed me, I'd wanted to tell him in person that there was no chance for us. After all, I hadn't exactly played fair with him either. But when another week slipped by without him coming to see Ava, or even give her a call, my heart hardened a little bit more – especially when she asked where he was. She asked about Cam, too, and he'd video called her from school with some of her classmates. He checked in on her progress every day, and made sure I didn't worry about work by telling me there was no hurry to come back, and that I could do short days with Ava even when I did. So when he'd offered to pick us up, when Ava was released from hospital, I didn't hesitate.

'I can't believe how well she looks.' Cam turned towards me, as we stopped at some traffic lights a couple of miles outside of Appleberry. Ava was in the back seat behind us, singing away with her headphones on, watching a Disney movie on the iPad Cam had brought for her to make the journey home less boring.

'I can't stop looking at her. No one would ever guess what she's been through.'

'And what about you? Are you okay?' He put his hand on my knee briefly, but then the lights changed and he took hold of the steering wheel again. It was ridiculous, but I missed the weight of his touch as soon as it was gone.

'I'm fine. Mum is just about speaking to me again, too.' I laughed. 'You could probably hear her shouting from your place when she found out that Ava had been rushed up to London and I hadn't told her.'

'You did it for the right reasons.'

'I know that, and you know that, but she didn't quite see it like that.' Mum had been up to the hospital every day since she'd been home, and it had taken all my powers of persuasion to get her to let us come home with Cam, rather than her and Dad coming to pick us up. I almost had to resort to a head lock at one point.

'She did ring me to tell me to drive carefully.' It was Cam's turn to laugh and I couldn't help thinking about what Luke's reaction would have been in the same situation. He'd have gone into a rant about my mother interfering, and him being perfectly capable of driving us home.

'Did you tell her what time we'd be back?' I crossed the fingers on my left hand, making a silent wish for just a bit of time to settle back in to the cottage, before she descended on us.

'I told her late afternoon.' Cam grinned again. 'I figured you could call her when you're ready that way, rather than getting home to find her waiting on the doorstep.'

'Has anyone ever told you you're a marvel at understanding women, Cameron Ellis?'

'It's a gift!' He was still grinning. 'I just thought you might need some time to yourselves. I wanted to do a bit of a welcome home party for Ava tomorrow, like I mentioned at Phoebe's place. Just a couple of hours with some of the kids from the school in the church hall, but I wasn't sure if it would be too much?'

'I think she'll love it, and if she gets tired I can just take her home.' I watched Ava's reflection in the mirror of the sun visor. She was still singing at the top of her voice and she even did an air-grab at one point. I could have watched her forever, absorbing every moment with a new appreciation.

'I'll make some calls tonight to confirm it's going ahead.' Cam pulled off the main road onto the narrow country lane that was the only way to get to Appleberry, just as Ava's singing reached a crescendo. We both started laughing again, and we'd have looked like the perfect little family to anyone watching us. And, just for a moment, it felt like we were.

* * *

Ava was tucked up in bed by eight o'clock and my parents had finally left at nine. Mum had cooked me enough meals to last us the first week home, and she'd even put a wholemeal pasta bake in the oven to heat up before she left. The fact that she'd made some meals with carbs in, told me how worried she'd been.

I was looking forward to getting our routine back to normal. The thought that Ava would be sleeping in the room next door, instead of in a hospital bed miles away, was even better. It was just another of those simple pleasures. The ordinary, everyday stuff that I had taken for granted before Ava's accident. Like sitting down with a plate of pasta and maybe even a glass of wine, in front of a gritty crime drama, and not being on tenterhooks just in case the hospital rang.

Pyjamas were a must too, if I was going to really relax into our first night home. But when I got up to the bedroom, it was as if I'd stepped into a crime drama of my own. Opening the end of my wardrobe that was filled with shelves, the hairs on the back of my neck stood on end. My clothes had been stuffed into the bottom three shelves, and the top three shelves were filled with somebody else's clothes. Pulling open the doors at the other end of the wardrobe, the same thing had happened. My clothes had been shoved to one end, and a man's clothes were hanging in the space that had been made.

Flicking through the hangers, I couldn't stop my hands from shaking. The sound of the water tank filling made me spin round momentarily, terrified that I might see someone standing there. But there was nothing out of place, nothing except the clothes on the rails and shelves in front of me. I didn't recognise any of it, until I got to the second to last hanger, and then I saw it. Luke's wedding suit. The one he'd been wearing in the photos that were now boxed up and hidden away – a part of the past that I was only holding on to for Ava's sake, so she could see that we'd been in love once. But now his clothes were hanging in my wardrobe, in a house he'd never even lived in.

I didn't have to guess how he'd got in. I'd made the same mistake as I'd made with my phone, keeping the habits I'd had when we were together. I'd bought a little hedgehog key safe, back when we'd lived in Cornwall, to keep a spare front door key in. It was where I'd put the spare key to the cottage too, and the little hedgehog sat in the flowerbed by the front door. It would have taken Luke less than a minute to find it and let himself in. But what was more of a mystery was *why* he'd done it, and *when* he'd done it, especially as he was supposed to be away on business. Maybe he thought he could railroad me into going along with what he wanted, like he had so many times before. Only this time I didn't need him, and I didn't want him, either.

What else had Luke touched whilst he was here? Suddenly the thought of sleeping in my own bed, with Ava just next door, had lost its security too. I wanted to throw his clothes out into the garden and set fire to them, then clean the house from top to bottom to make it feel like mine again. But getting rid of them would have to wait until the morning, I couldn't risk disturbing Ava. I was going to have to call him again, though, and let him know he'd really pushed it too far this time. Shutting the wardrobe door, I stalked past the dressing table towards the bedroom door. It was then that I realised everything on there had been moved too. My jewellery box was open and the contents strewn out. It was mostly costume jewellery anyway, and my wedding and eternity rings, which I'd taken off when I'd moved back to Appleberry, were still there, caught up on the beads of one of my necklaces. But I couldn't find my engagement ring. It was a five stone diamond ring that had been Luke's grandmother's and I'd planned to give it back to him – it was a link to his family, and I wasn't part of that any more. Only it seemed like he'd taken matters into his own hands and taken the ring back himself. If he was gambling again, and he'd sold the ring his grandmother had left him to fund it, leaving his daughter lying alone in a hospital bed, then he'd sunk about as low as a person could go. But the idea didn't shock me, not any more.

Running down the stairs, I wrenched the front door open and scooped up the little hedgehog ornament from the flower bed. Thank God, the key was still there. At least there was no danger of him letting himself in again when I was out, or even worse, asleep. How could I have been so stupid? Snatching up my mobile, I typed in the new code – something Luke would never be able to guess – and there was a message waiting.

✉ Sender not in contact list
Luke has made the right choice, now it's time for you to do the same. Stay away from him if you know what's good for you.

I shivered, my skin prickling as I re-read the words. Whoever was sending these messages was welcome to Luke, but I had a horrible feeling he'd dragged me into something I wasn't going to be able to walk away from, no matter how much I wanted to. And changing my number was never going to be enough.

* * *

'Ava and I could have made our own way to the party, Mum.' She was fussing around in the kitchen, washing up two breakfast plates I hadn't got around to.

'You look exhausted, and I don't want you driving Ava about until you're on top form.' Mum tutted. 'The last thing we want is another accident. I blame myself enough for the first one, and I'll not have another one on my conscience.'

'I'm fine.' I wasn't going to tell her that I'd been up half the night, emailing local divorce lawyers, and the tenants down in Cornwall to see if they were interested in buying the B&B before it went on the market. I'd also packed up all of Luke's stuff and sorted out a few photographs of him and Ava. There were no pictures of his parents with her but, if he didn't respond to my messages in the next few days, they'd be finding all of his stuff in a big heap in their front garden. I'd also looked into whether I could get a restraining order out against him if I needed to. If it was him, or someone acting on his behalf, sending the messages, then I had plenty of evidence. I wouldn't put it past his parents to be involved somewhere along the line.

'You don't look fine to me. If you gave up carbs you'd feel much better, and you'd have more energy too.'

'Funnily enough, changing my diet isn't my top priority right now.'

'Well, you can't look after Ava properly unless you look after yourself.' She put down the tea towel, gesturing towards the row of hooks by the back door. 'Is that Cam's coat? We could take it back to him, unless he's leaving things here now?'

'It's Luke's.'

'Please tell me you're joking. After everything he's put you and Ava through?' Her voice had gone thin and reedy.

'He left it here. Uninvited.' I'd told her as much as Cam knew about what had happened with Luke, but she didn't need to know about the clothes turning up in my wardrobe. I could deal with that myself. 'You could drop it off to the charity shop next week if you like?'

'Nothing would give me more satisfaction.' She smiled. 'Although I'm tempted to save it until Bonfire Night, so we can use it to dress the guy and then watch it burn.'

'Mum!'

'You just wait until Ava grows up and meets someone. I pray to

God she doesn't meet anyone who treats her the way Luke has treated you. But if she does, then you'll understand.'

'I already get it. Thanks, Mum.' I put my arms around her and we stood like that for a good ten seconds, just hugging – in a way we hadn't done for years. 'Shall we get to this party then before all the good buffet food goes?'

'Just don't eat anything brown. Pastry's the work of the devil.' Mum started listing all the reasons it was bad for me and I couldn't help smiling. Some things would never change.

* * *

Ava was giggling, sitting on a picnic blanket in the church hall, surrounded by her friends, all held spellbound by Cinderella. Even the boys.

'He's done a great job your Cam, hasn't he?' Kate nudged me, sloshing some of the wine from her plastic cup onto my arm, so that it ran gently down to my elbow before plopping on to floor. I made a mental note never to go out drinking with her and Phoebe at the same time, or I'd be soaking wet and reeking like a brewery. 'And there's me, counting myself lucky that Alan finally seems to have stopped wanting to spend all his time with his car, and is back to servicing me on a regular basis instead!'

'Kate!' I had to say this for her, she always made me laugh. 'I'm really glad to hear Alan is back to being your Channing Tatum stand-in, although I definitely don't need to hear the details. You're right, though, Cam's done amazingly well, but Natasha Chisholm booked Cinderella and she's got the kids hooked.' The woman dressed as Cinderella was apparently a professional actress, and her costume definitely wasn't the sort of cheap fancy dress outfit you could get for £9.99 from eBay.

'That was nice of her.' Kate's response was grudging. 'But it's easy to do something like that when you can just splash the cash.'

'Your cupcakes, and all the bunting Dolly and her kids made is much more personal.' I gave Kate a squeeze around the waist. I meant it, and I'd been overwhelmed by how much effort everyone had made to welcome us home. 'Even Claire Winters came up and told me her son missed having me as his teacher.'

'Jesus, it must be a full moon!' Kate wrinkled her nose and I had to laugh again. I'd missed Kate and Dolly, and almost everyone in Appleberry, but especially the kids in my class. I was looking forward to starting half-days with Ava in the next week or two, if she continued to make such good progress.

'What are you two giggling about?' Dolly walked over to join us, her four youngest children, whose adoption would be finalised in the spring, were making the most of the small bouncy castle that Cam had inflated inside the church hall.

'Claire Winters said something nice to Scarlett!' Kate raised her eyebrows.

'It must be a full moon!' Dolly echoed Kate's words from moments before.

'You two have been spending too long together without my supervision. It's a good job I'm back.'

'And you're home for good? In Appleberry, I mean?' Dolly looked serious for a moment. 'No deciding to go back down to Cornwall, after all?'

'That feels like another life. I can barely recognise the person I was then. I thought I could change Luke and make things work for Ava's sake, but watching her over there now, I know coming back to Appleberry was the best thing I ever did.'

'Why don't you go over and take some more photos, Scarlett, and I can help Ruhan and Cam get the food served up. You don't want to miss the chance before Ava gets too tired.' Dolly put her hand in the small of my back and gave me a gentle shove. For such a sweet person, she could be pretty forceful when she wanted to be.

'I feel guilty leaving it all to you guys.'

'Cam doesn't want you to worry about anything today.' Dolly shooed me away with a wave of her hand. 'And you know what a hard task master he is.'

'Yeah, he's a regular dictator these days.' Kate rolled her eyes and laughed. 'It'll be more than our lives are worth if he sees you anywhere near the kitchen.'

I took my phone out of my bag as I walked towards Ava, ready to take some more photos. I'd read a magazine article about mindfulness whilst I'd been sitting by her hospital bed. I'd barely taken it in, but one thing I'd remembered was that capturing photographs was supposed to help people enjoy experiences more. And I wanted to capture as many good memories for Ava as I could. I'd chosen a father for her, who seemed incapable of living up to the label of Dad, but I was going to do everything else I could to give her the best childhood possible.

'And they all lived happily ever after.' Cinderella finished telling the story just as I got to them, and some of the children had bought Ava presents that they were desperate for her to open next.

'Open mine first!' A little girl from Ava's class, whose name was Betsy, handed her a beautifully wrapped gift, which was easily the biggest in the pile.

'Thank you, Betsy.' Ava gave her friend a sweet smile and took the parcel, peeling the paper off so slowly and carefully that Betsy was hopping from foot to foot with impatience. I could see her point and I was almost tempted to rip the wrapping paper off myself.

'It's a baby!' Ava held up the box containing a scarily life-like baby doll.

'That's lovely isn't it, darling? What do you say to Betsy?'

'Thank you!' Ava stood up and hugged her friend. 'Isn't it cute, Mummy? I wish you could have a real baby like that, but remember I said at Christmas I only want a sister. I don't want a brother!'

'Your mummy can't have a baby, silly.' Betsy put her hands on her hips. 'Because you haven't got a daddy.'

'Yes I have. Mummy says he's been poorly but I just think he's not very good at it.' Ava gave a matter-of-fact shrug and I wanted to scoop her up into my arms. 'Anyway, I don't want my daddy to be the baby's daddy. Mummy's got Cam and I think he'd be much betterer.'

'You and me both kiddo.' I hadn't realised I'd said it out loud until Cinderella turned and gave me a wry smile. Thankfully the children were too preoccupied with moving on to the next present to notice. But sometimes children had a wisdom beyond their years, and Ava had worked Luke out a lot more quickly than I had. Whatever happened with her dad, she was going to be okay. And that was the greatest gift anyone could have given me.

21

By the middle of the week, a fortnight after the party, Ava could have auditioned for a remake of *The Exorcist*. Her head wasn't quite spinning around in circles, but she had taken boredom to an almost Olympic level and we'd agreed that she'd do half-days on the Thursday and Friday, and get picked up by Mum and Dad at lunchtime, so I could go back to work.

Ava had run into Cam's class on the first morning back, and her friends had cheered her arrival. I just hoped my own class would be as happy to see me. I needn't have worried, though. Ruhan had them all sitting and waiting, with the cards they'd made the day before, to welcome me back. Some of them got up to hug me too and I had to swallow hard when Claire Winters' son, Jules, told me he wanted me to be his teacher forever.

Ava coped really well with her first half-day at school, and had made Mum spend the afternoon baking, so I was pretty confident we'd be able to move to full days again by the following week. Luke had finally replied to my multiple texts and voicemails, and agreed to come down on the Friday evening. As far as I was concerned, it was to pick up his stuff and agree a plan for selling the B&B and starting divorce proceedings. He seemed to think it was to give us a chance to *chat about everything,* and I had a horrible feeling he still thought he could talk me around. But that was his problem, I had other things to focus on.

The family were all due to meet up with Auntie Leilah and her fiancé, Nicky, on Saturday, after the final dress fittings. Cam had been included in the dinner plans, and he seemed to have been sucked straight into my family's life. Luckily, he appeared to like it as much as everyone else liked him, and it was already difficult to imagine a future without him. He'd asked me if I wanted him to be there when Luke turned up, but I needed to stand up to Luke on my own. And when I did, not even he could doubt we were definitely over.

'Sorry to interrupt, Scarlett, but someone's here to see you.' Louise, the school secretary, looked apologetic when she came into my class on Friday afternoon, after the children had already left. I was just doing a bit of preparation for the following week, before heading home to wait for Luke. Ava was having a sleep-over at my parents' place and, according to the text I'd just had from Mum, she was almost bouncing off the walls with excitement at the thought of trying on her bridesmaid's dress again.

'Really, who is it?' If it was Luke, I was going to kill him. Turning up at the school would have been low even for him. But he was going to make the break-up all about Cam, I knew that already. Otherwise, he'd have to accept some responsibility for the fact that we were a million per cent over. And that would never happen. So there had always been a good chance he'd turn up at the school and confront Cam at some point.

'She said her name's Lily Dyson and she's a friend of your husband's?' Louise raised an eyebrow. Now that the whole world – or at least the world that extended to the boundaries of Appleberry

– knew about me and Cam, any mention of my husband was more than a little awkward.

'Thanks, Louise. Can you send her through, please?' The name didn't ring any bells, but maybe Luke had decided to get the jump on me and appoint a divorce solicitor of his own. Never mind shaking her hand, I might have to kiss her if that's who she was. But whatever she was here for, if she really was a friend of Luke's, I didn't want to have the conversation outside the school office.

'No problem.' Louise disappeared, but she was back in less than a minute with a petite blonde woman, standing behind her.

'Come in, please. Thanks Louise.' I closed the door and turned to face Lily Dyson. She didn't look like my vision of a divorce solicitor; she had wavy hair that framed her face, and big green eyes that gave her an almost doll-like appearance. But appearances meant nothing, and she could easily have been a cut-throat negotiator beneath that fluffy exterior. I wanted out of the marriage with Luke more than I could say, but I wasn't going to walk away and give him everything. I owed it to Ava to get us a fair deal. I could be a ball-breaker too, or at least I could pretend to be. 'How can I help you Ms Dyson?'

'Lily, please.' She bit her lip. 'Look, I'm sorry, this is going to be really difficult to say, but do you mind if I sit down?' She smoothed a hand over the woollen coat she was wearing, a discernible bump outlined as she did. She was either packing a basketball or a baby bump, and my money was on the latter.

'Of course, please sit down.' I sat behind my desk, trying to be patient as she undid the coat and settled herself into the seat. I just wanted her to come out with whatever it was she had to say. 'Louise said you're a friend of Luke's?'

'Actually, I'm his partner.' Lily looked straight at me. 'I know that's probably a shock to you, but we've been together for almost two years. On and off.'

'And the baby?' I stared at the bump again, trying to work out how I felt.

'It's his.' Lily put her hands over her bump in a protective gesture, as if she expected me to launch myself at her at any moment. 'I know he's been confused, and that he feels like he owes you and Ava something, especially after you begged him to give things another shot. But he's got another child on the way now, and I know it's me he loves. He just can't stop trying to look after you.'

'Look after *me*?' I actually wanted to laugh, but if I started, I might never be able to stop.

'When you got yourself into all that gambling debt.' Lily sighed. 'It was me who lent him the money to help you get out of it. We were at school together and we reconnected through a Facebook group about two years ago. He just started pouring out all his troubles to me, telling me about how you'd always wanted to have a bed and breakfast place, and he'd gone ahead with it because it was your dream. But then you started gambling when things went wrong. He said he thought you might have postnatal depression, too – he was at his wit's end.'

'The gambling debts were his, and so was the dream of running a B&B. And it was Luke who went out on a supply run for the business and just never came back.'

'The debts can't have been his, he said you kicked him out because you'd started seeing someone you met out clubbing.' Lily was shaking her head, and all I felt for her was sympathy. She was carrying Luke's baby and it sounded as though he'd told her even more lies than he'd told me.

'Clubbing? I was working all the hours God sent to run the B&B and look after Ava, and if I'd had a moment to myself, the last thing I'd have wanted was to spend it clubbing.' I took a deep breath. 'I don't know if you're ready to hear all of this, Lily, but since he showed up again, it's Luke who's been asking for a second chance with me and Ava.'

Lily bit her bottom lip again. 'It's just because he's confused, though, and he thinks you need looking after. But if you let him talk you into it, you'll be making a big mistake. Because he'll always come back to me. Ever since he started talking about getting back in contact with you last autumn, I've been trying to warn you that it be would a mistake. When I found your number on his phone I started texting you, and then I got up the courage to call. I know it was wrong and I didn't know what to say at first, so I disguised my voice in case Luke found out. I stopped messaging when I heard about Ava's accident but, once I knew she was okay, I had to make sure you were both going to do the right thing. But I had a horrible feeling you wouldn't, not without knowing the whole story. So I thought it was finally time I talked to you face to face and sorted this out once and for all.'

'The text messages and phone calls were from *you*?' I was right, she wasn't nearly as sweet as she looked.

'I was desperate. Nat told me that I should speak to you directly, and that Luke was playing us off against each other. But she's never *really* liked him, not even when we were at school together. He always said she was jealous of his friendship with James, and I get the feeling she thinks I'm an idiot for trusting him.'

'Natasha Chisholm?' Maybe Kate had been right about Natasha too. 'How long has she been involved in all this?'

'I messaged her a month or so ago, when I thought Luke might actually go back to you after Ava's accident. He asked me not to tell anyone in the Facebook group about us, until your divorce came through. He'd started using a different name on there too, that only a few of us knew about, so that no one could find him unless he wanted them to. But I had to speak to someone who knew you both. Nat tried to tell me that Luke was lying and that you'd met someone else anyway, but she doesn't know how torn he felt when Ava was ill. I know you've got a daughter together, and I don't want to stand in the way of that, but we'll have a little boy soon, and the chance to be happy together. You've got to let go of Luke and move on. He can still be Ava's daddy, but he doesn't love you any more. I'm sorry.' She held out a hand towards me. Any moment now the alarm would go off and I'd wake up and find out this had all been a dream – it was certainly surreal enough.

'I don't *want* Luke in my life, I can promise you that.' I touched her outstretched hand briefly; I couldn't just leave her hanging there. My fingers brushed against the ring on her engagement finger. It was the ring that had disappeared from my jewellery box – the same one Luke had proposed to me with. I wondered what he'd said when he'd asked her to marry him, especially since he was still officially my husband. But she wasn't going to hear anything I said, not really. She was so desperate to believe the lies Luke had spun her. 'But the messages you sent me... why didn't you just say who you were from the start?'

'I didn't want Luke to find out. He said you were too fragile, and that if you found out about us it could trigger your depression again.' Lily tilted her head to one side. 'I don't blame you for the gambling or anything else. I know postnatal depression can really mess with your head and I'm terrified about it happening to me after the baby is born.'

'Does Luke have any idea you're here, now?' I wasn't going to waste my breath denying Luke's version of events again, Lily was in too deep to even consider I might be telling the truth. But confronting him together could be one way of getting the closure we both needed. Whether he'd tell the truth when we cornered him or not, was anyone's guess. But at least Lily would hear me telling him that I didn't want us to try again, and the phone calls and messages might finally stop.

'He's got no idea. He's promised me that when he sees you again, he's going to explain once and for all that it's over, but I couldn't risk you talking him around again, because of Ava. So I had to let you see for yourself that it's already too late for you to try again with Luke.'

'I promise you that's the last thing I'd want to do.' I could tell by the look on her face that she didn't believe me. 'Why don't you come back to my place and wait for him to arrive? Then you can hear it for yourself and we'll all know where we stand.'

'Nat was right about you being nice, and I know this is going to be really hard for you. But I promise you're doing the right thing.'

'Believe me, I know I am.' I didn't think I could be any more certain than before I'd met Lily, but I was. And I had Natasha Chisholm to thank for that. Whatever Lily decided was up to her, but by the end of the day I was finally going to be free.

'You look great!' Luke leant in towards me as soon as I opened the front door, and I stepped back to avoid the lunge.

'You'd better come in.' The door led straight into the front room of the cottage and Lily was waiting in the kitchen – perched, bump and all, on one of the high stools that pulled up to the breakfast bar. 'Although I suppose I should be thankful you didn't just let yourself in.'

'I was going to tell you about me moving in, but work's been crazy and I thought it would be a nice surprise.'

'A *nice surprise*?' I was using my teacher's voice, the tone I used to carry to the back of the church hall in assemblies, in the hope that Lily would hear my message loud and clear, even if Luke still didn't get it. 'How did you think it would be *nice*, after I told you I didn't want us to get back together and that I'd only ever considered it for Ava's sake?'

'Because I know you, Lettie, probably even better than you know yourself. You just don't want to admit that you still want us. I get that I've hurt you before and I'm sorry, but it'll be different this time. I promise.' He dropped the bag he'd been carrying onto the sofa, like he owned the place, but I knew just how to wipe the smug look off his face.

'Why did you decide to come back when you did? Was it just because you got my letter?' I'd been turning it over in my mind – ever since Lily told me about how torn he felt, and the texts she'd sent to warn me off, long before I left the letter at his parents' place.

'I'd been thinking about it for a while, wondering how you might react. But I missed you Lettie, and when I got your letter there was no reason for me to hold back any more.'

'No reason at all?' I pictured poor Lily, overhearing that as far as Luke was concerned, she'd been nothing at all.

'None, I promise you.'

'That's interesting, because there's someone here to see you.'

'Ava?' He hadn't even asked after his daughter in the last couple of text exchanges, they'd been too filled with excuses.

'No.' Walking past him, I pushed open the door to the kitchen and Lily looked up at us. 'I think you've got some explaining to do, Luke.'

'What the hell are you doing here?' He stalked towards her, his face twisted with rage, and Lily immediately started to cry. All of a sudden, confronting him didn't seem like such a good idea.

'I can't go on like this, Luke. You keep coming and going between the two of us, and then I hear you out there, admitting it was you who wanted to move back in with Scarlett and Ava. You told me it was all her, begging you to come back.'

'It wasn't what it sounded like.' Luke's voice softened and he put an arm around her shoulder. She shrugged it off, but I admired her restraint. 'I've told you before that I have to tread carefully with Scarlett, this is all really difficult for me.'

'Difficult for you!' The sheer nerve of the man almost took my breath away, but I was determined to have my say. 'I know what you've told Lily about me, but I need you both to hear this. It's over Luke, I'm filing for a divorce and I think I've found a buyer for the B&B. If Lily wants to give you another chance that's up to her, but I don't know how to make things any clearer to you.'

'At last.' Luke nodded. 'See, Lily, I told you she'd get there eventually, if you were just patient.'

'Are you for real?' I couldn't believe she was actually going to buy this, but he had slipped his arm around her shoulders again, and this time she didn't shrug him off.

'We've all got what we want Scarlett, there's no point arguing any more.' Luke shot me a look and I stood there for a moment, opening and closing my mouth like a flounder in a net. But the words wouldn't come out. He was right. Whatever I said, Luke would find a way of persuading Lily that I was making it up. And because she so desperately wanted to believe him, she would. Ending it this way was cleaner. Luke couldn't use me as an excuse for messing Lily about any more. I was certain that was the reason he'd said he was feeling torn, and my letter had given him another excuse to break away from her. Perhaps things had been going too well with Lily, and Luke was self-sabotaging again. It was a pattern whenever he got what he thought he'd wanted, like starting his 'dream' business, but he couldn't cope when it didn't fill that void that seemed to lurk deep within him. I could blame his parents for that, as I had for so long, but he was a grown man now and it was time he started taking responsibility for his actions. Perhaps it was simpler than that, anyway. Maybe Ava suddenly seemed an easier option than a new baby, or maybe his ego had been hurt by discovering I had someone new and he'd wanted me back to restore some sort of twisted pride. I'd never know the real truth, but it didn't matter. Luke probably didn't even know himself – he'd lied so much, the lines between fact and fiction were blurred forever.

If Lily wanted to believe that I was a gambling addict, who spent every night out clubbing, and then begged Luke for a second chance, I could live with that. She'd come to realise who Luke really was for herself, or she wouldn't. There was a good chance he'd never fully commit to Lily either. But I wasn't going to confront him about any of that, it was none of my business any more and he was incapable of telling the truth anyway.

'I'll help you load up the car with your stuff. And Lily's given me your address, so the solicitor will be in touch.' I widened my eyes, daring Luke to argue, but he just nodded. 'And they can work out an arrangement for Ava too.'

'Okay, but things might be a bit busy when the baby arrives.' He put a hand over Lily's bump and she leant into him. Another wave of sympathy for her washed over me. He was so full of it.

'Just promise me you won't mess Ava around. If you can't see her, don't promise her that you can.' I searched Luke's face, hoping to see some glimmer of understanding there, and he finally nodded his head.

'Maybe it's best if we leave it for now, then.' Luke shrugged, as if he'd just taken a rain check on seeing a movie or something. Lily was welcome to him, but my heart ached for the baby she was carrying, and most of all for Ava. She'd coped without him before, though, and she would again. At least this time we knew exactly where we stood.

* * *

'I was hoping you'd come over.' The unexpected knock at the door, an hour after Luke and Lily had finally set off, startled me. I'd always had an over-active imagination, but the months of silent phone calls and threatening messages had made me jumpier than ever. So peering through the pane of glass in the door, and seeing Cam standing under the outside light, had been a welcome surprise. 'I wasn't expecting to see you, but I'm really glad you're here.' I couldn't help smiling at the warm feeling I got from just being around him, especially now that none of the other stuff was hanging over us any more. I'd sent him a text to let him know about Lily turning up and to fill him in on the basics of what had happened, but I was really pleased he'd come over. I needed to tell him everything, before I could really let myself believe it.

'I needed to see you.' Cam looked unusually serious, as I stood back to let him inside.

'Me too. I've got so much to tell you about what happened with Luke and Lily.' I was still on a high from finally seeing the back of my soon-to-be-ex-husband, and my words were coming out thirteen to the dozen.

'And you're actually going to give me the *whole* story this time?' Cam turned to face me and my scalp prickled. He'd never looked at me like that before, as if he didn't even recognise who I was.

'What do you mean?'

'I had a message from Luke. Apparently he kept my number in his phone when he deleted it from yours. He told me to be careful about what I was getting into with you.'

'And you're listening to him? After everything he's done?' I sat down on the sofa with a thud, struggling to understand what was going on.

'I'd have assumed it was all more lies, except he told me about something that happened at the local hospital, when Ava was first admitted, around the time you seemed to back away from me.' Cam shook his head. 'It all just made too much sense to ignore.'

'What did he say?' I looked up at Cam, knowing what was coming, but hoping against hope I was wrong.

'He said you talked about wishing you'd had more kids with him and giving things another go. And that you kissed. Or are you going to tell me he blackmailed you into all of that too?'

'No, I'm so sorry, Cam, I should have told you.' I wasn't going to try and lie my way out of it, that would have made me no better than Luke. I reached towards Cam instead, but my arm just hung in the air, like the tension between us. 'I was in such a state when Ava had her accident, and Luke was there when I found out I couldn't donate my kidney. He said he wanted to look after us both. And, for a little while, I did think some of the feelings I had for him were still there. But even when I wasn't sure about Luke, I never stopped wanting to be with you.'

'Even when you were kissing him?' Cam didn't even look at me.

'It was just once.' The excuse sounded pathetic, even to me. 'By the time Ava was at the Brompton, I already knew I was in love with you, not him. And he really did blackmail me into sending that text.'

'It doesn't matter how many times you kissed him. You lied to me, Scarlett. When I asked you at Phoebe's place if there was anything else I needed to know, you could have told me then.' He sighed, like the weight of the world was on his shoulders. 'I get that Ava being so ill threw the two of you back together, and some confused feelings were probably going to surface as a result. I could have handled it if you'd been honest with me. But now I don't know what else you're hiding.'

'I promise you there's nothing else.'

Cam shook his head again. 'How am I supposed to trust you when you say you don't want Luke any more? I've fallen in love with you, and Ava. But I can't risk getting any deeper than I already am, and then watching you walk away the next time he clicks his fingers.'

'It's not like that. When I kissed him, I knew for sure we'd *never* had what you and I have got. The only good thing that came from mine and Luke's relationship was Ava. I could have walked away as his friend at that point, I even felt guilty that I didn't love him the way he said he still loved me. But then he pulled that stunt at the Brompton, and I actually started to hate him. There didn't seem any point in telling you about the kiss, or any of the other stuff by then, because I didn't want to hurt you for no reason. There's absolutely zero chance of me wanting Luke back in my life, but it'll be up to Ava if she wants him in hers at some point in the future. Although the way he's acted, I honestly think she's better off without him.'

'I don't expect you to stop him seeing Ava, if that's what's best for her, but I just don't know if I can do this.' Cam was already moving back towards the front door. And when I got up to try and stop him, he shrugged me off. 'I need time to think Scarlett, I'm sorry.'

'I'm sorry, too.' He didn't turn as I spoke. And I wasn't sure if he even heard what I said next, as he slammed the door behind him. 'I love you, Cam. I honestly do.'

22

Ava sat transfixed in front of the mirror, as the hairdresser worked her magic with the curling irons and pinned tiny artificial daisies around the crown of her head.

'Can you keep an eye on her, please, while I go and check whether Mum and Auntie Leilah need any help?' I turned to Dad, who was sitting in his armchair, watching his only grandchild with a big grin on his face.

'Of course, love. I'm just happy to stay out of your mother's way.' He was all set for the wedding, already, and I felt a pang of envy. It was so easy for men; a suit, a shower and a shave, and they were good to go. Thankfully, the hairdresser had already worked a miracle on my hair and I just had to get into the dress that was hanging up in the spare room. I had no idea if Cam was going to be at the wedding or not. He'd accepted the invite before we'd rowed about me kissing Luke, but he hadn't turned up to the family dinner after the final dress fittings. I knew from Auntie Leilah that he'd sent his apologies and given some excuse about not feeling well, and it had been a relief to go along with the lie. I'd only texted him once to explain a bit more about what had happened with Luke and Lily, and to tell him the ball was in his court now that he knew the full story.

I hadn't been able to bring myself to tell Mum or Leilah about what had happened, but I'd confided in Phoebe, Dolly and even Kate. They'd all been certain that Cam would come around in the end, once he got over the shock, and that he'd eventually understand why I'd decided not to tell him about the kiss, or my temporarily confused feelings towards Luke. I wasn't so sure, but all I could do was give Cam the space he'd asked for and pray that my friends were right.

But it was Leilah's big day, so I tried to push thoughts of Cam to the back of my mind. I wanted to make sure Mum wasn't railroading her into anything she didn't want to do, like wearing makeup that would end up making her look like someone else entirely in the photos.

As I climbed the stairs, it sounded like a seagull was calling outside, but we were much too far from the sea for that. Stopping on the landing, I listened again – someone was crying, loudly. Not waiting to knock, I pushed open the door to my parents' room where Mum was sitting on the edge of the bed, sobbing her heart out.

'What on earth's going on?' I looked at Auntie Leilah, who shrugged her shoulders.

'I keep telling her it's going to be okay, but she won't listen.'

'What's going to be okay?'

'Don't tell her, Leilah, please.' Mum gave a big shuddering sob, and my throat started to burn as I sat on the edge of the bed next to her, terrified of what might be wrong.

'Are you ill? Mum, please, if it's serious I just want to know, or I'm just going to panic.' The worst possible scenarios were already running through my head. Maybe she'd been diagnosed with some-thing terrible, or Dad had, but when I looked up at Auntie Leilah again, she was smiling.

'I'm sorry, Chrissy, but we're going to have to tell Red what's going on. It's all a lot of fuss about nothing anyway.' Leilah moved to sit on the other side of me. 'We had all this out in Iceland, but she just can't seem to let it go.'

'Had what out?' She might as well have been speaking Icelandic for all the sense she was making.

'Your mum thinks that I'm settling for Nicky, because I'm really in love with your dad!' Auntie Leilah laughed, but I still didn't have any idea what she was talking about.

'What do you mean you're in love with Dad?'

'I'm not, you dafty!' Auntie Leilah pulled a face. 'He's a lovely man, and we did date for a bit when we were younger, but we weren't after the same thing.'

'You and Dad went out together?'

'For the best part of a year!' Mum interjected, her voice breaking again as she said it. 'And he finished it to go out with me.'

'Oh my God! How did I never know this?' I couldn't imagine my gentle dad, who worshipped the ground my mother walked on, ever being part of a love triangle. Especially with Auntie Leilah. He was such a homebody, and she was such a free spirit, I wouldn't have put them together in a million years.

'Because it's ancient history!' Leilah seemed to be finding it all ridiculous. 'I told you at the time I didn't care, Chrissy, so why you should think it bothers me now, more than thirty-five years later, I'll never know.'

'I'll tell you why.' Mum wagged a finger at us both. 'Because you told me back then that you never wanted to get married and that Steve was definitely the marrying kind.'

'And I meant every word. We realised early on that we didn't want the same things and we were always more like friends, who just drifted along pretending to be more than that. I think, looking back, that he only did it so he'd have an excuse to come to the house and see you.'

'But you lied about how you felt to protect me, I know you did. If you really didn't ever want to get married, then why are you marrying Nicky?' Mum couldn't keep her voice steady. 'I can't help feeling that you've been nursing this for all that time, and that's the real reason you didn't get married.'

'Chrissy, for God's sake, what is it going to take to convince you? I promise you I didn't want to get married back then. I really didn't think I ever would, and I was just happy that you and Steve had found each other, and I got to keep my friend in my life as my brother-in-law. It was only meeting Nicky that changed my mind. You've seen what we're like, the same fitting together of two halves that I saw with you and Steve. I just don't understand why you can't accept that.'

'Because I still feel guilty!' Mum got to her feet. 'I convinced myself that I hadn't done anything wrong by moving in on Steve. But then when you said you were getting married all that guilt came rushing back, and I felt as though I'd robbed you of the last thirty-five years and the chance of having a family of your own.'

'I've got a family of my own.' Leilah put her arm around me and reached out her other hand to Mum. 'I was never cut out to be a mum, but I've had the best fun being an auntie over the years and I've always had all of you to come home to at the important times. It's why I wanted the wedding to be here. I love you all – Steve included – but we'd have been divorced within six months if we'd ever taken it that far. It was me who told him to just get on with it and ask you out in the end.'

'You did *what*?' Mum thumped back down onto the bed. 'Why didn't you tell me that before?'

'I didn't think it was that important.'

'Is this why you were so upset when Leilah told us she was getting engaged?' I was suddenly looking at Mum through new eyes. So much made sense now about why she'd acted the way she had over the years, and why she'd always seemed so obsessed with Leilah's determination to stay single.

'I just couldn't stop thinking about what we'd done, and I tried to tell you when Ava was in hospital, because I felt like I was being punished for what happened back then. We'd been far too happy for too long, something had to come along and break our hearts.' Mum screwed up her face and I couldn't believe that was what she'd been trying to tell me. At the time, I'd wondered if she was going to confess to being behind the anonymous calls and texts, and I'd been terrified of what that might do to our relationship if she did. So I'd let it go.

'That's what's been eating you up all this time?'

'Yes, but knowing that Leilah pushed me and your dad together makes it a bit better.' Some of the tension finally seemed to disappear from Mum's face.

'Now can you finally accept that you didn't do anything wrong? I never loved Steve, not like that. And I've never felt the way I feel about Nicky, before.' Leilah took hold of both our hands again. 'Can we just get on with enjoying the day now? I've got to the grand old age of sixty-four without tying the knot, so I want to make the most of it.'

'I think we should all have a glass of champagne.' I didn't know about them, but I could definitely do with a drink.

'You pour them, Red,' Auntie Leilah got up first, 'and I'll fix your mum's makeup. We don't want her to frighten the children!'

'I don't know why I felt guilty, the way you talk about me!' Mum laughed through her tears and the atmosphere in the room seemed to shift. It just went to show that, whatever had gone on in the past, it was never too late for a fresh start. I was counting on it.

* * *

I'd spotted Cam as soon as I got to the venue. He was helping his best friend, Jamie, who ran the forest school, to make some finishing touches to dressing the patch of woodland where Leilah had chosen to hold her wedding. They'd done an amazing job of turning it into a forest wonderland. There were rows and rows of tiny fairy-lights strung in between the trees, and even the chairs were made from logs. Jamie had decided to diversify from just running the forest school and had started to offer part of the woodland out to hire for picnics and family parties. Holding the wedding there had meant a dash to the local registry office to get the official part of the proceedings sorted out. Mum and Dad had gone with Leilah and Nicky as witnesses, and I'd gone on ahead to the venue to make sure everything was going according to plan.

There was a marquee pitched in a field to the side of Jamie's farmhouse for the reception, and as a back-up venue for the ceremony. But even the weather was playing ball. It was a perfect spring day and a blanket of bluebells were spread across the forest floor, beyond the clearing where the wedding was taking place. Auntie Leilah might have waited sixty-four years to have her big day, but it had turned out perfectly. I didn't speak to Cam before the wedding, but at one point he looked up at me and smiled. Trying desperately not to read too much into it, I smiled back and somehow resisted throwing myself at him. Even a smile was a step in the right direction, after the way he'd looked at me the last time we'd met.

The ceremony was really personal, with Leilah and Nicky writing their own vows. Ava was a little angel and I wasn't sure who looked happiest, her or the happy couple. The wedding party wasn't huge, less than a hundred people. But some of Nicky's friends and family had flown over from the US, and they knew how to have a good time. We didn't have a big extended family, and the guest list on Leilah's side was mostly made up of her friends, which meant I didn't actually know that many people at the wedding – and I definitely hadn't expected to see Natasha Chisholm sitting in one of the wooden seats in the second to last row. But Natasha's mum, Brenda, was a long-term friend of Leilah's, and she'd been widowed the year before, so she'd obviously brought her daughter along as her plus one.

I hadn't spoken to Natasha since the showdown with Luke, but then again, I hadn't spoken to him either. Strangely enough, Lily had been the one to keep in touch and she'd even sent me a photograph of baby Sebastian's 3D scan. It had been an odd experience, opening up the attachment on her text and looking at the photograph of my husband's unborn son. Lily had texted me the day after we'd first met, asking if I minded her messaging me every now and then. She'd apologised again for the texts and calls, and to my surprise I'd found it easy to forgive her. I knew only too well what it felt like to be manipulated by Luke and left in the dark about what he was going to do next, so I couldn't bring myself to blame her. She'd said she wanted to keep the lines of communication open, in case the children wanted to meet one day. She didn't say whether Luke knew about it or not, but I'd have bet my last pound that he didn't. And I'd have bet my last working kidney she had no idea about his message to Cam, either. It might just have been a case of Lily wanting to keep her friends close and her enemies closer, but I was glad she wanted to keep in touch. It was important for Ava that the door to her father's new family wasn't slammed shut, and I'd thought long and hard about whether to tell her about the baby.

As it was, I still hadn't made up my mind. Luke wasn't someone I wanted in her life until he'd sorted himself out, and I could be sure neither him nor Lily would pull any more crazy stunts. Keeping in touch by text meant that things could change in the future, though, if Ava wanted them to. But only when I was certain seeing Luke was the best thing for her and that he was finally capable of putting her feelings before his own.

'Ava was a little star during the ceremony, wasn't she? I got a great picture of her on my phone when she was coming back down the aisle. I can send it to you if you like?' Natasha walked over to me, as I watched Ava playing chase with Nicky's great-nephews. Cam and Jamie were setting up for the live band that Auntie Leilah had booked for the evening, so I still hadn't had the chance to speak to him, even if he'd wanted to. It was typical of Cam, he was always doing something for someone and bit by bit I'd fallen in love with him because of it. It amazed me, after everything that had happened with Luke, that I'd been able to fall so hard and so completely for Cam. And not knowing if he could ever forgive me was almost unbearable.

'I'd love to see the photo, thanks.' I smiled at Natasha, pushing thoughts of Cam back down again. 'I think I fidgeted more than she did, but I kept feeling as if my bra strap was slipping down my shoulders. I seem to spend my life in leggings or jeans when I'm teaching, I'm just not used to dressing up like this.'

'You look stunning. Mum said she remembers you when you were about Ava's age, and she reckons you're like two peas in a pod.'

'I really hope so.' I didn't need to tell Natasha why.

'I wanted to find you, so I could tell you that Claire has finally had all the results of the genetic tests back, and she and Amber are both in the clear.'

'I'm so pleased for them, it must have been such a relief.' It if had been anyone else I might have hugged Natasha, but there was still so much I didn't know about her involvement with Luke and

Lily, and I couldn't help feeling slightly uncomfortable around her as a result.

'She was over the moon, especially about Amber.' Natasha took a deep breath and I knew what was coming. 'Have you heard anything from Luke?'

'No, but I've heard the latest about the baby, from Lily. He's due next month.'

'She told me what happened when she came to see you.' Natasha fiddled with her hair, which looked as perfect as always. 'I think she understands more about Luke than she wants to admit, but she's just in love with the idea of who she wants him to be. I didn't know what to do for the best when she told me she was expecting his baby, and I'm really sorry if all that made things worse for you.'

'Actually, it helped. I felt sorry for Lily and I could tell she didn't want to know what had really happened with Luke, but I'm glad I got the chance to say it, and I'm glad she wants to stay in touch. Ava and Sebastian might want to meet one day, even if Luke isn't in either of their lives by then.'

'Sadly, I can see that coming. James was Luke's best friend, but even he's had it with him now. Lily was mad about Luke, even when we were at school, and they were always flirting in the Class of 2003 Facebook group. But there was quite a lot of that going on, so I didn't think anything of it. Especially as, when he was staying with us, he swore blind there was no one else involved. I don't know if there really were any gambling debts, but when Lily got in touch to tell us about the baby and how long it had been going on, she admitted she'd lent him money. There's probably other stuff we don't even know about, but for what it's worth I think you've had a lucky escape and you deserve so much more. It looks like you've found that in Cam.'

'Even if it meant being on my own forever, I'd still have been happy to see the back of Luke.' I took two glasses of champagne from a passing waiter and handed one to Natasha. I could see us being friends one day, but there was no way I was going to confide in her about how things currently stood with Cam. Not when she was still in contact with Lily and Luke – even if it was only through the Facebook group that had so much to answer for. 'Do you think Lily will be okay if he doesn't stick around?'

'Once Sebastian arrives, I think she'll make him her priority whatever happens. Like I said, she always had a thing for Luke. But, when her marriage broke up, I think she was worried she'd missed the chance to be a mum. Luke came along at the right time, or maybe the wrong time, when she was desperate to have a baby. Part of me wanted to tell her that she'd made her own mess and she could just get on with it, when she told me about her and Luke. But she stood up for me a lot when I was being bullied at school, and I felt like I owed her.'

'Things like that can tie you to someone for life, can't they?' I thought about Phoebe for a moment and how often she'd run to my house when her mum was being particularly difficult.

'They can and you never forget the bully either. Unfortunately I haven't had the chance.' Natasha took a slug of champagne. 'The worst of them was Belinda Fincham, she'd tell me every day after she found out that I was adopted that I didn't have a real family and it was because nobody loved me or wanted me.'

'Dolly told us about that at the documentary screening. I couldn't believe it; Belinda always comes across as being so lovely when she's doing stuff for the Oaktree Forstal PTA.'

'She acts like butter wouldn't melt in her mouth now, but she still tries to get one up on me by raising more money for the federation than we do.'

'It must be hard trying to put the past behind you.' My eyes slid over to where Cam was standing, but I forced myself to look at Natasha again.

'Yep, she's a bitch.' Clapping a hand over her mouth, Natasha somehow kept the glass of champagne she was holding in her other hand completely steady. 'Sorry, I shouldn't have said that.'

'I think I'd say the same if I was you, but hopefully she's grown up a bit since then.'

'Hmm, maybe, but I've got a tonne of ideas for fundraising in the summer term. Will you be at the next PTA meeting?'

'Definitely, and I'm sure you'll do even better than Oaktree Forstal.' I looked over her shoulder, as Cam walked towards us, my stomach already twisting in knots. 'But you're so much more than that. You've got a great family of your own, so even if you didn't raise a single penny next term, you'd still have proven her wrong.'

'You sound like my mum now!' Natasha grinned.

'Sometimes mums really do know best.' As Cam waited behind me, I couldn't help hoping I was right. If he was coming to tell me we were finished, then bringing him into Ava's life, and having him walk out again, would be the second biggest mistake I'd ever made.

'I didn't know if you were even going to be here today.' I turned to Cam as we got outside the marquee, neither of us wanting to have the conversation we were about to have in front of the rest of the wedding party.

'I was never going to let Jamie down.'

'Of course not.' I shifted from foot to foot, the heels of my shoes digging into the soft ground outside the marquee. Away from the heaters inside the tent, goose-bumps were springing up all over my body – although it wasn't entirely down to the cold. 'How have you been?'

'Miserable.' Cam shrugged. 'I've been an idiot and I massively overreacted to Luke's message according to Mike.'

'You told your stepdad what happened?' My cheeks burned, despite the chill in the air. I hated the thought of Cam's parents thinking badly of me.

'I needed to talk to someone about it. As soon as I was outside your cottage, I wanted to turn around and sort it all out. But pride and sheer bloody-mindedness got in the way. Mike called me a moron, if that helps?' Cam laughed and I hadn't realised how much I'd missed that sound. We'd avoided each other like the plague at school, and I'd seriously wondered how I'd be able to carry on working alongside him, if we didn't manage to make things right again.

'And did he give you any advice?'

'He told me to follow my heart and that things were never easy coming into a ready-made family, like he did with me and Mum. But that it was the best thing he'd ever done.'

'And what's your heart telling you?'

'That it's already lost, to you and Ava. So I might as well man-up and deal with whatever comes our way. I'm not going to be happy with anyone but the two of you, so I don't really have a choice.' Cam took hold of my hand. 'But that's assuming you still want me around?'

'I do, and so does Ava. I've kept her busy doing things for the wedding, so she didn't realise we weren't seeing you after school.' I looked down at our intertwined hands. 'I didn't want to tell her things had changed, not until I *had* to.'

'And now you don't need to. I get now why you didn't tell me about the kiss, and the rest of it. You were just trying to protect me, too. But if I promise not to overreact and storm off like a twelve-year-old girl, can you promise just to be upfront with me from now on? Whatever happens?'

'I promise, but there really won't be anything else to tell.'

'There's something I need to tell you, though.' Cam looked serious again, and my heartbeat started whooshing in my ears. If there'd been someone else for Cam since we'd been together, or even a hint of it, I wasn't sure I could handle it.

'What is it?'

'I let Janey and Emily have first pick of the forest school slots for next year again, when I was still sulking like a kid. So you're back in the sub-zero slots.'

'Is that it?'

'You almost got the extra day of playground duty too!' He was grinning again and so was I – like an idiot.

'I think that's a fair trade-off. Does that mean we can we call it quits now and pick up where we left off, before we got ourselves into all of this?'

'Absolutely.' He pulled me towards him and I suddenly understood what Leilah had meant, when she'd described two halves coming together. Cam was who I'd been waiting for, before I'd even known I was looking. And, after everything we'd worked through, nothing would stop us making it work.

The lights inside the marquee looked almost as pretty as the ones outside as the evening wore on. Ava was still spending most of her time playing with Nicky's great-nephews and no one would ever have guessed that just weeks beforehand she'd been critically ill.

'I thought Ava would be flagging by now.' Cam led me off the dancefloor, where Ava was busy jumping up and down on the spot with the two boys. They might not have much rhythm, but their energy levels were phenomenal.

'Me too. She might not be, but I am.'

'It's been a great day though, hasn't it? And you looked so beautiful.'

'Thanks.' I brushed off the compliment, looking at the floor instead. 'You and Jamie worked so hard and I think it ended up as pretty much the perfect venue.'

'It was definitely perfect for Leilah and Nicky, but it isn't where I'd want to get married.'

'You've thought about it, then? I always assumed it was just us girls that did stuff like that.' I looked up at Cam and he pulled me closer towards him.

'I've thought about it a lot just lately. I know it's early days and you might not even want to do it again.'

'I wouldn't rule it out altogether.' I smiled, happier than I could ever explain that we were back to teasing each other again, in the way we always had.

'In that case, I was thinking about a castle somewhere. I thought Ava might enjoy playing at being a princess for the day.'

'I think she could get on board with that.'

'That's good to know, but there's no rush. I think we should just enjoy every moment after the drama of the last few months. I'm guessing we've got at least a couple more years before she grows out of the princess phase, anyway.'

'So seven's the cut-off point?' I smiled again, as I looked up at him. 'And there was me thinking I could get away with being a Cinderella bride.'

'If anyone could pull it off, you could. And when we're ready I don't care where we do it, or if you're wearing a wedding dress or overalls. I don't even mind if you don't want to get married. I just want to be with you and Ava for good. It's all I ever wanted.'

'That, Mr Ellis, is the nicest thing anyone has ever said to me.' I felt a tugging on my hand, as I spoke.

'Mummy, can you and Cam come and dance with me? All the other kids are dancing with their mums and dads.'

'Of course we will darling.'

I looked at Cam, who nodded, and the three of us headed back towards the dancefloor. We might be more of a mosaic than the picture-perfect image I'd always imagined, but I already knew we could face whatever life threw at as. Together. And no one could ask for more than that.

ACKNOWLEDGMENTS

A huge thank you to all of the team at Boldwood Books. With special gratitude to my brilliant editor, Emily, and to Cari and Candida for their excellent copy editing and proofreading skills.

Another massive thank you goes to everyone who reads my books and especially those who take the time to leave a review, including the amazing book blogging community.

This book is dedicated to the old school friends who are still part of my life and to the friends I made on the school run, who helped me survive ten years back in the playground. Thank you all for your friendship and the laughs we had along the way.

Finally, as always, the biggest thank you goes to my family for their patience, support and belief in me.

MORE FROM JO BARTLETT

We hope you enjoyed reading *Second Chances at Cherry Tree Cottage*. If you did, please leave a review.

If you'd like to gift a copy, this book is also available as an ebook, digital audio download and audiobook CD.

Sign up to Jo Bartlett's mailing list for news, competitions and updates on future books.

http://bit.ly/JoBartlettNewsletter

Why not explore the bestselling The Cornish Midwives series:

ABOUT THE AUTHOR

Jo Bartlett is the bestselling author of nineteen women's fiction titles. She fits her writing in between her two day jobs as an educational consultant and university lecturer and lives with her family and three dogs on the Kent coast.

Visit Jo's Website: www.jobartlettauthor.com

ABOUT BOLDWOOD BOOKS

Boldwood Books is a fiction publishing company seeking out the best stories from around the world.

Find out more at www.boldwoodbooks.com

Sign up to the Book and Tonic newsletter for news, offers and competitions from Boldwood Books!

http://www.bit.ly/bookandtonic

We'd love to hear from you, follow us on social media:

facebook.com/BookandTonic

twitter.com/BoldwoodBooks

instagram.com/BookandTonic

First published in Great Britain in 2021 by Boldwood Books Ltd.

Copyright © Jo Bartlett, 2021

Cover Design by CC Book Design

Cover photography: Shutterstock

A CIP catalogue record for this book is available from the British Library.

Paperback ISBN 978-1-80162-000-0

Large Print ISBN 978-1-80162-001-7

Hardback ISBN 978-1-80048-999-8

Ebook ISBN 978-1-80162-003-1

Kindle ISBN 978-1-80162-002-4

Audio CD ISBN 978-1-80048-994-3

MP3 CD ISBN 978-1-80048-995-0

Digital audio download ISBN 978-1-80048-997-4

Boldwood Books Ltd
23 Bowerdean Street
London SW6 3TN
www.boldwoodbooks.com

Printed in Great Britain
by Amazon